Deadly
Charm

Deadly
Charm

an amanda bell brown mystery

Claudia Mair
Burney

HOWARD BOOKS
A Division of Simon & Schuster
New York • London • Toronto • Sydney

Our purpose at Howard Books is to:
•*Increase faith* in the hearts of growing Christians
•*Inspire holiness* in the lives of believers
•*Instill hope* in the hearts of struggling people everywhere
Because He's coming again!

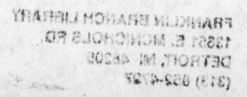

Published by Howard Books, a division of Simon & Schuster, Inc.
1230 Avenue of the Americas, New York, NY 10020
www.howardpublishing.com

Deadly Charm © 2009 Claudia Mair Burney

Library of Congress Control Number: 2008023836

ISBN-13: 978-1-4165-5195-9
ISBN-10:   1-4165-5195-6

10 9 8 7 6 5 4 3 2 1

HOWARD and colophon are registered trademarks of Simon & Schuster, Inc.

Manufactured in the United States of America

For information regarding special discounts for bulk purchases,
please contact: Simon & Schuster Special Sales at 1-800-456-6798 or
business@simonandschuster.com.

Edited by Lissa Halls Johnson
Cover design by Stephanie D. Walker
Interior design by Davina Mock-Maniscalco

This novel is a work of fiction. Names, characters, places, and incidents either are the
product of the author's imagination or are used fictitiously. Any resemblance to actual
events, locales, organizations, or persons, living or dead, is entirely coincidental and
beyond the intent of either the author or publisher.

Scripture quotations marked KJV are taken from the King James Version. Scripture
quotations marked MSG are taken from *The Message*. Copyright © 1993, 1994, 1995,
1996, 2000, 2001, 2002. Used by permission of NavPress Publishing Group.

For my father,
James Harold Hawthorne, Jr.
August 29, 1936–February 2, 2007
Because you'd want to know what happened.

acknowledgments

I AM ALWAYS GRATEFUL to my amazing family for their love and support. I extend the same gratitude to the friends— you know who you are—who helped and loved me on this journey.

And I thank you, dear reader, for trying me again with Bell's third adventure.

Lissa, the dance was lovely. I let you lead even more this time. No regrets on the ending.

Thank you, Chip MacGregor, for weathering all these storms with me.

And to my wonderful team at Howard Books, thank you, thank you, thank you.

Mair
July 11, Feast of St. Benedict

Jesus said unto him, If thou canst believe,
all things are possible to him that believeth.

—Mark 9:23 KJV

chapter one

ROCKY SHOWED UP at my apartment door with an offer that, in his words, I "no coulda refuse." Or maybe those were Marlon Brando's words. I couldn't be sure. My blond, dreadlocked former pastor slash ex-boyfriend locked me into a stare with those big brown puppy eyes. He'd puffed out his jowls to utter the Godfather's most famous line, while grazing his cheek with the backs of his fingers—an excruciatingly amiss imitation. I've seen newborn babies' smiles that were more intimidating.

"You look more like a hamster than a mobster, Rock."

"Hamsters are cool."

"But less compelling, you must admit."

Rocky grinned and wagged his finger at me. "Never underestimate the power of a furry little creature." He twitched his nose and started making hamster noises.

"Amen!" I said.

I thought of my vicious former pet sugar glider, Amos. Although he'd become my friend and hero, I had to give him away to another nocturnal creature—otherwise, I'd never sleep again. My husband's best friend, Souldier, had taken the murderous marsupial. Now Amos happily shreds *his* drapes.

"Come on in, my not-so-furry friend," I told Rocky, mostly so he would stop making weird rodent sounds.

I moved aside so he could enter my little slice of paradise: shabby chic meets Africa is what Jazz, my husband, called it. Rocky loved my funky, eclectically furnished place, too. He just didn't describe it as aptly as Jazz did.

Who was I kidding? Rocky didn't do *anything* as aptly as Jazz did. I had lost them both six weeks ago, and now here was Rocky, surprising me by showing up at my door like unexpected grace.

"Welcome back, Rocky," I said. I know I sounded lame, but I wanted him to know I was glad he'd come, no matter what the reason.

He muttered a shy "Thanks."

We stood in my foyer exchanging reticent glances until I got bold enough to take a long look at him. I'd missed him so. He wore a typical Rockyesque uniform underneath his white down jacket—khaki pants and a long-sleeved *Batman* T-shirt. A cupid earring dangled from his right ear. Every year about this time, he wore it to remind me to come to the Saint Valentine's Day feast.

Without thinking I blurted out, "I see you and cupid are still advertising our—" I bit my tongue. There'd be no "our" Saint Valentine's Day feast this year for prodigal Bell. "Sorry," I muttered.

"No problem," he rushed to say, and then an awful silence descended on us like a cold, gray fog.

When I was still a member of his church, befittingly named the Rock House, I never missed the event. Rocky would tell stories of Saint Valentine; we'd eat candy conversation hearts, listen to live music, and share abundant amounts of food and laughter.

It was Rocky's way of making sure the lonely hearts wouldn't spend the evening alone. There with my church family, not only did I get heaps of love, I could give out some from my meager supply.

That and we always had a chocolate fountain.

What was I going to do now?

I tried not to think about the sting I'd felt when Rocky kicked me out of his church. I didn't want to think about anything that had happened six weeks ago. Still, I figured whatever brought him to my door had an olive branch attached to it, and I'd be willing to do whatever he asked, short of sin, to reconcile with him.

Rocky hung up his jacket, kicked out of his Birkenstocks, and headed over to my rose-colored velvet sofa and sat. I followed, plopping down beside him.

"So what's the offer, Godfather?"

He stared at me. "Did you gain weight?"

Because I know it's rude to kill your loved ones, I let that one slide and gave him a polite smile, but I did grab a mud-cloth throw pillow to cover my expanding waistline.

"So what's the offer, Rocky?"

He gushed in a most *un*-Godfatherly way, "I want you to go to a meeting with me. It's only going to be the way-coolest event you've been to in forever."

I cuddled the pillow and eyed him cautiously. He didn't mean the Valentine's Day feast. I braced myself. Rocky's idea of way cool could be scary. "Can you be a little more specific?"

He didn't answer. Just reached out and touched my hand, rubbing his thumb across my knuckles. "I really missed you."

Oh, man. That small gesture—him touching the hand no-

body held anymore—had the effect of a pebble in a pond, creating ripples of unexpected sadness that circled out of my soul.
Lord, have mercy. I didn't fling myself at him, begging like a
rhythm-and-blues singer for him to keep loving me, not to give
up on me, but something in me wished I could.

I didn't want to *marry* Rocky, or even date him. He had never
been the love of my life. In that moment I simply wanted to
banish the nearly incarnate loneliness that had been dogging my
heels as a solemn, maddening companion, shuffling me through
all those days without my best friend Rocky.

And without my husband Jazz.

I gazed up at him with my own version of puppy eyes. "I
missed you, too, Rocky."

We let a bit of silence sit between us on the sofa like a third
and very quiet presence. Our heads hung low. Apparently we
were both still smarting over the pain of separation.

Minutes passed, our hands still clasped together, but Rocky's
merciful presence soothed the dry patches of my soul like
olive oil.

*Thank God. Thank God for every kind soul I don't deserve in my
life who loves me anyway.*

"Rocky." I made my voice as soft and small as a baby's
blankie.

He turned to me, his face as open and vulnerable as that
blankie's little owner.

I squeezed his hand. "I'm so sorry I hurt you."

Those puppy eyes shone with compassion.

"I'm sorry for the things I did, too, babe. For the things I said
that night."

"Don't call me babe."

He chuckled. "Some things never change." Again, those gentle peepers bored into me. "Why didn't you tell me you married Jazz?"

"At the time I didn't seem too clear on it myself. Things happened pretty fast, and the next thing I knew, I was a wife." I paused, the weight of that statement shifting just a bit with Rocky there to help bear my burden. "He's mad at me."

"Duh-uh. You were kissing your blond boy toy." He nudged me with his tattooed arm. "What's going on with the two of you now?"

"I've seen corpses on Carly's autopsy tables more alive than our marriage."

I wondered if I'd ever get over what I'd lost with Jazz.

"I can only imagine what his parents think of me. I guess they'd say I'm the nightmare that took his ex, Kate's, place."

He regarded me with the care and concern I'd seen him lavish on the fortunate souls he counseled as a pastor. Rocky may be only twenty-eight years old, but he'd been a pastor for two years. Two good years. He didn't have the life experience an older pastor would, but God had given him an extraordinary shepherd's heart.

"You're not a nightmare," he said. "You jumped into a marriage with no spiritual or emotional preparation."

Like I, the clinician, needed *him* to tell *me* that.

I sighed. "Yet another 'psychologist, heal thyself' thing." I looked away from him, guilt gnawing at me. "Maybe Jazz and I just aren't meant to be, Rocky."

"Have you talked to him?"

I shrugged. "Just once. He came over for a few minutes on Christmas Eve. I let him know I wanted him in a way I knew he'd understand. And then I waited. He never came back."

"Why didn't you go to him?"

"The same reason I didn't come to *you*. I wanted to give him some space to feel whatever he felt and then to decide on his own."

"But maybe he's not like me, babe."

"Ya *think*? And don't call me babe."

"Maybe he needs you to *help* him decide. Like some extra reassurance or something."

"That's crazy, Rock."

"It's not so crazy, babe."

I took back every nice thing I'd just thought about him. What did he know? Yes, he pastored a church of more than two-hundred members. He did missions work. He had a shepherd's heart. He took pastoral counseling classes in seminary, but honestly! His voice sounded just like Patrick's from *SpongeBob*.

Rocky glared at me. "Babe . . ."

"Don't call me babe."

"Babe! You gotta go to him."

"But he yells. Sometimes he cusses like a fishwife."

"What's a fishwife?"

"I don't know, but my great-grandmother used to say that and it stuck with me. Maybe only females cuss like fishwives. Maybe he cusses like the fish." Now *I* sounded like Patrick!

"Fish don't cuss."

"Okay, I know I should have reassured him."

He sighed. Looked at me with those eyes. Squeezed my hand. "Will you ever let anyone love you?"

"People love me, Rocky. My sister. My secretary. Sasha."

"I have doubts about Sasha."

I thought about that and chuckled with him. "You may be right. My mother *has* done a few things that make me wonder. Now I'm really depressed."

"I want to see you happy."

"I want to see you happy, too. Speaking of which, how are you and Elisa?"

He grinned, reddened, looked away.

"What? Did you marry her in six weeks? My goodness!" For the first time, I didn't feel jealous that someone was interested in Rocky. Well, not much.

"No. I'm not married. I'm . . ."

"You're what?"

"She's really special, but it hasn't been that long since she left creepy cult dude. I'm not sure I should be involved."

"How involved are you?"

"I'm involved, babe."

"You're in love?"

He wouldn't say anything, but his goofy grin spoke for him.

"Rocky?"

He nudged me. "Cut it out, babe."

So, Rocky was really in love. Wow. I always knew it would happen, but I didn't realize I'd still have the teensiest bit of pain knowing he'd moved on from me for good. The last time I saw them together, I could see a flower of astonishing beauty blossoming between them, even though it nearly killed me at the moment. But God knows Rocky deserved the biggest, juiciest love he could find. He needed to look beyond the nonexistent us. And he *still* called me babe.

"Just take it slow, Rock. Trust me. The cost of moving too fast is astronomical, even if you are in love."

I could tell he didn't feel comfortable talking to me about Elisa. I decided to let their love blossom without my tending, pruning, or pulling up weeds. I got back to the business at hand. "Are you ever going to tell me what your offer is?" I eased into the lush upholstery of my sofa.

Rocky's face lit up. Honestly, if that guy had a tail to go with those puppy eyes, it would be thumping my sofa with joy.

"It's gonna be awesome, ba—I mean, Bell."

Apparently our little chat about Elisa made him correct himself.

"You think everything is awesome, Rocky."

"I don't think *everything* is awesome."

"You said my Love Bug is awesome. You said Switchfoot's new CD is awesome. You said my new zillions braids are awesome, and you said the ice cream at Cold Stone Creamery is awesome." Okay, the ice cream at Cold Stone happened to be awesome for real. Lately I'd been craving it like the blind crave sight.

"But, babe . . ."

There he went again. Honestly! A holy war couldn't make that man stop calling me babe.

He went on. "Those things *are* awesome."

"*God* is awesome, Rock. 'Awesome' meaning the subject inspires awe, as in reverence, respect, dread."

"You *reverence* your tricked-out VW Beetle," he said. "And I *respect* Switchfoot, especially Jon Foreman, and your way-cool, African-goddess hair *inspired* me to get dreads."

I stared at him. Comments like these coming from Rocky tended to render me temporarily speechless.

He filled the silence with his proposal. "I want you to go see Ezekiel Thunder with me."

My eyes widened. Electroshock therapy wouldn't have given me such a jolt. "*Ezekiel Thunder?*" I screeched. I jerked up from my slouch. I'd heard the *un*-right reverend wanted to hit the comeback trail, bringing his miracle crusade with him.

Rocky gave me a wicked grin and smugly settled himself into the soft folds of my sofa. He knew I'd left Thunder's particular brand of Pentecostal fire many years ago and had no desire to go back.

Rocky bobblehead nodded, as if his physical movement would effect a change in my attitude.

"Stop all that nodding!"

"I'm just trying to encourage you."

I did not feel encouraged.

"It'll be fun," he said, blasting me with the full puppy-eyes arsenal. Oh, those eyes. Powerful! Mesmerizing! Like a basketful of cocker spaniel puppies wearing red ribbons. I could feel myself weakening.

"Rocky, that meeting will torture me. It will torture *you!*"

"No, it won't. Ezekiel is my friend."

"Your *friend*?"

"He led me to Christ."

"Ezekiel Thunder led you to Christ?"

"I told you I came to Christ at a Bible camp."

"Yes? *And?*"

"It was a Sons of Thunder Bible camp. I'm a Thunder Kid!" He beamed with what I hoped wasn't pride.

"You never told me that!"

Honestly! You think you know somebody! He was my ex-boyfriend for goodness' sake. We'd talked about *marriage*. I couldn't believe I had no idea he was close friends with the infamous Ezekiel Thunder.

"You can be kinda judgmental about guys like Ezekiel," he went on. "I didn't mean to upset you or trigger bad memories of your tongues-talking days."

"Then don't ask me to go see him."

"He's a different man. He and his family want to buy a house in Ann Arbor. He's living at the Rock House house until one comes through for him."

"God forbid!"

"He needs support. People to show up and cheer him on."

"Cheer him on? We should *stop* him!" Had Rocky forgotten that Ezekiel Thunder had fallen as hard as many of his televangelist contemporaries in the eighties—and for a tawdry tryst with a young intern? May it never be!

"How hard would it be for you to sit there and listen? Maybe say a few prayers for him."

"God bless *you* as *you* do that for him."

"I was there for you, supporting Great Lakes Seminary when

they were struggling and going to lose their building. I did it because of how much *you* love Mason May."

"Rocky! That's not even comparable. Mason is a fine theologian who trains good men and women for powerful, effective ministries. He's not a snake-oil peddler."

"It's not snake oil. It's miracle prosperity oil."

I stared at him. He'd stunned me to silence once again. I waited for Rocky to fill the silence with testimonies about the healing properties of miracle prosperity oil. Thankfully, he refrained. But he didn't look like he'd let me off the hook.

I tried to reason with him. "You shouldn't ask me to do this. You're *Emergent*, Rocky, not a dyed-in-the-wool charismatic."

"You don't like postmodern, postdenominational, Emergent folks, either."

"I like them more than I like Ezekiel Thunder."

"What's that thing you say about the Emergent church?"

"This is not about the Emergent church. I'd go to an Emergent meeting with you anytime. You name the place: Mars Hill, Ann Arbor Vineyard. How 'bout Frontline Church?"

He didn't budge. "Come on, babe. He's like a dad to me."

"A *dad*?"

"You always say Mason is like a dad to you."

"But Mason has a PhD. He doesn't sell 'miracle prosperity oil.'"

"Ezekiel doesn't sell it, either. He gives it away in exchange for a love offering."

"A considerable love offering, if I remember. It's plain olive oil he's pushing to gullible babes in the faith who don't know any better. How can I support his money-lusting schemes?"

"Ummm. By going with me?" Hope burgeoned in his voice as if I hadn't just accused his mentor of being a hustler.

"Did you hear what I said, Rock? Ezekiel Thunder is everything I walked away from."

"You walked away from a lot more than that, babe. And you've been known to hang out with people with worse theology than his. People way more dangerous."

He had a point.

"Rocky . . ." I didn't want to go. *Please, God, don't make me go.*

"He's changed, babe. Give him a chance. For me."

The eyes again, and a smile with an invisible tail wag.

I grumbled.

He grinned.

I gave him a dramatic sigh. "What time are we leaving?"

"If you're not busy, and you're not, we can leave in a few hours. I'll pick you up at six."

"How do you know I don't have plans?"

"Because you have antisocial tendencies."

"Don't hold back, Rock. What do you *really* think about me?"

"Don't worry," he said, ignoring my insolence. "You're gonna fall in love with Ezekiel."

I rolled my eyes. "Not likely."

He put his face right in front of mine until we were eye to eye. "You are feeling veeeeeery tired. You're getting sleepy. You're going to enjoy yourself at the crusade."

"No fair," I said. "Those eyes of yours are potent hypnotizers."

"You are going to love Ezekiel Thunder."

"I am going to love Ezekiel Thunder."

Rocky got out of my face. "You've gotta admit, babe. This will be safer than sleuthing."

No, it won't, a disembodied voice—also known as the still, small voice of God—informed me.

I tried to ignore it.

Couldn't ignore it.

What, Lord? Am I some kind of trouble magnet? Don't answer that, God.

I started rationalizing immediately to take the edge off what I truly hoped was *not* a prophetic warning. Maybe I *could* fall in love with the guy and respect him. Maybe he could even heal the egg-size growth on my lower abdomen, which scared me to death each time I ran my index finger across it. Maybe I could even find the keys to unlock the little room inside my heart where all the Ezekiel Thunders I'd ever known were locked. I'd stored them there to keep me safe from the particular brand of harm only they could inflict. Maybe I could forgive them. Finally.

I could feel my defenses shoot up as if propelled by a rocket.

I wished I would fall in love with Ezekiel Thunder.

I shouldn't have wished. My great-grandmother and namesake, Amanda Bell Brown, used to say, "Be careful what you wish for, baby. You just might get it."

She ain't never lied.

chapter
two

ROCKY PAID NO ATTENTION to my whining and pouting all the way to the rented building in Inkster where Thunder intended to hold his meetings.

"Why didn't you let him use the Rock House?"

"I offered, but he wanted to have a central meeting place so his Detroit audience could get to him easier. He's gonna have more meetings in Ypsilanti and Ann Arbor when he finds a house."

I wished I'd taken my Love Bug. It had my iPod. I needed comfort. I felt ill at ease to my core about this whole Thunder thing, and my car always enveloped me in a kind of feel-good safety that was difficult to explain.

Rocky's red pickup truck had an iPod, too, but he didn't want to listen to it. Instead he wanted to practice a method of relaxing and releasing his thoughts that he termed "contemplative catatonic."

"I don't think you should do that while you're driving, Rock."

He ignored me.

"I'm not comfortable with the idea of the driver being in an altered and, quite frankly, *DSM-IV*-scary state of consciousness."

He roused himself long enough to say, "I'm not *really* cata-tonic. I'm a *contemplative* catatonic person who is driving. You're completely safe. Now be quiet and go catatonic with me."

Fortunately, before I had time to zone out, we arrived at our destination. The rambling school building looked condemned. Graffiti adorned the wood covering broken windows and the white brick walls—at least they used to be white. I think.

"This is where Thunder is having his meeting?"

"Cut it out. Don't be a spiritual elitist. You know what Jesus thought about *them*."

"I'm not being an elitist. I just didn't happen to tuck my hard hat and steel-toed work boots in my purse."

"Can you be nice? Maybe God will speak to you."

"I hope He says, 'heads up,' before the ceiling caves in."

"You should be glad if He says *anything* to you. You certainly don't spend much time talking to Him."

"Ouch."

Rocky got out of the truck and opened the door for me.

"Lock your doors and take your iPod," I said, stepping out of the car.

"Quit it."

"Look at this neighborhood. You're in da 'hood, my friend. Did you notice the huge housing project across the street?"

"It's just some town houses."

If he wanted to call the brown-brick two-story burned-out, broken-down, drug-infested horror "just some town houses," sure. But I didn't.

"Rocky. Those town houses have a nickname. Little Saigon.

I interviewed many of its residents for Dr. Weston when I interned at Wayne County Jail."

He didn't lock the doors after he shut mine behind me. Ever the good guy and gentleman, he grabbed my hand.

"Rock, I'm telling you. Lock up."

"Whatever is not of faith is sin."

"I try to protect you, and what do you do? You beat me up with Scripture."

He ignored me and pulled me toward the building. A few weary sojourners ambled through a set of ancient double doors —psychedelic double doors, now multicolored from the chipping layers of paint. Probably lead paint.

Great. I get to die here in Lead and Asbestos Elementary School.

We walked through doors flanked by two Philistine guards. Where Ezekiel Thunder got the pair of seven-foot-tall mutants was beyond me.

"Hello, gentlemen," I said. "Nice evening."

Both growled an unintelligible greeting.

"Whoa," Rocky said, picking up his pace. He looked at them as if they were truly awesome.

"I don't think we have to worry now. If my great-grandmother could see those two, she'd say they could kill a brick."

"He didn't use to have bodyguards."

"Maybe the father of that intern he took advantage of is looking for him."

"That's not funny, babe."

"No, it isn't. And don't call me babe."

We followed crude handwritten signs down a long hallway with old-fashioned coat hooks halfway down the walls. It was like walking through a ghost town. I could imagine the children who'd once roamed the halls. My ache for a child burst into my consciousness. "God, have mercy."

Rocky stopped short. "What is it, babe?" He stood in front of me and cradled my elbows. His kind eyes looked into mine.

"I'm fine."

"Are you sure?"

A fine mist of sadness had settled over me. "No, Rocky. I'm not fine. Everything that makes me think of children and not being able to have a child upsets me."

My feelings jumbled inside me, colliding into one another. Joy and grief. Peace and turmoil. Love and walls to guard what was left of my heart. All stirred together.

"And I think I'm feeling emotional because you're here with me, and you keep calling me babe." My voice broke without warning.

I had to hold it together. It would be hard enough to revisit my Pentecostal past. I willed the tears to a place of quiet submission. "I'm so happy to be hanging out with you again. And this is so weird because we're about to see Ezekiel Thunder. It's been so long since I've been to anything like this. And . . . and . . ."

Too late. I kept talking and the sorrow I had barely held at bay seeped out. I blubbered all over his *Batman* T-shirt.

Poor Rocky. He stood there hugging me, rubbing my back, and praying the Ninety-first Psalm from *The Message*. Just the way I like it.

When he finished, he paused and then said, "Are you okay, babe?"

"*WAAAAAAH.*"

As we stood there, he stroked my back and the curtain of blond braid extensions I wore. I let him rub and pat the peace into me with the steady rhythm of his hand and his rock-solid love. I held him until my breathing slowed, my heart sighed with relief, and my arms were ready to give Rocky a squeeze—our signal that I was ready to let him go.

"I got snot on your shirt."

"That's okay," Rocky said. "Well, not really; this is my favorite *Batman* shirt."

I laughed. "I really, really missed you."

"Come on. Let's go get you some miracle prosperity oil."

"No, thanks."

"Last chance, babe. I'll put the love offering in myself. The only thing you have to lose is poverty and lack."

I chuckled. "Yeah, right."

He nudged me with his elbow. "You forgot to tell me not to call you babe."

"I actually liked it that time."

A smile like sunshine, like a bright new merciful morning, spread across his face. He grabbed my hand. "Let's not let anything keep us from being friends ever again, okay?"

"Okay, Rock."

"Shake on it."

I shook it like a Polaroid picture. He did the same.

We laughed, and I knew that with my husband out of the picture, it wouldn't be too hard for us to stay friends at all.

———————

With one glance I took in the gymnasium. *Oh, how the mighty have fallen.* The once wildly popular man of God failed to fill the gym of a tiny, dilapidated school in a ghetto neighborhood. Before I could give any more attention to the disgraced evangelist's fate, a rabid usher ambushed us, or rather, me.

Honestly, it felt like that old black woman clamped an iron claw around my entire arm. I feared she'd permanently branded her handprint across my biceps. The ancient but incredibly strong old church mother could have been my own great-grandmother, Ma Brown. Only Ma Brown was prettier. And less vicious. And smelled better.

Granny Hook reeked of Chantilly Eau De Toilette. I hadn't had a whiff of that since puberty. Even then I didn't think anyone other than adolescent girls wore it. The overpowering scent mingled with the mothballs she must have packed her clothes in and the Altoids on her breath, creating a noxious blend. I could feel myself greening as my gut did a back flip. Either I'd look like Kermit the Frog by the time I got to the seat she was dragging me to, or I'd end up spilling my guts—and not in the "confession that's good for the soul" way.

Of course, she'd chosen me alone as the focal point of her wrath. My blissed-out pal had smiled at her and skipped ahead to his seat in the VIP section—two pathetic, nearly empty rows in front.

"This way, *missy*," the evil usher hissed, with a snort that smacked of her disapproval. It was the race thing. I could just feel it. Rocky and I had been through this too many times before. Not everyone wanted to see Dr. King's dream of black and white together realized. Still, it wasn't her business.

Besides, we weren't a couple anymore, and I happened to be a "mrs.," not a "missy." I wanted to say so in an effort to defend myself against her snark, but I figured she'd *really* do me bodily harm if I had the audacity to be that brazen. As it was, she kept looking from me to Rocky. Her disapproval burned into me. Or was that heartburn? I couldn't tell.

"He's my pastor. Sort of." I didn't know what else to say. I hadn't necessarily replaced him.

That infuriated Granny Hook even more and elicited a tighter squeeze. She brought her face close to mine. "You ain't got no business goin' round with yo' pastor, *hussy.*"

Why did everyone find that idea appalling? Did somebody publish a church etiquette book stating that under no circumstances should one date her pastor? Did I miss a memo? And did that old bat just call me a hussy?

"Look, lady, I'm married. To someone else."

She glared at me. That did it. I could see my sinner status grow exponentially in her glassy eyes. I had become the whore of Babylon.

I tried to wrench myself from her grip to go sit with Rocky, but the guerrilla grandma yanked me to the center of the gymnasium. "Demon," she hissed.

"Look, I know you and I didn't get off on the right foot, but I hardly think—"

"*Shush.*"

I shushed.

Granny got very close to me. "You foul demon of interracial dating and adultery, come out in Jesus' name."

"*What?* Demon of inter—"

"Shut up." She slammed her open palm against my forehead.

"Ow! Lady!"

Must not have been the response she wanted. "Come out!"

Just then a few more faithful joined her in casting out my interracial-dating-and-adultery demon. I briefly wondered if that was one demon or two.

"Listen, everybody, I'm not possessed. I'm not even dating, interracially or otherwise."

This didn't sit well with Granny Hook. She pulled me to the front of the auditorium as if she were my mother threatening to give me a beatdown.

A cameraman, his camera mounted on a huge tripod with wheels, came over to us. I noticed Hook had strategically marched me up to stand in front of the Plexiglas podium with the new Ezekiel "Son of Thunder" Crusade logo. At the same time, a very well dressed man, much shorter than the giants that greeted us at the door, stuck a microphone in my face.

Grandma Hook spat her words at me. "You lyin' *demon*! Name yourself."

"I don't have a demon."

"*Name* yourself!" She grabbed my shoulders and gave me a brain-rattling shake.

"I'm *Amanda*!" I certainly wasn't going to let her call me Bell. "*Liar!*"

I started fishing around in my purse for my driver's license. I could hear someone call out from the audience, "Uhn-uh. Them demons be lyin'. Don't wanna lose they home. Gon' and cast it out, Sister Lou."

Sister Lou snatched my purse away from me and threw it onto the floor, no doubt for effect.

"Come out!" Her spittle showered my face. She gripped my head with her talons digging into my forehead. Honestly, her laying on of hands almost gave me a migraine, and I could feel slimy spit gliding down my cheeks like a bunch of slugs.

Not good.

Suddenly my poor stomach rebelled. Her Chantilly oh-the-toilet. The sludge that flew out of her mouth. Her green apple Altoid breath. All that laying on of hands.

One last command from Sister Lou and Company for the devil to come out, and something altogether different exploded out of queasy me. I hurled. In a big way. I'm not talking a dainty little gag. I mean I projectile vomited like a young Linda Blair puking up torrents of split-pea soup in *The Exorcist*. And they were filming me!

I wanted to cry out in protest but my retching required total participation. Sister Lou grabbed my braids and continued to rebuke and cast out, laying her iron hand all over my poor head.

"Ohhhhh," I moaned, looking down at a pair of alligator shoes. Very expensive shoes.

My head snapped up, probably because Sister Lou yanked me by the braids in that direction. Suddenly I found myself standing face-to-face with Ezekiel Thunder, the last of a dying breed of televangelists.

My first impression: Wowza! Tall, thin, and wickedly handsome, the mahogany-colored dreamboat with a slightly portly belly—probably from too many after-church fried-chicken dinners—looked amazing for a man who had to be sixtyish. A

legend stood before me—a man as well-known as R. W. Scham-
bach or T. D. Jakes. Fiery. Devil chasin'. Sin hatin'. Except for
when it came to his personal sin, apparently.

I remember when, as a frail teenager, I had holy lust for that
man's healing power. That was back when, in the summertime,
he would take his tent crusade to small towns, where he would
serve up miracles like lemonade. And now he's singing his signa-
ture song to me: "You Won't Leave Here Like You Came."

In Jesus' name.

Lord, have mercy.

He interrupted his song to grin at me with his Hollywood-
bright teeth. "How do you feel now, darlin'?"

My mouth opened, but apparently my voice had gone on
silent retreat. In the absence of protest, I got another laying on of
hands. Ezekiel Thunder himself smacked me upside the head.

I stood there stunned.

Again. *Smack!* "Be healed in Jesus' name."

I wondered if he and Lou had any concept of the idea of *laying* on of hands. Maybe slowly? Maybe gently? But no, he, too,
gripped my forehead and pushed me back with enough force to
slay me himself if the Holy Spirit didn't. A big, burly man, the
catcher, stood at the ready.

I righted myself and kept standing.

Then it dawned on me. I'd gone to Rocky's church so long,
I'd forgotten the charismatic rules. I should have been slain in the
Spirit at Ezekiel's touch. If I didn't fall down, I'd get delivered all
right, to the hospital to get care for a closed head injury.

Talk about not leaving like you came!

Okay, I repent. They didn't hit me that hard.

Finally I leaned back into the catcher guy and let myself fall. A woman standing by draped my already completely covered legs in a piece of silky red cloth.

Ezekiel Thunder gave me a big smile. Or maybe he was smiling for the camera.

I lay there thinking how I would kill Rocky. And how as soon as I got home, I'd find a plot of land and claw the dirt to dig my ex-pastor's grave with my bare hands.

Somewhere off camera a little voice cried, "Hi-eee."

While the cameras followed Ezekiel Thunder, singing like he was God's troubadour, up to the Plexiglas podium, my attention went to a little guy, a lighter-skinned, preschool version of the man, waving at me from the front row. He nearly stopped my heart with his crooked little smile. There was no doubt. This had to be Little Thunder Boy.

Suddenly I didn't care if I'd been exorcised on camera and left for slain, splayed across the floor of a raggedy gymnasium. The brown-eyed cherub, laughing and gesturing for me to get up, captivated me.

Rocky called it right. I fell in love with Ezekiel Thunder. I just didn't know he'd be the miniature one.

And speaking of Rocky. When I finally made it to my seat next to Rocky and behind Thunder Boy—only sitting next to Rocky so I could get to that baby!—Rocky had the unmitigated gall to say something to me.

"Babe! I didn't know you were *possessed*."

Following the style of my great-grandmother and namesake, Amanda Bell Brown, I didn't dignify that with an answer.

I smacked him upside his head.

chapter
three

THE WOMAN holding little Baby Thunder in front of us in the "Holy Ghost row" certainly didn't look young enough to be his mother. The honey-colored older black woman, much more elegant than the crazed usher, appeared old enough to be a great-grandmother to the child. She wore her salt-and-pepper hair in a neat chignon. Her suit, a cream-colored poly blend, sparkled from the intricate beadwork sewn across the trim. She seemed to engage the toddler as needed, but the furrow in her brow and her craned neck indicated a greater interest in the action going on around the child's father.

She didn't even seem to notice when I leaned forward and whispered my name to the captivating baby. "*You,*" I told him, "can call me Bell." He slapped his chubby hand to his lips and chortled, whipping his head back and forth with baby glee.

I didn't see anyone seated nearby who seemed to have motherly interest in the little boy, so I glanced up at the makeshift stage.

Aha. There, without a doubt, young Madam Thunder sat on a first-lady chair. The huge, ornate, ugly-as-sin monstrosity seemed to coordinate with a similar, equally hideous bigger piece of furniture next to it. Honestly, a pair of matching electric chairs held more appeal than that set of his-and-her thrones, or whatever they were. The chairs seriously activated my gag reflex, and my mother would have died on the spot if she'd laid eyes on them.

I gazed at Mrs. Thunder. She looked like a teenaged girl, with her flawless café au lait skin. Her auburn hair had been teased to impossible heights—a frightening eighties throwback. I had to admit, she had a figure to die for. She was not turn-your-head beautiful in the face, and I'd seen better makeup on the dead, but the outfit she wore shouted "high maintenance" as earnestly as a roomful of Pentecostals shouted, "Glory."

She certainly didn't look old enough to be the fallen intern. I doubted if she had even been born yet during that season of Thunder's life. I would have said the man had had a recent, raging midlife crisis, only he'd passed midlife by now. He knew better. The old goat!

I'm sorry, Lord. I had that whole calling-people-animal-names thing down pat. *All this judgment!* Rocky had assessed me well when he told me I could be a little judgmental. *A little?*

I mumbled another lame "Sorry" to God, but I still felt reluctant to release the flurry of criticism storming through my head. Those barbs served as a powerful defense mechanism.

I shot a look at Rocky, now in ardent worship as Thunder's velvet voice rang out, "Great Is Thy Faithfulness."

I marveled at Rocky and his own faithfulness. He may get a little smart-mouthed, but he never strays from honesty given with a hearty dose of love. He knew what it meant to forgive folks their debts. I could only imagine what Thunder must owe

people, including Rocky, but my former pastor responded to the
man as if he were Christ himself—sinless. I sensed not a hint of
judgment from Rocky. And I don't think he could have looked
more radiant if we'd been at a Billy Graham crusade. He shone
like a polished rock—no pun intended—and that brightness of
spirit had to be God's love.

Rocky loved him some Jesus, and nothing would diminish
that, but he also loved Ezekiel Thunder. And now I'd stumbled
once again into his good graces. I stood next to Rocky, debt-free,
loved as if that night I broke his heart had never happened.

I raised my head and began singing the hymn of God's faithful love and provision as passionately as Rocky. I forced the
skepticism prowling about my head like a wild animal to a dark
corner of my soul. Like everyone else in the room, I worshipped
God until I felt peace like my great-grandmother's quilt—soft,
warm, and comforting—around me. The music quieted. Several
people sang softly in what sounded like a heavenly language. I'd
been thoroughly trained in the structure of this kind of service.
I listened, because it still sounded lovely to me, and it had been
a long time since I'd found anything that made me feel like my
spirit sang with angels. I willed myself not to go analytical. At
least not too much.

How many years had it been since I'd been to a meeting like
this? Or sung in what I believed was my own heavenly language?
How far had I ventured from the idealistic young Christian
woman I used to be before Adam, my former abuser, stripped me
of innocence and a good deal of my sense of self?

Oh, it hurt to think of it. I missed the former Bell, the innocent who still believed in miracles and didn't know about the

kind of ugliness and evil that Adam possessed. Evil that could draw you in before you knew what hit you. I missed the girl who believed in the Ezekiel Thunders of the world. Before televangelists fell like a house of cards, while young Bell watched with a frightening blend of horror and shock, wondering if *anything* she *thought* she knew about God was true.

Don't think about it, Bell.

Tears stung my eyes. My throat tightened. I didn't want to cry again. I knew if I did, big, heaving wails would break the levee holding back the grief over those lost years that I'd contained for too long.

Oh, God. Don't let me fall apart.

But, man, how I wanted to believe in a God who healed *everybody* who asked, just because they named it and claimed it. I wanted the old-timers who'd left their walkers and crutches on the altar not to realize the next day that they still needed those walkers and crutches after all. I wanted to believe in miracle prosperity oil that would bring abundance and no lack.

I shouldn't have come here.

A hush fell over the room. In this sacred time, carved out in many charismatic meetings, the faithful listened reverently for a prophecy. A once-familiar eagerness seized me. I wanted God to speak some kindness to me. With a desperation I didn't realize I had, I begged God in my heart for just a whisper. A breath. Anything.

We waited in quiet stillness for the lone voice of the prophet to pierce the silence and give us a word. Instead, a tiny toddler voice filled the room now pregnant with anticipation. "I love you," the voice said.

Baby Zeekie. My head snapped up. My eyes met the little boy's. He smiled as wide as the sky. "You," he said, pointing a chubby little finger at me. He laughed, then smacked a kiss on his hand and flung it at me.

Schlepping along with Rocky afforded me his VIP status by default, which meant we got to go into the green room—a room that, in fact, had beige walls. It used to be a classroom and still had that weird school smell about it, which nauseated me. Ezekiel Thunder or Sister Lou needed to exorcise me again. I felt a distinct urge to vomit, and surely they'd want to capture that fine moment on tape as proof of my deliverance.

We stood around a few banquet tables covered with white paper tablecloths. The tables nearly buckled under a feast of soul food delights. Everything looked good—well, almost everything—but I wanted something that might settle my stomach.

"Rocky."

"Yeah, babe?" He cradled my elbow in his hand and drew me closer as he leaned in to hear me.

"I'm feeling sick. I think I'm coming down with something." For several weeks some kind of stubborn virus had clung to me, never burning itself completely through my immune system to become full-blown.

He gave me a wary glance, sizing me up. "You're not still possessed are you?" He stage-whispered this as if the twenty people in the room could not hear him.

"I'm *not* possessed," I hissed.

"Well, not *anymore*."

I wanted to smack him—again. "I wasn't possessed earlier! I've had flulike symptoms for the last few weeks, and—well, she got to me with all that cologne and . . ." My spidey senses told me Sister Lou lurked nearby. I snapped my mouth shut.

My spidey senses happened to be correct. Sister Lou sauntered up to me with a self-satisfied smirk on her face.

"Ummmm-hmm."

Her Chantilly wafted in my direction. I didn't respond. How could I? I had no idea what she meant by "ummmm-hmm," and if I opened my mouth, more than words might come tumbling out. I started using affirmative self-talk to keep from making a spectacle of myself once again.

You are in control.

You are fearless.

You are not going to puke.

Positive self-talk failed to help me. Nausea washed over me in waves. I stepped closer to the fried chicken for comfort and strength, this time asking God for a little help.

Can you just keep her away from me?

I had to shoot straight with God. I didn't have the energy for grandiose words that wouldn't impress Him anyway.

Chantilly Lou didn't move toward me or follow me. She seemed to fix her attention on Rocky.

Serves him right for bringing me here. Let him *get delivered.*

Only, she didn't exorcise him. Rocky smiled at her and gave her the puppy eyes. She didn't even get the full blast, and the next thing I knew she'd thrown her head back and was cackling like the Wicked Witch of the West and touching her hair.

Eww!

I picked up a plate and piled on a mound of mashed potatoes and spooned out gravy, trying not to look at Rocky and Wicked. Grabbed a few chicken wings. A piece of corn on the cob, lots of butter. I left the greens because I didn't like the look of the ham hocks floating in too much pot liquor. I stole another look at the terrible two.

Wicked pinched Rocky's cheeks, called him baby, and made his plate. I get interracial-dating and adultery demons cast out, but Rock doesn't. He gets the royal treatment. I tried hard not to be jealous—not that I coveted the affection of the despot prophetess.

"I could use a little tender loving care," I said aloud to myself.

"Well, let me give you some, darlin'." A sexy voice with a smooth Southern drawl, groomed from many years of working an audience.

I turned. There stood Ezekiel Thunder. He took the plate from my hand, looked at it, and smiled with his pearly white veneers that probably had cost more than the national debt. Like his wife, he had flawless skin, with very few lines to betray his age. He'd colored his hair an unnatural black. Still, I could see why young women fell for him. He could have been a movie star instead of a fiery preacher. He added macaroni and cheese and an anemic-looking three-bean salad to my plate.

"Thank you, Mr. Thunder." I tried to keep my cool exterior, but his eyes seemed to look into every cell in my body. I couldn't have been more affected if Errol Flynn were standing in front of me.

"Call me Ezekiel," he said with a wink.

"Okay, Mr. Thunder."

My mind screamed, *Don't trust him*. I tried to offer him a polite smile, but the war within kept my lips from fully cooperating. The edges curled up, and it may have appeared that I snarled at him. He didn't seem to mind.

"So *you're* Rocky's heart?"

"Rocky's heart is in his chest, sir. I'm his friend."

"Bell Brown."

"The name's Amanda." No way would I let Ezekiel Thunder call me Bell.

"Ow," he said. "I've heard about your name. You won't let me call you Bell, darlin'?"

"No offense, Mr. Thunder. It's reserved for my inner circle. And don't call me darlin'."

"Then that's Reverend Thunder to you." His eyes twinkled with playful mocking.

"I stand corrected, *Reverend*."

A broad smile spread across his face. "Call me Ezekiel, Bell." He winked again and sang as he handed me my plate, "*You. Won't. Leave here like you caaaaaaaaame, in Jesus' Naaaaaaaaame.*"

Rocky and Sister Lou walked up to us. I took my plate, stacked higher now thanks to Thunder's generosity. Sister Lou scowled at me, then grinned broadly at Thunder.

I wanted to shove her over to the housing project across the street, but I had a feeling Little Saigon was no match for devil-chasin', sin-hatin', Chantilly-stankin' Lou. Oh well.

I took a few not-so-discreet steps to get as far away from her

as I could without leaving the room or going near other people.
I ended up next to the beverages and desserts.

"Punch anyone?" I asked.

"I'll get it, babe," Rocky said, rushing to my aid.

He filled two cups from a bowl of red punch topped with
what looked like orange sherbet. He served Sister Lou first, then
me—age before beauty, obviously. He made another go of it and
served Thunder and himself.

"Thank you, son," Thunder said, his voice as smooth as silk.
His eyes shifted over to me. "Why don't you sit with me, Bell? I
want to get to know the woman who stole my boy's heart."

"Don't call me Bell. And I'm afraid Elisa's not here tonight."
I said this for both Thunder's and Sister Lou's sake, in case Lou
had a mind to cast out adulterous demons again.

Rocky's puppy eyes narrowed at me, no doubt because of my
rudeness. *"Babe!"*

"Don't call me babe."

Ezekiel Thunder chuckled. "He told me you always say that,
and that he still always calls you babe."

Honestly! What else had Rocky told him about me?

Thunder took the lead and glided over to one of the banquet
tables set up for dining. He gave us a quick glance to make sure
we weren't going to go rogue and sit at another table. "Walk this
way," he said.

Rocky literally walked the way he did, imitating the man
Three Stooges–style. He turned around and grinned at me. I figured you only live once. Like Rock, I glided over to the table mim-
icking Thunder. He and Sister Lou seemed oblivious to our fun.

We got to the long table and the three of us sat down, Ezekiel right next to me. Sister Lou initiated our next battle.

"You sho' got a lotta food, gal."

"*Excuse* me?" *Me. Lou. Parking lot. Now.*

Old smoothie said, "That's because she's pregnant."

chapter
four

I DIDN'T KNOW who would get worse whiplash, me or Rocky, the way our heads snapped up to look at Thunder. My heart dropped to my shoes and did a drum cadence. Rocky's mouth opened, but no sound came out. I, however, had plenty to say.

"I'm not *pregnant*!" I said it like he'd called me a dirty name.

He turned on the charm. "Bell, you're positively radiant with child."

Rocky stared at me like I'd grown a third head. "I thought she looked that way because she's not possessed anymore."

Ezekiel laughed. "Oh, she's possessed all right."

I started sputtering before I finally got out, "Mr. Thunder. I'm not pregnant. I happen to have a difficult time getting pregnant, and—"

"Her husband left her."

Make that *Rocky*, Lou, and me in the parking lot. I'd take 'em both.

I shot lasers out of my eyes at Rocky—only, they didn't really exist, so he remained unharmed.

"What I was going to say"—I frowned at Rocky—"was that

I don't appreciate your . . ." His what? Fake prophecy? Bald-faced lie? Insensitive lack of insight?

"But her husband still loves her." That from puppy eyes.

"He sure does, Rocky," Ezekiel said and then turned to me. "And he'll be restored to his rightful place as the head of his family. *God,*" he said—and because of his accent it sounded like *Gawd,* "is going to give you above and beyond all that you ask for. Thus saith the Lord." He did a little jerk, made a sound like "ha-ba-ba-shondo," and threw his hands in the air. "Hallelujah."

"I'm not pregnant!" I screeched. My mind riffled through my calendar and marked off the three pitiful days that I had my period *after* I made love with my husband. Days that I cried bitterly because I'd been profoundly disappointed at its appearance.

Sister Lou cut her eyes at me. "Thank God you got some of them demons out then." She looked at me with pure disgust. "Pregnant *and* fulla demons."

Before I could come up with an appropriately scathing reply, Ezekiel Thunder covered my hand with his. He leaned in so he could whisper in my ear. "Now, don't you mind Sissy. She means well." His breath tickled my ear.

I knew "Sissy" to be an old Southern endearment. I wondered if Lou could be his natural sister.

"She gets a little excited." His drawl extended the *sigh* sound in "excited." Honestly, if he'd nibbled my ear, I wouldn't have been surprised. The man could probably seduce a fruitcake. He pulled himself away from me and touched my chin with his thumb and forefinger—a tender gesture. Almost fatherly. *Almost.* If I didn't know he pitched snake oil and was subtly hitting on me as well, I might have liked him.

"Isn't he great, babe?"

I rolled my eyes at Rocky.

Again, Thunder's eyes met mine and seemed to permeate me. "God heard your cries like He heard Rebekah's. You *hay-ave*"—and yes, he stretched out "have" over two syllables—"the desire of your heart."

Dear God, I have cried like Rebekah.

His words caressed me like a pair of soft, skilled hands, but I knew this kind of man—this unholy hustler in his alligator shoes and suit expensive enough to feed a multitude. For a moment I felt confused. Oh, he was good. Intellectually, I knew I should feel angry, but his words were smooth and warm.

I wanted to believe him. The realization shamed me. Everyone around us seemed to disappear. My eyes locked with his. I could feel something inside of me wail and moan, and I couldn't quiet it. I whispered in my astonishment, "Why are you doing this to me?"

He squeezed my hand. "God heard you." Ezekiel Thunder reached up and stroked my braids, his every move hypnotic.

Without thinking, my hand went to my belly. "Endometriosis. I can't . . ."

"God can." He grinned like a used-car salesman. "Of course, Jazz had a lot to do with it, too." He winked at me again. When he said my husband's name, I snapped out of the weird dreamy state I'd been plunged into. A hot, suffocating anger surged within me. Its force took my breath for a moment.

Ezekiel Thunder sickened me. Confusion battled with a new bout of nausea in my gut. Heat rushed to my face. One way or another, I was about to lose it.

I spoke slowly, to keep my rage from roaring out. "How did you know my husband's name is . . ."

Rocky must have told him!

The anger I held at bay exploded out of me. I stood, knocking my chair out from behind me. "Listen here, Mr. Thunder. I don't know what Rocky told you about me, but I can assure you that I'm not pregnant and doubt if I ever will be. If you're under the impression your little *word of garbage* rather than *word of knowledge* is going to get an offering out of me, think again. You can play your head games with the poor desperate souls gathered here who need to believe there's some truth in your prophe*lying*. But I'm not one of them."

He simply smiled with his perfect teeth and said, "Jesus said, 'If thou canst believe, all things are possible to him that believeth.'" I couldn't tell if he'd said it for my benefit or because by now we'd gotten an audience with everyone in the room staring at us.

I reminded him, "The devil can quote Scripture."

Sister Lou stood up, probably to cast more demons out of me, but Ezekiel stopped her by moving one finger. She sank back down to her seat.

I turned to walk away. Where I'd go, I didn't know.

At that moment, Madam Thunder swept into the room like a tornado, little Zeekie in tow. The older woman who'd held the baby earlier when I'd talked to him walked behind her as if she were doing surveillance on her.

Mrs. Thunder walked up to her husband and shoved the child into his arms. "Take him." Apparently she had the maternal instincts of a Nazi war criminal.

I took a deep breath and chastised myself for my uncharitable thoughts. *Forgive me, Lord. Any mother can get tired.* I had judged everyone present and found them wanting before I even walked through the door. I turned to Rocky. "May we please leave?"

Rocky stood. Just then sweet Baby Thunder called my name.

"Bay-yell." He had his father's accent. From his father's lap, he reached his arms up, and Ezekiel Thunder picked up the boy and handed him to me. I took the little bundle of fun and squeezed him.

Little Zeekie put both hands on my cheeks and blew a raspberry on my lips with his wet mouth. My heart felt like it would burst from hope deferred. *Oh, God, please, if there's any way I can still have a child* . . . I imagined my body as hollow as a drum, the once-deafening sound of my biological clock now empty white noise. A tear slipped down my cheek. My throat constricted. I could barely croak out, "Rocky."

I guess First Lady Thunder misread me. She snatched the little boy away so roughly he cried.

I added her to the list of people I'd give a beatdown to. Ezekiel Thunder seized that moment to grab my hand.

"You have a tumor, Bell. It will cause a lot of problems."

I jerked my hand away from him. He couldn't know. God wouldn't have told this awful man what I hadn't even shared with my own doctor or with my sister, who was also a medical doctor, even though she worked with dead people.

I began to shake with rage. It was all I could do not to disobey the scriptures and lay hands on him *suddenly*! I turned on my heels and exited the room as quickly as I could. I stormed down the hallway, ignoring the ghosts of children past that haunted me in the little school. My lungs burned, and my heart felt like it would jump out of my chest. I had to remind myself to breathe in and out.

That insensitive cow wife of his has a baby, but I get a tumor! And I'm not pregnant! And never will be.

It felt so unfair. *How did that awful man know about my tumor? Nobody knows.*

All the terrible things that I'd ever done flooded my memory. I'd left Jesus for Adam. I'd opened up more than my heart to that nutjob. God *gave* me a baby, and I let Adam kill her. I didn't let Jazz help me. Love me. Now a tumor inhabited my belly. I hadn't told a soul about it, knowing that through my neglect I was committing suicide on the layaway plan. Who was I to ask God for help?

Confusion covered me like a burka. Thunder's words beat upon my brain.

You have a tumor.

You're positively radiant with child.

With child.

But I'd had my period. I couldn't be . . .

I heard Rocky call "Babe" from somewhere behind me. I didn't turn around. I snatched my cell phone out of my coat pocket and punched 411 for directory assistance. The operator could barely get out, "Information, what—"

"Yellow Cab, please. I'm in Inkster, Michigan." I didn't know if Inkster had a Yellow Cab company, but everywhere else on Earth seemed to.

Except Inkster. I sighed. "Any old cab will do. I just need to get outta here."

She must have heard the distress in my voice. The operator connected me to Big Four Cab, and I managed to squeak out my location through my sobbing. I tore out of the double doors, past the big, beefy guards, and into the icy night air.

Rocky trailed behind me until he trotted up to take my hand. "Babe, come back. He didn't mean to upset you. He said to tell you he's sorry. You don't have to call a cab. I'll take you home."

I put my phone away without canceling my cab. "Look around, Rocky."

He looked, confused. "What?"

"Do you notice something different?"

"Um. Nooooo."

"Your truck. It's gone."

Rocky stood there, mouth agape, scratching his blond dreadlocks.

I sighed. "I told you to lock your doors."

So much for the protection those two Goliaths offered. I felt sorry for Rock, but he was with his people. He'd find a way home, and his insurance would cover the truck. I didn't even want to offer to share my cab with him.

He used his cell phone to call the police. We waited outside in the freezing air, even though Rocky didn't have his coat on. By the time the police arrived, so had my cab.

"Are you going to be all right?" he asked.

I felt so vulnerable, I actually wished he'd call me babe. "As soon as I'm far away from here."

"I'm so sorry," he said. "I wanted God to speak to you."

"It was a very foolish choice for you to make for me, Rocky. I knew I shouldn't have come."

"Sorry. Babe . . ." I don't know what would have trailed behind that "Babe," but I didn't want to find out.

"Not sorrier than I am, Rocky."

"Let me pay for your cab."

"That's okay. I just wanna go."

He nodded, sadness brimming in those hound dog eyes.

Cost me sixty dollars to get home. I couldn't afford it, but it
felt like the best money I'd ever spent.

Thunder was right. I didn't leave there like I came.

chapter
five

FINALLY, IT'S FRIDAY. Friday means that the next day I wouldn't have to see anybody at the Washtenaw County Jail *or* my private practice. It means I could stay up until the wee hours of the morning watching season after season of *Columbo* on DVD. I could eat popcorn, Oreos, and Cold Stone Creamery Berry Berry Berry Good ice cream with nobody to tell me, "You should stop. You're getting fat."

This particular Friday had the distinction of being the day after I'd gotten the golden zillions braids taken out of my hair. I had my hair dyed off-black again—the closest I could get to my natural color, sans the streaks of gray—and walked out with a new set of braids that had taken three braiders four hours to weave onto my head. They looked fabulous, though. Long, tiny, flowing braids with the ends loose, falling just below my shoulders in soft, curly waves. The style, romantic and versatile, required little upkeep and allowed for Charlie's Angels–like hair shaking.

I arrived at my office parking lot, excited about showing my new hairdo to Maggie, my secretary, when a sinking feeling came over me—sinking as in the *Titanic,* with no fine Leonardo to take the edge off the tragedy.

I knew something wicked this way came. Every single car parked in the ridiculously small lot belonged to someone I knew.

Now what?

I shouldn't have wondered. Should have just said no, like Nancy Reagan told us in the eighties.

Go back home, Bell. I hadn't yet touched the ice cream in my freezer. The Godiva store had plenty of chocolate-covered strawberries—just in time for Valentine's Day—and I could make it there by the time they opened. No harm, no foul. Let Maggie handle the crisis.

But, no, I soldiered on.

My heart pounded, and I took a few steps toward the building, telling myself that it was *good news* that brought my loved ones together.

Not!

Good news, my eye! It was more likely that an episode of the *Jerry Springer* show awaited me! I didn't want Jerry Springer. I wanted my client Bill, who compulsively sang Chaka Khan songs. He at least was easy to deal with.

The conspicuous absence of the blue, unmarked, police-issued Crown Victoria that my husband, Jazz, drove didn't escape my attention. Whatever they'd planned to ambush me with, Jazz wasn't in on it.

I couldn't decide if that was a good thing or not.

I gathered my strength about me like I would pull my great-grandmother's quilt around my shoulders. If she were here, my namesake would say, "It ain't courage if you ain't scared." Besides, if they could ambush me at work, they could ambush me at home. I should be thankful they weren't all crowded into my apartment.

I got out of the Love Bug, fortifying myself with the Jesus Prayer: "Lord Jesus Christ, Son of the living God, have mercy on me, a sinner."

I went with the long version. I figured it couldn't hurt since I didn't know what awaited me. I slipped quietly into the corridor of my office. The scent of a special Valentine's Day coffee blend that Maggie got from Whole Foods greeted me. It had a sumptuous chocolate and raspberry flavor that made my toes curl inside my shoes. In a good way. It occurred to me that my heightened senses probably meant I'd been overcome by hormones and was now in the throes of a biological nightmare intent on barring me from motherhood for good. My poor, ailing biological clock. Every now and then I'd hear a cough or sputter from it as it marched in a funeral procession toward its premature death. Most days I pretended not to hear it. My marriage had crashed and burned. Why not my reproductive organs, too?

Nary a soul was at Maggie's desk. I'd hoped to find her holding court in the reception area as per usual, ready to give me a full report on what I'd be walking into.

"Maggie?"

She called from inside my office, "Amanda Bell, is that you?"

"Who else would it be? Everybody else is already here."

"Don't get smart with me."

Honestly! I'm about to get roasted and still have to watch my mouth.

I passed through the reception area and stepped into my office. *Everybody* indeed sat in there, and by everybody, I mean all the important people in my life, with two very notable exceptions: Jazz and my daddy.

Sasha, my mother, controlled the gathering from my favorite, way-cool purple leather office chair—which I'd bought myself as a belated birthday gift.

Both of the fine European wingback chairs Maggie had given me when I opened my office were filled, as well as the few cute, armless modern chairs usually in my reception area. Carly, in scrubs, sat in one of the wingbacks. Her black hair hung past her shoulders. An unlit cigarette dangled precariously from her mouth.

Next to her, my girlfriend Kalaya sat, tall, gloriously brown, with long legs crossed, resplendent in her class-with-sass style. She sat by her boyfriend Souldier, also known as cocoa brown, dreadlocked fineness. He also happened to be my husband's best friend. Souldier, a midnight-shift man, had probably just gotten off work. He still had on his heavy blue nylon Crime Scene Unit jacket.

My in-laws, Jack and Addie Lee Brown, were present and accounted for, along with my spiritual father, Dr. Mason May. Rocky sat next to him.

We were about to have a grueling group-therapy session. I just knew it.

"Did something bad happen? Because you all have to know it would be a terrible conflict of interest for me to see any of you as patients, even in a group session."

Carly lit her cigarette and began to smoke furiously. I noticed she'd taken a paper cup from the kitchenette to use as an ashtray.

"We're not the crazy person in your life," she said, puffing away.

"No comment on that," I said. "And this is a smoke-free office, Carly."

My mother stood up at my desk like she was about to begin a sales presentation. "This is an intervention, Bell."

"An *intervention*?" I didn't recall abusing drugs or alcohol. *What kind of addiction do they think . . .*

"You're getting fat."

"I told you," Maggie said to my mother.

Maggie, who did not get fat and always looked fantastic, gave her a triumphant nod. The snitch.

Fortunately, a few kind loved ones averted their eyes when Ma started in on my weight, except Addie Lee, my husband's mother, who intently stared at me. Still, my defenses soared.

"You're doing an intervention because I gained a few pounds?"

"A few?" Carly quipped. "It looks like you've gained about ten, maybe twelve."

"Seven! I've gained seven pounds."

"Have you seen your abs?"

"I haven't seen my abs since 1987. Abs don't count. I'm *bloated*. And I'm not addicted to food." Well, maybe ice cream, but did that mean I needed a 12-step program?

Kalaya spoke up. "We're not here about your weight, Bell, which I think looks great on you. Your mom just mentioned your weight to be . . ."

"Vicious?"

"Um . . . I was going to say motherly."

"How 'bout *truthful?*" Sasha said, her face looking like the innocent little lamb she wasn't.

Even Rocky agreed. "You do look a little fluffy, babe."

"Fluffy?" It sounded better than fat, but not much. "And don't call me babe."

Addie threw this jewel out there. "Sweetheart, are you pregnant?"

I sputtered. They were doing a pregnancy intervention? The wicked spawns of evil.

"No!" I shouted.

Rocky supplied. "Bell's very sensitive about her pregnancy."

"I'm not pregnant! What is this so-called intervention about? I. AM. NOT. PREGNANT!"

Sasha shook her head. "Umph, umph, umph. I *knew* someone would get pregnant. I had a dream about fish. I thought it would be your reporter friend."

"Hey," Kalaya said, "I'm doing the *right* thing with him." She nodded to Souldier, crossed her arms defensively, and scowled.

"Maybe it's Carly," I said. "She's the one with a sex life."

"Not anymore," Carly said. "And I wouldn't smoke if I were pregnant."

Rocky said, tentatively, because Carly hates him, "Maybe you should put that out, with Bell being an expectant mom and all."

I tried to reiterate. "I'm *not* pregnant."

Addie Lee didn't buy it. "I knew you were pregnant. As soon as you walked in, I could see it all over you." Tears welled in her eyes. Jack, who happened to be sitting near one of several boxes of Kleenex strategically positioned in my office, snatched up a tissue and handed it to her.

I tried to calm her. "I'm not pregnant, Addie Lee, honest."

I wanted to call her Mom like I used to, but I didn't know what Jazz had told his parents about me. I feared they thought the worst of me.

"Call me Mom," she said, relieving my fears.

Sasha just sighed. "Aren't you a little long in the tooth to be having your first baby?"

"I'm thirty-five. Thirty-five is the new . . . thirty-five."

"Didn't you say you couldn't get pregnant without some kind of procedure?" Carly jabbed.

"Yes, a procedure that I didn't have."

Rocky chimed in, "You had sex."

"I *married* him. *Before* we had sex."

"You could be pregnant."

"*Shut up!* I can't be!" I yelled at my former pastor. Again, I glanced around the room. "Why are you all here?"

"It's about Jazz," Addie Lee said.

"This is a Jazz intervention? You think I'm addicted to Jazz?"

Souldier popped up from his chair. "No, Jazz is addicted to you, Bell. You've got to go back to him. He's . . ."

"A nutjob," Jack supplied.

"Could you be a little more specific, Jack?"

"Don't call me Jack," he said. "I'm *Dad* to you."

"I'm sorry, *Dad*. What do you mean he's a nutjob?"

"First of all, baby. You look terrific. And Addie never calls 'em wrong. Congratulations."

"Dad, with all due respect to Mom's track record, I'm afraid I'm not pregnant."

Carly's cigarette smoke was starting to nauseate me. I shifted my weight on my legs. "Carly, this is a smoke-free office."

She kept puffing. "I'm under stress, and Timothy broke up with me. Is everything about *you*?"

All attention went to her. My own intervention, and things couldn't even be about me.

"When did you and Tim break up?"

"This morning. And where was my sister when I needed her? At home, doing pregnant things instead of answering *any* of her phones."

"I'm not pregnant! And sorry about the phones. I forgot to charge them." Again.

Maggie shook her head, her no-longer-blond hair swinging about. Her vivid blue eyes regarded me with a look of pity. "Why, you practically need maternity clothes."

"I do *not* need maternity clothes. I just need a size up. Maybe."

Dad Jack added, "You certainly are acting like a pregnant woman."

I screamed. One of those high-pitched, tormented wails like the comedian Sam Kinison used to do, God rest him. "I'm not pregnant, people, and I find it hurtful, as well as distasteful, that you're all persisting in this mass delusion because I've gained a few pounds."

Rocky shook his head. "Elisa's the same way."

"I said shut up, Rocky! This is not about your girlfriend. This intervention is about *me*!"

Jack scratched his head. "His girlfriend? You mean he's cheating on you already?"

"He's not cheating on me, Dad. We're not a couple."

"But I thought Rocky was in love with you," Addie said.

"I do love Bell, but she's married," Rocky said.

"You young people confuse me," Jack said. He looked at Rocky. "You mean your girlfriend doesn't mind if you're in love with a married woman?"

Kalaya answered. "No, Elisa isn't his girlfriend. Yet. See, Rocky didn't realize he loved Elisa until he caught Bell sleeping with Jazz. Really, she set him free to love again."

"Jazz and I are married! It wasn't a sin to sleep with him."

"Do I know you?" Rocky said to Kal.

I stomped my foot. "Hello. *My* intervention here!"

And speaking of Jazz . . . When I had everyone's attention, I continued. "What did you people come here to tell me about my *husband*?"

Jack spoke up. "He's in bad shape, especially at work. It's that whole thing about Kate's murder. He's still mad because he thinks everybody turned on him. Said he gave his life to that department, and now he can see who his friends really are."

I wasn't sure if *I* made the friends cut, despite the fact that I'd risked my life for him.

Souldier added, "And yo, he's missing you like mad, Bell."

Carly's smoke really started getting to me. My legs felt like rubber and my stomach lurched. "Can you all be more specific? What do you mean he's in bad shape at work?" *And missing me like mad?*

I stood in a room full of people who insisted I was pregnant, but could anyone offer me a seat?

"Will somebody please let me sit down," I yelled.

"Sorry," Jack said, scurrying out of his chair and seating me like the gentleman he usually is. "We were all so surprised to see you looking so . . ."

"Looking so what?" I plopped into his seat.

"Pregnant," Carly supplied, stabbing the cigarette butt into the paper cup. "You do have that glow about you." She stared at me. "I'm so jealous. And you do this to me just as Tim decides to leave me."

Rocky, having the misfortune of being seated next to her, put a reassuring hand on hers. Her icy glare caused him to quickly pull it back.

"Praying for you, Carly," he said sheepishly. He gave her a powerful hit of the puppy eyes.

I cleared my throat to get everyone's attention. "Will somebody please tell me more about Jazz?"

Souldier raised his hand, though nobody required that kind of decorum. "He talks about you constantly. Day and night. He's driving everybody crazy."

"Really?" My heart did a little dance.

Jack offered, "You gotta be kiddin' me, baby. If you don't go back to him, we're gonna have to shoot him."

Addie Lee nodded. "Put him out of his misery."

The image did not please me. "You all seem to have forgotten that *he* walked out on *me*."

With the exception of Rocky and me, all eyes in the room shifted to my former pastor, who furiously blushed.

He sputtered. "I . . . um . . . I didn't mean to kiss her."

Everyone glared at him.

"I mean, I meant to, but now I'm sorry."

Mason offered, "The question is why did she let you?" He and I had been through the whole sad story already. I knew he wanted me to put everyone else's mind at ease. I so didn't appreciate his comment.

Rocky came to my aid like the fine man he is, and by fine I mean he's a great person, not just a blondie-locked cutie. "She didn't kiss me back," he said. His earnest expression assured even me.

Now all eyes on me. "Well, I did. I mean, I didn't jerk away from him, but I didn't kiss him in the way he kissed me. I wanted to let him down easy."

Mason challenged me. "And?"

"And maybe I happened to be a bit self-sabotaging because I didn't feel like I deserved Jazz."

My mother looked outraged. "That's nonsense. That man is lucky to have you."

Addie nodded her head. "Honey, my son definitely met his match in you. You had no reason to feel that way."

I looked at Mason, who also nodded in the affirmative. "I told you, pumpkin. The only one who believed you weren't worthy of him was you."

"She tried to tell me how she was hurting," Rocky said. "She only wanted me to help her sort things out."

Mason spoke to Rocky. "She wanted the familiarity of your love because she knew you wouldn't fail her. Don't forget that, Rocky."

"I know that, sir, but with the things she's been through, I didn't mind offering her all the love I have. She's my friend. I should have been thinking more about her than myself."

The conversation pricked my heart. I felt a little weepy, but I held it in. "I still love my husband."

Addie chimed in, "It's not *us* you need to convince."

I crossed my legs, my defenses going up like gas prices. "I tried to let him know how I feel."

Jack laughed. "You mean when you ripped his bodice? Funniest thing I ever heard in my life."

Carly's eyes widened. "You ripped *his* bodice?" She looked confused. "You didn't tell me that. When?"

Kalaya brightened. "On Christmas Eve. First she kissed him like they were in the movies or something, and then she grabbed his shirt and ripped it off like she was gonna have her way with him right there in the doorway. It was totally major."

Carly whooped. "Way to go, baby sis. And she did this in front of you, Kalaya?"

Kalaya nodded. "Let's just say I stood at a discreet distance from the action."

I had to correct Kal before my legend grew any more. "I didn't rip his shirt *off.* I ripped it from the top button to his waist, but I never tore it off his body."

Souldier looked at Kalaya. "How come you never rip my bodice?"

"Because Jazz and Bell are married. And, um, we're not."

Jack couldn't resist. "Hint, hint."

This time Souldier blushed under all that cocoa brown beauty. He put his head down so his dreads covered his face.

I sighed. "Is there anything else I should know about Jazz?"

Addie said, "He needs you. You have to go back to him."

Souldier shot straight. "He's drinking too much."

I thought about the night Jazz had come to my house—the night before Kate's funeral. He'd had more than his share of alcohol. It concerned me then, but I assumed he'd buckled under the extreme stress of his situation.

My mother rolled her eyes. "An alcoholic husband. Fabulous. You married your father."

Her comment seemed to miff Addie. "He's not an alcoholic. He's just . . ."

Pastor Rocky supplied the appropriate word. "Lost."

Carly rolled her eyes at him and quipped to me, "Thanks to you, Bell."

By the time this intervention was over, I'd have put out more fires than the Ann Arbor Fire Department put out in a year.

"How about if we all remain calm and civil? I'm speaking mostly to Ma and Carly."

They grumbled.

"And don't you start up either, Maggie." I don't think she heard me. She'd pulled out her portable television and was probably waiting for the *Maury* show to start now that they'd switched it to afternoons. She'd already stuffed the earbuds into her ears.

"*What?*" she asked. Loud.

"Let me ask all of you this. If Jazz is the one who left me, and he's the one drinking excessively, why didn't you do the intervention with him?"

"Because all of this is your fault," my mother said.

"Ma, I warned you." Not that I'd do anything to her. She frightens me.

"Well it *is* your fault, and you're a lot easier to pick on than cranky Jazzy," Carly said.

"How is all of this my fault?"

"If he hadn't fallen in love with you, he never would have needed to tell Kate he was getting married. And Kate wouldn't have gone to his house, so she wouldn't have been killed. And Jazz wouldn't be a drunk."

"My son is not a drunk," Addie said, her voice like steel.

My mother chimed in, "And if you had stayed in the bed with your husband, instead of calling"—she frowned in Rocky's direction—"for backup, you—"

"Ma! I needed to process the experience. That's the only reason I called . . ."

Carly glared at Rocky. "Heaven knows what you thought virgin boy could do."

Rocky spoke up for himself. "I happen to be proud that I have stayed pure."

"Unlike Carly," I said in Rocky's defense. She had it coming.

I gave her a pointed look. "Maybe all of this is *your* fault, Carly. If you hadn't taken me to the crime scene, I never would have met Jazz."

"Then it's *your* fault. If you hadn't turned thirty-five and planned on sitting home being antisocial, I wouldn't have had to drag you kicking and screaming out of your apartment while I was on call." Carly picked up another cigarette and lit up. I could tell she still stung over my comment about her virtue. "I should have stayed pure."

"Can you keep your *lungs* pure by not smoking in here?"

She ignored me.

"How 'bout keeping *my* lungs pure?"

I felt sorry for her. I really did, but I didn't think it was the time or place for an impromptu counseling session. Actually, we were in my office and I'm a psychologist, so it *was* the *place*. But not the time.

"I expect a succession of my clients to begin arriving any time now. We can talk about you and Tim later, Carly, I promise. Even though you weren't supportive when I had love troubles, and you kept calling my husband 'murder boy,' even after he was cleared."

Addie shot a hard look at Carly.

"Maggie cancelled your clients," Sasha stated.

"What?"

"You can't see people after an intervention. You have to go to rehab or something right away."

"What kind of rehab, Ma? I'm not the one with the drinking problem!"

"Just go see your husband. And think of it as a long weekend. Your neurotics will be back Wednesday."

It's a sin not to honor your mother. It's a sin not to honor your mother. It's a sin . . .

I stood. If I didn't get them all out of my office, I *would* start drinking and need that rehab after all.

"So, to conclude this intervention," I said, giving them all my "I mean business, meeting adjourned, and please go home" look, "what I'm hearing you all say is that Jazz is exhibiting classic indicators of a major depressive episode—situational, of course —and possibly posttraumatic stress syndrome, with a maladaptive pattern of alcohol abuse."

Everyone stared at me. Dad spoke. "Uh. No, baby. You're hearing us say he's acting crazy and drinking too much."

Rocky gave me a manageable hit of the puppy eyes. "He needs you, babe."

Everyone present shouted, "Don't call her babe."

"Whoa," he said. "Sorry. Force of habit."

Maggie bolted up from her chair, clutching the miniature television in her hand. Her face flushed. "It's a breaking news story. The reporter is at Rocky's house."

"M-*my* house?" Rocky stuttered.

Everyone shot out of their seats and crowded around Maggie. She held out her portable television so that we could all see the screen and snatched the headphones from the jack. We could barely hear the reporter through the tinny speakers.

"Ezekiel Thunder, the once-disgraced television evangelist, staged a glorious comeback . . ."

Rocky turned ashen. "Whoa. Did something happen to Ezekiel? He's staying at my house."

Maggie shook her head. "No. Not him. It's one of his kids. A drowning."

Gasps and "oh no's" rippled through the room. Mason and Addie began to pray.

My heart thundered—no pun intended. "A child?" Oh dear God, not the baby. Not any of them! "How many does he have?"

Rocky answered. "He has five, but only three are with him on the trip."

A picture of Zeekie, my sweet little Thunder boy, appeared on the tiny screen.

"Zeekie . . ." Rocky said, with a sharp intake of breath.

I froze. *Oh, God. Noooooooooooooo.*

My stomach sank while my mind whirled. How could this child die? Where did it happen? The Rock House took excellent precautions to protect small children.

It's murder.

Immediately I tried to talk myself out of that notion. I had no factual basis from which to draw that conclusion. I wondered if I'd been infected by my husband, who believes all deaths are murders. Were my zillions too tight? Were the tiny braids affecting my brain?

Moments later the reporter showed the senior Ezekiel Thunder looking somber, but still working the camera, saying, "I believe God will raise my son from the dead."

I sighed.

I had work to do.

chapter six

NOTHING LIKE A TRAGEDY to disperse an intervention. Yet while that child's death horrified me deeply, God knows I couldn't wait to get rid of my loved ones.

We made quick work of saying good-bye, and I received several admonishments to get rest, see a doctor soon, and take prenatal vitamins.

I tried to follow Rocky to the Rock House, but like a good intervention participant, he urged me to go see Jazz first. He'd find out what happened at the house and would have a full report for me when I came by.

I could go back to the Rock House! An unexpected, undeserved grace, since six weeks ago Rocky practically told me to never darken the doorway of his church again.

Maggie and my mother locked up my office, and I headed to Detroit to see Jazz. I hated to see him at work, but everyone thought it best that I ambush him in the same way they did me.

I dreaded going to the Detroit Police Department. I had a bit of a reputation ever since all my business regarding my relationship with my husband had been published in a newspaper feature story in the *City Beat*. And the fact that I'd sorta taken down one of their own, proving their best detectives wrong—well, let's say I didn't win friends or influence people there.

I hurried out of the February chill into the building and marched right into the department, feigning nonexistent confidence. I identified myself to the uniform manning the front desk, a harsh, dry-looking man who inspired unfair comparisons to a Brillo pad. He called Jazz on the phone, heralded my arrival, and chuckled at whatever hurtful thing Jazz said to him about me.

Brillo Boy led me to the area where I could find my husband. He pointed, said, "Straight back," and returned to his desk. A buzz started as soon as someone recognized me. I heard it spread among the detectives and uniforms, making me as nervous as Jenny Craig on Fat Tuesday. I finally found Jazz standing, as he always does whenever I enter a room.

I saw his desk first; my poor eyes. It made me think of Bobby Maguire, the disheveled detective whom I drove crazy trying to prove my husband's innocence. If detective Bobby Maguire's desk was like the Grinch's heart, three sizes too small, Jazz's desk—a hulking monstrosity of steel and yellow formica—compensated. Horrid!

"Well, well, well, if it isn't my wife. Hast thou come to torment me before my time?"

"You might want to keep in mind that a demon said that to Jesus."

"Maybe it's *you* who should keep that in mind."

"Is that supposed to scare me, Jazz?"

"Not if you're the Jesus person."

We had no privacy. The men and women who usually milled

about looking cranky and bored now stood at attention, waiting for the drama between us to either come to blows, bodice ripping, or both.

He pulled out the chair beside his big honkin' desk for me, and I took his cue and sat.

My gorgeous husband, his fair skin somewhat slick and pasty, had seen better days. He looked unusually unkempt, like he'd taken hygiene tips from Bobby Maguire. I couldn't take my eyes off him, and the feeling seemed to be mutual. I felt my cheeks warm under his gaze.

I couldn't help asking, "Are you okay?"

"Are you?"

"You look different."

"So do you, not that I'm complaining."

Another expanse of uncomfortable silence stretched between us. When I could stand it no more, I tried to fill it with the free-floating monkey chatter occupying my brain.

"You're looking at me like I'm a figment of your imagination."

He gave me a sly smile. "I could touch you to make sure you're real."

Before I had a chance to protest, he reached out and grazed a hand through my braids, then buried his face in them.

"Actually, that's the only thing about me that's *not* real."

Into my ear, "That's the only part I can touch and be a good boy at work."

And speaking of being a good boy at work . . .

I could smell way too much mouthwash on his breath. An old, completely ineffective game alcoholics play to mask their drinking.

"My hair is real, but it's not mine. Well, it's mine. I bought the hair—real, uh, human hair. Extensions."

He released my hair, his glassy eyes studying me. "You abandoned the blond braids."

I nodded, even though it wasn't a question.

He cocked his head and regarded me with a smirk. "What's the matter, baby, Rocky blond enough for both of you?"

"I wanted to get back to black."

He gave me a wicked grin. "That's reassuring."

"I meant black hair."

"Of course you did."

I scooted my chair away from him. "I don't want to spar with you, Jazz. Nothing is going on between me and Rocky."

"So you said. I'm sure his tongue fell down your throat by accident."

"His tongue wasn't down my throat." I crossed my arms. Looked around to see if anyone heard and might be gawking at us. "I shouldn't have come here."

"You're right. You shouldn't have. This is my job."

"On second thought, yes, I should have." I whispered now. "It's bad form to drink alcohol at work."

"So I've been told, more than a few times."

"Jazz . . ." I didn't know what to say to him, where even to begin. I thought it might be a good idea to start over. I took another deep breath. "Jazz, do you know why I'm here?"

"Yes."

"You do?"

"What took you so long?"

"I didn't want to do this. Other people put me up to it."

"*Other* people?"

I waited for whatever biting response he'd have, but instead he shook his head. "Spare me the details. Do you want to go somewhere we can talk privately?"

I looked around. "And where would that be?"

He raked his hand through his brown curls. "Come on." I stood, and he put his hand on the small of my back, arousing the tingling he always stirs in me.

"Where are we going?"

"Somewhere private. You've already ruined my street cred by telling the metro Detroit area I gave your pet sugar glider CPR."

"I asked Kalaya not to print that part. She couldn't resist."

He led me to the interrogation room.

I stepped in reluctantly. A uniformed cop sat at the table positioned in the center of the room. He'd been listening to the radio and apparently filling out reports. When Jazz and I entered, he bolted upright.

"Sorry, Lieutenant Brown."

The cop looked at me and a smile played about his lips. Jazz glared at him.

"Out," he said, and the uniform scurried out of the room. Jazz closed the door behind us, the radio still blaring.

"Would you like to have a seat?" he asked. He stepped over to the table and flipped a number of switches underneath. "I'm making sure no one records us. We have the room set up for it."

Thanks for sharing. Now I feel really comfortable.

"I'll stand," I said.

When he was done securing our privacy, he came back to

me. Stood impossibly close. He shrugged. "Do what you gotta do, but don't be surprised if I do what I gotta do, myself."

I froze. I wasn't expecting him to say that, and I couldn't imagine what he'd want to do. Well, yes, I could, and what annoyed me was I'd probably want to let him. Jazz looked irritated at my hesitation.

He leaned into my ear. "Maybe I deserve something *good* from you before it's all said and done."

I'd lost control of the situation already. "I'm sure you do deserve something from me, Jazz."

"I said something *good.*"

He moved closer still, the space collapsing between us in his swift movement. Oh, man. I loved him. I needed him. And I didn't think I'd have any power left in me to resist him. The truth was we weren't ready for that kind of love. I think we both knew it.

The uniform had been listening to Detroit's public radio. They played amazing jazz. My husband stared at me while the DJ rambled on about Lady Day. The sound of Billie Holiday singing Gershwin's "Our Love Is Here to Stay" followed the man's velvet voice, the irony of the lyrics mocking us.

He slipped his arm around my waist. "Can you dance?"

"Uh—"

"You know what dancing is, don't you? Or maybe you don't. I know you're one of those brainy types—"

"I can dance, Jazz."

His eyes sparkled with mischief. "Are you sure?"

"Yes, but we're in the interrogation room. At the police station. Forgive me if I'm not wanting to play Fred Astaire and Ginger Rogers with you."

But he had already grabbed both my hands. Jazz pulled my body flush with his, ignoring any whit of decorum. He didn't have his jacket on, and he pressed so close against me that I could hear his heart pounding, as if he felt the same way I did. A tremor went through him and subsequently through me. He whispered into my ear, "I know you feel it, too."

I did, maybe more than he did.

I smelled his liquor breath, and the coarse whiskers of his un-shaven face scratched me. Again, he nestled his face in my hair.

Every cell in my body wanted to merge with him until there was no more him and me, just some glorious, ineffable *one*.

Our dance began.

Jazz moved like a dream, even though he was intoxicated, and for once I let myself follow his lead. No, we weren't playing Fred and Ginger, for just a moment we were Jazz and Bell, our dance in that room revealing more truth about the two of us than a full-blown interrogation would. He'd led me in a simple waltz, but never had the dance been so sexy. I closed my eyes and surrendered fully to him. Rockies and Gibraltars crumbled and tumbled on the radio, but my heart soared to new heights.

The music went on, but Jazz stopped dancing to hem me against the glass and trail kisses up and down my neck. I grabbed his face with both hands and found his mouth with mine. His hands sought the waist of my skirt. He tugged at my blouse until his hands roamed freely inside.

"*Whoa*," I said. "Isn't this a two-way mirror?"

He didn't answer. For a moment I didn't care. I missed him so. I ached for him, hungry for his scent, the rough texture of his brown curls between my fingers. I knew the alcohol he drank and his simmering anger most likely fueled this passion we'd gotten caught up in. But I felt bereft without his laughter and the toothpaste-model smile that had captivated my heart when we first met.

Still, his hands had gotten a little too busy. We didn't have that much privacy!

I pushed Jazz away, and again, he stared at me like he'd dreamed me. "Baby—"

"I can't do this, Jazz."

"Nobody is watching."

"You don't know that."

"Oh, yes, I do."

He tried to step toward me again but seemed to pause, perhaps doubting what his next move should be.

Tears sprang to my eyes. I had no control with him. "I have to go." I thrust my hand into my coat pocket and grabbed my car keys before I could make a bigger fool out of myself. I tried to hurry away from him, but like I always do around Jazz, I tripped in my heels. My ankle twisted and pain tore through my tendons. I yelped in agony, blind through my tears. I didn't crash into his chest this time. I fell on the hard ground.

For an intoxicated man, he moved quickly and made his way to my side in an instant, his arms reaching out to hold me. I slapped them away, near hysterical now. I kicked the offending high-heeled shoe off my left foot, pulled myself up, grabbed my keys off the floor, and ran as fast as I could out of that wretched place amid the laughter of his colleagues.

They *had* seen.

Jazz called my name. *Bell.*

I made my way outside, hobbling. The sidewalk stung my shoeless foot, and my ankle throbbed, hot with pain. I willed myself to keep going, too humiliated to stop until I got myself inside my welcoming yellow Beetle, still warm from my trip to Detroit. I slammed the door and tore out of that parking lot as fast as the law and the Love Bug would allow, still crying out my embarrassment and grief.

When I was a safe distance away, I pulled over into a parking lot, lay my head on the steering wheel, and wept until my eyes were sore.

The oddest thing came to mind when I stopped crying. I thought about my work. My clients never cease to amaze me. They hurt, but somehow they find it in them to seek help. What they don't realize is that I don't do much. Most of the time I simply remind them of what they already know.

So . . . physician, heal thyself.

I hurt, badly. In the interest of my own healing, I asked myself what *I* knew to be true. First things first: I knew God loved me, and I needed Him right now. I may not have been in mortal danger, but when it came to Jazz, my heart felt perched on a precarious precipice above a bottomless ache that I could fall into at any moment.

Next, I knew Jazz to be a good man—someone trying hard to do what's right—but I also knew that when Kate betrayed him, he cut her off without mercy. Although they divorced, for months they'd continued to enjoy a sexual relationship. I didn't want to go to that same place with him. Finally, my thoughts went right back to God. I needed Him to be my firm and loving Father. My own father left me to navigate my teenage years on my own. I hadn't had his crucial protection when I'd needed it most. He should have been there to say, "This young man isn't good enough for you" or "That one doesn't respect you. You deserve better." I may not have been a teen anymore, but I needed my daddy. God knew that a part of me was more than willing to be "easy" when it came to Jazz. Yes, we were married. I loved him. It felt right to be in his arms, but like Ma Brown would say, "If you want to drink the milk, you've gotta buy the cow." We'd be married in every way, or we'd be separated, and only one of those came with conjugal rights. I didn't trust myself with Jazz unless we were ready to reconcile.

In that lonely parking lot, I told myself to buck up. I righted my blouse as best I could and buttoned my coat again. I had to be strong. When Jazz and I met, we'd made rules to keep us safe. Sometimes we broke them, but other times we abided in a wild, green, springtime place that made it possible for us to grow a friendship.

I had a lot to talk to God about when we had our private time, but for now I had to go home and rest a moment, then hurry back to Rocky's house. I had hurt him, but he'd put that aside and come back to me. And when he thought my husband and I needed him, Rocky showed up at my intervention. I may have felt powerless when it came to Jazz, but I could walk Rocky through whatever sorrow had come to visit him.

That I could do.

chapter seven

I ARRIVED AT THE ROCK HOUSE HOUSE, and reporters —both local and national—had gathered, including CNN. I stepped out of my Love Bug and immediately the press surged at me, shoving at least a half-dozen microphones in my face. I remembered what Jazz had taught me, looked straight ahead, and said absolutely nothing.

I made it to the door, but I had to wait a long time before Rocky cracked it open and let me ease inside.

He slammed and locked the door behind me. I'd never seen Rocky so stressed. In the two years he'd been a pastor, he'd lost members when people went to other churches or moved away. He'd even had an unfortunate church split. Rocky had married church members but never buried anyone. Poor Zeekie would be Rocky's first funeral. *Lord, have mercy.*

I couldn't bear the sadness shadowing Rocky's handsome face. I've teased him about his eyes, bright and affecting as a toddler's. Now his silent tears flowed freely. I took him in my arms and held on to him. My own sadness, which I had tried to hold in check, spilled out of me anyway.

"What happened, Rock?"

"He drowned in the bathtub."

"But how?"

"Sister Lou said the kids were giving him a bath."

"Where are they?"

Rocky walked me into the dining room, wiping his eyes. The Rock House had the support of some of Ann Arbor's wealthier citizens. Some had donated lovely, classic furniture. The dining table could seat ten, but was empty of people except for Sister Lou, her arms on the shoulders of an inconsolable teenage girl. Sister Lou paid me no mind, but the girl looked up at me, regarded me briefly with a tearful gaze, and put her head back down.

She, too, looked like her father, but far too old to be his young wife's child. A boy, maybe twelve years old, clung to her. Another Thunder kid.

I left the children to their grief, effectively delaying having to deal with Chantilly Lou. I took Rocky's hand and guided him back to the foyer.

"How old are they?"

"Fifteen and twelve."

"Did they leave Zeekie alone?"

"They said just for a few minutes."

"Why'd they leave him?"

"Zeke—not his dad, the little guy, not the baby Zeekie, either—had to use the bathroom, and so Zekia stepped out. He closed the shower curtain, used the bathroom, and left. He thought Zekia would go right back in behind him, so he went back into the living room to play his PSP. That's when little Zeekie was alone."

"So, Zeke is the twelve year old—his name is Zeke, too, right?"

"Right."

"And the girl's name is Zekia?"

"Yeah."

"Are there any more Zekes?"

"All of his kids are named Zeke, babe."

"Excuse me?"

"All of them are Zekes. All the guys are named Ezekiel, and the girls are some variation on Zeke: Zekia, Zekiah."

"Don't tell me anymore. That's way too George Foreman." I sighed. "So, twelve-year-old Zeke closed the shower curtain, used the bathroom, and left him?"

"Right."

I shook my head. "That can't be right."

"That's what the kids told me. Maybe you can talk to them when they aren't so upset."

"Or when that gargoyle isn't hovering over them."

"Babe, that's not very kind."

"You're right. I apologize to gargoyles everywhere."

"If you're just going to give attitude . . ."

I waited to see what he'd say.

He paused. Looked away from me, then back. "I'm sorry, Bell."

"Me, too, Rock. I'm here for you." I swallowed hard before I let what I needed to say next come out of my mouth. "And for your godfather."

Rocky managed something reminiscent of a smile. He pulled

me into a bear hug. "Thanks so much, babe. Will you talk to the kids when they're ready?"

"Sure, Rocky."

"I trust you. You know?"

I put my hand on his cheek. "I know. I won't let you down."

He nodded. We heard a tiny feminine voice squeak out, "Um. Rocky?" Both of our attentions turned toward the dining room.

Very pregnant Elisa St. James stood in the doorway. I hadn't seen her since the day I'd gone to the Rock House and caught Rocky serenading her baby with the arrangement of "All the Pretty Little Horses" he'd composed for *my* baby. The baby I'd never have. She looked at me like she thought I owed her a beat-down.

I looked at her. This pretty young woman, a wheat-colored, green-eyed sistah, had saved my life. In an act of extraordinary bravery, she trusted me and fled the cult that would destroy us both. And she believed I saved hers since I gave her courage to leave. She'd probably give my buddy happiness he'd never have with me. I thought of all I knew about both of them. I should have matched them myself, only I was too busy holding on to the sad remains of what Rocky and I once had, and missing out on everything God had graciously put right in front of me.

I beckoned her over, and she flew into my arms and sobbed. I rubbed her hair. "Are you okay, sweetie?"

"I thought you were mad at me."

"Why would I be mad at you? Because this great guy sings you songs?"

I pulled away enough to look into her shiny green eyes. She didn't say anything.

"Elisa, you are one lucky—no, blessed—woman. I know things have been a little confusing for all of us, but look at what you've come through. Look at what you've survived already just getting away from Gabriel. He totally controlled your mind. Do you realize how few people in your circumstance would have left him like you did? I'm not mad. I'm your biggest fan, Okay?"

She nodded and charged at me again. That woman hugged me so hard I thought she'd hurt her baby. She cried into my coat collar. "It's so sad about Zeekie."

"I know." And we cried some more. In fact, Elisa and I cried an inordinate amount of time. I'd totally abandoned any professional presentation. But God knows we needed to have that little chat, and I felt like I needed to cry for Little Zeekie, for my own dead child, and now for my dead womb.

Elisa and I finally tore ourselves away from each other. I asked Rocky where Ezekiel Senior was.

"He and Nikki went to the morgue."

What irony. I lived in Ann Arbor, but had no access to the morgue there. Didn't live in Detroit and virtually had a free pass because of Carly.

There had to be a way for me to find out what that autopsy would reveal, because, try as I might, I was having a hard time seeing a precocious, total firecracker like Zeekie, almost three years old, drowning in a bathtub. I had to talk to Zeke and Zekia.

Gonna need a little help here, Jesus.

"We'll figure it all out," I said in the professional, reassuring tone I used at work, both at my job at the Washtenaw County Jail and at my private practice. I'd switched to psychologist mode as much for me as for Rocky and Elisa. I could handle just about anything except someone hurting a child.

I hobbled back to the dining room one more time and peeked in. Sister Lou stared at me with her stony gargoyle gaze, like I was about to violate the church she stood watch over.

Something strange about that woman. More than cast-out-devil strange.

Whatever. I'd have to come back. My ankle begged for relief. Maybe I'd have more success when the parents got back, anyway.

I thought about that. The infamous Ezekiel Thunder, claiming before his son's rigor mortis had set in that God would raise that baby from the dead. No, I doubted if I'd have any more success with them.

Be wise as a serpent. Harmless as a dove.

"Aren't I always?" I replied to that still, small voice of warning.

God went silent on me in answer.

Oh, yeah. This was going to be interesting.

chapter eight

FATIGUE OVERTOOK ME as I stepped into my apartment and closed the door behind me. I removed my coat, shoes, and hosiery, right there in the foyer. I worked my way to the bathroom, which I seemed to have to do every half hour, and finally to my bedroom. I laid my blouse across the chair beside the chest of drawers, right next to my great-grandmother's Star of Bethlehem quilt. Not much in this world offered the comfort that protective covering did. At times it had been my shield and armor. Sometimes it served as arms to hold me, other times as something to keep me warm.

Maybe it could be all of those now. I cradled it against my chest. I crawled into bed without bothering to put on my pajamas and wrapped the quilt around me. I scooted under the comforter and felt so safe and warm that I promptly fell asleep.

I'm at the Rock House. Children are everywhere. They're playing and running and sitting in the seats. Children of all ages and sizes, and it's a happy place.

A little girl walks up to me, and she looks like me. I say, "Hi, sweetie." And she says, "Hi, Mommy." When

she calls me Mommy, I realize she's my daughter
Imani, and I cry and cry because I'm so happy to see
her. She lets me cry and kisses me on the forehead.
For a moment I think that she doesn't look anything
like Adam, and I'm comforted by that. Then she is
holding baby Zeekie's hand. I bend down to kiss him,
and he blows a raspberry on my lips. I laugh, close
my eyes, and throw my head back, but something
is terribly wrong. My laughter sounds way too loud.
Forced. When I look down again, Imani and Zeekie
turn into skeletons—all the children turn into hideous
decayed bodies, and they all are screaming, "Help me,
Help me!"

I wake up screaming.

I felt arms around me—real arms, instead of my great-grandmother's quilt. My eyes hadn't adjusted in the dark room, and I
screamed like a madwoman, especially since I distinctly remembered going to bed alone. Adrenaline rushed through me, even
though I hadn't fully awakened, and I pummeled my intruder
with desperate punches until his arms clamped around me.

"Bell, it's Jazz. Stop hitting me."

"Jazz?" My body realized the truth of his statement before
my mind. His scent, mingled with cigar smoke and faint traces of
Jack Daniels invaded my senses. He loosened his grip a bit.

"I've got you," he murmured in my ear.

Still, my heart nearly burst out of my chest.

"What are you doing here?" I yelled, not intending to.

"I was asleep, until you had a nightmare."

"I don't mean what you're *doing*! I want to know how you got in here."

"You didn't lock the door."

"Not at *all*?" Oh, man. I must have been *really* tired.

"No, you didn't. What if I was some kind of psychopath?"

"According to the people I met with this morning, the jury is still out on that."

If his expression was any indicator—eyes narrowed, brows furrowed—I'd confused him. "What people? What are you talking about?"

"Never mind." I shuddered to think I had slept like Goldilocks while Jazz, or anyone, could enter my apartment without me noticing. "I can't believe you came inside my apartment and got in bed with me."

"You didn't notice when I touched you, either."

I realized I wasn't fully dressed and pulled the quilt around me more. "What did you do, Jazz Brown?"

"I *am* still married to you."

"Where did you touch me?"

"You know, the scriptures say the marriage bed is undefiled. And this, if I remember correctly, and I most certainly do, is our marriage bed."

"Jazz, quit playing. Where did you touch me?"

He rolled over away from me. Laughed. "Maybe I didn't touch you at all. Maybe I just wanted to see what your reaction would be so I can gauge whether or not I can get away with it if the opportunity comes up again."

"Didn't you get enough at the station house today?"

"Apparently not."

"You totally humiliated me."

He blew a burst of air from his cheeks. Brushed his curls with his hand. "I know. I came to say I'm sorry."

"Whatever! Just leave me alone."

He sighed. Looked away and back at me again. Then mischief appeared in those delicious brown eyes.

"Or maybe I did touch you."

I let out an exaggerated sigh. "Did you touch me or not?"

"Did your boy Rocky do that when he *kissed* you?"

"Absolutely not!"

"Maybe I'm not the gentleman he is. Or is kissing another man's wife gentlemanly? You tell *me*, baby."

I had no energy for Jazz's Rocky barbs. "If you want to have a *real* conversation about Rocky, I'd be happy to talk. But if you'd rather keep stewing, I'll leave you to do that alone." I looked around the room. From the bedroom window, I could see it had turned dark outside. "What time is it?"

"It's about eight."

"I can't believe I slept that long. What time did you get here?"

"Maybe six."

I pulled the comforter back over me. "Why are you here, anyway?"

He reached over to the floor on his side of the bed and pulled up the shoe I'd left behind. He dangled it in front of me. "Cinder*bell*a?"

I sighed. "Thanks." I took the shoe from him and put it on the floor on my side of the bed. He gave me a mischievous look.

"Guess who I am?"

"I'd say the prince, but he was *charming*."

"Aren't you *sweet*, my dear wife."

For a moment neither of us spoke. I waited for him to say something about Rocky, but he didn't, so the words "dear wife" hung in the air between us.

Again I sighed.

Jazz kicked me under the covers. "Hey."

"Hey what?"

"I really did come to tell you I was sorry. Will you accept my apology?"

"No."

"But you want me to forgive you your trespasses?"

"I most certainly do!"

He put his chin on my shoulder. "I'm sorry, Bell. I disrespected you, and that was wrong. Will you please forgive me?"

"As long as you don't do it again."

He slipped his arms around my waist. "I wouldn't have done that today, but I had a little help from my friend Jack Daniels."

"I don't think Jack is your friend, Jazz. Listen, I wanted to talk to you about—"

"You wanna tell me what you dreamed?"

I thought about whether I should override his veto. Decided how futile it would be to force him to talk about the drinking when he clearly didn't want to, and proceeded back to what my subconscious mind had dredged up.

I told him about the dream, chills running through me as I

relived it. He listened, nodded. Touched my arm during the hard parts.

His eyes searched mine. "Have you been listening to the news?"

"No. Not really."

"Ezekiel Thunder's kid really drowned today. At your boyfriend's house."

"I know all about it. I just left . . ."

Uh-oh. Suddenly I had myself a situation.

"Bell, if you tell me you were with . . ."

I stayed quiet.

"Bell . . ."

More quiet.

"Bell!"

"*What?* You never said a name."

"I didn't have to."

He jumped out of bed, and I saw he had on a white undershirt and his skivvies. Whew! That man's body made our vows, "with my body I thee worship" sound like a *plan.* I couldn't stop gaping at him.

"You were in my bed half naked?" I hoped he didn't hear the longing in my voice.

"You're my *wife!* I'm supposed to be in your bed. *However,* you're not supposed to be going out with . . ."

I didn't fill in the blank.

He waited. And waited. "Were you with him, Bell?"

"Who?"

"You know *exactly* who I'm talking about. *Say it.*"

"It?"

He stared at me. Yanked his pants on. He grabbed his shirt which he'd placed on top of mine on the chair. "I can't believe you. Have you been seeing him this whole time we've been separated?"

"Seeing who?"

"You're really irritating me, Bell."

"No, I haven't been seeing him."

"Who?"

"Who are *you* talking about, Jazz?"

"Say his name, woman."

"Whose name?"

He put his shirt on. Slowly. He looked like he wanted to say something to me, but he swallowed it and probably a massive bitter pill at the same time.

God's voice, that small, quiet presence that I *knew* was Him spoke to me.

Don't let him leave like that.

I needed to stop playing around. His family and best friend said he missed me like crazy. I could let him know I love him.

"Jazz, you shouldn't drive when you've been drinking."

Punked out again!

"And you shouldn't be seeing Rocky after what happened to us."

He'd buttoned his shirt and tucked it into his trousers.

"Jazz, don't leave like this. Please?"

He glared at me. "I'm out."

"I haven't been seeing Rocky. I saw him for the first time Wednesday when he invited me to Ezekiel Thunder's crusade.

And I saw him again today. I only went over there because of poor baby Zeekie's death."

"I'm supposed to believe that?"

"You can ask Rocky if you don't believe me."

"I don't have anything to say to blondilocks."

"He didn't know I'd married you, Jazz, that's the truth."

"And you didn't bother to tell him. Not even when I gave you an opportunity to."

"Do you want to talk about that night?"

Jazz suddenly developed Tourette's syndrome. Tics and expletives exploded out of him. Most of them having to do with Rocky. I let him rage on until finally I tried again to broach the subject of what we really needed to do.

"Why don't we talk about it, baby?"

More tics and expletives. And his own twist on my game. "Don't call me baby."

I crawled out of the bed and covered myself with the quilt. I may have gotten a peek at his tightie whities, but I didn't want him to see how my cup runneth over! But he saw just the same. Jazz actually blushed, pinking his ears and cheeks. He noticed my discomfort and looked away.

And speaking of discomfort. My ankle still buzzed with pain. I hobbled over to my chest of drawers. Jazz noticed I was hurt but didn't say anything.

I slipped on a long-sleeved T-shirt with a tattoo design on the front. I'd had to get that shirt in large to contain my new girth. When I was dressed, I spoke to him. "I know you aren't ready to deal with it, but when you are, I'll be here. I'm sorry I hurt you, Jazz."

He turned away from me again and stared into the mirror on my dresser. "I hate you, Bell," he said to his own reflection.

But he didn't leave me.

———————————

I got an idea. Like the Grinch I got a wonderful, awful idea. I knew exactly what to do! If only he'd go for it.

I'd holed up in the bedroom, and Jazz stayed in the living room, making it much easier for him not to talk to me. I finally eased into the living room, careful not to frighten him in case he'd bite.

He surprised me by speaking first. "You need to stop walking until your ankle gets better."

"You noticed I was hurt." I sat next to him.

"I *always* notice when you're hurt." He reached down and cradled my ankle in his hands. Placed it across his lap. Nice and cozy. "Do you want some ice?"

"I had quite enough ice when I packed it earlier. I'm still freezing."

He rubbed my shoulders. He felt so warm. I started plotting right then and there to keep him. I just had to bring up one teeny-tiny thing.

"Jazz, I want you to work for me."

He didn't acknowledge my comment.

He picked up the book he'd been reading when I came in the room, my dog-eared copy of Brennan Manning's *The Ragamuffin Gospel.* I'd always encouraged him to read it. I thought the book built a beautiful bridge between Evangelicals and Catholics.

Manning himself had once been a priest. And I was glad to see Jazz reading instead of watching television.

Now, I loved my true crime and detective shows, but other than that, I didn't have an addiction to any particular show. The only boob tube I owned—a thirteen-inch Wal-Mart special—was in my bedroom. While the living room was cable equipped, I never wanted TV, that big icon of the world, to be the center-piece of my home. Jazz probably would have chosen to watch television, but he wouldn't go back into my bedroom. Good! I blessed whatever made him pick up one of my favorite books. But I needed his attention. I wouldn't quit until I had it.

"I said I want you to work for me—as a consultant."

He continued reading my beloved Brennan.

Jazz appeared to be tame, so I ventured to rub his arm. "I think the dream I had was a sign." I'd hoped pulling the dead-child-dream card would garner me some sympathy. It didn't.

He looked over at me but didn't speak.

"What if that poor child is trying to tell me he was mur-dered?"

Jazz gave me a blank stare.

"Think about the way he turned into a skeleton and asked for my help. And all those other children turned into zombies or something, screaming for me to help them. What if Zeekie needs my help?"

He rolled his eyes.

I nudged him. "What do you think, Jazzy?"

"I think you need to watch what you eat before you go to sleep."

"Jazz, I really think Zeekie is asking for my help from beyond the grave."

"I'm not listening to this, Bell."

"Come on, Jazz. You're the murder police."

"In *Detroit*. So I'm *definitely* not listening to this." He turned back to the book.

I nudged him. "Why are you going to work intoxicated, Jazz? You're up for promotion."

"Yeah. I'm thrilled. I just love working in a place where everyone in the department thought I was a cold-blooded killer, even though I gave them the best years of my life."

"You were cleared of all those charges, and they got the killer." Thanks to me, but I didn't want to say that.

He set the book down on my end table, careful not to disturb my leg, and sank back into the couch cushions. He crossed his arms, putting on his emotional armor.

"All those years, Bell, I showed up on the worst day of people's lives. You don't know the unspeakable horrors I've seen. Or that I have nightmares like the kind you had tonight, three or four times a week. I've seen more death than anybody should have to see in one lifetime. And it has changed me."

I worked at a jail. I knew enough cops to know how it affected them, but I wanted him to share his heart with me. "How did it change you, Jazz?"

"It marked me like Cain, even though I've never killed anyone. It curses you to see all that evil. You don't look at people the same anymore. The things people *do* to one another!" He took a deep breath. "Not just strangers, people who supposedly love one another. I've lost faith in people. And I don't think it'll come back. My dad told me not to stay in homicide too long, but I was busy trying to be the department's golden boy." He let out a hollow laugh. "I'm nobody's golden boy. All I am is an angry man with a black heart and a haunted mind."

I've known from years as a counselor that sometimes it's best just to listen. Let the speaker know you heard them. Quietly acknowledge their pain. I touched his hand and then withdrew mine, in case he didn't want me to hold it.

He looked straight ahead. I waited to see where he wanted to go in the conversation. "Still wanna hire me?" he teased, but the sadness in his voice gave him away.

"I don't want to be insensitive to you, Jazz, but the truth is, I do still want you to look into it."

"No."

"But what if someone committed a crime?"

"People do every day."

"The murder of a child?"

"I can see you *really* listened to me just now."

"Two kids might get blamed."

He didn't want any part of this, but he couldn't turn off being the murder police. His hand went into his McDreamy hair, like it always does when he's bothered.

"How do you know this?"

"I saw them this afternoon after the intervention."

He definitely looked confused. "What intervention?"

"The one that a bunch of people had in my office."

"Who did an intervention on you?"

"Friends and family. And it was really more about you."

"Me?"

"Sure! Let's see . . . your parents and my mother. Carly. Souldier, Kalaya, Mason, and Rocky attended. Everybody seems to think you're having a mental breakdown and are exacerbating your pain by abusing alcohol."

"They told you *that*?"

"Yes."

"And what was Rocky doing at an intervention about *me*?"

"Everybody, including Rocky, urged me to go back to you. He may be in love, you know."

"Yeah. I do know," he growled.

"Not with me. I think he may be falling in love with Elisa St. James. I wouldn't doubt it if he asks her to marry him before that baby gets here."

"Oh, really? And then what will you do, Bell?"

"Buy them a wedding present and a baby gift shortly thereafter."

He picked up the book again. Flipped a few pages without looking. "Does Elisa know he has a love jones for you?"

"She probably knows he made a mistake. Rocky is pretty transparent. I can't imagine he didn't tell her everything."

"Good for her. Personally, I don't care to talk about it. At all."

"But, Jazz."

"I don't want to hear it, Bell. Say another word about your blond boy toy, and I'm out of here."

"Fine." I crossed my arms and sank into the cushions of the sofa.

Jazz glared at me again. "Go sit somewhere else."

"This is *my* apartment, and I want to sit by you."

He shook his head and went back to the book, never looking at me, but still talking smack. "You know, letting people cool off *away* from you can be a good thing."

"Yes, I do know that. I'm a therapist, but this is my house, and I want to be around you. So, I'm not moving."

I thought he'd get up and move, but he stayed put. He must have liked that talk about me wanting to be around him. I know he needed more reassuring than that, but I had to start somewhere.

"Go with me to talk to Thunder's children."

Jazz looked at me like I'd asked him to check himself into a psychiatric hospital. "For what?"

"I heard a story about what happened, and it feels wrong. I may be able to get some answers if I can talk to those kids. I've got a feeling there's more to this case than meets the eye. I want you to check it out with me."

"You mean you want me to check it out *for* you. I'm the one who's a cop, even though Ann Arbor is *not* my jurisdiction. And did I tell you I hate you, Bell?"

"You did. I don't think you mean it."

"I mean it."

"Will you work for me?"

"No."

"Please, baby." I drew circles on his thigh with my index finger.

His hand caught mine. He tried, unsuccessfully, to keep himself from smiling. "Didn't your great-grandmother say, 'Don't start no stuff and it won't be none?'"

"Yes."

"You're starting something, and don't think I'm not more than willing to finish it. Your ankle is hurt, but you're looking just fine—and I do mean fine—otherwise."

I slowly withdrew my hand. I had to remind myself whom I was dealing with. "Then I'll go by myself."

"Fine with me."

I stood up, carefully. "Okay. I'll see you."

"Bye. Careful with that ankle."

"I'm going now, Jazz."

"Be gone already."

I thought I'd pull the sympathy card. "My ankle hurts, baby."

He grinned. "Then get back here on my lap and we can cuddle."

"But that child may have been murdered."

"You just got less cuddly. See ya!"

"All righty then. I'm off to *Rocky's* house. Where I'll see *Rocky*. Spend time with *Rocky*. Just *be with Rocky*."

His already fair-skinned face blanched. His angry expression looked so comical I started to laugh. I'd infuriated him.

"Oh, you think that's funny, Bell?"

When I could compose myself, I said, "Do you remember that *Three Stooges* short with the scene in which, whenever some-one said, 'Niagara Falls,' this man—and you could tell he had issues—yelled out, '*Niagara Falls*'?"

Jazz tried not to engage me.

"Then he would go . . ." I started my imitation. "*Slooooooooowly* I turned." I actually turned, slowly, of course. "Step by step, inch by inch." I pounded on the floor with my feet.

Jazz looked really irritated. "What's your point, Bell?"

"Apparently the name Rocky combined with the idea of 'I'm going over there' is your Niagara Falls, triggering an immediate *episode*."

He scowled at me for an uncomfortable amount of time, no doubt plotting my destruction, then stood up and marched over to my closet.

"*Step by step, inch by inch*," I teased, in time with his feet hitting the floor.

He hadn't laughed. It occurred to me that I'd hurt him again. I sighed. *That's it. He's leaving and never coming back.*

I bounced on one foot over to him. "I'm sorry."

With eerie calm and precision, he took out his coat and slipped it on. Next he took out my coat and extended it to me.

I grinned like an idiot. As he helped me into my coat, I leaned over and kissed him on the cheek. "Thank you, Jazz."

A low, guttural sound, something between a grunt and a moan, emanated from him. Whether or not he meant it in the affirmative, I didn't care, nor did I ask. I got my boots on, and he reached out his hand and made another caveman noise that sounded remotely like "Keys." I put my keys in his hand with great pleasure.

Score another one for Bell.

chapter
nine

JAZZ AND I ARRIVED at Rocky's house, but before we got out of the Love Bug, I thought I should lay down a few ground rules. "Jazz, you may not beat up Rocky."

"Aw. You never let me have any fun."

"Promise me you'll behave."

"No."

"Jazz, Rocky didn't know—"

"Don't want to hear it, baby."

I looked out the window at the sky. Bursts of silver starlight sparkled in the black night. "Why can't we talk about this like rational adults?"

"Because nothing you say will make that scenario work for me."

"I'm so sorry, Jazz."

His silhouette turned grim. "Are we going in or do you want to go back home?"

"Home? Exactly where is *your* home these days, Jazzy?"

"In or no?"

"In. And no hitting Rocky."

"Fine."

"And no smart-alecky remarks."

Jazz didn't respond.

"Jazzy. Don't go in there talking trash. We're working on a case."

He blew air from his cheeks. "*We* are not on *any* case, especially you." He pointed to himself, doing a really good Tarzan imitation. "Me, *Detroit* cop." Then to me. "You, psychologist."

I grinned at him. "But if you look into this for me, I'll play Tarzan and Jane with you later."

A blush crept up his cheeks. "I'm gonna hold you to that, *Jane*." He must have had a zinger of a thought because he snapped back to being crabby. "No, I won't. In fact, I'm not even going to look into this for you. And you are not even going to think about sleuthing again because, one, this is probably a tragic accident, and, two, you end up almost getting killed every time you poke that pretty little nose of yours into police business."

My heart rate quickened. "So, *you* think this could be police business—a murder?"

"Bell, you know I think *all* deaths are murders. It's a sickness I have. And since when do you care what I think?"

I bumped his shoulder with mine. "I care what you think. Especially if you think my nose is pretty."

He glared at me, but it didn't discourage me.

I cuddled my head into his neck. "Do you think my face is pretty?"

He raked his hand through his hair. "Can we go inside?"

I nuzzled his ear with my lips. "Do you want to kiss me?"

"No, Bell, I want to knock you in the head, but I'd go to jail for that, and I don't like jail."

I laughed and nibbled his earlobe. He's so much fun to frustrate.

"Don't think it's lost on me that you didn't try these bold maneuvers at the apartment where you'd have had to back up your actions."

"Who says I can't back it up right here?"

"Bring it on, Bell. We could give a whole new meaning to 'Love Bug.'"

I eased away from Jazz. He suddenly seemed a bit menacing, in a very sexy way. And I liked it. "All right, Jazzy. Shall we go inside?"

He looked at me like an innocent little lamb. "What's the rush? Why don't you do that nibbling thing again? Then I'll show you something I can do."

Honestly! When he smiles at me, my bones melt. He unclicked his seat belt, opened the door, and stepped his long legs out into the frigid air. I thought a friendly reminder would be in order.

"Don't start a fight with Rocky."

"I won't." But he stepped out and slammed the Love Bug's door.

His irritation didn't stop him from being a gentleman, however. He opened the door for me, and our sleuthing officially began. Whether or not my husband knew it.

———

Jazz knocked on the Rock House door, and none other than Pastor Rocky Harrison himself answered. His face registered surprise upon seeing me with Jazz, and he opened the door without saying a word. That is, until a burst of Rockyesque enthusiasm spilled out of him.

He threw himself at Jazz and pulled him into a friendly hug. Way too friendly for Jazz.

"Dude, I'm so glad you're here," Rocky said.

Poor Jazz. He stood ramrod straight, a ghastly expression frozen on his face.

God knows I tried not to laugh . . .

I covered my mouth, my shoulders shaking with mirth. I may have been able to control myself had I looked away, but for Rocky's safety I kept my eyes fastened on the pair.

All Jazz could say—to me—was, "Touching!"

Poor Rocky held on for dear life, and Jazz progressed to saying two words. "*Touching*, Bell!"

That did it. Laughter exploded out of me. I peeled Rocky off my husband, and snorted in a most undignified manner. Honestly, I tried to pull myself together. I looked into Jazz's hard brown eyes. Let me tell you, not much good was going on in those Godiva chocolate peepers. He'd balled his hands into fists, and his mouth flattened into a hard line.

"Jazz, Rocky is *very* happy to see you."

Unintelligible grunt.

"I'm seeing this as an opportunity for reconciliation."

Growl-like utterance from Jazz.

"Can't we all just get along?" I waited for Jazz to call me Rodney King—like he always did whenever I quoted Rodney —but Rocky's affections must have compromised his ability to articulate.

Finally, Jazz said something understandable. "Kids," he growled. He hadn't unfurled his fists of fury, so we still weren't in the clear.

"Rocky, my *friend*," I said, very loud and extra friendly, hoping to inspire Jazz not to hit either of us. "We'd like to talk to Zekia and Zeke."

Rocky still didn't seem to understand that my husband was trying desperately not to kill him. He put his hand on my shoulder—a dangerous move. "You know I want you to talk to them, but their mom kinda wants everybody to leave them alone. The shock, you know. And they've already talked to the police."

I shot a look at Jazz.

He crossed his arms over his chest.

I turned my attention back to Rocky. "Did you hear what they said to the police?"

"They just repeated the same story I told you earlier."

"About Zekia leaving the baby so Zeke could use the bathroom?"

He nodded. "Right."

I pried Jazz's hand off his own elbow. He allowed me to hold it. "Take us to them, Rocky. Maybe I can pull the psychologist card and Mrs. Thunder will let us speak to them."

"I don't know, babe."

At "babe" Jazz nearly broke all the bones in my hand.

"Don't call me babe," I said with a broad, very tight smile. "And I *really* mean it this time." I hoped Rocky would take the hint.

He ventured a peek at my livid, reddening husband. "Right this way, Lieutenant and Mrs. Brown," he said.

I thanked God for the momentary discernment of spirits.

We followed Rocky to the living room, and Jazz's hand relaxed into mine. Having him with me felt more comforting than I'd realized. Man. I really needed to let my hubby know how much I loved him.

A sniffle arrested my attention. My gaze went to Zekia and Zeke. The poor babies had curled into each other on the sofa, holding on for all they were worth. Mrs. Nikki Thunder sat on the edge of the couch, as far away from them as possible. I thought it odd that the children weren't in her arms, then attributed it to a stepmother thing. But, if that was true, why was she so protective about who talked to them?

I stole a glance at my husband. I'd seen him in this mode before. He was taking everything in. My attention went back to the family.

Rocky made introductions. "Nikki, you remember babe—uh, *Amanda* from the crusade, right?"

Her gaze flickered over me, and she looked as if she smelled something unpleasant. Her head darted up and down in a curt nod. Her reaction to Jazz, however, couldn't have been more different. Nikki sized my husband up like she was trying to figure out whether he wore boxers or briefs.

Rocky obviously had no clue about her appreciative appraisal. "This is her husband, Jazz."

"I'm deeply sorry for your loss," my husband said, extending his hand.

He gave Nikki one of his Colgate smiles, and I could tell that heifer heated up like she'd been blasted with a warm front from the Florida coast. She took his hand, no doubt undressing him with the lusty gaze she'd fastened on him. She let him cradle her hoof in his hand longer than I felt was necessary for social intercourse.

I turned my attention back to my schmoozing husband, who gave her his sexy Denzel Washington narrowed eyes.

"I can't imagine what you must be feeling now," he murmured in a way that made it the hottest condolence I'd ever heard.

I could imagine what she was feeling. And I didn't like it!

She gave Jazz a demure nod and continued to ignore me. "Thank you, Jazz. I appreciate your being here."

I'll bet she does, the . . . child of God. Man, that wasn't as satisfying as "heifer." Not by a long shot.

Jazz dropped to his knees in front of her, as if *Mrs.* Thunder were the Queen of All Things. "Is there anything I can do for you?"

"I'll let you know."

I'll bet she would. I knew that look. I'd given him that look, and the next thing you know we were married.

Mind you, this played out in the most subtle way. Jazz giving her nonverbal signals. Her responding by discreetly answering and even matching his cues. Her eyes a little wider to take in more of him. Her posture a little more open. His move. Her move. A delicate dance I had no part in.

I plopped down in a chair across from the sofa where I could keep an eye on them.

Nikki sat up just a wee bit in her seat, her attention fixed on Jazz. She uncrossed her legs, and in the most telling way, opened them slightly.

I'd hurt that cow. Truly.

She spoke demurely, "The Lord giveth, and the Lord taketh away. Blessed be the name of the Lord." But her words didn't match her body cues, unless she was talking about ditching her husband for Jazz.

The Lord giveth and the Lord taketh away, my eye. And I almost meant that literally so I wouldn't have to look at the two of them.

Jazz finally got up from his kneeling position and sat in a chair beside me.

Don't get me wrong. I'm not disparaging her quoting the book of Job. I'm all for faith while suffering; but honestly, she came off with as much authenticity as a Milli Vanilli song. I still cry, even now, over the child I lost, and that happened more than a decade ago.

I took a shot at her. "Wow. You sure are strong, Nikki," I said. It came out a bit more acidic than I'd intended.

Jazz cut his eyes at me.

She waved my comment away like she would a mosquito buzzing around her head. "I have to be."

"Amazing," I said. "Most women would be crying their eyes out. And your faith," I said, "talk about moving *mountains*!"

"And speaking of moving, Amanda," my husband quipped, "why don't you and Rocky go get this poor woman something to drink."

"What? I'm the maid now?" Fortunately, Rocky pulled me up from my seat and away.

He dragged me into the kitchen. "What's the matter with you, babe? You're being very rude."

"Rude? They were flirting right in my face."

"Did it ever occur to you that he's just being nice? And maybe she needs some kindness right now?"

"Rocky, you always see the best in people. That's an admirable quality, except for when my husband is trying out his game on another woman right in front of me."

God, I'm awful. A woman has lost her child, and all I can think about is taking her behind the house and giving her a beatdown.

While I continued to plot Nikki's destruction, Rocky poured a Diet Pepsi into an ice-filled glass. He didn't offer me one. "May I have a Diet Pepsi, too?"

"You don't need any soda. You're pregnant."

I don't know why my husband chooses the most inopportune times to interrupt Rocky and me.

"Excuse me?" he roared.

I was momentarily silenced by the horror engulfing me.

Rocky, however, happily obliged Jazz. "I told her she couldn't have any pop because I don't think it's good for the baby."

"*What baby?*" Jazz shrieked.

"Du-uh. The baby Bell is pregnant with."

The news must have flabbergasted Jazz so much, he didn't even knock Rocky out for "duhing" him. I had to get the situation under control.

"I'm not pregnant."

Jazz stared at me, mouth open.

"I said I'm not pregnant."

"Yes, you are," Jazz said slowly. "That's why your body is changing."

"I only gained a little weight."

"Your Chihuahuas are bigger. I felt them."

"Whoa," Rocky said innocently. "Babe, did you get some *puppies*?"

"No. And don't ask." I glared at Jazz. "You said you didn't touch me!"

"I did it for scientific purposes. They looked bigger, and I wanted to make sure." Jazz crossed his arms, putting his armor back on. "I knew it. I could tell as soon as I saw you."

"You could not."

"I got the gift! Just like my mother. I can spot a pregnant woman like that." He snapped his finger. "How in the he—"

"*Dude,*" Rocky said, settling a hand on Jazz's arm in a pastoral gesture. "Watch the language, please. Bell is pregnant. The unborn might hear."

Jazz narrowed his eyes, and the general area of his jaw tightened noticeably. "He's *touching* me, Bell."

Rocky slowly removed his hand.

But Jazz's rant wasn't over. "And how did Boy Toy find out before I did?" He started giving me that Niagara Falls look. "Bell, if you tell me you told him first . . ."

Rocky tried to save me. "I'm not her—um—boy toy anymore, and even if I was, we'd be holy and stuff."

Jazz stared at Rocky in the way I do when he astounds me with something he thinks is perfectly fine to say. Rocky, remaining oblivious, continued. "I'm her friend, Jazz. That's it. She didn't tell me—"

Just then Ezekiel Thunder walked into the kitchen. He still had the smooth television-personality demeanor, but grief had left cracks on the surface of his façade. He must have sensed the tension sizzling between us like bacon frying in a cast-iron skillet. "What's going on here?"

Rocky answered. "We were just talking about Bell's baby." He pointed at Jazz. "Ezekiel, this is Bell's husband, Jazz."

Jazz didn't respond.

"There's no baby," I said. "And I'm sure Reverend Thunder can figure out who Jazz is since you've already told him about him."

Jazz opened his mouth as if to protest. Rocky hit me with the eyes. "Babe, I've never talked to Ezekiel about Jazz."

"Oh, really? Then how did he know my husband's name at the crusade?"

"I'm telling you. I've never spoken to him about Jazz. You can ask him."

I looked at Thunder. He shrugged. "Not a word," he said, his seductive Southern drawl calming me despite my anger.

Thunder put his hand on Jazz's shoulder, as Rocky had moments earlier. Like spiritual father, like son, I supposed. But Jazz recoiled.

"I don't know who you are, but I suggest you get your hand off me."

"I'm Ezekiel Thunder, son. God told me who you are."

Jazz shot an angry glance at me. Shouted, "He's *touching me*, Bell! Can you tell your spooky friends to keep their hands to themselves? And why do they all do that creepy, I-know-all-your-business-because-God-tells-me bit?"

"Ezekiel Thunder is not my friend. And I don't know why they do that. Maybe God really does talk to them! Which I'm all for, except for when God gets chatty about *my* personal life."

I felt a little salty with God.

Ezekiel kept touching Jazz. "I feel your pain, Jazz. But God only gives us insight so that we can pray for you. It's not creepy, son."

"Yes it is," Jazz said. "And I'm not your son. Move your hand."

Ezekiel Thunder took his hand away.

Rocky came to Thunder's rescue. "I know Ezekiel. God *does* speak to him. And you're my friend, Bell. So are you, Jazz, whether or not you know it. I'm sorry about what happened that night in Bell's apartment, but we lost a beautiful little boy today. This isn't the time for fighting, especially about something as joyful and blessed as a new baby coming into the world."

He had a point, even though he looked rather silly giving his speech while holding sweating glasses of diet cola. And then there was the fact that I wasn't pregnant.

Jazz looked at Thunder. Sighed heavily. "I'm sorry for your loss, Reverend Thunder. I see the kids are really taking it hard."

Thunder's face sobered. "They blame themselves for this awful thing that has visited us."

"Sir," Jazz said, "how about if I take Zeke and Zekia out of the house to Cold Stone Creamery to get some ice cream and a little fresh air? The press isn't out there right now. And the kids have to be exhausted from all this. I just spoke to Nikki a moment ago. She thinks it's a good idea, and she'll accompany us. *If* that's okay with you."

For a moment Ezekiel hesitated, then he nodded briskly.

"Good. I could use some ice cream," I said.

"I'll bring you back some. Want some pickles with that, *baaaaaaybeeeeee?*"

"I'm not pregnant, Jazz."

Ezekiel Thunder nodded. "You're pregnant, darlin'."

"What do I have to do to convince you people I'm not pregnant?"

Thunder flashed his blinding smile. "You could take a pregnancy test."

"It'd be a waste of time and money."

"I'll pay for it," Jazz said.

"Then it'd be a waste of time. And don't you have to pay for *ice cream,* Jazz?"

"I can handle it, *baaaaaaybeeeeee,* and surely you have time to make pee pee for a pregnancy test, since you go to the bathroom *all the time.*"

"Maybe I have a small baby," I said, defending myself.

Jazz jumped all over it. "Aha! A slip! You said 'small baby.'"

"I said I have a small bladder."

"You said 'a small baby,' darlin'," Thunder said with a shrug.

Jazz scowled at Thunder. "Hey, don't call my *wife* darlin'."

Rocky set the Pepsi down on the kitchen counter. He turned back toward us. "That's it. Everybody hold hands."

We so didn't want to hold hands.

"Do it," Rocky commanded, even though he sounded about as threatening as Keanu Reeves in *Bill & Ted's Excellent Adventure.*

Jazz and I grumbled but clasped hands. Ezekiel and Rocky did the same and reached for Jazz and me. We became a circle of unity. At least we looked the part.

Rocky said, "I want you all to let go of anger, pride, fear—everything. Just quietly release and go catatonic."

Rocky went catatonic. This seemed to fascinate Thunder. It embarrassed me and seemed to amuse Jazz. Still, Thunder followed suit, and I figured if Jazz and I didn't go catatonic, we'd look silly standing there conscious. I started letting go, in the order Rocky suggested: anger first.

I took a few deep breaths, and honestly, it felt good. Pride was a little harder, but after a few moments I began to feel it go. Fear? That would really be a challenge. But I focused on staying absolutely still. Breathing softly, in and out. I thought of Psalms 46:10: "Be still, and know that I am God." In that brief stillness, I began to sense God's presence—His "I AM"-ness in the midst of all my turmoil. Maybe Rocky was on to something with contemplative catatonic after all.

When we'd all gone quiet and still, Rocky's voice broke through our collective silence. "Can we just be kind to each other?"

We all released hands. The rest of us nodded.

I looked at Jazz. "Can I go for ice cream with you? Please?"

"There isn't enough room in the car, *Jane*."

I recalled what he'd said, earlier, *Me, private investigator. You, psychologist*. He was assuring me he was on the job. I sighed. "Okay."

Rocky looked confused. "Babe, did you change your name to Jane?"

"Just for Jazz," I said. "It's kind of like on the television show *Joan of Arcadia*. Remember how her boyfriend always called her Jane instead of Joan?"

Rocky had no idea what I was talking about. He was more into *The Sopranos* than the late, great *Joan of Arcadia* series that I now could only enjoy on DVD.

Jazz interrupted. "Stay here and chat with Reverend Thunder. I'm sure he's having a hard enough time."

I looked at the old slickster. His sorrowful eyes. Beneath that smooth exterior, Thunder hurt for his little boy.

He spoke. "I certainly could use some good conversation."

"I guess that settles it," I said. "I'll stay and chat with Ezekiel."

Man!

Jazz couldn't exit without a snarky comment. "What kind of ice cream do you want, *Ma Bell*?"

"I don't want any, thank you," I said. I *did* want some. But I wasn't about to give him any pleasure by letting him win this round.

"Aw, don't be shy. Think of little Jazz in there." He knelt and talked to my tummy. "If you weren't in there, son, I'd put your mommy over my knee and spank her big, blossoming behind for keeping you from me."

I crossed my arms over my belly. "I would *never* keep a baby from you, Jazz. And my butt isn't blossoming. It's merely . . ."

"Getting really big?" Rocky offered.

Jazz stopped still. Obviously another man talking about my butt had a Niagra Falls effect on him. Slooooowly he turned.

I snatched his wrist and yanked him to me. Stood on tiptoe to whisper in his ear. "I said no hitting. And I'm sure your *girlfriend* Nikki in there wants something sweet from you. Get going."

Jazz played along. Put his arms around my waist and yanked

me closer. He grazed my ear with his lips and whispered, "You just make sure you get all the information you can out of Thunder, your *other* boyfriend. Pay attention to *everything*."

"I'm not pregnant," I said when Jazz released me, hoping it would make Rocky and Ezekiel think that's what we were talking about.

Jazz pulled away from me. "I'm from Missouri, baby. Show me."

He waltzed out the door, leaving Ezekiel smiling at me.

"He's not from Missouri," I said, at a loss for anything else to say. "He was born in Detroit."

"Ain't love grand," Thunder said.

I seriously doubted it.

chapter
ten

JAZZ HUSTLED—and I do mean hustled—Nikki, Zekia, and Zeke out of the house. Rocky had some administrative work to do, which left me with the task of prying information out of a man I considered my spiritual nemesis.

Thunder helped me into the living room, my ankle still smarting. He placed his hand at the small of my back the way my husband does, emphasis on *the way my husband does.* I froze.

"I don't bite, darlin'."

"It's not your bite that concerns me."

He chuckled, seated me as if he was a perfect gentleman, then, smooth as silk, eased himself down beside me on the sofa. "Isn't this cozy," he said in a voice that could make a fortune in late-night radio. "Now we can get to know one another."

"*That's* what concerns me." I didn't want to know him. I needed information, that's all.

"We'll just talk. I promise not to do anything to offend you." He cocked his head and looked at me with a bemused expression.

"Let me pray for that ankle, Bell."

"Sir, I don't think—"

Too late. Thunder placed his hand on my swollen ankle and began an earnest intercession. Odd. His hand felt warm. Something akin to peace flooded me. It felt nice. Too nice! I pulled away from him.

"Thanks," I muttered. We sat for a few moments until he broke the uncomfortable silence.

"You know," he said, crossing his legs, "I've known Rocky since he was a boy."

I crossed my arms, legs, too. "I know. He told me he came to Christ at a Thunder Kids Bible Camp." I imagined the young towheaded boy Rocky must have been. Smiled at the thought. "What was he like back then?"

Thunder took a deep breath and lowered his gaze. Another heavy sigh and a shake of his head. Then he smiled. I could tell he'd gotten caught up in the kind of nostalgia that could conjure both joy and pain. "Rock was a good kid, even then, but he had it rough."

"Really?"

I uncrossed my arms. After all, besides angering me with his false prophecy about me being pregnant and his true one about the growth on my belly, he hadn't done anything to me. And Rocky loved him. Couldn't I give him a break for that alone?

"His parents practically let the television raise him."

I thought about all of the television shows Rocky loved and the classic TV T-shirts he often wore. "He never told me that. I always thought he just loved television."

"TV was his friend. His family. He was a lonely kid. And a bit silly."

I laughed and echoed what Rocky had said to me earlier: "Some things never change."

Thunder laughed, too. "The boy craved love. Made quite a pest of himself to get my attention."

"You must have been good to him."

"I liked him. A lot. He just wanted to be loved, like all of us. I saw a lot of myself in him."

I thought about that statement. All of us want to be loved, and some of us make such a mess of things seeking it. "Rocky is one of the most loving people I know."

"He loves the stranger, all right, but he's broken, too."

"You think so?"

"I know so, Bell. That's why he clung to you. He knew you'd never love him back the same way he loved you. He repeated his childhood with you. He kept trying to win you over like he did with his parents. Never worked, did it, darlin'?"

For all my astute knowledge of psychology, I'd never known Rocky's parents ignored him like that. When we dated, and even before that when we were friends and comrades in ministry, he preferred to talk about me or God rather than himself. When he spoke of his parents, he never breathed a word about any emotional neglect. He described them as hardworking and good providers. Busy, he said, but never anything worse.

That's my Rocky.

I'd met his folks a few times and could tell they didn't care for his being with an older black woman, but I'd always thought the awkwardness I experienced in their presence was more about me, my age, and my color than the fact that Rocky didn't have a great relationship with them.

I shook my head. My heart ached for my friend. "I do love Rocky, but I was never meant to be his wife."

More silence. I pondered my sweet friend's heart. "How did he become such a love bug?"

"He wanted love, so he gave it freely. God rewarded him."

"But not with me."

"Bell, we all try to right our past wrongs with the new people in our lives. As a psychologist, you know this."

I filed that bit of info: *we try to right our past wrongs.*

"You know, Rocky always tells me I don't know how to be loved."

"He has trouble with it himself, darlin'. That's why he could recognize it in you."

I went ahead and let him call me darlin'. "Anybody ever tell you that you're a good psychologist, Reverend Thunder?"

He placed his hand on mine, briefly, and pulled it away. "Call me Ezekiel."

We sat for a while, and I wondered if he'd lost himself in the thought of how hard simply loving is. When I could stand no more of my own reflections, I brought up what I wanted to know all along.

"What happened to your son, Ezekiel?"

"I don't know, darlin'." His soft, velvety voice could lull me to sleep. "They said he was having a bath when something went wrong."

"Who told you?"

"Nikki."

"What did you think?"

He gave me a quizzical look. "I'm not sure what you're getting at. She told me my baby was dead. *That's* what I thought about."

His defenses went up like Jazz's blood pressure does when I say, "Rocky." I needed to play this cool. Way cooler than I was. This time, I breached my own defenses and reached out to touch his hand.

"Of course that's what you thought about. I'm so sorry, Ezekiel."

Silence spread out between us once again. Ezekiel broke it this time. "Well," he stretched "well" out to two syllables. "I did think it was a little strange that Zekia had bathed him. Sister Joy usually does."

Bingo! "Who is Sister Joy?"

"She's like our nanny. Really she's been a lifelong friend. Stays with us."

"Is she the woman who was holding him at the crusade?"

"Yes, ma'am. She watches him while Nikki sits in the pulpit with me."

"Where was Sister Joy when Zeekie drowned?"

"She was in her room reading. She didn't know Zekia was giving him a bath."

I settled back in the beige sofa cushions to think. So the nanny was otherwise occupied when he died. "And you say Zekia didn't usually bathe him?"

"No, she's not a real motherly kind of girl. She'd never showed interest in giving him a bath."

Something struck me. "How often did Nikki bathe him?"

"Not often, as far as I know. She's not the motherly kind, either."

How could a perfectly healthy mother rarely bathe her own baby?
Maybe she's not perfectly healthy.

"Why do you think Zekia did it this time, Ezekiel?"

"I've gone over it in my head again and again. Zekia said she just felt like it. I didn't want to push her too hard. The child is all broken up about what happened. Nikki thought I should let her be."

"How was Zekia's and Zeke's relationship with Zeekie?"

"They were crazy about him. Zeekie was a handful, but he was the sweetest child God ever did make. He just loved on people. It was a gift he had."

I'd experienced that poor baby's gift myself.

Thunder's eyes misted. "Zeekie was the light of my life. I wanted to do everything right with him. And I tried. God knows I did. He had so much energy—all boy. Nikki couldn't handle him. She's young. These young women, the first thing they want to do is give a child medication. She wanted to put him on Ritalin. Did he seem like he needed medication to you, Bell?"

A bolt of anger surged through me. No way did that child need medication. "No, he seemed like a wonderful, normal little boy."

Again I got a little salty with God. Nikki Thunder wanted to drug her toddler into submission. *She didn't deserve that beautiful child. Why did that cow have a baby, but I didn't?* I tried to calm myself. I chastised myself for thinking of the woman as cattle again. I didn't know Nikki Thunder. Mothering isn't particularly easy. She may have been overwhelmed. Like Ezekiel said, she was young. I had no right to judge her.

But I did.

"Does she enjoy being a mother?"

"I think she does. Although it's hard for her to deal with them all the time. She wasn't mothered well. She didn't have any good examples to draw from."

"How is she with your other children?"

"My older children don't care much for her. She's younger than they are. Then again, they aren't too thrilled to have *me* as a father."

The corners of his mouth lifted in a sad, shy smile. I understood it. I had a smile just like it when I thought of my husband and the mountain of regrets I had concerning him.

"What about Zekia and Zeke?"

"They try to like her. Nikki has a strong personality. She's been through a lot. It takes a while for her to warm up to people, and vice versa."

"Didn't take her long to warm up to you, did it?"

Whoops. That just came flying out. I'd embarrassed him, but he handled it.

"Like many young women who've had a rough go of it, she wanted a father figure."

"Father figure, or did she want a sugar daddy?"

He shrugged. "She gave me something I needed. I gave her something she needed. It's not real complicated, darlin'."

"Don't call me darlin'." I tried not to think about what he needed from her. I needed to get back on task. I didn't know how much time I'd have with him.

"Ezekiel, are Zekia and Zeke responsible kids?"

"Heavens, yes. They're great kids. And they love their dad. I don't deserve them."

"How long have you and Nikki been married?"

"Five years."

Nikki couldn't have been more than twenty-five, and I doubted she was that old. I tried not to show my disgust that he'd practically married a child. I gave him my fake, professional smile. "How old was she when you got married?"

"She had just turned eighteen. I married her right after I found out she was pregnant."

I couldn't even muster a fake smile at that one. "You got a teenage girl—who you weren't married to—pregnant when you were in your fifties?" You animal.

"I'm no angel."

"I'm kinda noticing a 'no angel' pattern here." I chastised myself for my judgmental words. Looked at him. "I apologize." I sighed and waited for his response.

"My dear, a man can choose his sin, but God will decide the consequences."

"Meaning?" I asked, as if my great-grandmother didn't live by that saying.

"I felt like David must have when God took his baby. My punishment for cheating on Zekia and Zeke's mother with Nikki was losing the baby girl Nikki was pregnant with."

"I understand that kind of loss more than you know, Eze-kiel."

"The Lord told me that, darlin'."

"But, enough about me."

I cleared my throat, unnerved by him saying God had spoken to him about me. Why didn't he have conversations with God about his own raggedy life?

Back on task. "So, you were married when you hooked up with Nikki?"

"I had a long, very loving relationship with my wife. She stuck by me during some hard times. She died shortly after our affair started."

Convenient. For Nikki that is.

"How did you meet Nikki?"

"She came to work for us. I hadn't planned on anything happening between us."

"Don't tell me. She was an intern."

He snorted. "You're very sassy, Bell."

"Don't call me Bell."

He regarded me with a crooked smile. Like he admired me for disliking him. "I'm afraid there was no ministry to intern for at that time. We lived off the sales of my early books, and I did whatever odd jobs I could get. My wife hired her to help around the house. We didn't have much. We only paid her a handful of dollars, but she needed the money. Poor kid had some tough breaks. Lived from pillar to post. My Toni took her in—she had a big heart like that. You'd be hard pressed to find a soul like Toni in the world. Salt of the earth. I didn't deserve her."

"I'm inclined to agree."

"Don't get me wrong. Toni and I had our problems. She was one of those women who thought she was too holy to make love with her husband. And Nikki—well, let's just say she was precocious."

"I don't think 'precocious' is the right word, but go on."

"She was happy to meet my needs, and being the wretched sinner that I am, I fell into sin. Toni found out and took to her bed. One day I went to look in on her and found her dead. I felt like I killed her myself."

I felt like I killed her myself.

I had a few more nasty comments for him, but the painful reminders of my own moral failures immediately came to mind, and I swallowed my insults. His answers were becoming increasingly hard for me to listen to. I turned my head away from him, mulling his words "like I killed her myself" over and over.

"What did she die of?"

"I'd say she died of a broken heart."

"That's not quite the clinical answer I was looking for."

"She languished for a while until she finally wasted away. The doctors said natural causes."

A chill went through me. I realized once again how I thought too much like Jazz now. But I knew the high correlation between sick souls and bodies. People *did* literally die of broken hearts. Still, I found it odd that he'd said he felt like he'd killed her himself. Was that an unconscious confession?

"Where were you when Zeekie drowned?"

"I'd gone upstairs to an empty room for *lectio divina*. I do it every day at nine A.M."

I raised an eyebrow. "I don't think I know any fiery Pentecostals into *lectio*. Isn't that practice a bit too high church?"

"Rocky introduced me to it."

Rocky! Him and his Tony Jones books. He had a copy of *The Sacred Way* surgically attached to him.

Ezekiel looked almost shy about his *lectio* practice, like I'd discovered a dirty little secret. I wondered if he thought I was mocking him. "I take it that you don't teach this."

He smiled. "No. This is personal. The ancient traditions changed me. I've been slowly adding new practices to my life for the last five years. I know you don't have much respect for me, darlin', but this sinner is actually repentant."

"You're still a flirt."

"Just around beauties like yourself."

"I'm no beauty."

"Ah, but you're wrong about that, darlin'. And it's not just the outside that looks good to me."

"I suck."

He smiled at me. "Maybe that self-deprecating quality is just plain lovable. *Bell*."

"Cut it out, Thunder."

"Old habits die hard. My granny used to say, 'When you see a pretty gal, if you don't look once, you're not a man, and if you look twice, you're not a man of God.' I'm trying to be a man of God. That's the gospel truth."

Like I could judge him. I stumbled through the ruins of my own sinful sexual past every day, trying to make my way back to God.

Lord, give me your wisdom. How would you deal with a man like him?

And then the awe-inspiring voice of God: *The same way I dealt with you.*

I hung my head, thoroughly chastised by the Lord. A few moments of uncomfortable silence passed, and I went back to his *lectio* practice. "So what do you do during your time in the empty room?"

"I spend an entire hour in a place where there are as few distractions as possible." His excitement about the subject shone in his eyes. "You know there are four distinct movements? *lectio, meditatio, oratio,* and *contemplatio.*"

I nodded. I could see he loved the discipline.

"I take a passage from Scripture that I chose ahead of time, and I spend some time reading it, slowly. Several times."

"What else do you do?"

"Then I meditate on it. I try to make it personal, see how it relates to my own life. If a particular word or two stands out, I meditate on that."

Again, I nodded my encouragement, not that he needed it now. He had brightened like a child at Christmas.

"Next I respond to the passage. I open my heart to it. This is where the conversation with God begins."

His voice had such a soothing quality. This was the most authentic talk I'd shared with him. His obvious connection to God through this spiritual exercise charmed me. "And then what happens as you open up to God?"

He took a deep breath, as if he were breathing in God's Spirit. He released it slowly, like a sigh of pure pleasure.

"My favorite part is *contemplatio.* By now I've spent the better part of an hour getting my mind ready to meet God in this movement. I just listen to God, sissy."

He called me sissy, the Southern endearment for sister, and I doubted if he'd noticed.

"I free my mind of my own thoughts. I don't think about

holy things or the cares of the world. Just me and my Father."

I had to admit how much that impressed me—a former prosperity and deliverance preacher practicing *lectio divina* and loving it. He had a satisfied grin on his face. A spiritual romantic. No wonder women captivated him like they did King David. He was a lover at heart.

I had to focus, though. I didn't want this man's attractiveness to fool me into not seeing what he was—a suspect, until he was proven not to be. I thought about what he said about going into an empty room. To my knowledge all the rooms in the Rock House house were occupied.

"Which room is empty?"

"The attic. Rocky has been painting it, working on turning it into a nursery for Elisa's baby."

Okay. That shouldn't have made me feel like he'd kicked me several times in the stomach, and yet . . . some strange noise burst out of my throat.

Ezekiel took my hand in his. "Are you all right?"

I nodded, still unable to speak.

"You do know that God has heard your prayer, darlin'? You have what you want." He gave "have" an extra syllable. "Take care of your tumor, sissy."

"It's probably a cyst or something. I don't know how you knew about that. Maybe you have some kind of gift. Maybe you're just a great manipulator, but—"

"It's a tumor, and it *can* hurt you."

Honestly! He sounded just like he did on television. I cleared my throat. "You can drop the honey-coated voice of the prophet bit. We're not on camera."

He sat back. Grinned at me. "You don't like me, do you?"

"I don't know you, Mr. Thunder."

"Maybe you should get to know me. You might find that we're a lot alike, darlin'."

I gave him a tight, fake smile. "I don't think we are, Reverend. And don't call me darlin'." Again I reminded myself that I needed to stop attacking Thunder and get as much useful information as possible. "Who else was home when the accident happened?"

"Just my folks—Nikki, Lou, Joy, and the children. Rocky's staff and Elisa had gone over to the church for a meeting. Rocky was . . . I'm not sure where he was."

At my intervention. But I wasn't about to tell Thunder about *that.*

"Did anyone else know you were in the attic?"

"I'm sure everyone did. Like I said, I do it every day at nine A.M." The tone of his smooth voice only held a hint of irritation at my interrogation.

I didn't say anything. Just cataloged the facts he gave me in my too fatigued brain.

"Bell?"

I looked at Ezekiel. I didn't say he could call me Bell, but I suddenly felt too tired to play the name game.

Again, Ezekiel took my hand in his. "I appreciate your interest in my son, but this was nothing more than a tragic accident. If it's anything other than that, I'm certain God will swiftly and mightily avenge my son's death."

This from a man who told the media he expected God to raise his son from the dead.

"Good luck with that," I said.

I meant it, too.

I found Sister Joy milling around the kitchen. Her dress was casual today. She wore a simple denim jumper with a red turtleneck underneath. Her hair was pulled into a chignon; a few tendrils had escaped, grazing her neck. She'd made herself a sandwich and was turning away from the counter most likely to sit at the small kitchen table when she saw me. She started and her hand flew to her chest.

"Excuse me," I said. "I didn't mean to frighten you."

"Child, you scared me half to death." She fanned herself, though the room wasn't hot.

"May I sit with you for a bit?"

"I'd be happy for the company. Get my mind offa . . ." She waved her hand in front of her face as if the gesture would halt the tormenting memory and threatening tears. She took a handkerchief from the pocket of her jumper and dabbed at the moisture brimming in her brown eyes. This honey-colored woman reminded me of so many women in my family. She could be my aunt.

We both sat at the table across from each other. When she set the plate on the table, I reached out and squeezed her hand. "I'm so sorry for your loss, Sister Joy. My name is Amanda. I sat behind you at the crusade Wednesday night." I fought back my own threatening tears. Zeekie seemed to be a gift to all who knew him. I needed to be focused, or I'd never be able to help Zeekie as he'd cried out for me to do in my dream.

"Lorda Mercy!" she said. "I didn't think I could cry so."

"You must have been very close to Zeekie."

She rocked a bit. "Honey, don't you know, I loved him like he was my own child. I never married or had children. Zeke's kids are about as close as I ever got to being a mama. I took care of that child since *that girl* brought him home from the hospital."

Something about the way she said "that girl" gave me the feeling Sister Joy didn't head up the Nikki Thunder fan club.

"You must have been with Ezekiel for a long time."

"A long time," she repeated, voice full of nostalgia.

"Tell me," I said. "I love a good story."

She pushed the plate toward me, offering half her sandwich. I took it and thanked her. There's something about sharing a meal and a story, no matter how meager the meal may be. Maybe the heart opens with the mouth, as memories fresh and sweet as strawberries picked off the vine, still warm from the sun, spill out of souls.

"I grew up with him and, honey child, don't you know, that boy was as slick then as he is now."

I feigned ignorance. "Slick?"

"Oh, yes, ma'am. You know he is."

She grinned at me. Yes. I knew.

"Even as a boy, he knew how to charm the ladies. That was one pretty brown boy."

Her wistful smile said so much more than her words. She'd loved him most of his life.

"Was he ever your beau?"

She lay her palms flat on the table. "Oh Lord, no. We were just friends, but I was always there for him. I was the girl next door. We went to each other's birthday parties and to Sunday school together."

She smoothed imaginary wrinkles off her jumper. I wondered if she'd counted the cost of loving him, even back when she was still a girl.

"How did his ministry begin?"

This time she smiled broadly. "We'd gone to revival under the big tent when we were fifteen years old, and he gave his heart to Jesus that night. Cried like a baby on a makeshift altar that was just a handmade bench on the grass at the front of the tent."

Sister Joy sat quietly, hands crossed on her lap. She looked lost in reverie. I took a bite of the heavenly turkey sandwich she'd made—real turkey, not cold cuts. My taste buds rejoiced. I nodded, my mouth full, to encourage her to finish.

She touched her neck briefly. She didn't seem to know what to do with her hands. "Wasn't too much longer after that and he got to preachin' and teachin' himself. All the old folks said he was like a little prophet. Well, he loved the book of Ezekiel, and we got to calling him that. The old folks called him a son of thunder. He put them two together, and Ezekiel Thunder was born. That was his destiny." She had a faraway look in her eyes, as if she really believed in his calling.

"What was his name before?"

"Norman Dickson."

"Did you go with him when he went to pursue his destiny?"

"Wished I could have. But he'd always come back home, and I'd be there."

I wanted to let her know how grateful I was for all that she'd shared with me. "This is the best turkey sandwich I've ever had," I said.

She grinned and took a bite of her half. When she finished chewing, she blurted out what I'd already surmised. "I've loved that man since we were children."

Again I touched her hand. "I know what it is to love someone like that. I haven't known him most of my life, but I feel like I've waited for him. Always. Like there was a Jazz-shaped hole in my life that I was always keenly aware of. What I lack in time I've made up for with fierce passion. My feelings for him astonish me sometimes."

She gave me a knowing glance and a nod, then took another bite. "I went to work for Ezekiel when I was about twenty. His ministry was growing fast."

"You stayed with him throughout everything? Even when the ministry had all those problems?"

"Yes, ma'am. I believed in Ezekiel Thunder. I was there when he met Jesus, and that was real. All those things that came later, those weren't real. I *knew* him before all that, when he was just a boy who loved Jesus."

"Did he know how you felt about him?"

"He couldn't miss it. I didn't have to tell him."

"And he never even considered you?"

"He kissed me once. One starry night when we sat on a grassy hill talking about everything under the sun. It was my first and only kiss."

Poor Sister Joy. One kiss, and she was her beloved's for the rest of her life. I understood it.

"What happened to Zeekie, Joy? How did he end up drowning?"

Her face clouded with grief. "I don't know. Nobody gave that boy a bath but me. I have to wonder if the whole thing was that girl's fault."

I didn't think "that girl" was Zekia. "What makes you say that?"

"She didn't have a mother bond, if you ask me. She doesn't have a bond to anybody. She knows how to open her skinny legs, but not her heart. She's not right, that Nikki. You mark my words. That girl told me to relax and do some Bible reading and she'd handle things with the kids. She never handles anything with the kids."

She sat back against the chair, posture as straight and elegant as she. Shook her head and pressed her lips into a flat line. "I blame myself. I shouldn'ta trusted her." A fresh wave of tears spilled down her cheeks. "I'd told myself I wasn't those children's mother, but I *was,* Bell. I was his mother. I shoulda given him his bath. He'd be here today if I'da given him his bath."

"Do you think she would intentionally harm him?"

"That gal isn't right. I wouldn't put anything past her. I can't stand her, I'm ashamed to say. I hate the day Toni brought her home."

"So you were friends with Ezekiel's late wife, Toni?"

"She was like a sister to me. I helped her with Zeke and Zekia. She was frail. A real nice lady, but she took sick real easy. But you'd never meet a sweeter soul. She was the salt of the earth."

"That's what Ezekiel said about her."

"Truer words have never been spoken."

"Her death must have devastated you."

"I never trusted what they say happened to her."

"How do you explain her death?"

"I can't explain it. But I can't help thinking somebody didn't want her around anymore. That's all I've got to say."

Point taken. "What about Sister Lou? Could she have been involved in Zeekie's accident?"

"All I know is she and *that girl* are thick as thieves. Louella is a sick woman. She's always been a little strange, but she's flat-out crazy most of the time now. It's no telling what she could have done."

She stood up. Our talk was over. "Well, I can't sit around running my big mouth all day. I've said too much as it is. I got to see to it that when Zekia and Zeke get home they got what they need to go to bed right away." She turned and looked at me, and she looked strangely, wonderfully ferocious. Like a lioness. Or a good mother.

"God help me, but I think I'd kill somebody if they tried to hurt those kids now." Again she pulled out her handkerchief and wiped her eyes. "You'll excuse me please."

"Sister Joy?"

She paused and looked at me.

"If you ever need to talk, please let me know."

"Like I said, I've already said too much." She swiped her hand across her mouth, as if the gesture would erase her words. "Don't you pay me no mind, you hear? I just miss my baby, that's all. Don't you pay me no mind."

"Sleep well, Sister Joy."

She smiled shyly, shook her head, and walked out of the kitchen, leaving me at the table pondering all she'd said.

———————

After dwelling on Sister Joy's interesting information, I began to get a bit agitated that Jazz was still gone. I don't know about Ezekiel, but the idea of my spouse hanging out with Ms. Brick House disturbed me more than I cared to admit.

I returned to the empty living room and sat on a stuffy old chair that wasn't old enough to be an antique but was uglier than one. I chose that chair so I could pull aside the sheer curtains every few minutes and peer out. By now Jazz could have gone to Rome and had ice cream with the Pope. Okay, maybe he hadn't been gone that long. But it felt like it. I picked up a book off the coffee table—*Cosmas or the Love of God*—and tried to read it. It looked like it might be good. Rocky was always reading good books. I read and reread the back cover, still not sure what it was about.

When I heard car doors slam and muffled voices drifting my way, I perked up. Ezekiel must have heard them, too. He materialized at my side and helped me get through the hallway as steps sounded on the porch outside. We stood in the foyer waiting on our spouses and the kids to come through the door.

They sauntered in looking like one big, happy family. Ever the gentleman, Jazz led Nikki into the house by placing his hand at the small of her back. She held on to Jazz so tightly that he practically had to wrench her off him once they'd gotten inside. For a grieving mother, Nikki positively glowed. I knew that glow. That was *my* glow! She had Jazz magic all over her!

The children went right into their father's arms, smiling, and for a moment they looked like normal children without a hint of tragedy marking them. Zekia clutched her daddy's waist. "Mr. Jazz got us whatever we wanted. I had cheesecake ice cream. Daddy, it tasted so good."

Little Zeke agreed with a vigorous bobblehead nod.

I did notice something amiss in this little family reunion. Mrs. Thunder did not readily embrace her own husband. She seemed far more interested in mine. I gathered my wits about me.

"What did you have, Nikki?" I asked, hoping she didn't say, "Your husband."

She looked at me like I was the scourge of the Earth. "I had to be a good girl," she said. "I think it's a woman's duty to watch her figure."

Better her than my husband watching it.

She seemed to study me. "I admire you women who let yourself go and eat whatever you want."

I stood there willing myself not to kill her. Jazz put his arms around my waist. "Personally, I like a little something to hold on to."

God bless that man.

Nikki didn't seem to appreciate his comment. Suddenly her husband existed. She took his hand. "I'd like to have a hot bath and get my husband to bed now."

"*Really?*" I screeched.

Jazz didn't acknowledge me but kept his attention fastened on Nikki. On the sly he pinched my waist, a move that said to me, "Don't start." I didn't let the Thunders see me react to the pinch.

Jazz cleared his throat. "It's been a long day. You folks had better get some rest." To Nikki: "I'll be back tomorrow to check on you—and the kids."

Yeah. Real smooth, Jazz.

"Me too," I added in case Jazz had the mistaken impression that he'd be coming here alone.

I turned my attention to Ezekiel. "It was . . ." What was I supposed to say? It was *good* talking to you? I don't think so. I settled for "Thanks for your time, Ezekiel. I'll be praying for your family."

"You do that, Bell. And I'll be praying for yours."

Jazz opened the door for me, and I tried to step out, but . . .

I turned back to Nikki. "I don't mean to keep you. I know you want to get upstairs for that bath, but may I say you are one extraordinary woman, Nikki."

She raised her chin and looked down her nose at me. She didn't reply.

"I mean, if my child—my *baby*—drowned this very day in that bathtub upstairs, the only bathtub in this house . . . well, I think it'd take a few strong men and an injection of powerful drugs to keep me from tearing that tub out of the wall, plumbing and all. I'd probably become a rabid shower person after that. It'd be a long time before Calgon would take me away. What amazing strength you have." I waved. "Good night, everybody."

Jazz let me out the door and gently settled me into the Love

Bug. He went to the driver's side and burst out laughing as soon as he opened the door.

"What are laughing at, crazy man?"

He shook his head. "You really are living up to your name."

"Bell?"

"No, girl Columbo."

He got in the car, shut the door, and off we went.

chapter eleven

N O SOONER had we pulled out of the driveway of the Rock House house than I started seething at Jazz's antics. I mocked him in my head. *I'll be back tomorrow to check on YOU—and the kids. Yeah, well, so will I. I'll be checking on you a lot, cow!*

Must repent. Must not call women farm animal names.

My complete silence on the way home should have made Jazz acutely uncomfortable. He didn't seem fazed by it or my simmering anger. However, I'd made the mistake of letting him drive, so he had to go with me back to my apartment. He parked the Love Bug and grabbed my iPod, placing it in a Kroger grocery bag. Jazz shut the door behind him and came over to the passenger side to open the door for me.

I didn't move. "What are you doing?"

"Opening the door for you."

"Why didn't you drive over to where your car is?"

"I'm not ready to leave yet, Bell."

"What if I've had enough of you for one day?"

"Oh, I happen to know you can take more of me than that." He said this with a wicked grin.

"Is your head always in the gutter?"

He leaned toward me, his arm resting on the top of the Love Bug. "Get out of the car, baby."

"No."

"I know you're mad. We can talk inside."

"I don't want to talk to you."

"You asked me to look into this for you, and that is what I did. Will you get out of the car so I can tell you what I accomplished this evening?"

I took a peek at him. "You were just working?"

"I was."

"You're not attracted to that Cruella De Vil stick figure?"

"Hardly."

"And you don't think I'm too fat?"

"Bell, get out of the car. It's cold out here."

"You were supposed to say something romantic that made me believe you don't think I'm fat."

"Bell, if you don't step out of the Love Bug right now, I'm going to drag you upstairs."

"That fell way short of romantic, not to mention you still haven't said I'm not fat."

He sighed and raked his fingers through his hair. "You're not fat. I think you're stunning. You're so hot that I can hardly resist you, even though I'm still mad at you."

I grinned. "You think I'm hot?"

"Perhaps you should focus on my saying I'm still mad at you."

"You'll get over it. About me being hot . . ."

"You'll be hotter inside your apartment."

"Do you want to ravish me?"

"No. I want to throttle you. Please get out of the car."

I stepped a leg out. "I'm only letting you inside so you can report what happened with your girlfriend Nikki."

He moved back, took my hand, and helped me out of the car. "Fine."

"I don't want you getting fresh just because you're my husband. We're separated."

"You grill me about whether or not I want you, and now you insist that I not flirt with you."

"I have my standards."

"Spare me the details," he said. "Let's go inside and *debrief.*"

I shook my head in disgust. "Must you make everything sound nasty?"

"I'm suggesting we go inside and discuss our experiences tonight. So, who's the nasty one?"

"Are we going to discuss your attraction to Ms. The Lord Giveth, the Lord Taketh Away?"

"And to think I thought that shade of green you turned was because you have morning sickness."

"I'm not pregnant."

"Bell, let's get you out of the car. It's cold out here."

"I don't have to go in there with you."

"Yes, you do, it's your apartment."

"Jazz, sweetie, I want you to zoom in on the fact that I don't have to go in there *with you!*"

"Bell, if you don't step out of the Love Bug right now, I'm going to drag you upstairs."

"Very romantic, Jazz. Turns out you're the Neanderthal I thought you were."

He sighed and ran his fingers through his curls again. "Not really. If I was, you'd be unconscious and upstairs by now."

I gave him my most withering glance. "I hate you."

"The feeling is mutual. Now step into my hating arms and let me carry you upstairs."

"I can walk."

"Bell!" And then his Tourette's syndrome flared up. After he finished cussing, he said, "You can't walk with that bad ankle. I'm taking you upstairs. And we're going to talk about tonight. Can you just cooperate since you're the one who vowed to God that you would obey me?"

"Don't pull the sacred vows card!"

His eyes burned into me like lasers.

"Fine!"

"Fine!" He took my hand and helped me out of the car.

"And keep this in mind, Mr. Debrief, my great-grandmother always said, 'If you want the milk, you gotta buy the cow.'"

"I *did* buy the cow."

"Then you have to milk it, or something."

"I'm trying to."

"Okay, that one didn't work. I'm just trying to say you don't get any lovin' if we're separated."

"You made that clear to me, cow!" He laughed.

I would beat him. As soon as I got my ankle back in order, he would be so spousally abused.

He locked the Love Bug and strained to carry me up the three flights to my apartment. Honestly! I needed to cut him some slack, if only for the Herculean efforts he made to take care of me. It had been a long day. I'd gone through a full gamut of emotions, from the surprise and irritation I felt at the intervention this afternoon to heart-wrenching grief at finding out about Zeekie—a grief that seemed to multiply as the hours passed. For a moment I let my head rest on his shoulder and pretended that we were all right. We loved each other, and we were going home.

When we finally arrived at apartment 3B, Jazz put me down and opened the door for us. He took my hand and pulled me inside. I winced when my throbbing foot touched the ground.

Concern slipped through his anger. "I'm sorry, baby, are you okay?"

"Yes," I lied. Then, "No."

He closed the door, locked all three locks, *and* put on the chain. He unbuttoned my coat, his tenderness moving me. I took the chance to let him know. "You're very sweet sometimes."

"I happen to like undressing you."

"You had to go there, didn't you?"

He slid my coat off. "I've just gotten started. I'm really anxious to get that body-hugging tattoo T-shirt off of you." He pulled a hanger out of the closet and hung my coat on it, then placed it in the closet.

I put my hands on my hips. "What? No dinner first? No movie? You think I'm a cheap date?"

He took off his own coat and hung it up. "Cheap date? Not you, Bell. You're *incredibly* high maintenance." He stepped out of his Florsheims.

"Like Nikki Thunder?"

"I don't really know Nikki Thunder, but based on first impressions, I'd say you're nothing like her. You've got your own brand of high maintenance that I worry about."

"Meaning?"

"People keep trying to kill you when you get involved in what you don't seem to realize is *police* work." He carried me over to the sofa, and both of us plopped down. He helped me gently pull off my boots. Propped my foot on the coffee table. "Can I get you something?"

"I'm not very hungry, but I could use something to drink."

"Coming right up."

He went into the kitchen. I could hear him rooting around my cabinets. He emerged a few minutes later with a tall glass of milk for me, and something that looked suspiciously like alcohol for him.

He handed me the milk. "Mooooooooo," he said. Sat down beside me.

"You are so evil."

He laughed again, and darn it, I laughed, too, because his laughter affects me that way.

"What's that you're having?"

"Jack Daniel's."

"I don't have any Jack Daniel's."

"I do."

"Jazz, didn't you have enough to drink earlier?"

"Apparently not."

"I'm concerned about you."

"I can handle my liquor."

"Other people seem to think you're having a problem."

"They're wrong."

For a few minutes neither of us spoke. I sipped on the milk, not really enjoying it.

"Why did you give me milk?"

"I didn't think you wanted whiskey."

"You could have gotten me a cup of coffee or a Diet Pepsi."

"Bell, maybe you should hold off on caffeinated drinks until you . . ."

"Until I what?"

He didn't mince words. "Are you pregnant?"

"I told you I'm not. That's something our weird friends and family concocted."

"Rocky seems to think you are."

"Rocky believes in Santa Claus."

He took my hands in his. "I bought a pregnancy test while I was out."

"It wasn't necessary. I'm not pregnant."

"Take the test for *me*." He took my hands in his.

"No."

"Baby—"

"I said no."

"What harm would it do?"

I snatched my hands away. "What harm? Maybe I've already been through this. Weeks ago, when my breasts were tingling and sore and nausea blindsided me. When I was scared to death to hope, but did anyway because I kept feeling these incredible things happening in my body."

His own body armor went up and he crossed his arms. But I hadn't finished my rant.

"Oh, I tried not to get excited, but I couldn't help it. I got a pregnancy test, Jazz, and before I had time to take it, I bled. I lay in my bed curled up like a fetus and cried my eyes out because I wanted your baby so badly. And I went through that all alone. You were busy being mad somewhere else."

He didn't say anything for a moment. Then, "You should have told me if you even suspected it."

"Oh, I wanted to tell you. I had all these fantasies about how I would let you know I was pregnant. I would make you a steak dinner. Man food! Medium rare, just like you like it. And I'd have a battle of nonalcoholic champagne. And I'd *nonalcoholic* wine and dine you, put a rattle on your plate. And you were going to realize we were made to be together, and it was all a terrible mistake what happened with Rocky, and we'd live happily ever after. You, me, and our baby."

For a moment I felt like I couldn't breathe. My throat constricted and tears stung my eyes. I whispered, "We were going to grow old together, like Jack and Addie."

A few errant tears slid down my cheeks. I swiped at them, angry that I'd been weak enough to let them fall. "Shoot. I said I wouldn't cry about this anymore."

Jazz didn't say anything.

I grabbed a mud-cloth pillow and put it between us like it was a wall I'd erected. "So you see, Jazz, I already have a pregnancy test I don't need in my bathroom closet. And if you don't mind, I'd like to have myself a Diet Pepsi. Because I'm not having a baby, and I never will. It's too late."

When he didn't respond, I tore into him, "Make it fast, Jazz, or I'll have some of that Jack Daniel's with you."

He got up and went into the kitchen and grabbed a Diet Pepsi out of the refrigerator for me. I'd gotten myself so upset that I'd started to shake and couldn't control the free flow of tears bursting out of me.

Jazz came into the living room, placed my Pepsi on the coffee table, and sat by me, immediately taking me in his arms. He ran his hands down my shoulders and arms and let them settle at my waist. He pulled me on to his lap. "Aw, baby."

"I don't feel well! All this craziness at the Rock House going on with these good Christian folk! It's hard to tell saint from sinner. I'm suspicious of the whole Thunder lot. Well, maybe not the kids or Joy."

I took a deep breath. "And that whole ticking biological clock thing? It's not ticking like it used to. In fact, I don't hear it at all, and how could I over the cacophony of voices tormenting me by telling me I'm pregnant when I'm not? And then there's you! And this insane *thing* we have." I furiously swiped tears away.

"This *thing* is a marriage. It's raggedy, but we *are* married."

A sob escaped my mouth.

He rocked me until I calmed down, and my breathing matched his, my heart beating in time with his. He murmured in my ear, "You don't have to worry about anything. Why don't you just sit here with me and rest?"

He kissed my cheek and went back to my ear. "I thought you came to ask me for a divorce today, baby. I groped you because I was hurt and angry. And crazy. I missed you, Bell."

I clung to him. I loved him so, but I never knew exactly what we were doing together.

"Baby," he said. "About Jack and Addie. They uh . . ." He

seemed to search for his story. "They aren't perfect. They got married a month after they met. Even though they loved each other, they had a lot of fights. They really didn't know each other yet, and it wasn't always easy for them. He thought Mom should be more motherly, and to be honest, she wasn't always a great mom. She was an artist. We ate a lot of peanut butter and jelly while she painted, sculpted, or made jewelry. And that food she cooks that you love so much? She started cooking in her forties!"

I laughed. Unbelievable.

"Dad worked all the time. And, once, he got confused and did more than kiss another woman."

"Really, Jazz?"

"They were a bigger mess than us, and that's saying a lot. But they got through it. They're the love of each other's lives."

I couldn't deal with this kind of revelation. Jack and Addie fighting like us? An affair? I had hoped life could be easy and great for some of us.

"I need to wash my face."

He nodded. "My shirt could use a go-round in the washing machine since you're in a cleaning mood."

I'd soaked part of his shirt. Thank goodness I'd abandoned makeup that day. "I may have ruined it if I had on mascara."

"You've ruined my shirt before."

I blushed at his reference to when I ripped his bodice.

"You paid me back for that today when you felt me up in front of your friends."

"Those aren't my friends. And I didn't do it in front of them. Bell, I said I'm sorry for that. I was—"

"Drunk."

"Yeah. Drunk. Let's just say I'm kinda like your Brennan Manning. Not to imply he's a drinker. I'm just saying, maybe my cheese slid off my cracker today."

"That's makes two of us. My cheese seems to have found a permanent home elsewhere."

"Don't get me wrong, baby," he said. "You've spoiled me. Touching you wasn't *all* about being drunk. I like a good bodice ripping now and then, too, though I think it'll be so much simpler if we just took our clothes off in the privacy of our bedroom. And I'll be happy to help you with that tonight if you have any trouble."

"I've been dressing and undressing myself since my preschool days. I think I can manage."

"I don't trust you. Let me see for myself."

"I'm afraid that won't be happening tonight, Jazzy."

He began to unbutton his shirt, slowly, with a seductive grin.

"What are you doing, Jazz?"

"Modeling healthy undressing. You did ruin my shirt again." By now he'd finished unbuttoning. He slipped out of his shirt and handed it to me. A wet circle of moisture from my tears stained his undershirt, giving me a new appreciation for "wet T-shirt." He pulled the undershirt over his head in one swift motion. Held it out to me.

I couldn't stop staring at his amazing torso. And he knew it.

"Your turn," he said sheepishly.

I took the shirts from him. "I'll put these in the wash. Do we have a baby's death to discuss or not?"

"Why not? You're not paying me to look pretty for you," he said, grinning at me.

That would totally be worth it.

"What exactly *am* I paying you, Jazz?"

"You don't have to pay me at all."

"Yes, but I *will* compensate you for your time and effort. This is business."

"I'm a little more interested in pleasure right now."

"We'll deal with pleasure later."

"I'll hold you to that, Mrs. Brown."

"You'd better," I said.

Jazz put his shirts in the washer for me, and afterward settled onto the living room sofa with me again. God knows I could hardly concentrate with a bare-chested fine man in my presence, especially since I could actually have him without committing a sin. At least not technically. I thought. Maybe.

Okay, if I couldn't be clear on it, we definitely shouldn't do anything. I had to get my mind in order. It was time to work.

Jazz stretched his legs out and crossed them at the ankles. "So, what's the first thing you ask in a homicide case?"

"Who stands to profit from the kid's death?"

"And who would that be?"

"Nikki Thunder."

"Why her?"

"She's not the motherly type."

"So I see."

"Do tell, *husband.*"

He sat back and grinned at me. "At no time did I forget that I'm your husband."

"You were flirting with her right in my face."

"It's not like I *kissed* her or anything. Oh, wait. We *can* kiss other people in our marriage, can't we?"

"I made a mistake, Jazz."

"You certainly did."

"I'm sorry."

"Are you? Because I would have thought that, being sorry, you would make some effort to communicate with me. I gave you several weeks."

"I tried to let you know that I want you."

"You tore up my favorite dress shirt. That was supposed to let me know you're ready to be faithful to me?"

"I didn't cheat on you."

"What do you call what you were doing?"

"A mistake."

"That's funny. Kate said the same thing."

"I'm not your skanky ex-wife."

"No, you're my skanky current wife."

I wanted to slap him. In a different time I would have, but Mr. Cool couldn't hide his raw hurt from me.

Still, he looked repentant about his comment. "You were supposed to slap me," he said. "What happened to my feisty woman?"

"If that's your opinion of me, slapping you wouldn't do much to change it. Besides, you did tell me not to hit you again."

"Do you want me to leave now?"

He was fishing for me to tell him how badly I wanted him to stay. Not a chance. "You just put your shirts in the washing machine, but you can take them out if you'd like. You can go home with wet clothes on and die of pneumonia for all I care."

Then he asked a silly question. "Did I hurt your feelings?"

"That was your goal, wasn't it?"

"Actually, my goal was to get you to convince me of how wrong I am. You were supposed to be outraged and say . . ." He cleared his throat and imitated me, hands on hips and all. "I'm not skanky. I'm a woman of God!" He sounded more like Flip Wilson's Geraldine than like me.

"Maybe I *am* skanky, Jazz. I've certainly made all kinds of mistakes with men, including you, maybe especially with you. You had your hands in my blouse in front of a two-way mirror, and I was only in that room with you for a couple of minutes."

"You put a stop to it."

"You may find this hard to believe, but sometimes I actually want to do the right thing. Every now and then I have a rare moment of clarity in which I want to act like somebody who believes she's worth something."

"Do you think my being intoxicated and trying to touch you means you're not worth anything?"

"C'mon, Jazz. I'm convenient to you now. You didn't even have to make much of an effort. Dance with me, and put your hands in my blouse. You didn't hesitate because it's like you said, I'm skanky. No need to respect me."

"You've got me all wrong, Bell, if you think that's my opinion of you."

"*You're* the one who said I was skanky. And *you're* the one feeling me up in public."

"It wasn't in public."

"You've got *me* all wrong, too, Jazz. I let one of my dearest friends kiss me because I knew I broke his heart. I didn't stop him because he's been one hundred percent there for me for the last ten years. He was just a teenager when we met. I didn't want to hurt him any more than I already had."

Jazz turned his head away from me.

"And maybe I was a little confused, too, but it wasn't about whether I wanted to be with you or Rocky. I didn't think I deserved you, Jazz."

His gaze came back to me. "What are you talking about?"

"I'm not the kind of woman gorgeous men like you choose. You know it, and I know it."

"I don't like you talking like this."

"You're out of my league."

"That's crazy."

"Is it? I'm not that young, and I don't have a flawless body like Kate's. Or Nikki Thunder's."

"Don't do this, Bell."

"Would you have kissed me if I hadn't kissed you first that night we met?"

"Yes, I would have."

I felt a little hopeful. I always thought it was my boldness that got us started. "Really, Jazz?"

In answer he leaned into me and gave me a long, lingering kiss, as gentle and tender as the first one we shared. "I would have kissed you. Maybe not that night, but I'd have come back. I keep coming back to you. I am my beloved's."

I hung my head.

He lifted it up. "You gotta say your part, too."

"I can't."

"Say it, Bell."

I whispered the words. "My beloved is mine."

"I am yours. And you're not skanky. You did hurt me, though."

"You hurt me, too."

"Don't we have a dead child to discuss?"

Let the debriefing begin!

Again.

Jazz's fingers meandered lazily up and down my arm while I sat on his lap and cuddled with him. I thought we might end up debriefing for real!

"Who are the players here?" he asked.

My sofa felt tiny, and I liked it that way. "Ezekiel said Rocky's crew had gone to the church for a meeting, so that leaves the Thunder gang."

"Which consists of?"

"Ezekiel; Nikki; Sister Lou; the nanny, Sister Joy; and the kids Zekia and Zeke."

"Where were they?"

"According to Thunder, Nikki was asleep. He was upstairs doing lectio—"

"Ezekiel Thunder does *lectio divina*?"

I smiled. Sat up and turned to face him. "I'm impressed you know what that is."

"I'm impressed that *you* do, charismatic girl."

"I'm kinda Emergent. I happen to dig the spiritual disciplines. But back to brainstorming."

I settled back against his chest. "Sister Joy was reading, Sister Lou was probably cavorting with the demonic—Thunder didn't say. Little Zeke was somewhere with a full bladder, and Zekia was giving Zeekie a bath for the first time in her life."

"Why start now?"

"Good question, and one that didn't sit right with Sister Joy, their nanny."

Jazz rested his chin on my shoulder. "So have you heard the kids' story?"

"I heard a third-hand version from Rocky, but the gist is Zeke needed to use the bathroom and Zekia stepped out. Zeekie allegedly drowned after Zeke finished his business and left Zeekie alone, presuming Zekia would go right back in."

"That's what I heard, too, and I heard it right from the children."

"Did Cruella De Vil actually let them tell you themselves?"

"Cruella was very accommodating to me."

"What do you think of it, Jazz?"

"They told it the *exact* same way. Using the exact same words. The likelihood of two *adults* doing that is slim to nil. Two kids do it, and I'm sure it's scripted."

I went on, "And what's the likelihood of a teenage girl who never gave her little brother a bath inexplicably doing so? And him ending up dead?"

"It could happen. What if the teenage girl is a sociopath? That kind of thing shows up around that age sometimes."

"Come on, Jazz. Zekia is a sweetie pie. Nikki Thunder is responsible. I just know it."

"How?"

"Look at her reaction. It was . . . off. And that whole 'The Lord giveth and the Lord taketh away' thing? How many mothers of dead babies have you heard say that?"

"Not many, and I've had to deliver bad news to a lot of mothers."

"Have you heard *any*?"

"Bell, I've known some people to have extraordinary faith in the aftermath of a homicide."

"Does Nikki strike you as being extraordinarily faithful? And what about that thing she said about taking a bath?"

Raucous laughter burst from his mouth. He cocked his head and regarded me. "I still think you're letting your jealousy get the best of you."

"Who said I'm jealous of her?"

"Oh, come on. You saw her scoping me out as soon as we walked into the room. She judged me to be an alpha male and you the inferior female."

"Inferior?" I climbed off his lap and scooted away.

He grabbed at my waist. "Hey, where are you goin'?"

I pouted on the cushion next to him, a little mad that I no longer shared his warmth. "I'll have you know that in no way am I inferior to that woman."

He grinned, enjoying my irritation. "I said *she* thought you were inferior. That's why she sized me up right in front of you. She didn't see you as a worthy adversary, that is, until you went Columbo on her right before we left."

"I wonder what made her think I'm *inferior*? Could it be your *flirting* right in front of me?" I thrust my fists inside the crooks of my elbows, body armor firmly in place.

"It was very subtle."

"Not too subtle for me to see."

"You were watching very carefully. You think I didn't know that? I wanted to see how far she would take things."

"How far did she take things, Jazz?"

"Far enough for me to form a less than flattering opinion about her."

"I'm not paying to have women ogle you."

"You're not paying me at all."

"I plan to. What are your consulting fees?"

"I don't have consulting fees. I have more work than I can handle at my job. Besides, I wouldn't take your money, Bell."

"What? Is my *money* inferior, too, alpha male?"

He laughed. I fumed.

"What are you laughing at?"

"The fact that you're in a rage."

"I'm reacting to your insults."

"I didn't insult you. I told you what Nikki Thunder thinks of you."

"Let me tell you what I think of *her*. She's a deeply disturbed, utterly self-absorbed, wholly narcissistic cow."

"What makes you think so, Columbo?"

"That's *girl* Columbo. You saw. She wouldn't let me talk to those kids, allegedly because she was protecting them, but they sat there huddled in grief and she didn't so much as touch them."

"Anything else, Bell?"

"She's skanky. While she was still a teenager, she lured Ezekiel Thunder away from his wife. After Mrs. Thunder had gone out of her way to help the little ingrate. Then *Nikki* conveniently became Mrs. Thunder, probably before the woman's body was cold—not that being Mrs. Ezekiel Thunder is a peak experience in life. Now she's on the make for *my* man before her son's rigor mortis has set in."

Jazz leaned over and kissed my pouting lips. I couldn't help smiling—the man did something to me.

"What was that for?"

"You remember the rules? A kiss for a good insight when we brainstorm."

"So you agree that Nikki is the most likely suspect?"

"I didn't say *you* had the insight."

I hit him with my mud-cloth pillow, eliciting another round of laughter from him.

"Best to look at all the facts. Everybody in that house, including the kids, may have a motive. Everybody is a suspect. Quick judgments only worked for Columbo, baby."

"He was never wrong."

"He was a *television* character. Writers made sure he always got it right. Real police work ain't so neat."

"Does this mean you'll keep looking into this case?"

"It's not a case at this point. It could be an accident."

I sighed. "Jazz, you know what I mean. Are you going to consult for me?"

"We'll see what the coroner says and what the Ann Arbor police do. I *will* continue to look at things for you, though. Will you do something for me?"

"Maybe."

"You just have to give me a hard time, don't you?"

"That's what wives are for."

"Wives are for a lot of things, baby."

I had to go straight Ma Brown on him. "Don't start no stuff, and it won't be none."

"You brought it up."

"Drop it. This is about business. What's your consulting fee, Jazz?"

His gazed flickered over my body. "I'll think of something. You just make sure you're willing to pay when the time comes."

I tried to ignore the tingling his gaze caused. "I can pay."

"I know you can, but I want you to let *me* do the work here. I'm the cop. You're *Jane*."

I sighed. My husband was a very naughty man. Nothing got by him.

———

He didn't waste any time asking. "May I spend the night?" He said it without the mischievous gleam in his eyes that appears when he teases me.

I was about to go to the bathroom for the fifth time that night. When he asked, I stopped in the hall like a deer in head-lights, my eyes blinking wildly in confusion.

"You want to spend the night?"

"It's late. I've had too much to drink. I shouldn't drive."

"I could take you home."

"You're tired. You have to pee a lot. It's easier if I spend the night."

"I'm not too tired to take you," I lied. "Or I could give you cab fare."

"I have money, Bell. I don't want to catch a cab to Detroit."

I decided to get to the brass tacks. "Your alcohol consumption shouldn't impose on me."

"Is my being here that big of an imposition?"

"Where will you sleep?"

And then the gleam was in the eyes. "I'll find someplace." This he followed with that brilliant smile of his. He didn't have a shirt on. The combination made me much more willing to share my space with him.

I stood in the hall deliberating.

Jazz kept grinning. "What could happen?"

"Nothing." I hoped. Or *not*.

"There you have it," he said, as if he didn't know how much he tempted me.

"Okay," I said, resigned. "Do you need something?"

"I believe I have both a toothbrush and a change of clothing here."

"What will you sleep in, Jazz?"

"I don't think you really want to know that, Bell. It might overstimulate you."

Was he kidding? The *thought* of him overstimulated me. "Do you need a blanket?"

"Your great-grandmother's quilt will be fine, if you don't mind sharing it with me."

"Okay," I said.

"I'll get it myself," he said. "Why don't you go on to the bathroom."

"Okay," I said.

In an instant he was in my face. Swooped me into a passionate kiss. "Good night, baby."

"Okay," I said again, like an automaton. But I doubted if I'd get any sleep, and that could be for a number of reasons, none of which I wanted to think about. I glanced at his sexy face again.

He winked at me.

"Okay," I repeated, though things didn't feel okay. Jazz Brown was a total threat to a sistah's chastity belt, even if we were married. And he knew it. Probably liked it that way.

I knew I shouldn't have let him stay. His being there only made things more difficult for both of us. We seemed to be perpetually on a collision course, slamming into each other, causing all kinds of damage to each other in every crash.

I lay in my bed ashamed of how my body burned for him. I think by force of my desire I willed him to knock on my door. Or maybe his own desire drove him. I couldn't tell. It felt too big to bear, this burden of lust we had for each other.

Just a few raps on the door, and once again, I became his Shulamite. Hearing the beloved. As undecided as she must have been a few millennia ago about whether to let him in. I lay there thinking of all the reasons we shouldn't be together tonight and knowing how much I needed him just the same.

Just go for it, Bell. Nobody will get hurt.

A lie and I knew it. I didn't care.

I threw off the covers and hopped over to the door to unlock and open it.

Jazz had obviously spent the last hour drinking. He staggered into my bedroom.

"Can I watch the news?" he slurred. He still had the bottle in his hand, and for a moment, I really, truly hated him. Revulsion rose up like bile in my throat. But I let him in. I loved him. I had become my mother in the worst time of her life, with an alcoholic husband.

We sat on the bed, him watching the news, both of us with grim expressions frozen on our faces. Images of Rocky's house and descriptions of the Thunder tragedy flickered across the screen. Jazz kept chugging liquor, growing more moody and morose. When I nagged him about it, he offered, "I'm Irish."

"You're on your way to becoming an alcoholic, if you aren't one already."

"You wouldn't say that if I was Bono sitting here drinking. You'd probably join me."

"You're not Bono. If you were I'd make you sing 'All Because of You' instead of sitting here embalming yourself."

He sighed. "Just leave me alone. You're a psychologist. You know all that twelve-step stuff. My drinking is *my* problem. Which means it's not a problem."

"Jazz, when your family and friends start being affected . . ."

"You worry too much. All of you."

"And you're drinking on the job."

"I'm at home now."

"This is *my* home, Jazz. Not yours."

He ignored that. "I got dealt with at work. Okay? I don't make a habit outta getting twisted at my *house*." The anger surging in his voice prevented me from pressing him to admit he had a problem.

I'd seen my mother try to reason with my father too many times. "You can't talk to a drunk," she'd say and give up. Her words burned into me and guided me in this moment.

I've said to several children of alcoholics I've counseled that if they were put in a room full of people, they'd gravitate, unwittingly, toward an alcoholic. I'd proved this true with Adam. A few others after him. My only non-alcohol-or-drug-abusing boyfriend was Rocky. And he was the one I let go of. Now here I was with the finest man I knew, and he was a drunken mess.

He clumsily put the cap back on the bottle. "Why can't you just love me?"

He didn't wait for me to answer, or he would have found out that I did love him, enough to have him in my bed when I knew better. We were courting the very thing I'd told God I didn't want.

Jazz lunged at me. Not violently; awkwardly. His hands got busy with my waist and hips. He tried to kiss me. Missed. Swore. I'd noticed before how alcohol seemed to bring out his aggression and how he had to fight against the haze of booze slowing his reflexes.

"Stop it, Jazz."

"I wanna kiss you, baby."

"You stink. I don't want to kiss you." My mother's words. Her exact words.

"Come on, baby. I love you." My father's words.

I clamped my arms around his neck as hard as I could.

"Ow. Baby, that's too tight."

"Shut up." I whispered in his ear. "I don't have the energy to wrestle you all night. And nothing, and I do mean nothing, is going to happen between us." I tightened my grip again.

"Ow, Bell."

"You go to sleep, Jazz Brown. I'm going to hold you until you go to sleep. And that's all the lovin' you'll get from me tonight."

"Bell," he whispered into my neck.

"What?"

"I'm sorry." His voice cracked and my big, tough cop husband began to sob in my arms.

I loosened my grip, but I didn't let him go. "Me too, baby."

I let his hot tears fall on me, and I rocked my baby—my poor sweet, confused baby—until both of us cried ourselves to sleep.

chapter twelve

I FELT SOMEONE KICKING ME. Fortunately I remembered that I had a houseguest—one who was drunk last night and was most likely hungover this morning. And he still reeked of liquor. Another nudge with his foot.

"Leave me alone, Jazz."

"Wake up, you need to see this." Another kick.

I tried to rub the sleep out of my uncooperative eyes.

"See what?" I asked. "And stop kicking me."

"It's headline news."

"You woke me up to—"

"Shush." He pointed at my thirteen-inch television. "It's about to air again."

"What is this about?"

"Thunder Ministries."

That perked me up. We stared at the television, and I tried my best to stay focused on CNN rather than wondering if Jazz still had on underwear. The underwear question definitely held my attention more, that is, until the reporter started in on Thunder Ministries and the recent tragic death of two-year-old Ezekiel Thunder IV. My heart ached seeing his picture on the screen, and then the focal point of the segment shifted to Thunder's "controversial" ministry.

Jazz nudged me in the ribs. "Watch this. It's my favorite part."

Suddenly Amanda Bell Brown was on the screen. And Sister Lou. And the caption "Woman Gets Demon Cast Out." Then the crowning moment when I spewed vomit across the room.

I couldn't speak. I couldn't breathe. I sank down in bed and covered my head with the quilt.

Jazz laughed like a loon.

"I'm finished," I moaned. "My life is over."

"How did you get that puke to go, what, twelve feet?" Another burst of laughter exploded out of him.

"I hate you, Jazz."

The man laughed so hard, tears streamed down his face. Meanwhile, the world as I knew it turned upside down, leaving me dangling precariously on the edge.

I squeaked out, "How many viewers does CNN have?"

"Probably not that many," he lied, cracking up. Several minutes later, when he could catch his breath, he said, "All this time I thought you were still pining for Rocky. Turns out you were riddled with adultery demons. It wasn't your fault, you poor little demoniac."

My cell phone rang right before I could curse generations of his future offspring. He tried unsuccessfully to straighten up. "That's your mother."

"How do you know?"

"I called her and told her to watch."

I would do karate on him. He'd think I was Ralph Macchio by the time I finished with him. I answered the phone.

"Hi, Ma."

"I'm having a heart attack," she wailed. "Don't call nine-one-one, just let me die."

"Ma, you're not having a heart attack. *I* am."

"You've finally killed me."

"You're not dead, Ma."

"I'm cutting you out of my will, Amanda Bell. I will never speak with you again. From now on you have one parent. He won't care that you were exorcised on national television."

"Okay. Bye, Ma."

"I told you not to speak to me. And don't call me Ma!"

Gladly! I snapped my phone shut, effectively implementing her suggestion.

I glared at Jazz. My looking at him inspired another round of the giggles. I had just the cure. I took my pillow and began to clobber him, which only made him laugh harder despite his hungover state. He didn't even seem to mind that I had violated his no-hitting rule.

It was going to be a long day.

After I hung up with my mother, my cell phone, landline, and pager chirped, rang, and chimed as if it were the end of the world. Carly screamed at me because she thought I should have dressed nicer for television. Kalaya called to make sure I didn't have any urges to harm myself. Addie called to console me and to let me know that lots of really great people were possessed at some time in their life, and Jack got on the phone and laughed so hard he couldn't speak. The fruit indeed does not fall far from the tree.

Now that I'd made my husband's day, and he'd filled his laugh quota for the next two years, I decided to torment him by stepping my scantily clad body out of bed, allowing him to have a bit of eye candy. My ankle felt significantly better, so I got sassy and moved with style and a healthy swing of my hips.

He stopped laughing. Looked a little disoriented by my perfect beauty. Okay, who am I kidding? Beauty must have been far down on his list of my best attributes. The Chihuahuas and my backside held him captive.

"Good morning, lovely wife," he said, and honestly, the way he looked at me made me think it might be good after all. "Nice view."

"I'm glad you're enjoying it. Don't you have to go to work this morning?"

"Nope. I'm all yours today."

"Then we have work to do, drunken master."

"I see you don't want to play nice today. Have it your way, Bell." Jazz stepped out of bed wearing only a wicked smile. I saw the fullness of his glory.

Another notch on my chastity belt slid loose.

God, I'm not sure what Jazz and I are doing, but can we speed up the process so whatever it is gets done really soon?

I hoped my heavenly Father was listening, because if I kept seeing Jazz in his undiluted, natural, red-blooded fineness, a sistah was gonna get herself in trouble.

My great-grandmother used to say, "You make a hard bed, you turn over more often." If ever there was a time in my life when I needed a soft bed—just for sleeping—it was now.

———————

Completely clothed—though, oh, the memories that remained, at least for me—we took the Love Bug straight to the Rock House. Jazz had on the wonderful cashmere turtleneck sweater he left at my place weeks ago and the jeans that fit like they'd been tailor-made for him. The man looked delicious in anything. Or nothing. And he'd showered, so his scent had improved dramatically.

I'd pulled on an artsy little number that reminded me of a dashiki shirt, only it was a little less seventies inspired and cuter. I wore my "fat" jeans, which were now my "getting too tight jeans" and sat there berating myself for my lack of discipline. My waistline continued to expand despite my best efforts to watch what I ate. As it was, I had almost no appetite for anything except ice cream and turkey—real turkey, not luncheon meat. Nothing in between. Lately I'd felt like I had a prolonged bout of the flu, only the symptoms were so low-grade they were more flu-like than full-blown flu. And then there was the tumor.

I'd progressed to considering the merits of Slim-Fast versus those of Jenny Craig when Jazz interrupted my thoughts.

"So who is this woman we're going to see?"

"Sister Lou. She was the one who performed the exorcism on CNN."

Jazz tried to choke back another round of laughter.

"Can you please let me try to forget that millions of people worldwide have seen me projectile vomit?"

"Not just any old vomiting. You were gettin' the *devil* cast out of you!"

I cleared my throat so he would cease and desist. "Warning, Pentecostalphobe. She's kind of a nutjob."

He smirked. "What would give you that idea, Bell?"

"Hmmm. Maybe because she cast imaginary demons out of me, and she almost cracked my skull open by her sudden laying on of hands. Doesn't the Bible say something about not doing that?"

"You wouldn't know it by the way some of you Pentecostals act."

"We're not all the same. Some of us have tempered our excesses with age and wisdom."

"And others have not."

"She's a strange woman, and Joy says she's in cahoots with Nikki."

"I thought you were under the impression that Nikki Thunder alone is the mastermind behind Zeekie's death."

"I think she is, but what if she got her evil, obsessed henchwoman to do her bidding?" I thought about that. At the crusade Sister Lou was glued to Ezekiel Thunder's side. But after the drowning, she hovered around the children. Unlike Nikki, she actually touched them. Seemed protective of them. Then again, could she have been hiding what really happened by using the kids as a distraction?

Jazz scratched his head. "Sounds far-fetched to me."

"Being possessed by an interracial-dating-and-adultery demon sounds far-fetched to *me*."

"No, that was believable, baby."

I scowled at him. "Thunder Ministries is a virtual laboratory of religious pathology."

"If you ask me, you just described all Pentecostals."

"Jazz! Your own mother is Pentecostal."

"That's how I know."

"Then you might want to keep in mind I didn't ask you." I chuckled. "Addie would be very disappointed if she heard you talk about her like that."

"I don't have a problem with Mom. I have a problem with the nutjobs she forced me to endure. You wouldn't believe! I could tell you stories—"

"No need. I've got my own charismatic tales I could thrill you with, including my glorious appearance on television this morning."

"Yeah. You got shot with Sister Lou's Holy Ghost machine gun."

Jazz suffered a similar fate at the hand of Benny Hinn himself. It scarred poor Jazzy for life.

I sighed. "Are you going to be able to handle her, Jazz?"

"I'm Joe Friday, baby. Just the facts, ma'am, and I'm out."

Or so he said.

We reached the Rock House and headed inside. The church was bustling with meeting after meeting going on, and a visibly upset Rocky was trying to prepare for dealing with the media and the now high-profile event that would be Zeekie's funeral.

After a bit of looking around, we finally found Sister Lou

in the sanctuary. She sat, a frail-looking, solitary figure, in the first pew, which my great-grandmother always called "the Holy Ghost pew." She believed things happened at an altar, and the first row put you right in front of the action. The better for the Holy Ghost to move on you.

Sister Lou sat with crossed arms, holding herself, and rocking back and forth. The attitude I'd come to hate seemed to have abandoned her. She looked about as intimidating as a five-year-old girl. I shot a look at Jazz. He shrugged his shoulder and gestured for me to speak to her.

"Sister Lou?"

Her attitude arrived as soon as she turned and saw it was me calling her name.

"What you want, gal?"

"I wanted to talk to you about Zeekie."

She turned her head away and faced the cross hanging above the pulpit before her. "Ain't nothin' to talk about. The Lord giveth, and the Lord taketh away. Blessed be the name of the Lord." She punctuated her scripture quoting with a burst of unknown tongues that, quite frankly, sounded like Klingon. She did look and act like Worf from *Star Trek: The Next Generation,* only she wasn't as attractive or likable.

I couldn't afford to get too close to the Chantilly smell. "I'm trying to figure out exactly how the Lord tooketh away."

With a sharp turn of her head, she faced me. "You know 'bout all there is to know."

"I just want a few more details."

"Why?"

Sister Lou was definitely a hostile witness.

I used my calming psychologist voice. "The death of a loved one is hard, Sister Lou, and the death of a child even more so. I'm trying to offer my meager skills to help everyone come to terms with this tragedy. It's the least I can do." I meant that sincerely. Mostly.

"Ain't no terms to come to." She turned her attention to Jazz. Looked him up and down, and I can't say I blamed her.

She crooked her finger at him. Jazz shook his head no. He slanted his body away from her and crossed his arms. Emotional body armor? Check!

Sister Lou narrowed her eyes when he didn't respond to her "come here" gesture. She got up and pointed her claw at him.

"You ain't right," she hissed at Jazz.

"Ma'am," Jazz said, tight-jawed. His voice remained steady, as if he were dealing with a mob of angry thugs rather than an old prayer warrior. "We're inquiring about Zeekie because we're concerned."

She didn't buy that anymore than the thugs would.

Again she hissed, moving closer to him. "I can see it all over you."

Jazz looked at me. I could tell Sister Lou was about to add another chapter to his book of Pentecostal horror stories. I tried to stand between the two of them, having known this woman's wrath. My own humiliation at this woman's hands, now complete after CNN, ensured I had nothing left to lose.

"Sister Lou," I said. I tried to get her to back down. With Jazz's history of Pentecostals giving him the willies, I didn't know what would happen if he had another spiritual trauma. "Why don't we just slow down?"

She seemed to consider what I said. She backed up and returned to the pew where we'd found her when we arrived. Only, rather than sit down, she reached beneath the pew and pulled out a few miracle prosperity oil packets, packaged like convenience condiments at a hot dog stand. She tore one open with her teeth and rubbed it on her hands.

"Ummm hmm," she uttered. "I'm gon' need some reinforcements for this kind. This kind don't come out but for fasting an' soaking prayer. I been intercedin' all mornin' for him."

Goose bumps rippled across my arms. "Awww, shoot."

Sister Lou stalked toward us again, speaking in Klingon. "HIja HIgos." I'm not going to make a case for or against the gift of speaking in other tongues, but honestly! I'm almost sure Worf said that exact thing in the second season of *Star Trek: The Next Generation.*

The only thing standing between Jazz and Klingon lady happened to be me, and as soon as she stepped closer, her Chantilly oh-the-toilet hit me.

Oh, the toilet indeed. I was gonna blow again, and I'd enjoyed too many beautiful services at the Rock House to hurl all over the carpet. I stepped away for environmental protection purposes, leaving Jazz wide open.

His voice boomed with authority. "Don't come any closer!"

Sister Lou got closer.

He held his arm out to keep her at a distance. "Drop the miracle prosperity oil, lady."

"I'm 'bout to anoint you, boy."

Jazz backed away, but at an angle that caused him to bump into a pew. Quicker than you could say, "nuqneH," which is Klingon for "What do you want?" she'd lunged for my husband's forehead.

Jazz had just enough time to cry out, "*Bell!*"

Klingon tongues of fire rolled effortlessly out of her mouth. She smacked Jazz in the forehead and said, "Name yo'self, you foul demon."

"*What?*" Jazz screeched.

"You got a *sechal* demon."

"I got a *what?*"

Even I didn't know what that was. I riffled through my limited knowledge of demonology. Sechal . . . Hmmm. Is that some kind of medieval thing? What could it mean?

She hissed at Jazz, "You got a sechal demon all over you."

I interrupted. "What's a sechal demon?"

"A *sechal* demon. You know what a *sechal* demon is, hussy!"

Oh . . . no . . . she *didn't* . . . just call me a hussy again. Now, it's one thing to refer to sistahs as hussies in the privacy of your own thoughts, but it's quite another to call a sistah out like that. She didn't know me like that.

My ghetto roots started showing. "I'm just sayin', lady, maybe I want to know what it is so I can pray with you." I figured if I could convince her I was her ally, maybe Jazz could escape while we prayed.

"*Sechal!* S-E-X-U-A-ayell!"

"Ooooh!" I said. "She thinks you have a *sexual* demon."

Jazz looked mortified. "A *sexual* demon?"

I tried not to laugh. Really I did.

Again, Sister Lou seized him. She grabbed his arm with one claw this time, while the other claw rested—if you could call that resting—on top of his head. "Come out in the name of Jesus!" she yelled, as if the sexual demon was hard of hearing. "Come out!"

Jazz didn't fall out under the power of God, so she tried to help him. Apparently he's not used to being slain in the Spirit at his Catholic parish. He resisted. She overpowered him.

Sister Lou started slinging Jazz around like a Raggedy Andy doll. Poor Jazz's arms flailed about wildly. Honestly! If I hadn't heard it for myself I wouldn't have dreamed a big, tough guy like Jazz could scream like a girl.

Her Chantilly didn't seem to have the same effect on him as it did me. Poor Jazz wouldn't give her the satisfaction of throwing up. I wondered if we'd be there for hours, Sister Lou jerking Jazz around while he flopped helplessly.

When I could take it no more I shouted, "Look, a demon!" I pointed to the pulpit area.

Sister Lou stop slinging Jazz long enough to look behind her. I grabbed Jazz by the hand, and we hightailed it out of there. Thankfully my ankle felt better, and—hey! My ankle felt better.

When we'd gotten outside, he stopped. He put his hands on his knees and began to hyperventilate. That or he had an asthma attack. His breathing sounded painful. I tried to encourage him.

"Don't stop now. She may be behind us."

He started gasping for air. "I can't breathe!" he shouted. "I can't breathe."

"Of course you can breathe. You're talking. Now, let's go."

Too late. Sister Lou had torn out of the church after us.

"We're going to have to make a run for it," I said, yanking him by the arm. He didn't even protest about his breathing or my ankle. He let me pull him, running like a girl in his infirmity. I hoped he wouldn't fall like girls always do in horror movies. I could just see it. Attack of the Holy Klingon Prayer Warriors.

We made it to the Love Bug, and I clicked the button on my remote opener, swung the passenger-side door open, pushed him inside, and slammed the door. I hurried to the driver's side, jumped in, shut the door, and locked the car. Sister Lou started pounding on my windshield, miracle prosperity oil in hand. I turned the engine on, thrust the Love Bug in gear, and we sped out of the parking lot practically on two wheels. We didn't even put on our seat belts until we reached Huron Street.

"Are you okay, Jazz?" I took a quick look at him. I didn't think he'd describe himself as "okay." "Jazzy . . ."

I continued down Huron until it changed into Washtenaw, and we headed toward Ypsilanti. Poor Jazz was not just shaken; he was actually shaking. He really did have a pathological fear of Pentecostals.

A small coffee shop, the Java Joint, was ahead in a strip mall. I wanted to get off the road and see to Jazz.

It seemed to take forever to get to the mall, and Jazz had truly begun to hyperventilate. "Breathe, honey," I said over and over.

I finally got to the coffee shop and parked the Love Bug. I undid my seat belt and took him in my arms. I kept whispering "breathe" to him. The poor baby's heart felt like it was going to slam out of his chest.

"I've got you," I said, patting him on his back. I held him for a long time.

Finally he pulled out of my embrace. "I'm sure you'll have a big laugh at this."

"It's not funny when you're terrified, Jazz."

"I *hate* that. I hate the way those people make me feel. Sexual demon! What is that, anyway?"

"I don't know. Then again, I wasn't aware of interracial-dating demons, either. They must have been popular in the days of yore when interracial dating was against the law."

My attempt at humor fell flat.

"Does that mean I want to have sex too much? Or that I think about sex too much?"

"It doesn't mean anything, because you're not possessed."

He didn't seem to hear me. "I'm not into porn or illicit affairs. And that one time we were together was the only . . ." He rubbed his hand across his forehead, smearing the spot of olive oil Sister Lou had left. "Maybe I think about making love to you too much." His eyes searched mine, as if I had the answers to his questions.

Again he crossed his arms, but it looked like he was giving himself a hug rather than putting on the protective gear. "Sometimes I relive our wedding night. Not . . . not the Rocky part. Being with you—over and over." He stole a glance at me and looked away again. "It's just you I think about that way. I try to keep my mind *right*."

His Tourette's syndrome returned momentarily. Apparently, to Jazz, cussing was allowed when you have a right mind. Then he shook his head. "Maybe I shouldn't have dwelled on it. Maybe I . . ."

"Jazz?" I took his hand in mine. He still wouldn't look at me. "When we made love, it was singularly one of the best experiences of my life. That time with you was as sacred as being in church." I tried to think of a way to explain that he would truly relate to. "You know how when you take Communion and you believe it's truly the blood, body, and divinity of Christ?"

He nodded, still not looking at me.

"Our loving was like Communion. You and I were completely one body. I was yours, and you were mine, and we were joined together in this beautiful, mystical way. And you know what?"

This time he did give me a shy look.

"I've relived that sacred time in my head, too."

"You've thought about it?"

"I met you there every day. I longed for you when you were gone, and the only place I had you was in my memories. Sure I thought about it. And it had nothing to do with the devil. What we shared was holy, and it's perfectly acceptable to God to meditate on good, holy things, as long as they don't become idols."

"I'm not possessed?"

"No."

"But I still think about being with you probably more than I should. What does that mean?"

"Would you say you thought about it a *lot*? I mean a *whole* lot?"

He nodded, a fearful look etched in his beautiful face. "What if I did?"

"It would have to be *a lot*, Jazz, for me to be concerned about it."

"What if it were a *lot*? What does that mean?"

"I'm afraid to tell you." I pretended to really be afraid.

"Bell, you have to tell me so I can get help."

"It can't be helped, Jazz. I'm sorry. I mean, you can change it, but the cost would be prohibitive. And this isn't something insurance pays for."

For a moment he looked hopeful. "What's wrong with me? I'll do whatever it takes to fix it."

"You sure you want to know? It's not easy for me to tell you this."

He yelled like Samuel L. Jackson. "Just tell me!"

"If you think about making love to me a lot . . ."

He blew air from his cheeks. "What?"

"It means . . ."

"Just spit it out, woman."

"It means you're a *man*! My man, to be specific."

I cracked up, and he couldn't help himself—he smiled, too. "I'm going to get you, woman."

"If you're thinking about me that often, I guess you *are* planning to get me."

"Will I succeed?"

"Time will tell," I said.

I prayed that time would be as chatty as the church gossip, and that it would get to telling soon. After seeing him naked . . .

Real soon.

chapter
thirteen

FTER COFFEE—to go—Jazz and I headed back to my apartment. I made sure to let him know not to start flirting again, despite what I had said in the car. We needed to focus. He didn't seem to mind my "no hanky-panky" rule. I think the idea of a sexual demon still spooked him, and he played extra nice.

My ankle felt so much better, I insisted on climbing up all those darned steps to get to my apartment myself. Honestly. Management should have free bottled water and a giant bowl of candy on each floor to reward the weary sojourners who make their way up those stairs. Halfway up I said, "Jazz?"

"What?"

"Do you think Ezekiel Thunder healed me? I shouldn't be feeling this good."

He groaned, "Baby, baby, baby! Please don't make me think about that. Please. I've had way too much supernatural power of God today."

"I don't think you had *any* supernatural power of God experiences today."

"Whatever! I don't care. I don't want to think about healing and miracles and your spooky friends."

"She's not my friend."

"I don't care. Stop talking to me about it!"

By now we'd reached my floor. "Fine," I said, letting him guide me with his hand on my back.

He looked a bit repentant about his harsh tone, stuck my key into the lock, and glanced over at me with kind eyes. "Sorry."

"Don't worry about it, Jazz."

"Tired?"

"I'm always tired. I think I'm going through the change."

He raised an eyebrow.

"What?" I said, my horns sprouting. "Does that bother you? Do you need a younger wife? Maybe one Nikki Thunder's age, which is, what, twelve?"

"You're thirty-five. You're not going through the change."

He turned back to the door, ignoring me. I didn't feel ready to let go of the issue since my defenses had shot up like bottle rockets and exploded over my head.

"Older women have something to offer, too," I said, as if it weren't me who suggested he wanted a younger woman in the first place.

He opened the door, put his hand at the small of my back, and guided me inside.

"Some men prefer older women," I said in defense of sistahs over thirty-five everywhere. He closed the door behind us and locked the three locks.

He tossed this little question over his shoulder: "Men like Rocky?"

No, you wicked, evil man, because even he had gone on to fall in love with Elisa, who is younger than he is.

But all I said was, "Among others."

I could tell he wanted to have a bit of fun with me. I could also tell I wouldn't have fun with whatever he had in mind.

He gave me that dazzling smile of his. "Your dance card is full, huh, baby?" He took my coat off and hung both of ours in my closet.

"I was speaking in general, not about me."

"Older men are into you, too. Like Thunder."

"He's not into me. He's into *women*. As a whole."

"He looked at you like he's into *you*, as Amanda Bell Brown."

"He's not."

"Maybe we can switch. He can take you, and I'll take Nikki. Everybody is happy."

I froze. My animal nature kicked in, and I had a powerful urge to pounce on him and claw him about the face and neck.

He kicked out of his shoes and stepped over to my sofa smirking. Until he saw my face. "Bell, are you okay? You're not moving."

I couldn't speak, either. My own latent Tourette's syndrome came dangerously close to activating. *If I don't speak, I can't cuss. If I don't cuss, I may be able to keep my rage in check.*

He laughed and plopped down on the couch, among my throw pillows. "You're so easy to frustrate." After having a chuckle at my expense, he went on, despite the fact that I was still livid and cemented to the spot.

"We need to do a background check on everybody," he prattled on. "I'll need their names—their *real* names. And why do I think "Thunder" is made up?"

I stood as still as Lot's wife after she'd turned into a package of Morton's salt. I'd had crampiness off and on in the past month, but nothing comparable to the sharp pain now twisting in my gut. I wondered if he'd made me so angry I'd gotten physically ill. Again, pain seared my entire abdominal cavity. It felt like my insides wanted to go outside. *Jazz made me burst my tumor!*

He stood, concern shadowing his face. "Baby?"

I shut my eyes. Someone had put a giant vise across my waist and squeezed. Hard! "Oh." Just a tiny sound escaped my mouth.

"I was joking," he said. "I didn't mean it."

Another "oh," only this one was soundless. I buckled at the knees. "Something is wrong," I whispered.

He rushed to my side. I decided to let out my secret.

"I think I have a tumor, Jazz. It's on my abdomen close to my bikini line."

"A tumor! What kind of tumor?"

"I don't know. I haven't really told anybody, including my doctor."

"Baby! You can't . . ." He looked confused. Angry at me, yet compassionate. "I'm taking you to the emergency room."

"No!"

"Why not?"

"Take me to Tiernan McLogan."

"Dr. McLogan is an hour away. And he's probably not even seeing patients today. It's Saturday."

Tears spilled from my eyes. "He's open on Saturday. Please, Jazz."

He looked torn.

"I want to see Dr. McLogan."

"Fine," he said. What happened after that, I couldn't say. I fell unconscious in his arms.

———————

According to Jazz, I woke up, moaned miserably, and promptly passed out again. Unconsciousness was a mercy. When we got to Dr. McLogan's office, the pain hit me with such force, I thought it would kill me.

Jazz parked the car as close as he could without taking a handicapped space. He held me in his arms, slammed the Love Bug door shut with one of his long legs, and locked the doors with the remote locker. I curled my body into his. "It hurts, Jazzy."

"We're going to take care of you. Don't you worry, love."

"This is it. I'm going to need a hysterectomy."

"I don't care what you get as long as you stay here with me."

"I won't be able to have a baby. Ever."

"You alone are a handful. With my luck we'd have a girl. I probably couldn't handle two of you anyway."

I rested my head on his shoulder. He carted me into Tiernan's office. I had to be the envy of every woman there. I had a strong, gorgeous man who had no problem carrying me across a threshold. I only wish I felt well enough to enjoy the full benefits of having him. Instead, pain shot through my belly and radiated down my thighs.

I whispered to Jazz, "I'm scared."

"Don't be. Whatever this is, we'll handle it. We've gotten

through everything else. We'll get through this, too, but you should have told me. A *tumor!*"

Dr. McLogan's nurse opened the door to the clinic. Tiernan had prepared a room for me as soon as he got the call. An ultrasound machine was already set up. We passed Dr. McLogan in the hall. He touched my arm and assured me he'd be right in.

He ordered Jazz, "Get her out of those clothes and into a gown."

Jazz didn't even say anything flirty to me after those directions.

The nurse settled us into the room, and I lay down on the gurney, clutching my belly.

Jazz pried my hands away and started undressing me. "Now, I have to take off your clothes. You're sick, baby."

I moaned.

He sighed. "It must be pretty bad if you don't have a sharp comeback for me. It's okay, though. I'm here."

He slid my groovy dashiki shirt over my head and peeled off my tight jeans.

He took a pale pink hospital gown—Tiernan totally has a chickcentric practice—out from under the gurney.

"I have to *completely* undress you, baby."

"No!"

"Bell, I've seen it all. Trust me." He stroked my hair. "I'm not in danger of having a sexual demon flare-up."

I grinned despite my pain. "Okay."

He pulled off the last of my clothing and put the gown on me. He tied the back, carefully supporting me, and gently laid me down again. He stood at my head, rubbing my hair. His pinched expression conveyed his concern.

Dr. McLogan came into the room with a nurse, and they rolled the ultrasound machine over to me. Dr. McLogan was kind enough to perform the ultrasound himself.

My elfin doctor friend, the sweet Irishman who'd taken my father's place and given me away at my wedding, held a tube of gel in his had. He muttered, "Warm, dear," to me, before squeezing the preheated goop onto my stomach.

He guided the ultrasound probe gently across my aching abdomen. I wailed at being touched there.

"Hmmmm," he said.

"What?" Jazz said. "Is she going to be all right, Dr. T?"

"Oh, yes, dear one," he said, "but we have some concerns."

"Concerns?" I squeaked. I craned my neck up to peek at the screen, which he'd turned so I could see it. I couldn't make out a thing.

"Do you see this mass?"

I did when he pointed it out. Jazz and I nodded.

"It's a rather impressive fibroid tumor. The last time I saw you, dearest, it was the size of a grape. It's a grapefruit now, and there are several small grape-size ones that weren't here before."

Great. My womb had turned into a fruit basket.

Jazz bordered on hysterical. "Grapefruit?"

"I take it that your clothes don't fit anymore, yes, Bell?"

I chuckled through my hurt. "Definitely not."

"Your uterus has expanded to make room, that's why it's so distended. It's benign, glory be, but there are two more concerns I have to tell you about."

"Two more!" Jazz screeched.

Dr. McLogan gave me that silly little leprechaun smile and

scratched one of his mouse ears. He turned back to the ultra-sound screen. "This baby and this one."

He'd shocked Jazz and me into silence. For a few moments we watched the areas he pointed to on the screen. Two little heartbeats pounded away.

"I'm *pregnant*!" I'd taken over the hysteria department.

"With *twins*?" Jazz said, matching me emotion for emotion.

Dr. McLogan grinned at us. "Congratulations, dear ones. God has given you above and beyond all you can ask or think. And they look absolutely perfect."

That moment will stay with me all of my days. Chains fell away, and I felt light and dreamy. I felt in my body the first heady experience of Jazz touching me. The first time he whispered something in my ear. I felt the first time he prayed the Lord's prayer with me and the gentle pressure of his hand holding on to mine. Our first kiss. The first and only time we made love. Everything about loving him had become quite literally embodied inside of me. I touched my belly. My babies'—*my babies!*—new home.

Did I look different?

Could the whole world see me glowing?

They'd definitely see me growing, changing into a woman so loved that we had made two people, *and I carried them inside me.*

Another "oh." This one filled with wonder. It caught in my throat and stayed there tickling and delighting until it turned to holy laughter. Jazz and I looked at each other. Great big, sweeping waves of happiness flowed into and out of me, and for a moment I forgot the pain. Jazz reached down and kissed me. "I knew it." His own voice broke. "You surprised me with two, though." His eyes shone with unshed tears.

I laughed, letting tears stream freely down my cheeks—silly, joyful tears. Even Dr. McLogan's eyes misted.

"I'm *pregnant*," I said over and over.

"And you have a fibroid gone wild from the estrogen surge, dearest. Let's get you out of pain," my wonderful doctor said.

But pain had taken a backseat to the overwhelming gratitude bursting through my heart. I thought about my great-grandmother Ma Brown. She used to say, "Every shut-eye ain't sleep, and every good-bye ain't gone." Just when I thought the fat lady had warmed up and was about to start belting out blues songs for my womb, God pulled a fast one on me.

He sure knew how to surprise a sistah. And for one of the first times in my life, I was thrilled to have been wrong about something.

———

Dr. McLogan admitted me to the University of Michigan hospital. It seems that the wild and crazy fibroid fed off of my increased estrogen and had outgrown its blood supply, which is why the pain started. The bleeding that I'd mistaken for a light period had been implantation bleeding when the babies first attached to my womb. Even though I felt like I was in some magnificent dream, I really was pregnant. With twins!

I was grateful that Tiernan was also a U-M doctor. I didn't want to be far from home and the people I needed. And, thank God, my people came out in droves.

Jazz was the first to appear at the hospital, having followed the ambulance. Once he made sure I was comfortable and in the care of Addie Lee and Jack (who must have broken traffic laws to get there that quickly), he said he should get to the office soon to wrap up some things so he could take the next couple of days off.

"Take as long as you want, son," Jack said, patting my leg through the sheet. "We'll take good care of her."

Addie couldn't stop crying and fussing over me, bless her heart. As Jack settled Addie, my mother blew into the room—Hurricane Sasha.

She flung herself onto my bed. "My poor sick baby. Look at you. You look like death eating a soda cracker."

Before I could recover my self-esteem, the good news burst out of Addie Lee. "She's having twins, Sasha. Twins!"

Sasha bolted upright. "You're having twins?"

"Yes, Ma."

She put her hand to her chest like she was going to have a heart attack. "And you couldn't tell me this on the phone so I could bring something for the babies?"

Never mind that I, her own baby, was half-dead. "I tried to tell you, but you said you were having chest pains about my CNN appearance. We ended up talking about you having 'devil girl' for a daughter."

Carly made a grand entrance, carrying two steaming cups of Starbucks. "What'd devil girl do now?"

Ma answered. "She's having twins."

Carly looked outraged. "You're having twins! What do you mean you're having twins! I'm the oldest. Do I have twins? Do

I even have a single baby? Even a small one? I do not! And my fiancé broke up with me!"

"Is one of those lattes for me?" I said.

"No. You're pregnant, and these aren't decaf." She scowled at me like she'd discovered God loved me the most. I knew he loved us the same, not that I'd argue. After all, I was the one laid up in the hospital. And I wanted that coffee. I tried to sweet-talk her and slide my java request in on the sly.

"But you're amazing, Carly. Gorgeous, smart, and, you know, *enhanced*. Besides, Tim will come back. And a little caffeine won't hurt me."

"I can't take chances like that Bell," she said, enjoying it. "Your eggs were old."

The *cow*. Sorry!

Kalaya popped into the room. "I'm not pregnant, and my eggs are great—as far as I know." Carly handed her my Starbucks—the traitor. Or should I say *traitors*.

"Don't any of you people have something to do?" I complained.

"But you're in the hospital," Kalaya said. "Thanks, by the way. I was bored to death at home."

"No problem. Let me know anytime you need my uterus to explode."

"It didn't explode," Carly said. "You're so melodramatic. And selfish. Two babies!"

"Not that she told me herself," Ma said. "What did I do to deserve your hatred, Bell?"

"I don't hate you, but since you asked, this is what you did: You obviously favored Carly all my life. You constantly criticize me. You favored Carly all my life, and you constantly criticize me. Finally, you favored Carly all my life."

Jack quipped, "But did she constantly criticize you? That's what I want to know."

"Oh, yeah," I said. "You constantly criticize me."

He burst out laughing. Addie and I joining him.

Ma wasn't amused. "That's no reason to keep two babies from me."

"You got the best legs," Carly said to console me. She had a point. I did have good legs. Of course she added, "Too bad you have no clue how to show them off."

She just *had* to say that. Couldn't leave it with me and good legs. Then she planted a kiss on my forehead. "But I love you, lamb chop."

"Hmph" rumbled out of my throat. I turned to Sasha to reassure her that I did not purposely keep the twins a secret to destroy her, but Jazz walked in carrying two teddy bears as big as Canada. Honestly. Jazz must be one of those people who think bigger is better.

"Jazz, where in the world did you get those?"

"If I tell you, I'll have to kill you."

He set one bear in Addie's lap and another at the foot of my bed. He avoided Sasha.

"I've got some interesting news," he said.

"Do tell."

"Sister Lou is a nutjob."

"What else is new?"

"I mean certifiable. First of all, her name is Louella Dickson, and she's Ezekiel's never-married sister."

"So that's why he called her Sissy." *That doesn't explain why he called me that.*

"Norman Dickson legally changed his name to Ezekiel Thunder when he was not much more than a teenager."

"I know, Sister Joy told me all of that."

He looked surprised. "Well, weren't you busy?"

"Just tell me about Sister Lou, player hater."

"Bell, are you using slang to compensate for your weaknesses as an investigator?"

"No, I'm using slang because you were *hating* on me because of my superlative skills as an investigator *player.* Now, continue, please."

"About twenty-five years ago, right before that thing with the intern that blew his ministry apart, Louella was one of his key staff."

I nodded for him to go on. Jack and Addie looked riveted by the story already. Even Sasha sat up, snuggling closer to me, with her arm around my shoulders.

"There was an incident."

Jack whistled. "That doesn't sound good."

"You're right, Dad. Turns out the good Sister Lou was known for her popular 'deliverance' ministry."

Addie jumped in. "So she specialized in casting out demons?"

"Allegedly," Jazz said, shuddering.

Jack looked as if a chill went through him as well. "Spooky."

"You have no *idea,* Dad." He and Jack seemed to have some kind of united front. Jack must have his own charismatic horror stories.

I looked at Addie. "Mom, did your husband get shot with a Holy Ghost machine gun, too?"

She rolled her eyes. "That poor man had to endure a lot worse than anything Benny Hinn could come up with. Let me say, in hindsight, I can see why he never converted."

Jazz went back to his story. "Anyway, some foul stuff happened with some chick she was trying to deliver."

"Saints preserve us!" Jack said.

"She ended up holding the girl hostage for three days. Wouldn't let the kid use the bathroom. Tied her to a cross."

"Holy guacamole!" I said.

"That's what I thought. Somebody in the ministry took pity on the girl and let her go when Louella had gone to replenish her miracle prosperity oil supply."

Jack shook his head. "Freaky weird." Addie Lee nodded her agreement. Sasha squeezed my hand.

"The girl never pressed formal charges because her parents had taken her to the ministry for help. Even though they were told that techniques the ministry used could be dangerous, they believed in Thunder's ministry enough that they gave permission for the ministry to do whatever they thought necessary. The family didn't know any better. The girl was only thirteen at the time and severely depressed. Big mood swings. Didn't really have a voice, if you know what I mean, so she couldn't even protect herself from her parents."

"Was she bipolar?"

"You guessed it, Dr. Brown. Apparently mental illness is a no-no in deliverance ministries."

"Among other things." I winked at him. Red crept up from his neck to his cheeks. Jazz's eyes seemed to plead with me not to betray his "secret." My so-called deliverance gets broadcast on CNN and made him laugh like a lunatic, but I can't mention the ol' *sechal* demon.

I decided to be the bigger person. The twins would make me the bigger person eventually, anyway. "Seriously, in many of those kinds of ministries, mental illness would be considered demonic oppression or possession. What else did you find out?"

"Unfortunately that wasn't the first complaint about her unorthodox methods, my love."

He called me his love. I grinned at him. "Am I your love?"

"All day, every day, baby, but especially today."

Jack sighed. "Can you two love birds continue that in private? Addie and I just had lunch, and I don't want to puke like Bell did on TV."

Jazz opened his mouth, momentarily speechless.

"Look who's talking!" I said. "Nobody is more lovey-dovey than you and Addie."

Jazz rolled his eyes. "Let me finish my story, people. Anyway, after all these complaints, and there were *several,* Thunder had to act. His board talked her into going to the loony bin for a few weeks. They thought that would cover their behinds in case somebody wanted to sue them. They could just point to her hospitalization and say, 'She's a nutjob. It's not her fault. Plus, we got her help.'"

"Could you go easy on the negative terms for hospitals and

mentally ill people? I'm beginning to think you don't respect my work."

Jack quipped, "I ain't touching that one with a ten-foot pole."

Nor did Jazz.

I considered that Thunder actually had an interesting strategy in regard to his Sister Lou problem. It didn't ultimately work. Poor Lou got the short end, along with the girl she tried to help, but I tried to think like Ezekiel Thunder would. He couldn't sever all ties with his sister—well, he could have, but he didn't. Odd person to place his loyalty with. Why couldn't he be that loyal to his wives?

I asked my husband, "Did you find out Lou's diagnosis?"

"Paranoid schizophrenia. And they might have a point with that."

"Sounds about right, but I've seen far worse cases," I said. "Jazz, when I got to the house Friday, Lou was with the kids, and earlier this morning at the church, she parroted what Nikki Thunder said to you—'The Lord giveth' bit."

"I think that kind of faith is admirable," Addie said.

"When it comes from the faithful," Sasha said. Shrewd woman.

"That's what I mean, Ma. Neither one of them are the salt of the earth, if you ask me. Sister Lou has some serious issues, and Nikki Thunder is just . . ."

"Cold," Jazz interjected.

"So what does all this mean?" Addie asked.

Sasha answered. "It means somebody is going to try to kill my daughter and grandbabies—like every other time she's gotten involved with crazy people. Why, oh, why," she wailed, "couldn't you choose a safe job? You could have gone into retail with me. At least you'd have better clothes. I need my nitro." My mother fanned herself.

"She's not getting hurt this time, Sasha," Jazz said. "I'll see to that if it kills *me*!"

"Calm down, everybody," I interjected. "Nobody is going to get hurt. Least of all me."

I thought for a moment, still not completely surrendering my sleuthing. "Sister Lou used the exact same words Nikki did, in the same scripted way the kids told their story. She also gave us the brush-off, not really answering any of our questions."

"Yes?" my mother said.

Jazz added, "I know what she's going to say. She's going to say Nikki and the children are covering for *Lou*. Maybe she's the one who drowned Zeekie."

"I can't really see Nikki covering for anybody, but we need to take a much deeper look at Lou. Ezekiel told me Nikki couldn't handle Zeekie and wanted him to be medicated. Maybe she thought he was possessed."

Jazz's face scrunched up. "Possessed with what?"

"A *little boy* demon, knowing those two. Maybe she looked to Sister Lou to help her."

Jack quipped, "Heaven help that kid if she did."

Jazz sighed. "There's one more thing."

"What's that, Columbo?" I teased.

He gave me a crooked smile. "The ME's office finished the autopsy. His death was ruled accidental."

My heart sank. "No way!"

"Bell, that kid had no signs of abuse. No bruises. No fractures. Except for the drowning, he seemed perfectly healthy and well cared for."

I thought about Zeekie. He did appear to be healthy and well adjusted. Not once during the crusade did I think he was abused, not even when Nikki snatched him out of my arms. She didn't win any good-mama points with me for that, but I didn't see her battering her son.

"But that story . . . the daughter suddenly wanting to give Zeekie a bath with no precedent for it. Him drowning because Zeke walked out of the bathroom. He wasn't eight months old. He was almost three."

"Bell," Jazz said, "you already know from Kate's murder that sometimes even cops don't want to work hard. Even more so if the case is ruled accidental. Think about it. If anyone presses this family after the ME ruled the baby's death accidental, the Thunders can cry religious discrimination."

"But what about Thunder talking about God raising his son from the dead?" I asked Jazz. "Can't you see they're trying to get attention for their ministry? I wouldn't be surprised if the whole thing, including Zeekie's murder, was planned."

"It ain't a crime to believe that or even to say you believe that. The funeral is Tuesday morning at the Rock House, and it's going to be televised. I guess we'll all see what God is going to do."

Lord, have mercy. It will be a dog and pony show! I felt an almost unbearable heaviness at the thought of it. I didn't know if I could stomach their antics, but I had to say good-bye to my little Thunder boy. I had to.

Sasha got up from my bed. "That's enough about this awful

situation. My baby needs her rest and to keep her head clear of all this horror." She touched my hand. "I'll call your job for you, Amanda Bell, and Maggie will take care of rearranging your schedule for your private practice." She kissed my cheek and turned her attention to her fellow grandmother. "Addie, let's go to the gift shop and pick up some more presents for the babies."

Addie looked so eager to go baby shopping, she jumped up like she'd been sitting in an ejector seat.

"What about presents for me?" I said. "I'm the one laid up, in pain, hanging on to the babies by my fingernails. Like a cat! A weak, tired, slipping-off-the-edge cat."

Sasha rebuked me. "Stop being so self-absorbed, Ms. Kitty. You're going to be a mother. Nothing is about you now or for the rest of your life."

I didn't mention that *nothing* was about me anyway when it came to my mother, unless it was negative. Negativity was about me, but the *damage* my negative attitude, lifestyle, or fill in the blank caused was *always* about Ma and Carly.

At least her "heart" condition had improved with the news of the twins.

Jazz leaned into me. "I'll buy you some presents, Catwoman. Let them do their grandmother thing." He kissed me on my cheek, and for a moment I thought nothing could interfere with my happiness.

Nothing.

For a moment.

I should have known by the pensive look on Jazz's face that trouble was brewing. I'd stayed in the hospital overnight and most of Sunday until Dr. McLogan finally cleared me to go home late in the evening. I still had residual pain, and I didn't feel like participating in the battle of the sexes with Jazz. I just wanted to get out of the Love Bug, go into my apartment, and crawl into bed with my Bible and the Sunday edition of the *Ann Arbor News*. Instead we sat in the parking lot, Jazz neither making a move to open the door nor even looking at me.

I sighed. I didn't want to ask for fear that he'd answer in the affirmative, but I had to. "Is there something wrong, Jazz?"

"I don't think so."

"Which suggests that perhaps *I* will?"

"It's nothing. I mean, we're trying to do the right thing, right?"

"What exactly do you mean by 'do the right thing'?"

He drummed his fingers on the dashboard. "Yo, we do what we gotta do to stay on point and make sure the babies are straight. That's how we roll. Right?"

"That was an awful lot of slang there. What exactly are you compensating for, soul brotha?"

"Who said I'm compensating for anything?"

"That's not how you usually communicate with me. What have you done? What are you trying *not* to tell me?"

He unbuckled his seat belt. "Let's go inside. I'll come back for all the toys and flowers once we get you settled."

I didn't argue with him. I knew whatever he had to tell me I'd hear soon enough.

Ever the gentleman, Jazz carried me up the stairs once again, God bless him. I nestled my head into his neck. *God, I love this man.* He smelled of something woodsy and manly. He never needed to wear cologne. His own scent intoxicated me—when he didn't smell like a distillery.

"Ummmmm," I said into his neck.

"Don't start."

"I like the way you smell."

"I like the way you smell, too. But let's not smell each other until Dr. McLogan says its okay."

"Is that sexual demon trying to rear its ugly head?"

"Not funny."

"I was teasing."

"No, you were teasing when you were talking all up in my neck about how good I smell. Mention that I'm the spawn of Satan and you kill that loving feeling in me."

By now he'd climbed two flights of stairs. He needed to save his breath and concentrate, or I'd be walking up the last flight —which I was perfectly capable of, even if it meant I'd suffer a wee bit.

Again I curled into him, enjoying the ride. We finally made it to my apartment, and he gently set me down.

He huffed and gasped. Finally, "You okay, baby?"

"I am, but you sound like you may need to be resuscitated."

"I'm all right."

Honestly! Men cannot admit weakness. They have to have rigor mortis setting in before they'll think they're sick enough to go to the doctor.

He thrust the key in the door, unlocked it, and repeated the action two more times. Finally, he put his hand on the door, looked at me sheepishly. "Welcome home, Bell."

"Thanks, Jazz. Open the door."

He did. Reluctantly. And to my shock and horror.

A fifty-two-inch television overwhelmed my living room. Paintings were all over my walls—Addie Lee paintings—and a treadmill stood as stoic as a soldier next to my rose-colored velvet sofa. I had new throw pillows made of indigo-wax-dyed cloth that looked vaguely familiar. I scratched my head and turned my attention back to Jazz.

"You got me some new stuff?"

"Go inside, Bell."

"But what is all this stuff?"

"Maybe you should sit down."

I walked over to my sofa and slowly lowered myself down. My heart began to palpitate. The Addie Lee paintings were originals. And was that a Gilbert Young painting over there on the floor by my bedroom door? I'd kill several people to get some of Gilbert's work. The art fairy had also propped a huge Synthia Saint James painting next to the big-screen television. Elisa idolized her. *She'll be thrilled to see . . . But why are these things . . .*

Jazz eased himself onto the couch beside me. "Bell, baby."

"Yes?"

"I moved in with you."

"What?"

If I thought seeing the beautiful art quickened my pulse, hearing Jazz say he'd moved in nearly took me to meet Jesus. "Whaddya mean you moved in?"

"I mean while you were in the hospital, I brought all my stuff over here."

"Jazz, I was only in the hospital overnight. I'm gone all night and you felt like you had to drag all your stuff over here? Now you're going to have to take it all back."

"I sold my loft, and I had my stuff at my parents' house."

"So, why did you bring it *here*? What? Do you think I'm Bell's Storage now?"

He shifted in his seat. "I've been living with my parents since Kate died, but Jack and Addie put me out when I told them you were having twins. I mean, they actually put my stuff in a U-Haul they rented."

"What?" My voice went up about twelve octaves. I could have launched my career as a soprano opera singer after this conversation.

He didn't say anything about my spectacular voice. "I prayed about it, and the Lord spoke to me."

"What?" Another twelve octaves. I could sing with the cherubim now.

"What? Do you think God only speaks to Pentecostals?"

I shook my head. "I don't think that at all, Jazz. I just don't usually hear *you* say things like that."

"All the more reason for you to hear me out. Where is your copy of *The Message*?"

"It's on top of my armoire, wherever that is now."

"Bell, you can see I made a big effort to keep your things as close to how you had them as possible." He got up and went over to my armoire, which was now in a corner, having been displaced by Jazz's gigantic *movie screen*!

He grabbed *The Message* and came and sat beside me again. He turned to the third chapter of Hosea.

This was going to be bad. As soon as I saw he'd gone to the Old Testament, I knew there'd be trouble, but *Hosea*?

"It's the third verse," he said. "Like I said, I prayed and asked God for some kind of guidance. And he answered my prayer perfectly."

Usually, I'd enjoy thinking of my husband as a praying man. That God answered his prayer should have pleased me to no end. So why were goose bumps creeping up my arms? My throat went dry. He began to read.

"Then I told her, 'From now on you're living with me. No more whoring, no more sleeping around. You're living with me and I'm living with you.'"

My mouth flew open. It felt like the air had been squeezed out of my lungs. My eyes twitched wildly. I wanted to scream, but no sound came out.

He smiled in obvious triumph. "It's perfect! When I read that, I knew God had spoken. He wants us to live together."

"Ooooh," I moaned.

Jazz grabbed my elbow. "Are you in pain again?"

"*Eugene!*"

"What?"

"*Eugene!*"

He looked puzzled. "Who is Eugene?"

I started rocking to comfort myself. "Eugene Peterson. He's the paraphraser of *The Message*. He's *failed* me."

Jazz gave me another quizzical look. "I don't know what you mean. How did he fail you?"

"That paraphrase. It allowed you to use my beloved *Message* against me. Ooooh." I flung my hand, palm facing out, against my forehead and let my head fall back. Then I jerked my head back up and pointed a finger at Jazz. "And I take issue with that whole *whoring* thing!"

Jazz shrugged, the rat! "I'm just sayin' . . . that's what God told me to tell you. I think what we need to focus on is the 'you're living with me and I'm living with you' part. Your whoring demon got cast out."

He ducked, no doubt waiting for me to batter him. I jumped up to stand over him, trying to assert some nonexistent power.

"It was an interracial-dating-and-adultery demon. And it didn't even exist! I'm pregnant and that horrid cologne she wears made me ill. But that's not the point. You can't move in with me."

"Sure I can. God said so."

"That is a blatant example of twisting the scriptures to support your argument."

"What argument? As soon as I knew the babies were coming, I thought we should get our act together. I thought so before then, to tell you the truth. And why is it twisting scripture when God speaks to *me*? If God gave you some kind of answer to your prayer, you'd hang up a sign and declare yourself a prophetess."

"I would not! And don't try to get off the topic."

Jazz stood, too. Since he was a head taller, he instantly had the advantage over me. "Like Eugene said, 'You're living with me, and I'm living with you.'"

"You are impossible, Jazz!"

"And you're rebelling. That's like the sin of witchcraft. *Witch!*"

"Oh, I'm so going to hurt you. I'm going to jack you up, Jazz Brown." I tried to calm myself. Impossible. "You don't listen to anything I say. Charging in here like a bull in a china shop."

He ignored my insults and stood there glowering at me. I wondered if he'd say, "What else you got?" I didn't have a thing.

Weariness settled on me, and I felt crampy again. "I need my pain medicine now!" Oh Lord, now I sounded like Sasha. "You've stressed me out. I'm going to bed."

His hard expression softened. "May I get you anything?"

Despite my anger, my heart softened when my alpha male went beta and so beautifully offered to serve me. "No, Jazz. You can get *yourself* some blankets, a sheet, and a pillow, unless you want Ma Brown's quilt instead of blankets."

"I'd like to use the quilt, please."

Those eyes. He had naughty eyes. I'd have to keep an eye on him. "I'll get it for you," I said. I didn't want him rooting through my stuff. I tried to keep my voice soft, to turn away any stubborn wrath between us. I wanted to make peace with him.

He simply said, "Don't worry, baby, I'll get it myself."

"It's no problem, Jazz. I'm happy to serve you."

Okay, God, you see I'm trying. I used the "s" word.

"You'd like to serve me?"

I shrugged my shoulders. "I made vows."

A sexy grin tugged at a corner of his mouth. "So you did."

I felt silly standing there, the focus of his heat-seeking eyes. "You're sure I can't get you anything?"

"No need, baby. I'll be sharing the bed with you anyway."

I gave him my most beatific, albeit fake, smile. "Um. No, you'll be sleeping on the sofa."

"Baby, I'm sleeping with you now and until death, travel, or hospitalization do us part."

All kinds of alarms sounded inside of me. "We're not sharing a bed, Jazz."

"In that case, you can feel free to sleep on the sofa, Bell. I'll bring you a pillow and the quilt."

"I can't sleep in the living room. I'm the one who just got out of the hospital and is pregnant with twins."

He stepped closer to me and massaged my shoulders. Honestly! His hands are magical. "But, baby," he murmured. "I'm the one who married you. I *will* sleep with you. But don't worry. Since you just got out of the hospital, we can postpone our love-making. We'll see how you feel tomorrow."

I jerked away from him. "Jazz, the least you could have done was talk to me, you Neanderthal! You know I'm not comfortable with strong-arm tactics—not with my history."

"Bell, you're afraid to be happy. You don't know how to be happy, either."

His words rang so true, the gong could be heard round the world. It shot right to my heart, my soul, my spirit, my everything. I looked away. I couldn't let him see he was right.

"You don't trust that you can have good things in your life," he continued. "You don't trust that I meant what I promised in my vows to you. You can't accept what God says is good, no, excellent, because of what some nutjob named Adam did to twist what sex means to you. You can't *be* with me because you're afraid it's a sin to love your own husband."

"Isn't it wrong to sleep with your husband if you're separated?"

"We're *not* separated, Bell!" he shouted. "I'm here. I *want* to be here. I *want* to be married to *you*. And you want to be married to me. So how is being together wrong? I don't get it."

I didn't know. The messages about sex were muddled inside my head, and I couldn't sort them out. Not now. I needed to wait.

He shook his head. "And you're supposed to be the psychologist who helps people figure these things out."

I wanted to be mad. To be furious. To walk out on him. But he'd dismantled me, top to bottom. He *knew* me.

And loves you anyway . . . just like I do. That still, small voice in my soul—the one that shows up whenever I *don't* want to hear from God—spoke gently to me. It added, *Don't let the sun go down on your wrath.*

The sun had already gone down, but I got God's point, although I wanted to run from God, too.

"I'm going to bed," I said, not looking at him. I walked to the doorway of my bedroom, turned, and said, "Sleep tight, Jazz. And don't let the bedbugs—"

"Bite me!" he said.

My mouth flew open. Jazz cracked up.

"I couldn't resist," he said.

So much for Jazz knowing me. Or not letting the sun go down on my wrath. I went to bed spitting fire. And I went *alone,* locking my bedroom door behind me.

chapter
fourteen

MONDAY MORNING. Ma had called the jail for me on Saturday and informed them that I'd been hospitalized and wouldn't be back in until Thursday. I wanted to sleep in but ended up waking early to the sounds of Jazz—not the music; the man. He'd gotten into my bedroom somehow and sat beside me with his legs under the covers.

I prayed that man had something on. Anything, and it didn't look like he did from what I could see. He had his cell phone to his ear. Sounded like he was trying to schmooze someone into running fingerprints through AFIS—the Automated Fingerprint Identification System. I propped myself up on my elbow, wild-eyed, braids all over my head like Medusa, and still mad from last night.

"Jazz," I stage-whispered, "what are you doing in my bed?"

He put the index finger of his free hand to his lips. I hated when he shushed me, even if he hadn't actually *said* "shush." At least waiting to speak with him—okay, yell at him—gave me a chance to eavesdrop.

"If you get a hit let me know."

He waited. I couldn't hear what the other person said.

"Thanks a lot, okay?"

Pause. He laughed. "Cut that out, girl. You know I'm not on the market."

I sat up. "Who *is* that?" I said. Loudly. Honestly! Women seemed to have no regard for married men actually being *married*. What is up with the world?

He laughed again and nudged me with his elbow. "Bye, now." He flipped his phone closed. Looked at me. "Good morning, Mama."

"How did you get in here when I locked the door?"

"That lock is useless. All you need is a wire hanger to open it."

Man! Why didn't I listen to Joan Crawford when she said, "No more wire hangers"? I chided myself for my lack of foresight.

"So my boundaries mean nothing to you?"

"Bell, some boundaries are good. Noble. Others are dumb. We're married, and I'm going to sleep with you. No need to play hard to get anymore. Just accept this and be happy."

"What? You think sleeping with you is a gift?"

"Tanya Stevenson would think it's a gift."

"And who is Tanya Severenson?"

"Tanya Stevenson."

"That's what I said."

The mischievous eye-twinkle thing returned with a vengeance. "You didn't say that."

"Could you just tell me who Toni Anderson is?"

"I don't know anybody by that name."

"You just said she would think sleeping with you is a gift."

"No, I didn't. You got the name wrong."

"You know who I mean. Tessa Jefferson."

He chuckled. The sound delighted me. "You're doing that on purpose."

"I don't have all day to play the name game with you, Jazzy. Please, tell me who Tonya Harding is."

"She's the chick who got her ex-hubby and his boys to crack Nancy Kerrigan in the knee."

"She wants to sleep with you? Ew."

He chuckled again and bent over to kiss me. "You're so much like Sasha sometimes."

"That's not what Ma and Carly say. They say I'm just like Artie, my dad. Neither of them likes him."

"I'd like to meet him."

"Yeah. You can knock back a few drinks together. So, who is Tanya Stevenson?"

"She works for the crime lab for the Ann Arbor Police. I need to start networking and establishing relationships with them."

"Okay, networking is one thing. You need to go easy on the 'establishing relationships' thing, especially when Tanya Stevenson wants to bed you down."

He threw his hands up. "I'm not the one with an adultery demon."

"No, but who knows where that sexual demon will take you?"

He reached out and smoothed my braids. "Don't worry. You're cuter than she is."

"Am I smarter?"

"Yes, dear."

"Funnier?"

"Definitely."

"Breasts bigger?"

"I didn't look at her breasts."

I smiled at him.

He laughed. "I knew that was a trick question. You won't see me taking a beatdown from a hormonally driven pregnant woman. Jack Brown did teach me a few things about women."

I cocked my head to the side and studied him. "You don't miss a thing, do you, Jazz?"

"Sure I do. But you can help with that, can't you?"

I perked right up. "I know! Maybe we can be private investigators *together*. We'll be the black version of *Hart to Hart*. Chic, fabulous—"

"And filthy rich."

We got quiet for a moment. Jazz must have been seriously contemplating the possibility of us working together. He frowned and shook his head. "*Psych!* Don't even get your hopes up. Me, plain ol' homicide detective with police force. You, *Jane*. Me, have dangerous job. You, mommy now."

I lightly slapped his arm. "You downsized me! Jane used to be a psychologist."

"I *upgraded* you. Being a full-time wife and mother is a noble vocation."

Full-time wife and mother hit me like Niagara Falls! Slowly I turned . . .

Jazz deftly diverted my attention. "I'm running Nikki's and the kids' fingerprints through AFIS."

I filed that full-time wife and mother bit in my mental "important" file. We'd finish our discussion later. I'd make sure of it, but for now . . .

"How'd you get their prints?"

"I let them finish their ice cream in the car. I asked Nikki to collect the trash, so she touched both their cups."

"Good work, detective."

Jazz winked at me: "It's what I do. Besides, that's not what she was checkin' me out for."

I frowned.

He rubbed my arm. "I don't want her, Mama. I'm here in my bed with you, where I belong."

"I'm not going to touch that one right now."

I felt hopeful. Not only was Jazz investigating for me but he was sharing everything he did with me. I appreciated that as both client and jealous wife.

"So do you think Nikki could have murdered Zeekie?"

"I admit, a woman on the make when her son is at the morgue makes me leery of her, though honestly, people have been known to do worse and not be murderers. Bell, people use sex for a lot of things, and if what you told me about her is true, she probably isn't a stranger to that kind of behavior. That doesn't make her a murderer, though."

"It doesn't make her an innocent little lamb, either. Consider this, Jazz: since the ME ruled his death an accident, whoever killed him may now have a false sense of security. They'll think they got away with murder and won't be on to a continuing investigation."

He nodded, not bothering to hide his frustration.

"Why do you do this, Bell? I can see why I look for murder

everywhere. I've been in homicide way too long, but not you. Why do you insist on this? I don't like it. It puts you in a position where people hurt you. We can't afford that now."

"But she might get away with murder."

"She might not have murdered anyone, Bell, and you know what? Sometimes people get away with murder. I hate it, but they do."

"If you hate it, don't let it happen."

"There's no proof. Come on, Bell. You don't like her! Maybe you're seeing things."

"People thought I was seeing things when I saw that somebody other than you killed Kate, Jazz. I fought for you."

"I know you did, baby. I'm grateful. You saved me from prison, but you also almost got your neck broken."

Jazz lifted my chin with one of his fingers. "I can't let anything happen to you. She might have killed her baby, but she won't kill mine."

I didn't know what to say to that.

He took my hand, kissed my open palm.

"I'm still looking, Bell." He held my hand.

"It's Nikki, Jazz."

"I hate to say this, but you may be right."

"What do you think her motive could be?"

He looked uncomfortable. Very uncomfortable.

"You know something!"

"Why can't you just be normal? Why don't you bother me about money or for not spending enough time with you?"

"Tell me. I'm pregnant. I have to *know* things."

"I don't want to discuss this with you. Isn't it enough that I'm still looking into this?"

"I kept you from prison. You'd be up in Jackson right now if—"

"I would not!"

"Would, too!"

"Shut up!"

"What do you know?" I screamed.

He harrumphed.

I always break him down.

"She had a life insurance policy for him. And we ain't talkin' small change."

"Aha!" I said. "Familial murder, especially when a mother kills her child, is often motivated by insurance money. Other motives include a woman wanting to please a husband or boyfriend who's not the child's father, or she's frustrated and can't handle the child."

He agreed with this solid assessment.

I continued, "Ezekiel said she couldn't handle Zeekie. This wasn't an impulse killing like if she beat him to death in a rage. I'll bet she planned to drown him. Maybe that's how she got Sister Lou involved. She knows Lou hasn't got 'em all."

"Lou ain't got none!" He shuddered again.

"Maybe she coerced Lou to make her responsible for it and Lou is none the wiser. Nikki would know Lou's history of mental illness and about her unorthodox deliverance methods."

He agreed. "This could also mean Nikki was smart enough not to get her own hands dirty. Maybe Lou really did kill him in another exorcism gone wrong, but if she did, it really would be an accident. Actually it was brilliant. If anybody ever found out what happened and prosecuted, Lou's defense attorney could cop an insanity plea and nobody would even go to jail. Lou might even get the help she needs."

"What do you think of Nikki as a grieving mother?"

His brow furrowed. "I think she overdid the stoic yet surviving bit—when she wasn't brazenly putting the moves on me. That's the thing about murderers. They don't realize how fake their acting is."

"She must have fooled the police."

"Maybe not. Like I said at the hospital, they'd be inclined to go with the autopsy report, especially with this being a high-profile case. You, however, have an in with the AAPD. Why don't you ask your friends what they think?"

"Good thinking."

"Bell. She calls me."

"What?"

"She calls me several times a day. She's not a nice girl on the phone."

My heart sank. "Why are you taking her calls?"

"Because you keep your friends close and your enemies closer. How am I supposed to watch her if I don't watch her?"

"I don't like this, Jazz. She's got a freakin' personality disorder and deadly charm."

"You have nothing to worry about. I'm in love with only one woman." He rubbed my thigh, like seeing me jealous put him in the mood for love. "What's that you were saying about Nikki's deadly charm?"

I could hardly concentrate. He really did have skilled hands. "What, honey?"

He drew circles on my thigh. My bed felt really, really small. "Personality disorder? Deadly charm. What you think Nikki has."

I had to snap back to attention. I moved his hand. "In a way I was kidding when I said she had a personality disorder."

"You said 'in a way.'"

"Well, maybe I wasn't kidding. Jazz, she has a coldness about her. From the things Ezekiel told me about her coming on to him when she was a kid? How many teenagers do you know who throw themselves at old geezers?"

"I wouldn't call him that. He's pretty smooth."

"He was her sugar daddy."

"Many people like that arrangement."

"She had no regard for his wife, who ended up getting sick and dying two seconds after she found out they were lovers."

"Luuuceeee!"

"I didn't imply anything. The things Ezekiel and Joy said about her just give me pause."

Jazz rubbed his chin. "That's not a pause. That's practically an accusation, Bell."

"There could be something to it. Maybe she poisoned her. I can talk to Thunder. Get more information."

He rubbed his temples. "What? You just gonna ask your boyfriend flat out if Nikki's been knocking off hookers and transients?"

"Are you turning a little green around the edges, Jazz?"

"Maybe I don't like how the old hustler looks at you."

"He looks at all women like that."

"But you're *my* woman."

"Not if Jack Daniel's is your new best friend."

He turned away from me. Bit his lip, probably to keep from saying something I'd have deserved.

"I'm sorry."

He didn't say he accepted my apology. Just plunged into confessing. "There's something I really need to tell you." Concern shadowed his face.

My teasing mood sobered in an instant. "What is it, Jazzy?"

He lay back on his pillow and stared at the ceiling. "Like I said, I'm no fan of Nikki Thunder, and I'm not saying you're wrong about her, either, but . . ." He took a deep breath. "I guess I'm thinking about grief. How people can grieve in different ways. Like, some people might deal with their losses with a glass of Jack Daniel's, or three of them. Every few hours. For six weeks." He reached his hand over to touch my arm, as if he needed the contact to go on. I wanted to encourage him.

"Go on."

"I've been fighting you on it, but I know I'm drinking too much."

"You're self-medicating. There are healthier ways to deal with loss."

He pulled his hand away and my skin cooled, immediately missing his touch. If I didn't do something, a wall was going to go up between us. I leaned over and took his cheeks in my hands. "Hey."

He kept his eyes downcast. Didn't speak.

"Look at me, Jazz."

He inclined his head upward and fixed his eyes on me.

I tried to pour all the love I had in me into my words. "I love you."

"You love me, but what?"

"No buts. I love you. That's all."

"I got suspended. The chief suspended me for drinking on the job."

"Oh, Jazz."

"I'll get it together. I mean it."

He meant what he said, but that didn't mean he'd be able to do it. Then again, I couldn't tell whether I was seeing Jazz sitting in front of me all miserable and repentant or my father. They looked about the same in this instance.

"We'd better get up."

"Yeah, we'd better. I'm not good for layin' up in bed with you. Gives me ideas."

"None of which I can help you with today. I'm ready to get over to Rocky's and deal with the suspects."

"You're not going anywhere today, young lady."

"But, Jazz . . ."

"Your job today is to take care of those babies."

"They're not here yet."

"And if you go traipsing around the globe trying to solve crimes, they won't make it here safely. I ain't having that."

"I would hardly call sitting down at Rocky's talking to people traipsing around the globe. And did you hear that I said *sitting*?"

"You'll sit at home, wife."

"But . . ."

"No buts!"

Then that man stepped out of the bed in his birthday suit. He turned from me and walked toward the bathroom.

"I thought you said 'no butts'!" I cried.

He laughed all the way to the bathroom.

———————

The naked detective left me to my own devices with a stern warning to order in, tip good, and intimidate the delivery person because I never knew who could be a psychopath. He also insisted I not attempt much beyond going to the bathroom, though I was allowed to grab a few books and bring them to bed.

I didn't want to read. I didn't want to watch TiVo. I couldn't stomach any of my romantic DVDs, and Jazz said crime shows were off-limits, especially *Columbo*.

But a sistah had to do what a sistah had to do. I picked up my phone and called my *other* partner in crime solving, Kalaya Naylor, ace reporter for the *City Beat* tabloid newspaper. At least we could brainstorm some more.

I punched her numbers, excited before she even picked up.

"Bell!" Her voice rose in what sounded like a mix of surprise and excitement.

I grinned. "Happy to hear from me?"

"I'm always happy to hear from you. I'm at the Gap in Briarwood Mall looking at babyGap stuff for my godchildren."

I acted like I didn't understand the massive hint she'd given me. "I didn't know you had godchildren, Kal."

Pause. "Don't start no stuff, girlfriend."

Kalaya loved my Ma Brownisms as much as Jazz and I did.

I laughed. "Relax. It won't be no stuff, especially if you pur-
chase said godchildren something like matching itty-bitty jeans.
Little pink cowgirl shirts. That would be so cute!"

She gasped. "I see some totally major ones." She whooped
and cracked up. "They're, like, so little." I pictured her studying
the tiny denims. "This is dope. I so have to get pregnant *before* I
turn thirty-five. No offense, girl."

"None taken. Just make sure you and Souldier get married
before you get started on that. Can you pick me up an Auntie
Anne's pretzel?"

"Yep, especially since you implied I'll actually marry the man
of my dreams."

"And hurry."

"I'm working on him."

"No, hurry and get here. Jazzy wouldn't let me go on inter-
views with him today."

"I'll be there soon, you big, whiny baby."

"For that you have to bring me a Mrs. Fields cookie, too."

"Chocolate chip, oatmeal raisin, white chocolate macadamia
nut? What'll it be?"

"Yes, please."

"Which kind do you want me to bring you?"

"You mean I have to pick *one?* Out of those great choices?
Just get all three and I'll decide when you get here. Or not."

I could imagine Kalaya shaking her head. "If you weren't
pregnant . . ."

"Just get over here."

We rang off.

I looked around my apartment, crowded now with my things

hastily moved around to accommodate my new housemate. I hoped within the week I'd feel well enough to arrange things a little nicer. I'd be spending much more time at home, and I wanted to be comfortable.

Dr. McLogan had already let me know he considered my pregnancy high risk. Twins practically ensured an early delivery. I didn't mind that, as long as they stayed inside long enough to live and be healthy outside of the confines of my womb.

Tiernan also informed Jazz and me of the challenges the large fibroid tumor growing on the outside wall of my uterus might pose. Estrogen would continue to feed it, which would keep it growing. If it grew too fast, I'd get that pain again. I knew I could expect more bed rest. How much, no one could say yet.

Honestly, I could see the value of Jazz's moving in. But how he did it grated on my nerves. Not that I didn't drive him crazy as well.

"God, will we ever get it right?"

I tried to quiet my mind long enough to hear his answer. I closed my arms and rested my head on the pillow.

"I love him, Lord. Help me get it right."

I'm giving a lecture somewhere, and I'm disturbed because only Jazz and a few of my friends attended, and they keep asking me to talk louder because they can't hear me.

My talk is on women who kill.

I look out at my audience, and now Nikki Thunder is there and she's telling me to be quiet. I keep going over the characteristics female sociopaths share, and she's yelling for me to shut up, and my friends are yelling for me to talk louder.

I open my mouth to speak, and nothing comes out. Nikki laughs and laughs, and my friends disappear one by one until no one is left but Nikki—laughing.

I feel something trickle down my legs. I reach down to touch the moisture sliding down to my feet, and when I look at my hands, they are drenched in blood.

I try to cry out that my babies are dead but nothing comes out of my mouth. I see Nikki leaving, and she takes Jazz with her. He's wearing a red suit, and she has on a black wedding dress.

Jazz says, "I'm going with her." And he looks so sad.

I'm trying desperately to say "Noooooooo" but nothing comes out.

My own voice crying aloud "Noooooooo" startled me out of sleep. I jerked my body up and heard Kalaya's voice screaming with me.

"Holy Moses!" she said, after I realized it was only a dream and stopped screaming. "You almost scared me to death."

I couldn't quite catch my breath. My heart rattled rapid-fire like a snare drum.

Kal eased beside me on the bed. She pulled me into an embrace. "Girl, you're about to shake right out of your skin. Are you cold?"

I nodded. I didn't feel ready to talk yet, so I squeezed her.

Kalaya pulled the quilt around my arms. "You want me to get your pretzel or the cookies?"

I shook my head. Rarely at a loss for words, I knew my silence worried her. Frankly, she should have called an ambulance when I turned down a Mrs. Fields chocolate chip cookie.

"Can I get you a drink?"

I knew my poor girlfriend spooked easily. If I pulled myself together, she'd feel so much better. But I could no more bring myself to act on my intellectualism than I could bring Zeekie back from the dead. I squeezed my eyes shut. Tears slipped out the sides and Kalaya wiped them with her thumbs, cradling my face.

"What's wrong, honey?"

I didn't want to say. Didn't want the horror of the dream to materialize in real life. If only I could stay quiet, maybe . . .

Kalaya hugged me more fiercely than she ever had. I knew I'd scared her, but I couldn't help her anymore than I could help myself. I started rocking my body on the bed. Still shaking. Silent as a stone.

She seemed reluctant to move away from me, but she whispered, "You hang on to me, okay? I'm just going to make a call."

Her cell phone hung off a chain on her jeans. She unhooked it, flipped it open, and furiously dialed a number. She tapped her foot as she waited for the other person to answer.

"Jazz?" she said.

My heart dropped. I wanted to see him so badly.

"Can you come home? Bell is looking bad."

I couldn't hear Jazz's response.

"I'd have called an ambulance first if that's what I thought she needed. You just need to come home and see her for yourself."

She flipped the phone closed. My guess is that he hung up and was on his way before she had time to say good-bye.

Thank God.

———————

I'd been a single woman for so long, it was second nature for me to give Kalaya all the phone numbers of the important people in my life. I did this just in case she knocked on my apartment door and I didn't answer even though the Love Bug was outside. Being an avid consumer of truTV, I had the worst images in my head. I could picture Kalaya using the key I gave her and coming into my place welcomed only by the smell of death wafting about the room. There'd I'd be. Dead! Having lain there for six weeks because nobody loved me and nobody noticed when I didn't call them or show up for work or hadn't been seen in the land of the living.

I hadn't died however. My remains were not decomposing, and I did not bear the stench of the not-so-recently departed. Yet Kalaya must have felt inspired, because she called all my in-case-of-emergency people. I didn't complain, but only because of the emotional trauma clutching me in its evil grip.

Jazz, being closest, arrived first. Honestly, I'd never heard him unlock my locks so fast. My whirling mind fixated temporarily on the fact that it was he who insisted on all those locks. *Bet you wish you didn't have to go through all those locks, huh, Jazzy?*

By lock number three, Jazz's frustration must have got the

better of him. He pounded on the door, just about knocking it off its hinges.

Kalaya pried herself out of my hug and went to open the door for him, though I'd have been interested in seeing if he'd have gone so far as to kick the door open like a television cop.

She unlocked the third lock and flung the door open. Jazz exploded into the apartment like the Tasmanian Devil—the cartoon one—and was at my bed faster than if I'd had on that silver nightgown he liked so much and was saying, "Come hither."

He stopped cold when he saw me. I'm not sure how I looked, but it must have been compelling, since Kalaya called my entire family to come help. He eased over to the bed and sat down next to me. He spoke in soothing, therapeutic tones, which scared me. I'm used to macho man speaking to me in strong, authoritative tones. Or sexy Marvin Gaye "Let's Get It On" tones. He rarely deviated from the two.

He may not have puppy eyes, but his Godiva chocolate yummies looked at me with such compassion and concern that my lip trembled, and I lunged at him like a linebacker at the quarterback.

When he could breathe again, he stroked my hair. "Baby . . ." Soft, soothing tones.

I buried my head in his coat.

He tried, unsuccessfully, to peel me off him. "Baby, tell me what's going on."

I didn't feel ready to disclose yet.

Being the stronger of the two of us, he eventually succeeded in wrenching me away from him. "Bell, will you tell me what's going on?"

I wanted to tell him. I opened my mouth to speak, but how could I explain the unspeakable horror that had enveloped me? There are dreams, and there are Dreams, and I hadn't confused the two since I was a teenager. To do so could mean the death of someone I loved. I'd had a Dream, with a capital "D," and for me Dreams were real in a way that life sometimes wasn't. And I couldn't lose Jazz right now, even though the Dream said I would, and Dreams really did come true.

I squeezed him again, praying with all my being—albeit silently—that God would intervene. It was my only defense, crying out to God.

———

Hurricane Sasha arrived with Carly in tow. Neither of them seemed surprised that my apartment now overflowed with man stuff—and had a resident fine man. Traitors! They must have all been in on this move, while I lay helpless and vulnerable in the hospital, carrying my precious bundles. Evil people!

Sasha and Carly hung their coats in my closet. Jazz, Kalaya, and I had taken our little party to the living room. They thought tea would cure me and I'd spill the whole story over a steaming mug of Hot Cinnamon Sunset. I had to admit, they had chosen my favorite tea. Only, they'd have to pull out bigger guns than that to get me sharing.

Sasha breezed across the room and sat opposite me on one of my upholstered chairs. Her eyes locked with mine, but she directed the question to Kalaya.

"What did you say happened, Kalaya dear?" Ma used her

tough, efficient queen voice to get answers. Kalaya sat trembling in fear, terrified of her. Most of the time I was, too.

"Um—Mrs. Brown—"

"Sasha!"

Kalaya sprang up to a standing position. "I'm soooo sorry. Mrs.—uh, Sasha."

"What *happened*?"

Words spilled out of Kalaya like wine pouring out of a bottle. "Bell called me over because she was mad because Jazz wouldn't let her investigate with him."

Ma's eyes narrowed. She didn't take kindly to any notions I had about involving myself in crime solving, particularly when it involved a murderer or someone who could beat me up.

Kalaya went on, never missing a beat. "And I hurried up and got the baby stuff from the Gap. She was asleep when I got here and didn't hear me knocking, and I got scared thinking maybe a nutjob came in and killed her, but I didn't smell any decaying flesh. I smelled lavender candles. I came in with the key she gave me and when I saw she was asleep I said, 'Coolness. I'm hungry.' I raided the refrigerator because I thought she'd have real food now that Jazz lives here, and—"

Carly yawned. "We'll be here forever."

Sasha wouldn't. "Dear," she said. I knew that "dear." The first dear had been a *real* dear, but this second one, especially since it was accompanied by the insidious expression of polite yet controlled rage, wasn't. If Ma didn't get some answers fast, she'd blow with such impressive force, Mount St. Helens would applaud her.

Sasha sighed, an ominous release of breath. Kalaya had

crossed the line and gotten on Ma's last nerve. "Did she say what she dreamed?" The tundra had more warmth than Ma's voice.

Kalaya sank back down on the couch next to me. "Um. No, ma'am. She woke up screaming, 'No!'"

Jazz pulled one of his arms from around me to join the fun. "She had a dream the other day that made her wake up screaming."

Ma's head snapped in his direction: "And why were you present when my daughter woke up? Mr. I'll Leave You High and Dry Whenever I Feel Like It." The devil himself would have been frightened by her withering scowl. "Or shall I call you Mr. *Unavailable*?"

Jazz's cheeks reddened. He pulled his other arm from around me, no doubt to protect himself if my mother threw a few blows. "Ma."

I think any variation of the word "Ma," coming from anyone besides Carly and me—oh, who am I kidding? She rankled when Carly and I referred to her as our mother, too—but coming from anybody else . . .

She roared like she was a demon possessed. "Call me *Sasha*!"

"Sasha!" Jazz shouted. Addie had raised him well. He tried to regain his swagger, not content to let an old lady best him. He lowered his voice. Spoke slowly, as if she were not in her right mind. "I left *temporarily* so I wouldn't *really* kill someone, namely her puppy-eyed sidekick, Rocky. You're aware, since we discussed it at length, that I am completely committed to honoring your daughter, who I love. I can assure you that although I *feel* like leaving *right now* with all this *drama*, I won't be going anywhere."

Honestly, I found his effort to control his voice modulations honorable. I'd be screaming if it were me.

Sasha opened her mouth, probably to lash out her acidic retort, but Jazz interrupted her. "My point being," he said, loudly, then softer, "she woke up screaming from a dream she had Friday."

My mother must have realized there was a time to exchange sharp zingers and a time to find out why her daughter's behavior hovered just shy of catatonic—and not in a contemplative way. She turned her gaze back to me. "Did she tell you the content of her dream, Jazz?"

"Yeah. She said she had gone to the school building where Thunder had his crusade thing. She said the building was full of kids of all ages. She saw her daughter, Imani, and Zeekie, and for a minute she felt happy and was laughing. Then the kids started turning into zombies and skeletons, and they were begging for her to help them."

"Ewwww!" That was Carly's profound contribution.

Kalaya shuddered.

Ma pursed her lips. "But she told you everything?"

Jazz nodded. "Right."

"Then it was a dream. Not a Dream."

The difference must have escaped Jazz. Again he tried to control his volume. Slowly. "Sasha, what do you mean it was a dream, not a Dream?"

She sighed and hugged her arms. Released a deep breath. "Dreams, with a capital 'D,' are from God."

Jazz's face brightened. "Okay. From God is good, right?"

Sasha's darkened. "I've never known them to be."

Kalaya wrapped me in a tight hug, as if she could protect me from God's wrath. "This is gonna give me the willies. I can feel it."

Carly waved her concern away. "Nonsense. Some of the women in our family, including Ma Brown, had this weird God Dream thing."

Jazz's mouth hung open. "'Weird God Dream thing'?"

"Right," Carly said, as if creepy God Dreams were as common as varicose veins. "It seemed to skip generations. Nobody in my father's generation had it, so the old folks started speculating which of us would be dreamers. Everyone thought it'd be me, since God obviously gave me so much more than Bell."

I would hurt Carly. I would spend many hours planning her ruin.

Kalaya, ever the reporter and probably driven by "the willies," asked Carly, "So do you have the creepy God Dreams?"

She sighed, "God didn't want to burden me. He knew that I was meant to be a butterfly, spreading peace and happiness wherever I go."

I rolled my eyes, even though she'd spoken the gospel truth.

She got up, rounded my coffee table and got on her knees beside me. She placed her hand on my thigh. "No," she said, "I was spared, but our little Bell is *not* a butterfly."

"She is!" My husband lied. "She's my butterfly."

Although Carly sat on the floor, she managed to tilt her head back just so and stare down her nose at Jazz seated next to me on the sofa.

She shook her head at him as if he should be pitied. "You sweet boy."

I don't think Jazz enjoyed her calling him a boy, especially a sweet one. He bit his lip as if the gesture would keep curses from flying out of his mouth. "Does my wife have weird God Dreams or not?"

Kalaya, the youngest Christian among us, took this moment to show off her Bible prowess. "Maybe it's like Acts, chapter 2, verse seventeen says: 'In the last days, God says, I will pour out my Spirit on all people. Your sons and daughters will prophesy, your young men will see visions, your old men will dream dreams.' Only, Bell isn't an old man." She thought for a moment. "Does it count if Bell isn't an old man? I can be a literalist sometimes when it comes to scripture."

No one bothered to answer her.

Carly finally said, "She has weird God Dreams." At this she got up and went back over to her chair next to my mother and sat down.

Sasha rubbed her chin. "It's been years since she had one this bad, but when she was about eight, she had her first one about a neighbor of ours. The woman was traveling, and Bell dreamed she was on her way to her wedding, and she had on a red wedding dress."

"So what ended up happening?" Jazz asked.

"The woman ended up being murdered."

"Holy Moses!" Kalaya said.

My mother went on. "When Bell first had a Dream, we all told her that it was probably something she ate. She agonized over it. She asked anyone who would listen if she should tell our neighbor about it." Ma shrugged. "At the time, nobody knew Bell would have the gift."

"Or curse," Carly said.

"Shush!" Ma said to Carly. "It's not a curse. It's a very difficult cross to bear, but if you ask me, God chose well. At least Bell cares." She looked around the room at everyone. "Anyway, she was just a child. She didn't know what to do, and we all counseled her to forget about it. We didn't want Carolyn, our neighbor, to needlessly worry. I guess we were mistaken."

"How often does she have a Dream?" Jazz asked.

"Thank heavens they're rare. She had a few in her twenties. And the last one a few years ago. It was so terrifying, she wouldn't even speak it. In fact, for days she didn't utter a word. When she spoke again she said one word, 'Daddy.' We had an all-night prayer vigil for him, though frankly, I wonder if we shouldn't have let him go on to meet his maker."

"Ma!" Carly said.

"So she will talk again in a few days?"

Ma shrugged. "It doesn't have to take days. She's capable of talking. She's just scared. We have to pray that whoever she dreamed about will be protected."

Kalaya looked relieved. "So you mean nothing happened to her dad?"

"Unfortunately God answered our prayers. He's fine."

Carly finally had something useful to add to the conversation. "When we found out she was a dreamer, Ma Brown took her under her wing, taught her about what she used to call 'praying through.' Bell was just a kid, but she took it all in. But once Ma Brown was gone, she'd get discouraged. If anything happened to the person she dreamed about, she'd blame herself."

Jazz shook his head. "That sounds like a terrible burden."

"We don't get to choose the gifts God bestows on us," Ma said.

Carly quipped, "I hope she didn't dream about me." She pulled out a package of cigarettes.

She wouldn't have the nerve to light up in my apartment after all the fuss I'd made in my office. She knew that not only was I in the throes of misery from having a prophetic Dream but also I was pregnant. With twins.

Carly fished around her sky blue Chloé Paddington handbag that had to have hit her for a grand. The purse had an adorable padlock on it, and honestly, I hoped that lock would keep her from accessing a lighter. Unfortunately it did not.

I waited for someone, anyone, to tell her no smoking. My husband seemed a logical choice. The lion protecting his lioness carrying their cubs. But he didn't pay attention to her. My mother kept staring at me as if her gaze would compel me to speak. Kalaya rocked me in her embrace, and while I loved her, I needed my delicate fetuses protected more than me.

Carly lit up. Honestly! Nobody rushed her on behalf of my babies. She went into the kitchen and came back carrying my *last* Addie Lee mug. She sat back down in her chair and took a long drag of her Newport.

I yanked away from Kalaya. Everybody looked surprised. I tried to stare Carly down with an icy gaze. She paid me no attention whatsoever. I jerked my head around, scowled at my husband, and then looked at Carly again.

"What?" he said.

Sheesh! What does a girl have to do to get some respect

around here? Again, I looked from Carly to Jazz with exaggerated movements.

Carly flicked an ash into my beloved mug.

"*Carly!*" I screeched like a maniac.

She laughed. "Look, it talks!" She cracked up all the way to the kitchen. I heard water running. She came out a few minutes later, sans cigarette. She looked triumphant. "I knew that would get her talking. And the Addie Lee mug effect. Brilliant."

Everyone laughed, except me.

"I washed it out. No harm done. But who has three days for you to speak? We want to know what you dreamed."

"I don't want to talk about it," I said.

"So we see," Jazz said. His voice had an edge, but he grabbed my hand and held it, tenderly stroking it with the pad of his thumb.

"What did you dream, ladybug?" Ma said.

No fair. I loved it when my mother acted like a mother and not a drill sergeant. "Awwww, Ma. I don't want to say."

"Let us help you pray. Was it another wedding dress dream?" I nodded.

My mother scooted to the edge of her chair. She leaned toward me. Not like a drill sergeant at all. "Baby, what color was the dress?"

"It was black."

She nodded. "Good girl. Now, baby, did you have on the dress?"

"No."

"Who wore the black wedding dress?"

"Nikki Thunder."

Ma nodded again, showing no sign of shock or surprise. "What else happened?"

"I lost the . . ." I couldn't say it. I placed my hands on my belly.

Ma didn't ask me to clarify. "Anything else?"

Tears sprang to my eyes. I quickly wiped them away. "Don't make me say, Mama." My voice cracked.

I rarely called her Mama. Sasha stood up and walked over to me. Both Jazz and Kalaya got up from the sofa to give my mother plenty of room to comfort me.

She sat down beside me. Cradled my hand in hers. She lifted my chin with her finger until my eyes met hers. "Baby, you have to tell Mama what you dreamed. We have to pray."

I didn't say anything. My tears fell on her hands. She stroked my hair. "You know that God will do His will. You get the Dream so that you can pray. What else happened?"

I whispered. "I can't say it, Mama."

She nodded. "It's okay. You don't have to tell me what happened. Can you say who we need to pray for? We really are concerned."

I looked at her. She meant it.

"Bell, who else should we pray for?"

"The babies. And Jazz."

Gasps.

"We will pray," my mother said. Without hesitating she began a very lengthy conversation with Jesus. We all joined in, praying for dear life.

Literally.

chapter
fifteen

THAT NIGHT Jazz and I had our honeymoon. We didn't make love. Jazz insisted that we wait until we were sure I was physically well enough. He told me we had the rest of our lives for lots of lovemaking. I hoped he was right. Instead, we held each other and listened. I heard secrets he had never shared with anyone, and I told him mine. We talked until the wee hours of the morning.

Even after Jazz had gone to sleep, I stayed awake. I didn't want to go to sleep again. Thoughts of Zeekie's funeral filled me with anxiety, but I had to focus on the case, not my own feelings. People from Nikki's past could be present who could tell us more about the enigmatic cow.

Cow again? Goodness gracious, I'm gonna have to watch my thoughts!

Finally, my pregnant body forced me to slumber. I had a mercifully dreamless sleep. I woke up the next morning feeling the chill of Jazz's absence, his warmth no longer beside me. For one irrational moment I panicked. "Jazz!"

He rushed into the bedroom. He already had his suit pants

on and a white undershirt. Shaving cream was slathered on half his face.

"Are you all right?" He brandished his plastic razor like a gun.

"I'm fine. I got scared when you weren't in bed."

He sat on the bed next to me. "Baby. I know the Dream spooked you, but we prayed, and we'll keep praying. You have to trust God that I'll be all right."

"I do trust God. But God's idea of all right and mine are sometimes two different things. I want to grow old and naughty with you. I want us to be like your parents."

He got up and went back into the bathroom. My place was small enough for me to hear him without either of us significantly raising our voices. "Then keep talking to God about it."

"But what if He wants you for Himself?"

"I've been a cop almost half my life. He had plenty of opportunities to get me if that's what He wanted."

"But what if it's only now that He wants you?"

"You can't live in fear, baby."

"Tell my brain and heart that."

"How's the pain this morning?"

"Mostly gone. I'm more tired than anything."

"Why don't you stay home and rest?"

"Maybe I will."

Jazz came out of the bathroom with his face shaved clean. His skin looked as soft as a newborn's. He leaned against the doorjamb, watching me.

"I hate baby funerals." The look of revulsion on his face made me shudder. He nearly spat out the words. "You know what I hate the most? Those itty-bitty caskets."

"What I hate are those itty-bitty bodies in those itty-bitty caskets."

We didn't speak for a few moments. Jazz pierced the silence, but his voice had taken on a soft, sympathetic tone.

"Did Imani have a funeral?"

The question cut into me. I wondered if I'd ever get over her death, but I wanted to share everything with him. "No. They put her in a hole in the ground in Adam's backyard. Adam was as high as a California redwood that day. He got nice and coked up for the occasion. And I couldn't even make it to the backyard because he'd nearly killed me. I couldn't walk for weeks, and the other wives didn't think I should attend."

"They didn't think you should attend your own baby's funeral?"

"Jazz, they didn't think I was worthy of medical attention. They certainly weren't concerned about my feelings." I paused as the feeling of nausea that always accompanied this memory washed over me.

And forgive us our debts, as we forgive our debtors. Help me out, Lord.

I had to forgive all of them, seventy times seven. All day, every day.

"Are you relating this case to your past? You know what that does to objectivity, not that you've been objective *at all*."

"I'm not making it personal. But you know that woman isn't thinking about her dead baby if she's trying to hook up with you. And since we're on the subject, I'd better watch my back. Nikki got it in her head that she wanted Thunder, and the next thing you know, his wife was dead. Not to mention I had that dream . . ."

He came to me, gathered me into his embrace. "Then don't mention it. Just pray."

"I'm afraid that if you have to rely on my paltry prayers, you're going to end up pushing daisies."

"You're not the only one praying, so don't worry." He kissed me on my neck. I wished we could stay that way forever, locked in an embrace, completely safe from all the Nikki Thunders in the world. But we couldn't do that.

Jazz got right back to business. "I've been thinking about what you said. There's definitely something that's not right about Nikki Thunder. I get a bad feeling . . ."

"I had a bad Dream. A God Dream. I hate that I asked you to get involved in this now."

"Are you sure it wasn't just a pregnant dream? My mom said expectant mothers have very vivid dreams. You know she has mystical inclinations."

"Then her mystical inclinations should clue her in to the fact that my Dream was from God. Besides, I've had pregnant dreams before. There's a difference."

"You said prayer affects the outcome."

I sighed. "I did."

He took my hand and stroked it. "Then pray already; but I gotta look at this case harder."

"Maybe we should let this be the Ann Arbor Police Department's problem and step off."

"Your local boys in blue are done with this, unless we give them a reason to look back into it." He looked into my eyes and continued his gentle hand massage. "I know you're scared about the dream, but you can't do a three-sixty now and ask me to stop. I'm in this, Bell. And I'm going to see it through to the end."

"I don't want it to be *your* end."

"What did I just tell you to do?"

"Keep praying. I know."

Jazz's expression changed to a boyish, reticent look. Like he wanted to tell me something I'd spank him for. And not in a good way.

"What?" I said. "What are you thinking, Jazz Brown?"

"What do you mean, baby?" he said with absolutely no sincerity.

"You have to tell me something I'm not going to like."

"Who? Me?"

"Spill it."

"I was just wondering if you're going to go back to work tomorrow."

"I'm thinking of calling in."

"Fox isn't going to like that."

The only thing my boss, Dr. Eric Fox, hated more than me poking around in police business was me missing work because I got hurt poking around in police business. I'd been on probation ever since a nutjob almost took my head off strangling me. Eric didn't have an issue with me being injured. He had trouble with the fact that I'd brought it upon myself.

"I don't think the jail will fall apart because I won't be there to give someone the MMPI."

"It won't fall apart if you don't go back at all."

"Don't go back at all?"

Uh-oh. His emotional armor went up. He crossed his arms over his chest. He took a deep breath. "Don't get mad."

When someone starts a conversation with "Don't get mad," you can be sure they're about to tick you off. "Don't get mad at what, Jazz?"

"Maybe you should quit."

"*Quit?* My private practice doesn't bring in enough income for me to live on. It doesn't have benefits, either."

"Let me take care of you."

"No offense, Jazz, but I'd like to keep my job."

"What about your high-risk pregnancy? Wouldn't you *like* to keep our babies?"

"I'll work until I can't anymore."

"I want you to quit the jail."

"No."

"I demand it, Bell."

"You're not trying to pull the 'I'm the head' card again, are you, Neanderthal man?"

"You seem to forget that I *am* the head, woman. It's my job to protect and provide for you. Some women would kill for a man like me."

"Nikki Thunder?"

"She probably would, which is why I'm going to take her down if she killed her kid. I'm not going to let that nutjob hurt my family, and you happen to be my family. One thing I can say for her, though: *she* seems to *want* a life with me."

"I don't recommend you have kids with her."

He got up. The pinched expression on his face made it clear that I hadn't pleased him. "I gotta go."

He stormed out of the room and went back into the bathroom. I got up and went to him. He stood in front of the mirror adjusting his tie, a grim expression on his face. I tried to sweet-talk him, taking over the tie business.

"Baby, I didn't mean to offend you. I just don't think it's a good time to quit my job."

"No, Bell. You didn't mean to offend me. You never mean to offend me, but you do. Your problem is you don't trust me to be a man—a good man. Not to worry. Do your thing. I'm out. I've got work to do. Apparently so do you."

When his tie looked perfect, I gave it a pat. He jerked away from me. "I need to get to Zeekie's funeral early. We don't need to talk about this anymore. Looks like you've made up your mind."

"We can talk about it later."

He didn't acknowledge my existence. Jazz walked to the foyer, opened the closet door, and put on his coat.

I grabbed him as he put his hand on the doorknob.

"Wait."

He turned around. His being mad at me was one thing, but I'd had a Dream, and he was on his way to where Miss Black Wedding Dress held court.

I reached up and put my arms around his neck. He didn't lean down to kiss me, but I didn't care. I simply pulled his head down. I didn't force him out of my apartment permanently by giving him the full treatment while I still had morning breath. I pressed my lips on his until I could feel him relaxing and yielding to me. I trailed kisses to his ear. "I'm sorry," I whispered.

He looked at me. "I have to go."

"I love you." If he was the man I thought he was, he wouldn't leave without saying it. He knew the Dream worried me.

He shook his head as if I alone were the source of all his problems. "I love you, too. Why, I don't know. You're stubborn, hardheaded, and insubordinate."

"Aren't those all pretty much the same thing?"

"*Yes!* That's my point."

"Have a great day, Jazz. Stay safe."

"I will."

"I love you more than Columbo," I said.

"I bet you say that to all the detectives." A half smile tugged at his lips. "Get some rest, and call me if you need anything."

He pressed a kiss on both my cheeks and gave me a peck on the lips. "See you later."

"Okay," I said.

I'd make sure he would. And it would be sooner than he thought.

———

For a few moments I played "I'm going, I'm going *not*" with one of the carnations I had gotten as a gift when I was in the hospital. Finally, I abandoned the childish game.

Man up, girl! You had a Dream! You can't let Jazz go out there on his own.

Not that I'd offer much protection, but God knows I'd do

what I could. Jesus asked his disciples to watch with him. If I could do anything at all in this case it was to watch the predator intent on making Jazz her own.

I made quick work of dressing and grooming and got ready to meet my Jazz at the funeral. I stopped at the closet before I put my coat on, and placed my hand on my belly, silencing my guilt about our argument. I prayed that I hadn't miscalculated what my body could do.

You up for this, Mama?

I couldn't help smiling. I still couldn't believe I was going to have babies. *Babies!*

"Lord, don't let me do anything that could harm them. Give me wisdom."

I waited, fine-tuned to my intuition and the small, still voice of God's leading. I didn't hurt at the moment. I felt tired, but I didn't feel any pain. Just to be sure I padded back to the bathroom and opened the medicine cabinet behind the mirror. I grabbed the bottle of Tylenol that Dr. McLogan assured me was safe for the babies and took it with me.

See. I can be proactive.

Again I waited for something, anything, to tell me I shouldn't join him, but nothing did. I got my coat on, locked the doors, and headed over to the Rock House.

———

As Kalaya would say, "Holy Moses."

I arrived at the Rock House a little before nine. The Thunders had planned for the wake to take place an hour prior to the ten o'clock funeral. Cars overwhelmed the parking lot at the Rock House, spilling out into the streets. The media had come out in unbelievable numbers. When Jazz had been accused of murdering Kate, the media descended on him like vultures. The attention they gave Jazz didn't begin to compare to this. News vans bullied the SUVs and cars for parking spaces.

Oh, man. I hoped I could get in without being hassled, especially since most of the people present had probably obsessively watched all kinds of media coverage of the story—including my infamous appearance on CNN. Maybe no one would recognize me.

I gathered my courage and headed to the church. I had to press through the throngs—easily a thousand people—huddled all around. At last I neared the door to the church. That's when I heard it.

"Look!" a disembodied woman's voice said. "It's devil-vomit girl."

A crowd of reporters rushed me, thrusting microphones in my face. They fired questions at me. "Are you still possessed?" "Do you support Ezekiel Thunder?" "Do you believe God is going to raise Ezekiel Thunder the fourth from the dead?"

Jazz had taught me well. I kept walking, showing no emotion, offering nothing of myself.

Devil-vomit girl! I experienced no guilt for ignoring them.

When I finally got inside the church, I had to inch through more crowds of people to get to the sanctuary. While everyone could come view Zeekie's body, only certain people could stay inside the sanctuary with the family. I got in a long line and tried to gather enough courage to actually view Zeekie, my little Thunder boy, dead in a tiny casket. My knees shook.

Dear Jesus, please help me to endure this. And please help the Thunder family get through this terrible day. Let us celebrate his short life, Lord. And grant us peace. If Zeekie was murdered, please give us wisdom. Do as his father said, Lord. Speedily avenge his murder. Justice, Jesus! Please.

After my short prayer I felt stronger. Still I dreaded this funeral in a way I had dreaded few things in my life. After about fifteen minutes, I made it to the door of the sanctuary. I spotted Elisa. Her green eyes were red and swollen from crying. When she saw me, she greeted me with a warm hug. She'd come to see me at the hospital, delighted to hear my good news. She'd regaled me with her stories of morning sickness and wild kicking, and we both laughed about what it would be like to have two babies playing soccer inside of me. We had bonded in a special way, and being in her embrace gave me a bit more courage.

"I'm so glad you're here, Elisa."

"We pregnant women have to stick together." She gave me a final squeeze and released me. "Bell, this is the worst thing I've ever seen, and I've seen some terrible things in my life."

She'd lived with a madman in a cult. I knew she spoke the truth when she said that.

"I don't think I can take seeing him," I told her.

"You can. He looks beautiful. Like a sleeping angel." She released me to continue in the procession.

My gut twisted, and not from fibroid pain or morning sickness. I looked to the front of the sanctuary. Zeekie's terribly small silver coffin drew me like a moth to a flame. Oh Lord. I thought I'd die to see him like that. Again, I thought of my favorite ancient prayer—the Jesus Prayer. It was made famous by a book called *The Philokalia,* about a pilgrim who desired to learn what it meant to "pray without ceasing." For centuries the words to the prayer, "Lord Jesus Christ, Son of God, have mercy on me, a sinner," have been to pilgrims everywhere a continuous, uninterrupted calling on Jesus. My great-grandmother hadn't taught it to me; Rocky had. I'd never needed my beloved Jesus Prayer— the abbreviated version—more.

Kyrie eleison; Christe eleison; Kyrie eleison.

Lord, have mercy; Christ, have mercy; Lord, have mercy.

I shuffled with the line toward the casket, the prayer looping through my consciousness and out of my mouth. *Kyrie eleison; Christe eleison; Kyrie eleison.* Another step closer. *Lord, have mercy; Christ, have mercy; Lord, have mercy.* Repeated the sequence over and over.

Tears stung my eyes. I kept praying. Walking. Trying to keep breathing in and out while grief staggered me. Someone took my hand. Jazz. My rock—no, my *boulder.* My anchor. My mainstay, my rear guard, my protection. The man I'd do any good thing for, including quit my job. I squeezed his hand. "I don't think I can, baby."

"I've got your back."

More steps. The warmth of Jazz's hand. His strength. His intoxicating scent. His nearness until we made it to the front and stood before the casket.

A part of me wanted to look away, but my gaze stayed riveted on him. Oh, what a beautiful boy. Wheat-colored skin like

Elisa's. Endless eyelashes. Face like an angel. The few memories I had of him flooded my consciousness. Him saying my name, *Bay-yell.* Holding my cheeks with his tiny hands. Blowing a raspberry right on my lips. Zeekie was a love bug. But not my stupid yellow Volkswagen.

I thanked God for Sister Joy being his mother. Nikki Thunder had to be a psychopath. Only a crazy woman could resist this child's unadulterated, loving spirit.

"Good-bye, Zeekie. Tell Imani that I love her. Blow a raspberry on her lips for me."

I used to pray, "Come quickly, Lord Jesus," because once upon a time, my highest hope was for the day I'd meet Jesus face-to-face and He'd take me by the hand and lead me to my baby girl. Now I wanted Jesus to tarry long. I still wanted to see her, but I wanted to live. I was going to have her brothers or sisters or one of each! I wanted to stay here because I'd finally found my beloved. I was his, and he was mine. No more passive suicidal ideations—like letting that tumor grow without getting it checked out. *God, forgive me.*

Nikki Thunder didn't stand a chance.

I touched Zeekie's face, and Jazz led me away from the casket. Rocky had saved a seat for us, in a pew just behind the Thunders. My heart went out to Zekia and Zeke. Both were inconsolable, their cries shattering my heart. Tears spilled out of my eyes, and Jazz held on to me.

A peculiar memory occurred to me at that moment. I thought about being a teenager and attending the Church of God in Christ. At the end of every service, Elder Johnson would ask us to stand, lift our hands, and repeat after him. First, he'd say,

"What I say unto one, I say unto all." We would repeat after him, "Watch and pray. Live holy every day. Most of all obey."

I got the distinct impression that that is exactly what God wanted me to do.

I gently pulled myself out of my husband's arms and got started on my divinely inspired task. The first thing I did?

Watch.

chapter
sixteen

MOURNERS AND GAWKERS alike shuffled past Zeekie's casket, and I tried to keep my eyes off the silver box that would hold that dear boy's remains until Jesus called for him in the resurrection. The horror and the heartbreak of his death, the evil of the very idea that he died, senselessly, at the hands of his loved ones—all culminated at that tiny coffin, where Zeekie, wearing his little white suit, slept in Jesus.

The Jesus Prayer continued to roll around in my soul. I was thankful for the spiritual disciplines and the simplicity of practicing what the ancients did to root themselves in the things of God. I wondered about Ezekiel, seated in front of me. Did he know the Jesus Prayer like he knew *lectio divina*? What enabled him to bear the weight of this day? He'd buried a wife, lost a baby like David and Bathsheba had, and now had to surrender one of the most beautiful children—body and spirit—that I'd ever encountered. Or would he surrender? No one, other than the media, had mentioned his claim that God would raise his child from the dead.

I had to wonder if he meant God would raise him at the second coming of Christ, the hope of all believers. Or if he expected

a miracle today, and by his comments ensured that the event
would be televised. Was he sincere? Was he working the crowd,
the camera? I couldn't tell. By now the wake was just beginning.
We had a whole hour before the funeral, or resurrection celebration, would begin.

I turned my attention back to the mourners and noticed
a young woman tottering in red stilettos toward the Thunder
family. The voluptuous woman looked to be in her midtwenties—
plain features, skin the color of coffee grounds. She seemed to
compensate for her bland features with clothing that made her
look like a streetwalker. She wore a gold nose stud and a half-
dozen door-knocker earrings in each ear. She'd poured herself
unmercifully into a cheap red dress, a nightclub special. Her face
bore the pockmark scarring of a woman once hooked on heroin,
yet she had a hopeful air about her, as if she was finally getting
her act together. Her elaborate coiffure, a mound of slick black
curls piled high, looked like it had been shellacked into place. I
prayed she wouldn't go near the candles, which cast a soft glow
in the sanctuary. If that hair caught fire, the thing would flame up
and turn the poor woman into a human matchstick.

She stopped in front of Nikki, leaned over, and touched her
knee—a gesture of familiarity. "Girl," she said, "I seen you on TV.
I'm so sorry 'bout yo' baby. I 'ont know how you can do it after
you lost them other two."

Nikki turned into a block of ice. "I don't know you," she
said.

The woman looked confused. "Girl, it's me, Neicy. You know
who I am."

"I don't know you."

Nikki turned her head to catch the attention of one of the bodyguards flanking the Thunder family. Goliath and Jolly Green got on the job immediately. One of those mutants seized the offending woman's arm, but sistah did not go easy. A stream of expletives exploded out of her. Among the cuss words, this gift: "You ain't no Nikki Thunder. Yo' ol' skinny behind is Yawanza French. You ain't foolin' nobody." She exited the sanctuary shouting, "You ain't right, Wanzie. I'ma remember dis."

My husband and I exchanged glances. He had that "I told you so" gleam in his eye. With his head he motioned toward her. I stood up and excused myself.

"I'm going to the bathroom," I stage-whispered, in case anyone took a notion to tackle me, thinking I was out to take down Nikki.

Fortunately, media teemed outside the sanctuary. Nikki's manservant released "Yawanza's" former friend, probably not wanting to be immortalized on video manhandling a black woman. However, the sistah didn't want to forgive and forget. She hauled off and threw a punch worthy of the *Jerry Springer* show.

For a moment, it looked like the clown would retaliate, but Sistah Spitfire pulled out her *Karate Kid* moves and lifted one knee, her arms extended up in a crane pose. I walked up to her before she busted a move on him.

"Neicy!" I said.

She turned around confused.

"Girl, whatchu doing here? Where you been? I haven't seen you in, what . . . ?" I grabbed her arm. She followed me like a lamb to slaughter. I led her into the ladies' bathroom.

"I'm sorry, Neicy. You don't know me. I thought you had a little trouble with Big Boy there, and I didn't want to see you have to mess up your hair over him."

She patted the stiff monstrosity on her head. "Girl, this style cost me sixty-seven dollars. But looka he-ah, looka he-ah." She patted it for effect.

I watched in horror as she crooked her neck in some bizarre pose that made me wonder if she wasn't a contortionist. She placed her palms together and put them under her cheek like a makeshift pillow. "If I sleep like this . . . girl, this thang can last for 'bout two months."

"Now that's a bargain, Neicy." Pity she'd pay the difference to a chiropractor. Thank goodness she righted her head. "My name is Amanda Brown. I'm a psychologist."

She now looked leery of me.

"I'm investigating little Ezekiel Thunder's death. I couldn't help overhearing what you said to Nikki. I've been thinking that she may not be who we think she is. You say you know her as Yawanza French?"

"Um-hmm. I came all the way from Philly to see that no-good . . ."

Let's just say she failed to call Nikki a complimentary name.

"Would you mind going somewhere we can talk privately? I used to be a member of this church. I know where we can sit quietly, and I can get you back into the sanctuary if you want to pay your respects at the funeral."

"I ain't studyin' that ol' . . ." More unflattering names.

When she had exhausted her impressive range of expletives,

she continued, "I been to two of her baby funerals. And I came all this way to be here for her. We use to be cool."

"Tell me about that, Neicy."

She rolled her eyes and neck, not particularly at me. "I might as well. I ain't got nothin' to do now."

We went upstairs to one of the Sunday school classrooms—a room that filled me with nostalgia. Once upon a time, I taught Sunday school here, back when I didn't feel guilty every time I stepped into the house of God. *Lord, have mercy.*

Elisa had recently painted a Noah's Ark motif on the walls. That young woman had a phenomenal gift. I wondered if she'd do some work like this on the room Rocky was preparing for her baby—their baby if God kindly answered some of our prayers.

I motioned for her to sit in the adult-size chair. It didn't seem wise for either of us "substantial" women to try to sit in those little plastic chairs. Fortunately, each Sunday school class had a desk in the corner for the teacher to prepare his or her lessons. While Neicy sat in the chair, I hoisted me and the twins within onto the desk. "Tell me about Yawanza French," I said.

She didn't hesitate. "I ain't always did as good as I'm doin' now. I got in some trouble when I was younger. I ain't gon' lie. I'ma from aroun' the way, girl." She looked me in the eyes. She'd made peace with her past. "I knew Wanzie from the 'hood. We use to hang. Do some hustlin' together."

"What kind of hustling?"

She cast down her eyes, and her gaze shifted to the right. She wasn't lying. She was remembering.

"Like, one time Wanzie was staying with this old lady. Helping her out. She always got hookups like that. People would let her stay with them and stuff. Anyway, the lady died or some-thing, and Wanzie used her ATM card like she owned it. The lady musta had a lot of money. Wanzie went buck wild. Got me some stuff, too. We use ta be cool. She kinda liked the fine things in life."

Like my husband.

"I've noticed that," I said.

"She wasn't nothin' but a hood rat—just like the rest of us—but she gon' act like she all that."

"Tell me some other impressions you had of her at that time."

"I 'on't know. I guess she was greedy. If you had something she wanted, she went for you. I 'on't think she can be no real friend, 'specially after how she just played me."

"I'm sorry you came all this way and got that kind of treat-ment. But, Neicy, you may be a godsend. Tell me about these babies of hers that died."

"She was always after some older man."

I noticed that, too, but I let Neicy tell her story.

"She got with this brotha when she was fourteen. He was 'bout twenty-eight. Big baller in the 'hood. Got the bangin' ride, always lookin' fly. He da dope man, but be actin' like he legit. He one of them brothas that always be talkin' 'bout ideas he got for a business, but he don't do nothin' but sell dope and talk smack."

I nodded. I knew the type. They came to the county jail and held court before they went to prison, only to find out what their rank truly was. God help them.

"Anyway," she said, head rocking as she talked, "she hooked up with him, and they was s'posed to open a boutique. She gets pregnant, and it don't look like no boutique is gon' happen. She had that baby, and he died from SIDS, girl."

I shook my head. "That's tough."

"And you know what? She ended up with this other guy, this one was this white man 'bout forty. Now, this one really did seem to have it together. He had a house, a business, drove a nice ride, hooked Wanzie up, and she was in a nice truck. He gave her all his money, but you know. He ain't satisfy her, you know?"

"I can imagine."

"She would cheat on that poor man. He would come all up in the 'hood, looking for her. He kept giving her money tryna buy love, but she ain't love him. They had a baby, too. I guess when that baby came, she got sick of her ol' man. Kept talking 'bout leavin', but she ain't wanna give up that money. Anyway, she had some bad luck, because that baby died of SIDS, too, and right after that the poor man killed hisself. Least that's what she said. Police said it was *inconclusive*."

A chill went through me. I knew lightning sometimes strikes twice, but I thought an unsettling *pattern* had emerged. I couldn't wait to get back to Jazz, and to my reference books at home.

"How old was she when this happened?"

"Sixteen."

Meaning the following year she met Ezekiel Thunder, and shortly thereafter his wife inexplicably died.

Shazam!

"What city did you and Yawanza live in?"

"We was in Philly back then. She moved to Detroit after the white guy died, 'specially when all his estate went to probate and she ain't get nothin'. I ain't seen her since, until I saw her

on TV talkin' 'bout her baby drowning. I came all the way from
Philly . . ."

The rest of what Neicy said sounded like Charlie Brown's
schoolteacher. *Wah wonk wah wah wonk wonk* . . .

"I don't have any more questions, Neicy. Thank you for your
information. Can you give me a number I can contact you at?"

She dug in her big red Coach knockoff that every urban
beauty-supply store on Earth sells for sixteen bucks. She fished
out a piece of paper littered with tobacco. Scrawled her cell
phone number on the paper with a black kohl eyeliner pencil.
She turned to the mirror and used the same liner to trace her lip
line and then filled in her lips with a glistening white gloss.

"I'll be in touch. God bless you, Neicy."

I reached in my own purse—my Birkin knock-off that cost
considerably more than sixteen dollars—and gave her the business card for my private practice. I took out two twenty-dollar
bills and handed them to her. "Buy yourself a good lunch before
you head back to Philly. It's on me."

"Thanks, Miss Brown."

"Mrs."

I smiled. I was *Mrs.* Amanda Brown.

Neicy torpedoed her girth toward me and squeezed me like
we were the best of friends. "Least I got to meet you," she said. "I
spent my last tryna get a ticket here. I thought I was gon' eat after
the funeral. Girl, this a blessing."

"You keep doing the good work you're doing on yourself,
Neicy. Call me anytime."

"Watch yo' back around Yawanza. She ain't right."

An understatement.

The image of my great-grandmother flashed in my mind, comforting and familiar, as full of feel-good as a childhood song, now a part of me. Ma Brown came quoting one of her favorite scriptures.

For the Lord will go before you, the God of Israel will be your rear guard.

I whispered, *Thank you, Jesus,* in my soul. Neicy didn't have to worry. My back was taken care of.

Nikki, however, had better watch hers, because if what I was beginning to think about her was true, I'd personally take her down. She'd be in a black wedding gown, all right. But she'd take my husband with her over my dead body.

I meant that.

But first, I had to pee.

————

When I sat back down with Jazz, a fierce determination seized me. I leaned into him. "I love you. You're mine, and nothing and nobody is going to take you away from me."

He grinned. "I'd send you to the bathroom more often if you didn't already go a lot anyway." Jazz flung his arm around the back of the chair then inclined to whisper to me, "Did you get anything?"

I nodded.

"Good girl."

I don't know how many people came out to pay respects, but so many came through the doors of the Rock House, I didn't think the place could bear the weight. I thought there would be more time for people to talk to the family during the hour set aside for the wake, but not too many ventured to make conversation. Ezekiel stood to hug and chat with a guest here and there, but that's about it. When Zekia and Zeke saw familiar faces, they'd break again, poor kids. People kept telling those babies that this wasn't their fault, and they'd shrink a little more. How they'd endure for another hour, I didn't know. Nikki Thunder stayed seated, wearing a mask of stoic serenity. She sickened me.

Finally the funeral started. I didn't know how Rocky would hold up. The Rock House had never been filled to capacity and beyond, and the media brouhaha had to unsettle him. Rocky's style of simple, honest relationships with God and others didn't leave room for ministry superstars who had basketball players on steroids as bodyguards and who hawked miracle prosperity oil for a love offering.

As a pastor, Rocky's strength lies in his being the greatest *servant* in the church. Here at the Rock House, you were as good as the love you gave. It astounded me that he'd stay involved with someone like Ezekiel Thunder. Then again, his loyalty knew no bounds. He'd forgiven me. He'd surely forgive the man who'd led him to Christ. It was no stretch to imagine Rocky encouraging Thunder to go back to the Jesus he'd met as a young boy when he knelt on the grass by the crude wooden bench and surrendered all.

Rocky looked uncomfortable as he approached the microphone. He had on a suit! In all the years I'd known him, he'd worn a suit only once—when he was ordained. He had done it then for his mother. I smiled despite the solemn occasion. He must have worn the suit this time for Ezekiel. His tie was askew,

probably because he had no clue how to tie one, and his dreadlocks were pulled back by a black band. He had his acoustic guitar in his hand.

He cleared his throat and began to exhort us. "Brothers and
sisters in Christ. This is not a funeral. It's a celebration of life—a
life taken away too soon."

A few "Amens" floated toward him. Heads nodded their
agreement.

"I don't have any clichés to offer. I don't understand this
death. I don't like it. I wish I could turn back time and—" His
voice broke, and he swallowed. Took a deep breath to regain his
composure. Spoke softer. "I would turn back time and protect
him."

He locked eyes with his spiritual father. "Ezekiel, I'm a little
mad at God today." A few gasps from the crowd. "God knows
how I feel, so I won't pretend otherwise, but you taught me a
long time ago something I never forgot."

Ezekiel nodded and wiped his eyes. Tears slid down Rocky's
face as he shared his mentor's burden of grief. I thought I would
come undone at the sight of them.

Rocky wiped his eyes. "You taught me that God is faithful. I
was a little boy when you told me that, and it stayed with me. I've
seen God's faithfulness again and again."

He propped his guitar against the podium. Walked down the
few stairs from the pulpit and went to his mentor. Rocky knelt
before Ezekiel. "You have been a father to me. I love you, Ezekiel.
God never forgot the good deeds you've done, even if other people have. He loves you." He took Ezekiel's hands in his. "Where
you and I aren't faithful, God is. We fall from the right hand of

God, but, Dad, He catches us in His left hand. Your favorite scripture is Mark chapter nine, verse twenty-three. You always liked the book of Mark. You used to tell me it was the *power* Gospel. Remember?"

Ezekiel nodded, letting his tears flow freely. Rocky's tears trailed down his face, too.

"And you loved that scripture in the King James Version. I teach using NIV, *The Message*—almost anything but King James, but I always remember that scripture in the King's English because you taught it to me. 'Jesus said unto him, If thou canst believe, all things are possible to him that believeth.'"

Still kneeling, Rocky scooted closer to Ezekiel. "All things are possible. I believe with you that God can raise little Zeekie from the dead."

More gasps across the sanctuary, including my own. And speaking of raising, my blood pressure must have spiked along with my heart rate. Without thinking, I moved to the edge of my seat, waiting in horror for the fiasco that was about to happen.

"And we know God is faithful. Zeekie is with Jesus now. He is happier than he's ever been. He's kissing Jesus the same way he kissed *everybody*."

All of us who knew Zeekie laughed.

Rocky placed his hand on Thunder's knee. Again his voice broke with emotion. "Let Him stay with Jesus, Dad, knowing that God is faithful and your baby is safe in His loving care. Jesus will raise him up again when He raises all of us who belong to Christ. God will resurrect him. Let Him do it in His own time. In God's time."

The two men embraced. People began to stand and applaud.

I don't think there was a dry eye in the house. When Ezekiel released him, Rocky humbly walked back to the pulpit, stood before the mic, and began to serenade God with *Great Is Thy Faithfulness*. He sang every verse, and like a good prophet, he ushered us into the throne room of God. Our collective tears became like baptismal waters, and God's tender presence raised us from our grief. With every verse, I felt renewed, and I doubted if I alone experienced such grace.

My own thoughts became psalms. I placed my hand on my baby bump and sang with gusto. My faith was smaller than a tiny mustard seed, and yet God gave me *more* than what my heart desired most in this world. I hadn't been faithful, but God stayed faithful. He didn't change, and His compassion hadn't failed, just as Rocky sang. I'd received the new mercies that every day came with the promise of a new morning. I looked at my husband, my beautiful model of a husband. *Dear Jesus, look what you've given me.*

I closed my fists and squeezed them together with all my might. I'd used this technique many times in therapy. My fingernails dug into my palms and I burned into my heart the memory of this sweet moment with God. Most of the time I used the exercise as a physical symbol of letting go. Uncurling my fist acted as the release. This time I used it to hold on, as Rocky did, to God's faithfulness.

I took a deep breath, and a scripture I'd memorized long ago, Isaiah 46:3–4, came to me. I hadn't thought of it in ages. It rolled in waves inside of me.

You who have been borne by Me from birth and have been carried from the womb; even to your old age I will be the same, and even to your

graying years I will bear you! I have done it, and I will carry you; and
I will bear you and I will deliver you.

I slowly released my nagging doubt. I felt bound by love, carried by God, and free. Oh Lord, I wanted to go confidently with God for the rest of my life, knowing He loved me.

Zeekie's voice came to me in that moment. "Bay-yell. I love you."

"I love you too, Jesus," I said.

Zeekie would have wanted it that way.

As Rocky sang, Nikki Thunder stood. She walked to the pulpit and stood right beside Rocky, waiting patiently until he was done. He noticed her and graciously sang the last stanza, bowed to her, and surrendered the microphone.

I didn't think they'd planned this. I had to wonder if the attention Rocky gave his spiritual father hadn't incensed her, since he hadn't included her in the moment. I know Rocky would never purposely slight her. I assumed what he had to share was for Ezekiel Thunder, and him alone. Rocky would love on all the appropriate parties in their time.

Nikki Thunder looked immaculate. She had on a black chiffon and knit dress with three-quarter-length sleeves and an empire waist. It looked a little soft, a little goth, and a little playful and sexy. Not quite the understated black suit I'd have worn. Her hair fell down in soft Miss Clairol auburn waves. Her voice was steady. "I want to testify."

She had our attention with her looks alone.

"My mother and father were drug addicts who neglected me and my little brother . . ."

Nikki went on to astound us with a powerful testimony of

how she'd found her parents dead from an overdose when she was thirteen. How she'd tried to care for her little brother until he caught pneumonia and died and she was placed in a foster home.

She spoke kindly to Zekia and Zeke, saying she'd always felt responsible for both her parents' and her brother's death, so she understood their feelings about being responsible for Zeekie's death. She said when she had no one, she met Ezekiel, and he loved her for who she was.

She told about how she'd been misguided and promiscuous. How she'd had two babies but lost them. God had taken her third because of her sins. And now her fourth baby was gone in a tragic accident. "The Lord giveth, and the Lord taketh away," she said. She lifted her hands. "Blessed be the name of the Lord."

Her sex appeal, her flawless delivery, the crying in exactly the right moments—the cameramen would love her. She walked down those few steps from the pulpit and stood before her step-children, freeing them from any responsibility for Zeekie's going to be with Jesus. She put her hands on each of their heads and pronounced blessings.

Cameras flashed wildly. She was being videotaped, broadcast via satellite, globally podcast, and heaven only knows what else.

I nudged Jazz. He subtly nodded to acknowledge me. We continued to watch Nikki intently. The entire audience was captivated.

Then she addressed her husband. "Daddy," she said, revolting me because she called him that as an endearment. "I vowed to God that I would love, honor, and obey you for the rest of my days. Not once have you let me down. Not once have you been unfaithful. I continue to honor you, but, baby, Rocky is right. We've got to let Zeekie go."

Tears streamed down her face. "I didn't think I could take losing another baby, but Ga-*awd*!" She raised her hands. "Ha-ba-ba-shondo!" That's the same tongue Ezekiel Thunder used. In fact, I'd heard that word a lot! Did it mean something? Was there a Holy Spirit interpreter in the room who could clear this up? Is that something widely said in heaven by the cherubim? I'd have to ask Mason about it. He knew Greek and Hebrew.

My mind actually meandered back to Nikki. After she made God a two-syllable word and spoke in unknown tongues, she said He was going to give her all her babies back. One day. She said, "Let him go, Zeke. God will give him back."

Honestly! I thought she'd break out into a few verses of Diana Ross and the Supremes' "Someday We'll Be Together." She did have that same diva quality as Diana. But she didn't sing. She riveted us for another half hour with stories about her hard life.

Yowza Yawanza. And speaking of Yawanza, she didn't mention that was or had ever been her name or that her first two babies had died of SIDS.

I sure hoped she'd tell us something about Zeekie. I backtracked and thought about what Neicy said.

She was all about Wanzie, you know?

That's all I knew for certain. If Nikki/Yawanza was truly what I thought she was, I'd have to dig to prove it. But unlike on television, a *real* homicide case calls for good police work and strong allies everywhere in the community. I'd need to make my case, first to my husband and then to the Ann Arbor police.

I listened to Nikki again. Even I had to admit how compelling she was. Some of what she said gave me chills.

Still, she could be a psychopath. Ted Bundy proved murderers could be effective speakers. I stared at Zeekie's casket.

Did your own mama kill you, baby? Did she make it happen?

Am I wrong about all of this because I had misgivings about Nikki from the start?

Am I a spiritual elitist like Rocky said?

I closed my eyes and saw Zeekie in his little white suit.

You deserve somebody to look at the hard things. I'll help you, my little Thunder boy.

Maybe I'd prove myself wrong. If I did, more than just Zeekie would rest in peace.

I may have wished for Zeekie to rest in peace, but he'd do no such thing at his funeral. After Nikki's remarks, Elisa waddled to the stage and wept through reading his obituary. Why they'd ask a pregnant woman to handle that task baffled me. I couldn't have done it! The obituary wrecked me, too. Jazz had to be my official Kleenex dispenser, handing me tissue after tissue.

Rocky gave a short eulogy, and more friends gave remarks. Truthfully, no one made the impact Nikki had. That is, until people were asked to pay their last respects before they closed the coffin.

I stood to have one more excruciating moment with Zeekie. Jazz grabbed my arm and gently pulled me back to my seat.

"What?" I whispered.

He leaned toward me. "Baby, I know he meant a lot to you, even in the short time he touched your life, but if you go up there knowing they're about to close the casket, I'm going to have to scrape you up off the carpet. It'll be bloody. It'll be messy. It'll leave a stain. Why don't we skip that drama?"

"But, Jazz . . ."

"You're pregnant. Emotional. And crazy. I need you to trust me on this."

I pouted. He grinned, and goodness me, I felt all warm and fuzzy. "Will you hold my hand?"

"I'll do more than that, *Jane.*"

Honestly! We were at a funeral! Flirting at a funeral just seemed wrong.

So why couldn't I stop smiling?

He'd called it right. Pregnant. Emotional. Crazy. But I trusted him enough to listen. Thank goodness, because Sister Lou blew a gasket.

It happened after the crowd said good-bye and the Thunder family huddled around the casket—Sister Lou and Sister Joy included.

Carly and I made a deal a long time ago that whoever died first, the remaining one would, as Ma Brown used to say, "cut a fool" at the funeral. The surviving sister would cry out in agony, try to crawl into the casket, shout with fist pounding the air, "God, *whyyyyyyyy?*"

We'd make sure to have on hand some of those nurses you see in some churches. The kind that aren't really nurses but are trained to bring water to the preacher, circle individuals in the throes of ecstasy, and shout—by that I mean dance—with wild abandon as led by the Holy Spirit. They could also discreetly drape knees—covered and otherwise—of females slain in the Spirit. They were most needed, however, at funerals, where someone would inevitably faint. I think they may be licensed and certified to wield powerful smelling salts.

And then the dedicated, surviving sister would let out a piercing scream and fall into a dead faint. Nurses to the rescue.

Someone must have made Sister Lou the official "cut a fool" person. That woman's plaintive wail should have shattered the stained glass.

Jazz almost jumped out of his skin.

He muttered something foul about Pentecostals. Honestly! Did he have any respect for the house of God?

Lou paced the floor, speaking in tongues, arms flailing about, until she got to Ezekiel Thunder. That woman pounded him with her fist. "You was s'posed to raise him from the dead. You was s'posed to raise him. She said you was gon' fast and pray. These kind only go out with—"

Before anyone could overcome the shock of seeing her beat up her brother right in front of the baby's casket, poor Lou started jerking and screaming. Incoherent babbling replaced any utterances one could attribute to the Holy Spirit.

I jumped out of my seat.

Jazz yanked me back down. "Jazzy, I think she's moving out of her normal repertoire of crazy. I think she's about to have a psychotic break."

"Today you're not a psychologist."

"It's unethical not to help her."

"I'll call nine-one-one."

He whipped his cell phone out of his pocket, punched the three digits and waited for the operator. Some of the funeral attendees had gathered around the front like they were in Jerry Springer's studio audience. Since Jazz was occupied calling for help, I slipped away from him.

"Jane!" And when that didn't work. *"Luuuuuceeeeeeee!"*

I wasn't so pregnant that I couldn't be fast. My center of gravity may have shifted, but my gait hadn't been significantly altered. I pushed through the crowd shouting, "I'm a doctor."

Yeah. Well. I did have a doctorate! And I had dealt with psychotics.

Rocky must have seen me coming. He grabbed my arm and maneuvered me through the masses to Sister Lou. Two or three men held her down.

"Get this crowd to back up."

Goliath and Jolly Green made themselves useful by frightening all but the media back. I certainly didn't feel up to being a television personality again, but I had to do what I had to do.

I dropped to my knees in front of Lou, who was fighting wildly. "Hold her," I said to the impromptu orderlies.

I got close enough for Lou to hear me over the hullabaloo. "Sister Lou. It's Amanda. Remember when you helped me? Remember when you cast that interracial-dating-and-adultery demon out of me?"

She kept fighting. Didn't respond.

"Lou, I'm Amanda. You *helped* me. Now I want to help you."

Her hair had fallen out of the bun she held it in. Her skirt had hiked up her thighs. I tugged at it. "I want you to listen to me,

Louella. You have to stop fighting, because no one wants you to hurt yourself."

Tears rolled down her cheeks. She howled in pain.

"Honey, I know you wanted to help Zeekie, but he's with Jesus, and that's a good place for him. He's not in any pain. He's probably playing with my little girl."

She began to rock back and forth.

"Will you let me help you, Louella?"

She didn't speak, just rocked back and forth.

I scooted closer. Someone shouted, "Hey, isn't that devil-vomit girl?"

I ignored them. I motioned for the men to keep holding her, and I gently placed my arms around Lou. I had never heard such mournful cries. I held her like I would a child. She cried and cried in my arms.

I didn't feel like a psychologist. I felt like what I imagined a mother must feel, a little helpless, trying to be strong when I just wanted to sit on the floor and cry with her—right in front of Zeekie's casket.

The family proceeded to close the lid. The soft thump and Zekia's resultant gut-wrenching cries felt like a stab to my heart. The knowledge that no one on Earth would see his beautiful little face again plunged me so deeply into grief that I didn't know if I'd ever see my way out.

I'd lost the professional distance I desperately needed to cling to. No matter that I'd only met him once, he seemed to be a part of me. Inside me.

Jazz had tried to keep me from this. Pregnant. Emotional. And crazy. At a baby's funeral—a recipe for disaster. I kept holding Lou, rocking with her, trying not to break down. My clinical skills abandoned me. All I could think about was Sasha. I did what my mother taught me.

I sang "All the Pretty Little Horses" softly to Sister Lou until the ambulance came. I accompanied her to the University of Michigan Psychiatric Emergency department. The staff knew me from times when I'd come in with an inmate from the jail. They let me stay with her, and I ended up staying several hours.

By five in the evening I called a cab to go home. I wasn't in a hurry to deal with an angry husband.

I wondered if he'd be willing, despite his anger, to scrape me off the floor, because that's exactly where I was.

chapter
seventeen

I DIDN'T HAVE to put my key in the door. Mr. Intuition whipped it open just like he had the night he'd broken into my apartment and ordered Chinese. That time he'd gone to the door and yanked it open, leaving a deliveryman standing, mouth agape, with his fist poised in the air, ready to knock.

I expected him to be angry, but he wasn't.

He pulled me into a hug and kissed my forehead. He pulled away from me enough to look into my face. "How do you feel?"

"I think you're going to need that scraper you talked about."

He shook his head, but not in disgust. It looked more like pity. He bent and planted a kiss in my braids. I got teary again.

"I'm so tired, Jazzy."

"I know. Are you hungry?"

"No."

"Can't you eat a teeny-weeny meal, for me?"

I shook my head.

"I'll let you slide this time. How 'bout a nice hot shower?"

I loved baths, but he was sensitive enough to not mention soaking in a tub when we'd just laid Zeekie to rest. I didn't know when I'd want to take a bath again.

I slid my boots off. I hadn't taken my coat or purse when I went with the ambulance. Jazz hadn't questioned me as I left with the paramedics. I knew he'd collect my things and bring them home.

He didn't yell at me for getting involved or being gone for hours or risking my personal safety by dealing with what he'd call "a nutjob." He'd become a beta male, at least for now.

Jazz led me by the hand into the bathroom. He turned on the shower and checked the water for a comfortable temperature. He had a fluffy towel waiting for me. And fresh flowers. Not that the house didn't already look like a botanical garden with the flowers from my overnight stay in the hospital.

We faced each other as he unbuttoned my blouse, unzipped my skirt, and removed both. Then my slip and everything else.

He walked me to the shower and urged me to get in.

"When I hear the water go off I'll bring you your spa bath-robe."

"I don't have a spa bathrobe."

"You have one now."

He gave me the Colgate smile, and I marveled at the wonder of this man.

"Thank you, Jazz."

"No problem."

I stepped into the shower and let the hot water soothe me. It didn't offer the womb-like environment of soaking in a bathtub, but the cold air and the chilly hospital waiting room had nearly numbed me, and I welcomed the relief the shower offered. He'd gotten new soap for me, in my favorite lavender scent. I almost expected him to join me.

I turned off the water, and just as he'd said, he had a brand-new white spa-quality bathrobe waiting for me. I didn't even bother with the towel. "Come to Mama," I said.

"Me or the bathrobe?" he teased.

"Both of you."

He helped me into the robe, and we strolled back to our bedroom. A week ago it was *my* bedroom, and I hadn't known I was pregnant. Hadn't seen Jazz in weeks. The changes delighted, frightened, and disoriented me all at once.

He'd changed the bedding. We now had a new comforter—a colorful Indian-inspired pattern with little plastic mirrors sewn to the surface—and new soft Egyptian-cotton sheets in red. He'd placed one of his mother's paintings of a man and woman embracing on the wall above the headboard of my bed—*our* bed! The man was fair-skinned like Jazz, the woman, while not peanut-butter-colored like Jazz insisted I was, was darker than her lover. Red roses rested in a vase on my night table. I loved it all.

I sat on the bed. "This is all so beautiful. I thought you'd be mad at me."

"I am mad at you, love. I'm always mad at you."

"Do you still hate me?"

He nodded. "I hate you *very* much."

"'Hate' is a strong word."

"My feelings for you are very strong."

I lay down on the bed and cuddled with one of the new paisley throw pillows. "Stay with me. I need you."

"I'm not going anywhere. You need rest."

"I want us to make love."

He startled. "*Jane!* What's gotten into you?"

"You do realize I could give you a very naughty response."

He blushed. "It's too early. You just got out of the hospital."

"I feel fine." I reached for his thigh. "Please."

He looked away from me. Thought for a few moments. "Are you sure you're okay? We won't hurt the babies?"

"I don't think so, Jazzy."

He looked nervous. Shy. I didn't know what to think. This is Mr. Naughty himself and now . . . I withdrew my hand.

His head hung down.

My tummy did a flip, and it wasn't the babies moving. I willed the tears of humiliation stinging my eyes not to fall.

"I guess I'm emotional." I spoke with the forced enthusiasm of a person trying to save face. I turned my body away from him. "Just forget I asked."

He touched my shoulder. *"No!"* He'd said it louder than he needed to. Spoke more softly, "No, I'm just . . . I'm going to take a shower. I'll be back in a few minutes. Don't go anywhere, okay?"

He squeezed my arm, leaned over, and kissed my cheek, then headed to the bathroom.

I heard the water go on as my eyelids tried to blink away the heaviness threatening to overtake me. I fell asleep waiting for Jazz to come to me.

———

His kisses awakened me. I had to touch his hair, tangle my hands in his rough brown curls. I drank in his scent . . .

Wait. That wasn't his scent. Part of my brain remained in a

sleepy-headed fog, but the smell had triggered a vague olfactory memory. A bad one. But this was Jazz. My eyes fluttered open. Jazz was kissing me. My hands were still in his hair. The smell was liquor seeping out of his pores.

I glanced at the clock. I'd slept for hours, and Jazz had clearly imbibed more than his share, once again.

"Jazz?" I said slowly. Trying to process what was going on between us.

But he didn't stop kissing. And I couldn't stop wanting him.

My mind went to war with my body, went to some dark memory of my father's drunken affection—nothing inappropriate. He didn't molest me or any such thing. He's what one would call a "happy drunk." But when my mother would see him in that altered state, she'd lacerate him. Sometimes for hours. I'd listen in my bedroom to her crush his spirit. The more she trashed him, the more he drank. The only time they got along was when they went into the bedroom and locked the door behind them. Like Jazz and me?

Oh God.

A woman always rues the day she turns into her mother. My constant stream of acrid thoughts, calling women who annoyed or threatened me cows and heifers, my flair for the dramatic when I was *not* onstage—all those things I attributed to Sasha's influence. But I'd married an alcoholic. All the warnings she'd given me. All the awful stories she told me to poison me against my dad. The fear of imbibing alcohol that made me mostly a teetotaler. My psychology degrees. All of it rushed to my mind.

But not my body.

The smell of alcohol on him sickened me, while my husband's touch thrilled me. I never asked him to stop.

I wanted him anyway, and hated myself for it.

———————

I threw up. It's a little difficult to explain, after being so passionate with Jazz, but his essence of Jack Daniel's finally got the better of me. I came back to the bed, and he'd gone into the living room. He'd poured himself another drink and turned on the television loud enough to annoy me.

I wanted to say something to him, but I'd been blindsided by the thought that instead of pouncing on me when I first approached him, he'd hemmed and hawed and had to get drunk before he could bring himself to touch me.

We kid sometimes that we hate each other, but in that blistering moment of reflection, when I believed with all my heart he couldn't stand to make love with me without medicating himself, I truly did hate him. Or was it myself I hated?

He didn't look thrilled with me, either.

I turned to go back to bed alone. He could get his own blanket and pillow. Or not.

I closed my bedroom door and locked it, even though I knew he could get in with minimal effort. A vicious headache throbbed at my temples and I put a pillow over my head. Shoot. Maybe I could suffocate myself with my pillow.

Who was I kidding? While I felt bad enough to die, I had no intention of doing so. I wanted to see my babies!

Instead, I let the pillow muffle the sound of me crying myself to sleep.

———————

I made morning prayer a simple affair: "Help."

It didn't surprise me that I woke before Jazz. I showered and put on a simple dropped-waist dress. I'd gotten it at the art fair last year, and it had a funky African-inspired pattern painted on the front. Most of my pants had gotten too tight at the waist. Not even two months along, and Maggie had called it right: I needed maternity clothes.

The thought of it saddened me. Sometimes, as much as I reveled in it, I wondered if I was really pregnant or just coming down with a virus. I couldn't feel them move yet. I felt their presence, and they'd certainly changed my body, but I longed for the day I could feel their kicks.

I went into the bathroom and closed the door so I could look at myself in the full-length mirror behind the door. I turned sideways to look at my baby bump. I put my hands on it.

"Thank you, Jesus."

As soon as my thanks slipped out of my mouth, that still, small inward voice whispered to me, *Thank me for Jazz.*

I sighed. Grumbled. Surrendered. "Thank you for Jazz. Help me not to throttle him."

I waited for my rebuke. It didn't come.

"Okay. Now you've got me self-rebuking. I'm sorry. Please help me to see that, like many adult children of alcoholics, I'm simply reacting to an incident that triggered memories of some traumatic events that . . ."

I took a deep breath. Then another. Slipped a ponytail holder off my wrist and gathered my braids into a ponytail. I really loved the long hair, even if it was extensions. *I should have let my hair grow like Sasha said.*

The still, small voice decided to be chatty.

Don't avoid me.

I put my hands behind my neck to massage away the tension. "I know I tried to hide behind intellectualizing. I don't want us to be like Ma and Daddy. Jazz hurt my feelings. It can't be wrong to want him to desire me . . ."

Frustration flushed my cheeks. "Shoot! Don't make me do this right now. Please."

I didn't feel anymore prompts from God.

I went back into the bedroom and pulled a small suitcase out of my closet. I wasn't sure how long I'd be gone. Not that all my clothes still fit. I grabbed my favorite shirts and a dressy blouse for work. I'd go shopping for some maternity slacks.

I didn't cry as I packed. I told myself that I'd be back in a few days. I just needed to clear my head. Zeekie's death. My pregnancy. Jazz moving in. Last night. All of it swirled around and clashed in my mind like colors in a kaleidoscope. I wanted to rest. To think, that's all.

When I'd finished, I quietly shuffled through the living room. I didn't want to wake Jazz. I didn't have to worry. He wasn't on the couch anymore. My stomach did a back flip. I'd hoped to slip out and leave him a note. The toilet flushed. I set the suitcase next to the door and went back into the living room, sat on the couch, and waited for him.

He didn't come out of the bathroom naked, thank the Lord, because it's possible that I'd not have made it out the door. As it was, the sight of his bare chest made my heart palpitate. He had on a pair of sweatpants, and his white athletic socks slouched at his ankles. When he saw me on the couch, he headed for the kitchen.

"Jazz?"

He stopped, sighed, and turned to me. "Do you think I can have a cup of coffee before we square off and come out fighting?"

When the first thing he said to me in the morning hurt my feelings, I could only guess that the conversation would head south from there.

"Go ahead."

As if he could read my mind, he addressed my hurt. "I didn't say that to intentionally hurt you, Bell, but let's be honest. We're not going to have a pleasant little chat. I'm taller, stronger, and meaner than you. Let me have a cup of coffee so that I'm not the total jerk I'm capable of being."

If he put it that way . . .

Even mean, coffeeless Jazz had a thoughtful side. "Would you like something?"

"No, thank you."

"Have you eaten, Bell?"

"No."

"How are you supposed to feed my babies?"

"I'll eat later."

"Later? When you leave?"

I slouched into the sofa cushions, exhausted already. "Just get your coffee."

"No time to feed my children? You must be *anxious* to get to where you're going."

"So you *are* ready to fight?"

That comment must have knocked the wind out of him. He retreated to the kitchen. I had no idea what I'd say to him. I'd tried to come up with a little speech in my head. Nothing I thought of seemed adequate.

Jazz came back into the living room a few minutes later. He sat down in one of the chairs opposite the sofa. I tried to mask my disappointment that he didn't sit on the sofa with me.

He took a few sips of coffee. A few more. Went straight for the jugular.

"Why are you leaving me?"

"I'm not leaving you, I—"

He slammed the cup on the coffee table. "You're dressed, even though you don't have to go into work, your suitcase is at the door, and you want to"—he crooked his index and middle fingers on both hands in the gesture for quotation marks—"talk."

"I don't think I'll be able to"—I repeated his gesture—"talk." I placed my hands on my lap. "If you keep interrupting me."

"Look. I'm hung over. I really don't feel like any crap. You're leaving me, and I want to know why."

"Last night—"

He groaned. "Why do we have to have a Cecil B. DeMille epic whenever we sleep together? We've done it twice. The first time, I catch you making out with your *boyfriend* afterward. We do it again, and you pack up to leave me."

"May I remind you that the first time *you* were the one who left. After you threw your keys at me and told me to go to hell."

"I didn't throw my keys *at* you. If I had, I wouldn't have missed."

"Jazz, I don't want to fight. I just want to go—"

"Are you going to see a lawyer? Because I know a great one. He can get you right out of a disastrous marriage that lasted all of five minutes. Ask me how I know."

"You weren't kidding about being a jerk."

He picked up his coffee and took a long drink of the hot liquid. "Why didn't you ask *me* to leave? Wouldn't that be easier?"

"Would you have gone?"

"No."

"Why not?"

"Because God told me to live with you. You want to be disobedient, go right ahead."

The man exasperated me to no end. I probably did the same to him. I tried to keep my growing frustration in check. "Jazz. I'm merely trying to—"

"Why don't you go already and stop tormenting me with your endless discussions."

My mouth flew open. "Hey, Jazzy, I know! Why don't you toss me out the door and throw my suitcase right on top of me."

"Why can't we just be normal, Bell? Be together. Cuddle. Say I love you. Go to sleep."

I'd had enough of him. Enough! "You know what the problem with that is, Jazz? We weren't *together*."

"I beg to differ."

"Oh no, beloved. We weren't together at all."

"Is this some kind of semantic thing?"

"No, it's not. Being together means you're fully present. You were in a drunken stupor, and my mind kept tripping over the thought that you had to get drunk before you could be with me. We were on two different planets."

"Bell—"

"No, I'm going to talk now, Jazz. My father was an alcoholic. And last night I saw my life stretched out before me, with this gorgeous man who doesn't really want me but tolerates me because I'm the mother of his children."

"Bell, wait. It wasn't—"

"Shut up!"

He actually did.

"I don't know what we did last night, because I don't understand us. For all my knowledge of human behavior, I'm a total idiot when it comes to Bell and Jazz. You flirt outrageously with me, move yourself in here, parade around naked, and insist on sleeping in the bed with me. You take care of me and romance me. You bombard me with *all that Jazz,* and when I finally trust you enough to *ask you* to make love, *you have to get drunk to do it*!"

Jazz took his turn. "I'm sure that made you feel bad, Bell. Almost as bad as I felt after you got up and puked. That made me feel like a real love machine, baby."

"I'm pregnant. Pregnant women get morning sickness."

"You don't want me! That's why you kissed Rocky after we were *together*! That's why you didn't come back to me. That's why you threw up. That's why you take every opportunity to resist and defy me, and that's why your suitcase is at the door and *you're leaving me!*"

"Oh no, *beloved,* I wanted you, all right. I wanted you badly enough to . . ." I froze. I felt like I was turning into a sieve, leaking water everywhere all the time. I ached from wanting him and craved his arms around me, not the shouting match we were having. Tears had sprung from my eyes before I realized I needed to cry. I furiously wiped them away. Anger. Love. Hate. Grief. All surged within me. "The worst thing about last night was that I wanted you *despite* thinking you couldn't stand to be with me without getting trashed. I'm ashamed that a part of me doesn't care that you can't stand to touch me."

That last confession took me right over the edge. I ran to the closet, got my boots on as quickly as possible and threw on my coat.

I snatched up my suitcase.

He finally got to the closet, his face red and full of rage. "And just where do you think you're going, Bell?"

I unlocked those stupid locks, looked at him, and answered. "Niagara Falls. And you'd better be gone when I get back."

chapter
eighteen

F I WERE A REFUGEE or a battered woman or a homeless teen or fleeing a cult, it wouldn't matter. Rocky treated the stranger like Christ. He treated the friend like Christ. He treated family like Christ. I was family.

I showed up at the door a mess. Pulled together on the outside, but my eyes betrayed me. They constantly leaked. They shouted my sorrow like a herald.

The night I'd called him, right after Jazz and I made love on our wedding night, when I was a bundle of confusion, I sat on the floor in the corner of my living room. He had accepted my fragile state, even though his own heart broke, knowing he would finally have to release me. A million little things like that made me call him my *Rock*.

When Rocky saw me standing there with my own puppy eyes, he took my suitcase, linked his arm through mine, and led me to Elisa's room. We prayed and cried—that is, Rocky prayed, and Elisa and I cried. They didn't ask any questions, just hurt with me and talked to Jesus.

Rocky told me that he'd make some arrangements in the house and have a few of the men bunk in the same room so that

I could have a room to myself, for as long as I needed. Then he winked at me. "It won't be long."

After that, they prayed for respite from the throbbing ache in my soul. I felt so sleepy. Kept yawning.

Rocky laughed. "Pregnant women," he said with a shake of his blondilocks.

Elisa took my hand. "The baby is due in two weeks," she said.

"*If* you make it that long," I teased. "And you probably won't."

"Rocky and I wanted to talk to you about something."

I knew what it would be. What else?

Rocky got on his knees in front of Elisa and me. He took Elisa's right hand and my left. I stole a glance at Elisa's left hand to confirm my suspicions. A princess diamond gleamed on her ring finger. I wanted to jump up and down. Not a trace of jealousy remained in me. I knew Elisa was Rocky's beloved.

Rocky hit me with a weakening blast of the puppy eyes. He didn't need to. I could hardly keep a straight face.

He addressed me first. "Babe."

I shot a look at Elisa. She laughed. "He's never going to stop calling you that. It's burned into his brain."

Their kindness and acceptance overwhelmed me.

She put her arm around me. "Don't worry. He calls me Babykins."

"Babykins! I love it. It suits you."

Lord, how I'd come to love this woman. I thought about how I had found her in Gabriel's house, rail thin, her honey-colored skin pale and ashen. She'd been so afraid but was clinging to that last spark of life. I recognized her frail state because once I'd been her. I fought for her to choose life, and in choosing, she saved *my* life.

She came to the Rock House like shattered glass, transparent and beautiful yet broken with edges that could make you bleed if you weren't very careful. Rocky had been careful. He loved her back to herself. I always thought that was the best love gift, giving someone permission to be exactly who they are.

I turned my attention back to Rock.

"So what do you have to tell me?"

"Babe, I want Babykins Junior to have my last name."

Oh Lordy, tears stung my eyes again. My heart felt so full I thought it would burst.

"Harrison is a great last name, Rocky."

"And I want Mama Babykins to have my last name, too—"

I couldn't help it. I grabbed him and nearly asphyxiated him, hugging his neck before he could even get the rest out. Elisa joined our embrace. We group hugged; wiped tears, sniffed, and giggled like we'd had too much wine. We let one another go, and details flew out of Elisa like doves soaring skyward.

"We're going to have the wedding at the Rock House and Ezekiel is going to perform the ceremony." The words fluttered out of Elisa so fast I could hardly keep up. "First I didn't want to until after the baby, but Rocky really, really, really wanted to do it this way and I'm gonna look like whale girl, but I'm sooooo happy." Her green eyes shone both from tears and joy. "Bell, we want you to be our best person."

I giggled. "Best person?"

Rocky's invisible tail wagged and his puppy eyes assaulted

me. "Dude, who says we have to be traditional? We want a best person, and you're one of the best best people we know."

Elisa finished me off with, "We're bringing out the chocolate fountain."

"But we only use that . . ."

When it dawned on me, my grin stretched almost to my ears.

Sly Elisa slowly bobbed her head. "Uh-huh."

A Valentine's Day wedding. The day Rocky celebrated love without a beloved for all those years. Our feast this year would be a wedding feast.

"Okay, you talked me into it," I said.

Another round of laughs.

Rocky said, "It means so much to us. I wouldn't have my Babykins if you hadn't brought her to me, babe."

"She made it worth the trip, Rock." I wagged my finger at Elisa. "But you're so going to paint my picture when I'm close to delivery."

She clapped her hands, "You know I will, girl."

Finally, peace settled on me. Somehow I knew we'd all be all right. Rocky had found his real babe. God gave Elisa both a husband and a father for the baby.

I want that too, Lord.

You already have him.

"I'm really tired," I said. "I know it's early in the morning, but I can hardly keep my eyes open."

Rocky jumped up, hoisted Babykins off the floor first, and took my hand to help me up.

He squeezed my hand. "How long do you need to stay, babe?"

I had no idea. Already I wanted to get back home. "I dunno, Rock. Maybe for as long as it takes for him to come for me. Maybe. I'm a little confused right now."

He swept his hand across the back of my head and leaned in to kiss my forehead. "If you're planning on staying until Jazz comes for you, I wouldn't unpack if I were you. I'd expect him here in like ten minutes, and that's only because he'll have to obey the traffic laws."

"You think so, Rock?"

"I know so, babe." He put his hands on both my shoulders. "Do you remember how you felt when your father left home? You said you cried and begged him not to go."

The memory pricked me in the heart. "I remember it well."

He inclined toward me a little more. "You said you weren't the kind of person anybody would fight for. You said no one would ever beg you to stay."

I hung my head down, "Yes. I did say that."

He took his hands from my shoulders. Lifted my chin with his palm. "He'll come here fighting to have you back."

"Impossible," I said.

He sighed. "Babe. Will you promise me one thing?"

"Anything, Rock. I'm your best person after all."

"Promise me you'll play hard to get. Let him work for you. You'll be surprised to see how much he'll be willing to do to have you. Promise?"

"Promise," I said.

But all I could see was Jazz going on with his life, without me.

––––––––

It took him twenty-seven minutes to get to me. Without looking out the peephole, I knew it was him by the way he pounded on the door—as if he was the police. I sprinted like Flo Jo to the door, but Rocky stopped me.

He grabbed my arm. "Babe, remember what we talked about?"

"Rocky, he's going to leave if you don't open the door."

"He's not going to leave. Go into the living room and sit down. Wait. Okay?"

"But, Rocky—"

"I'm asking you to trust me, as a pastor—your pastor if you'd like—and a friend."

"What if he's angry?" The way he pounded? He *was* angry. "What if . . ."

Rocky shooed me away and answered the door.

I eased down onto the sofa. My heart pounded with an intensity that matched Jazz's attempt to knock the door off its hinges. My hands trembled.

Please, God, don't let him start a fight with Rocky.

I had no idea how things would play out.

I couldn't hear their conversation. I wanted to tear my tiny braid extensions off my head, one by one, out of frustration.

Finally my husband shouted loud enough to blow Rocky's dreadlocks back. "Where is she?"

Rocky raised his voice just a bit. "She's here, but you can't see her unless you calm down, dude."

"Why is it that my *wife* has to come to you every time we make love?"

Rocky challenged him. "Why do *you* think that is, Jazz?"

"She obviously still has a *thing* for you."

"Dude, if she had a thing for me, she wouldn't be *your* wife."

"Just let me see her, Rocky, and I won't hurt you."

"I'd like for you to answer the question, Jazz."

Expletives flew out of Jazz's mouth. I gripped the cushions because I anticipated him cracking Rocky's skull. I stood up. Walked toward the foyer. Turned around again. If I went out there, it would only make him more angry if I didn't leave with him. I hugged myself. Forced myself to sit down again.

Lord, have mercy; Christ, have mercy; Lord, have mercy.

Rocky raised his voice again. "Dude, you can cuss all you want, but that won't get you anything. Answer the question, Jazz. Why does your wife come to me after she's been with you?"

Silence. I wondered if Jazz was strangling him. I strained to hear, but they were quiet. I wondered if Jazz had killed him.

Finally, my husband's voice. "She probably thinks you're the better man."

"No, friend. That's not why she comes to me."

Then a miraculous moment of humility. "What am I doing wrong, Rocky? I don't know how to make her happy."

"Dude, she just needs a safe place to be unsure."

"Unsure about what?"

"Everything. You, herself, marriage."

Rocky's answer swirled around my head like the smoke from

incense, and I breathed the words into me. For a moment I didn't think about Jazz. I thought about how *unsafe* everything in my life felt sometimes. Rocky called it right. I came to him because he lets me be a mess. I never have to be a psychologist with all the answers about human behavior with him.

For a long time, I could hear only soft voices. I couldn't make out what they said to each other. I asked myself what Rocky would likely do. If they'd come this far and Jazz hadn't left or stormed into the house to find me, Rocky would most likely be praying with him.

More soft voices. The door opened, then closed. I stood up and walked over to the hallway and sneaked down the hall to the foyer. I spotted Rocky walking toward me, alone. I didn't understand why Jazz wasn't coming to me.

"What happened?"

Rocky shrugged as if a shouting man demanding his wife came to the house every day. "We talked."

"You talked?"

"And prayed."

"You talked and prayed. Rocky! He sounded like he was ready to bludgeon you."

He nodded, blondilocks bobbing. "He was, but he didn't because it would have hurt *you*."

"That was risky."

"No it wasn't. He doesn't want to hurt you. The dude is crazy about you. He's just scared."

I snorted. "Scared? Of what?"

"He doesn't want to lose you, babe. He thinks he already has."

I couldn't wrap my mind around the idea that Jazz was afraid to lose me. I shook my head and wanted to disagree, but suddenly I was way too tired. My own fear slipped out of my mouth. "He left me here."

"He'll be back."

"It's just like my father. He won't be back. He doesn't have to come back. He can go on and get any woman he wants."

"He only wants one woman, babe."

I shuffled back into the living room and flopped down on the couch. Rocky sat beside me. I turned to look at him. "Rock?"

He gave me a pastoral dose of puppy eyes. "What is it, babe?"

"You told Jazz that I need a safe place to be unsure. Why isn't Jazz safe for me?"

"Because he's as unsure as you are. You both want to protect yourselves, and you're not listening to each other. Babe, he loves you. And you love him. That's a great place to start. Everybody is going to be okay."

"Are you sure, Rock?"

"I'm way sure, but, dude, you both got homework to do. And you did good with yours."

"I barely made it."

He laughed. "Oh, I know, but I had faith that you were going to sit there and play hard to get, and you did it."

"What's Jazz's homework?"

"I can't tell you that."

I hit his arm. "Rocky! Tell me."

"Nope!"

"Why not."

"Sometimes, God wants to surprise you."

"Do I *want* God to surprise me?"

He so didn't pay any attention to me. "You're going to have to figure out if you believe God loves you. In the process, figuring out if your husband loves you will get easier. For now, play hard to get. Seek God. Believe He wants you to have this."

I thought about Zeekie's funeral, something Rocky said to Ezekiel Thunder, "*Jesus said unto him, If thou canst believe, all things are possible to him that believeth*."

In that moment, I knew Jesus was saying the exact same thing unto me.

chapter
nineteen

LUNCHTIME and I wanted to hide out in my room, but Elisa wouldn't hear of it. "Girl, we gotta eat. We're with child."

She had a point. She waddled and I walked into the dining room. The Thunders were already seated.

Ezekiel stood when we came to the table. "Well, look who's joined us. It's good to see you, Bell."

He seemed sincere, and God knows I didn't have the energy to spar with him. I couldn't even muster a "Don't call me Bell." Nikki didn't look pleased to see me. I noticed the kids weren't present.

Ezekiel walked around the table and seated Elisa. I waited, knowing I'd offend him if I didn't allow him to seat me as well.

"Where are Sister Joy and the children?" I asked.

"Joy's in the kitchen. She's serving us lunch this afternoon."

"That is very thoughtful of her."

"Yes, Lord," he said. "She's got the heart of a servant. And can cook, too." He pulled the chair out for me, and I sat.

"Thank you, Mr. Thunder."

He inclined toward me. "Now, you call me Zeke, sissy."

"Zeke," I said as I scooted my chair up to the table. That

seemed to satisfy him and irritate his wife. I gave him an extra big smile just to annoy her.

Sitting with all of the adult players—Sister Lou being the exception—gave me a chance to play Columbo. I'd have to play it cool, as my television hero would. I didn't know if I could pull it off with the finesse of the master detective, who never seemed to get beat up, like I always did.

I'd already established a rapport with Ezekiel and Joy. They'd been generous with information. Joy spoke to me out of her grief. And though, I suspected, Ezekiel knew my questions went beyond mere morbid curiosity, he still spoke freely. And that made me wonder if he, on some level, wanted someone to dig for answers to the troubling questions that had to be eating at him and Joy. I wondered if I could make him an ally in this investigation, and if so, how?

A pitcher of water sat in front of Ezekiel. "Can you please pass me the water, Zeke?" While I was all for staying hydrated, I really didn't need the water at the moment, nor did I need something to make me have to go to the bathroom more than the twins already demanded. I wanted to see if he would serve me.

Ezekiel didn't disappoint. He did exactly as I thought a Southern gentleman would. He stood, picked up the pitcher, and came to my side of the table to pour me a drink.

"I certainly appreciate your chivalry," I said. I tried to put on an air of being a *Northern* belle—pun intended.

Ezekiel responded with predictable charm. He flashed the veneers. "Darlin', I'm always happy to serve a pretty woman."

I looked at Nikki. "Wow," I said. "I can see why you snagged this one. Did he turn on the charm like that for you?"

Her smile didn't quite reach her eyes. "He's like that with all the ladies." She didn't seem to care.

"My husband is the same way," I said. "Women practically throw themselves at him to get his attention. It drives me crazy." I wagged my finger at her. "But you, Nikki, you don't seem to care one whit about your husband's flirtatious ways. That amazes me. You must be so secure in his love that you *know* he'll never stray."

She looked me right in the eyes. "Unlike some women who are obviously insecure and don't know what to do with the man they have, I don't have anything to worry about."

Oh, she wanted to spar? She had no idea who she was dealing with.

"That's true. You're young. Good-looking. You could easily have a man your own age, but you're with a man who's probably older than your own father. He must have had something you *really* wanted."

She opened her mouth to say something, but I kept talking.

"The moment I saw Jazz—and come on, look at him!—I thought he was the finest thing I'd ever laid eyes on. Then he smiled, and my goodness, I was a goner." I took a sip of water. "I so enjoy hearing love stories, especially about how a relationship started. What was it about Ezekiel that captivated you?"

Poor innocent Elisa chimed in. "Yeah, tell us how you knew he was the one."

Since I'd lived in the house before, I knew that if I spoke loud enough, Joy would hear me from the kitchen, and I certainly didn't miss the ball on that. Joy charged into the dining room with three plates and set one in front of Ezekiel, skipped Nikki, and set the other two in front of Elisa and me. I had to bite the inside of my cheek to keep from chuckling at Sister Joy's obvious diss.

"Sister Joy," I said. "Hurry back with Nikki's plate. She was about to tell us how she and Ezekiel fell in love."

She harrumphed. "*That* I'd like to hear."

I shook my head in amazement. Looked at Ezekiel. "Joy is an absolute delight, isn't she? Hospitable. Loyal. Kind. She told me she's been with you for a long time."

"She's the salt of the earth, darlin'," he said. I'm sure that sounded like fingernails screeching across a blackboard to Nikki. "She's one of the best people I've ever known."

"She told me she and your wife Toni were good friends."

"They sure were. 'Course Toni was just like her."

"Must have broken her heart when Toni died."

"It was very hard for her to accept."

Joy made it back to the table carrying two plates and slammed Nikki's in front of her. She moved around the table to an empty chair.

Ezekiel rose from his seat, and headed over to Joy, pulled the chair out from the table, and waited as she eased herself into the chair. He spoke kindly to her. "This looks absolutely delicious, sissy."

She glanced up at him shyly, clearly affected by him. "Thank you, Ezekiel."

Then I saw it. Just a moment, but a *moment.* They exchanged glances, and what passed between them was so subtle that you'd have to be rather astute to catch it. *He loved her, too! In* that *way!*

Poor Ezekiel. He'd chosen the wrong woman to marry. I

thought about what Joy had told me. Once they'd shared a kiss. She'd followed him throughout most of his ministry, throughout most of his life. Yet they remained star-crossed lovers, even though she would have been the obvious best choice as a spouse for him after his first wife's death. Maybe she didn't take his garbage. Good for her, but it was kinda sad, too.

Then again, how many men could resist a seventeen-year-old hottie coming after him?

I needed to find out his financial particulars. Five years ago, he and Toni had enough to offer a wayward teen assistance, but how much would that be? She'd lived with them. Seemed to me that she'd have to earn her keep, and they perhaps gave her money for incidentals. Those books he wrote couldn't bring in a lot of money, so it seemed unlikely she wanted him for money. What had she wanted? Why did she stay five years with him?

Lord, keep revealing everything Jazz and I need to know. Give me some sign that I'm on the right track here. I need wisdom, Jesus. Please provide it.

Nikki cleared her throat. "I'm going to pray over the food."

We all bowed our heads. I didn't close my eyes, however. My great-grandmother used to say, "Baby, Jesus said, *watch* and pray—sometime you got to pray with yo' eyes wide open." I always thought that sounded a little paranoid. But the older I got, the more I realized how wise Ma Brown was.

What I noticed? Nikki Thunder kept her eyes open, too. She said all the appropriate words. Her voice rose and fell in just the right Pentecostal rhythm, but as she prayed, she watched me intently, shooting daggers at me with her cold gaze. I had the distinct feeling she hadn't quite figured out what I was about. Was

I the inferior female whose alpha male she thought she could effortlessly lure away? Or was I a shrewd adversary, one who could take her?

She said, "Amen," and everyone began to eat.

I took a bite of the grilled chicken wrap Joy had prepared. She'd marinated the chicken with a delicate blend of herbs and a robust rosemary infusion. I think the babies danced with joy inside me. I couldn't wait to dig into the spinach and mandarin orange salad she'd prepared as a side. After I complimented Joy on her culinary delights, I fixed my attention back on Nikki Thunder.

"Nikki, you didn't finish telling us what made you fall in love with Ezekiel."

She gave me an indulgent smile, as if I were a child that she had to be patient with. "I think it's obvious." She looked at Ezekiel, maybe to bail her out of this conversation.

I waved away that lame response. "Aw, come now, don't be shy. We want *details*."

Ezekiel cocked his head to the side and gave her a sexy gaze. "You don't have to tell me. I already know what got us together, sweetheart."

"I'm sure you do, Daddy." She sounded like Ginger on *Gilligan's Island*.

The answer seemed to satisfy him. Didn't do much for me. "That doesn't tell us a thing, Nikki. Joy and I want to know when the magic started."

Joy didn't hide her disdain. "Yes, *girl*. Tell us about the magic."

Nikki must have sized us up and judged us both as inferior

females. She leaned forward in her seat, knowing she had our full attention. "I really don't want to share something that personal. I'm a pretty private person."

"I am so sorry." I touched my hand to my heart. "I'm a psychologist. I get so used to asking personal questions that they come flying out of me. Please forgive me."

She didn't say anything; stabbed at a piece of spinach that refused to be impaled by her fork. She finally discarded the leaf for a mandarin orange. The rest of us ate in silence until Ezekiel came to my rescue.

"Sweetheart, I don't think Bell meant any harm."

She put down her fork and placed her hand boldly on his thigh. She inclined her body toward him, revealing her ample cleavage, which he did not miss. "I know, Daddy. I'm fine."

"I think you're an *amazing* woman," I said. "I mean, here you are, this private, reserved person, and yet, yesterday at the funeral, you shared the most intimate details of the terrible tragedies you suffered with, what?, three-hundred people, not to mention the viewing audience."

Ezekiel beamed. "Folks were so impressed with my girl that she's been asked to share her testimony on the Good News Network."

"Wow," I said. "That show has an audience of millions. That's what I mean." I gestured toward her. "When most women would be too devastated to say *anything* at their baby's funeral, Nikki shares her story with millions. She stole the show, so to speak. That's a whole lot of attention for such a private person."

Ezekiel looked uncomfortable now. "And did you hear that anointed exhortation she gave?"

"I heard it. Gave me chills." I rubbed my arms to prove it. "Honestly. I had a physical reaction in my gut."

"I think she may be the next famous preacher in the Thunder family."

A broad grin spread across her face.

Shazam!

She was a Joyce Meyer wannabe, and she wanted to relegate *has-been* Thunder to the back pew.

I placed my elbow on the table and leaned toward Nikki. "Nikki Thunder," I said. "I have no doubt in my mind you are going to be famous. If you think people are talking about you now, you just wait. You're going to be unforgettable."

She sat back, a satisfied expression on her smug face. I again became inferior in her eyes. But I hadn't finished with her.

"In fact, let me just say, I don't know how you *did it,* all those tragic *accidents* in your life, but I'm determined to know. How did Nikki Thunder *do it*! You know, Nikki? I'm going to figure it out, because the things that happened to you don't just happen to people. It's amazing. I'm going to make it my personal mission in life to figure out what makes you the *unbelievable* woman you are. You can count on that."

Score one for Bell.

Nikki lifted her chin, and in that maddening manner she had of looking down on me, no matter what position she was in, she smiled and said, "Why thank you, *Amanda.* But I'm nothing special. Accidents can happen to anybody. They could even happen to someone *you* love. You have to be very careful—much more careful than I was, God help you."

Was that a threat?

Yeah, it was. One I wouldn't take lightly.

After lunch I retreated to my room. I plopped down on the bed I hadn't made yet. I still felt tired, and I had a lot to think about. Jazz stuff, Nikki Thunder stuff, my Dream. So she understood my threat and made one of her own. And I couldn't help being concerned about Zekia and little Zeke. It was well after one o'clock in the afternoon, and neither had come down from their bedrooms. My paranoia began to devise all kinds of diabolical schemes Nikki Thunder could have executed—no pun intended—to hurt them. But she wouldn't just go on a spree, killing all kinds of people. Not with her in the spotlight now. Would she?

I needed to talk to Jazz. I wasn't sure how to proceed from here. He always tempered my wild ideations with his wisdom and experience.

You need his strength.

Man! People say God comforts you, but He seems to be adept at disturbing me.

I'd steeled myself for the little chat God seemed to want to have with me when I was saved by the bell. My cell phone rang. I'd kept it with me more than I usually did, hoping that Jazz would call me, even if it meant we'd end up screaming at each other. How pathetic was I?

I picked up the phone and flipped it open. Jazz's cell phone number appeared on the screen. My heart did an Irish clog dance.

"Hello," I said, trying to hide my enthusiasm. I was supposed to be playing hard to get.

"Hello," he said. I could tell he was trying to play it cool, too. "My name is Jazz Brown, and I'm a homicide detective. May I speak to Jane?"

I tried to keep from laughing. "Jane?"

"Yes, please."

I wasn't quite sure how to answer him. Several possibilities existed. I settled on "Which one?"

He paused. I could imagine him grinning with that brilliant smile of his. "How many are there?" he asked.

"Three that I know of."

"Do tell."

I reclined on the pillow. This was going to be fun. "There's psychologist Jane."

"She sounds *smart*."

"Yeah," I quipped. "She's overwhelmed with phone calls from Mensa. But I find her boring and prosaic."

"Tell me about the other Janes."

"Well there's the sexy come-hither Jane."

"Now she sounds intriguing. Can I speak to her?"

"I'm afraid she is *unavailable*."

He laughed. "Score one for the Jane who answered the phone."

"That leaves only one more Jane," I said.

"That you know of. Which one is she?"

"Full-time wife and mother Jane."

He sighed. "I think I like that one best. But you missed one."

"I did?"

"Yes."

I scanned my mind's archives, riffling through all our Jane discussions. I couldn't think of a single other one. "You've got me, detective. Which Jane would you like to speak to?"

"My partner, private investigator Jane."

I smiled so wide my cheeks hurt. "This is she speaking."

A boisterous round of laughter burst out of him, so infectious that I laughed along with him. It felt so good to be happy with Jazz, even if it was for a few minutes of silly conversation. "I'm calling to see if you've got anything, PI Jane."

"I've got a lot, Jazz."

"Are we still talking about the case?"

"Get your mind out of the gutter. I want to tell you what I discovered at the funeral. I also had lunch today with the adults in Thunder's camp. I made some interesting observations."

"Jane?" I could hear the apprehension in his voice.

I didn't know what he'd say. I didn't feel ready to resume our marital drama. It felt so much safer to just deal with the case.

Safer?

I sighed. "What is it, Jazz?"

"I think we really need to talk more about the case. I'm serious now."

"Okay."

"May I please pick you up and take you out for coffee?"

I didn't want to answer too soon. I didn't feel ready to be with him, even though I yearned to. But time was ticking away, and we needed to get enough on Nikki so the police would take another look at her.

When I'd left Louella at the hospital, she was alternating between incoherent babbling and hysteria. Most likely she'd be there at least three days, until they scheduled a hearing for her, where her doctors would decide if she could be released. I had no idea how long the Thunders planned to stay at the Rock House house now. As it was, I'd caught a break when Ezekiel decided to bury his son in a family plot in a Detroit cemetery. I hoped they'd be around a little longer.

Jazz must have taken my hesitation for lack of interest. "I just want to talk about the case, Jane."

"How long are you going to call me Jane?"

He hesitated. "I miss my Bell very much. But you're a lot easier to talk to right now. Bell and I keep bumping heads. Once I told her that I wouldn't push her to do anything she wasn't ready for, but you know what, Jane?"

"What?"

"I did push her. I pushed her right away from me. And I can't lose my Bell. I'd die for that woman." He chuckled softly. "I can't live *with* her, but I'd die *for* her."

"I think she'd rather you live with her."

He snorted. "Not if you saw her reaction when I moved in. So what do you say, Jane? Can we talk about the case? I'll even let you have a small latte."

"*Let* me?"

"You *are* pregnant, private investigator Jane."

"If you put it that way. I'll see you in a half hour, detective."

"I'll see you in fifteen minutes, Jane."

I was waiting at the door with my coat on fifteen minutes later.

Score one for Jazz.

FELT LIKE AN OVERPROTECTED TEENAGER having to explain to my dad that I'd be a good girl when I went out on a date with the bad boy. Rocky didn't look convinced.

He stood by the door with me, arms crossed, tapping one Birkenstock-clad foot on the floor.

"I won't be more than an hour or two."

"Babe, I thought I told you to play hard to get."

I couldn't very well let him know Jazz and I were plotting to take down the evil wife of his godfather.

"He needs some forensic psychologist insight into a case he's working on." That happened to be true. Fortunately, Rocky bought it. "I promise I'll be good."

His puppy eyes regarded me warily.

"And I won't go home with him."

"Babe."

"Really, Rock. I'm not in a hurry to go there without counseling, spiritual direction, a guru, an angelic visitation, burning bushes, disembodied hands writing on the wall . . ."

I'd opened the door to be on the lookout for Jazz. When his car pulled up, Rocky peeked his head out the door with me. "Rocky, you're not going to say anything to him, are you?"

"I sure am."

"But, Rocky . . ."

"What's your job, babe?"

I grumbled. "Play hard to get."

"Excellent!" he said. He sounded just like Mike Myers in *Wayne's World*.

Jazz swaggered to the door. Heavens to Betsy, I could eat him up like a bag of M&M's. I unsuccessfully tried not to grin. Suddenly I felt as girlish as a teenager, which Rocky happened to be treating me like.

I'd let my hair down, and the braids hung in soft black waves to my shoulders. I'd lost the dropped-waist dress and had put on a wine-colored velvet shift, which I'd absently packed with no real intention of wearing. I borrowed an embroidered shawl from Elisa, a fabulous piece that matched her artsy personality.

Jazz shook Rocky's hand. If I hadn't believed in miracles before, I'd changed my mind. They did the complicated soul handshake. I didn't even know Rocky could shake like that. He's white! I decided complicated handshakes must be some primal urge men as a sex shared.

Jazz gave me a quick glance—head to toe—and a half smile, and I knew my appearance pleased him.

He didn't reach for my hand. Greeted me with a nod. "Jane."

"Hello, detective."

Rocky looked at me, confused. "Are you sure you didn't change your name to Jane?"

"Just for him," I said.

"Is that some kind of married thing I should know about?"

Jazz raised an eyebrow. "The last thing you want to do is get marriage tips from either of us."

"Actually," I said, "I can give great marriage tips in my office as a practicing psychologist. I just don't seem to be able to implement those positive behavioral choices in my own life."

Rocky turned to Jazz. "I expect you to have her back by dinnertime."

"Yes, sir," Jazz said.

"And don't try anything sneaky, like pretending you've run out of gas or something."

"I wouldn't dream of it."

"This is supposed to be a business meeting. I expect you to conduct yourselves with the utmost professionalism and—"

Jazz interrupted him. "Rocky, we're going to talk a little business, and then I'll promptly bring her back. Don't say any more, because I can hurt you."

Rocky's face reddened. "Right." He still didn't look ready to surrender me. He paused. "This is, like, so trippy, isn't it?"

I could tell Jazz still wanted to throttle him. "It's trippy. May we go now?"

Rocky stood back. Sighed. "Be good, young lady."

"I will, Rocky," I said.

Jazz extended his arm, and I went to him. He placed his hand at the small of my back and led me to the Crown Vic.

Like so many other times when he touched me, my feet didn't touch the ground.

———————

I thought he'd take me to Starbucks or Seattle's Best, but leave it to Jazz to take me somewhere off the beaten path. He'd found a coffee shop called Espresso Royale. It had more local color and better parking, and best of all, we didn't have to brave the crowds of slick Ann Arborites barking orders at baristas they'd deemed too slow in delivering their grande Caffè Mochas.

I sat across from him, trying not to stare at his beauty. Of course, several other women in the place didn't share my reticence. I half expected one of them to walk up and slip him her phone number. He disappointed them all. He only had eyes for me.

"So, what have you got?" he asked after we'd sipped what amounted to a cup of hot milk for a while.

"Jazz, what do you think about the possibility that Nikki's babies really died of SIDS?"

"My mom is Alpha Kappa Alpha. Her sorority sponsored a workshop on SIDS in the African-American community. She came back fired up about saving babies. One thing she mentioned is that our babies have a higher incidence of SIDS deaths."

"That's true; just like African Americans have higher incidence of certain diseases: cancer, high blood pressure, et cetera. But what are the chances, statistically, that she'd have two babies die of SIDS?"

"It could happen."

"You're right. In rare occasions, lightning really does strike twice. However, Nikki seems to leave a trail of bodies behind her wherever she goes."

"Do tell, Jane."

"I never got to tell you this, but at the funeral, Nikki's former friend told me that Nikki had lost two babies to SIDS, oddly enough, right after she'd had enough of her current boyfriend and after her previous boyfriend had mysteriously died. An alleged suicide. Inconclusive."

"Not good, Jane."

"And Ezekiel Thunder's wife died shortly after Nikki and Thunder had their affair. He said she got sick and sort of wasted away. Joy, who was good friends with her, didn't think so."

"Go on."

"Thunder also told me he'd gotten Nikki pregnant, and that, like David, he lost his infant. I thought about that Bible story and finally looked it up. Are you familiar with it?"

"Very. Remember, until we found out Kate's baby wasn't mine, I thought I had my own 'dead baby as punishment' story."

"And you know I've got mine. Well, at least I thought it was punishment at the time." I shuddered to think of the horrible tale of David and Bathsheba's loss, told in 2 Samuel. "The prophet Nathan told David that he'd given his enemies great occasion to blaspheme the Lord, and his child by Uriah's wife would surely die."

Jazz shook his head. "It's kind of a trip that he called her Uriah's wife. By then, Uriah was already dead and she'd become David's wife."

"It was a pretty fearful judgment. I admit I don't understand those kinds of God things."

Jazz reach across the table and took my hand. "I grew up doing church two different ways. One way tried to make God fit into man's ideas, the other accepted God as a mystery. You can't make mystery manageable—at least not the God kind."

I looked down at the table. He lifted my chin.

"Bell, David's sin is not our concern, neither are the sins we committed a long time ago and have long since repented of and been forgiven for. Dr. McLogan said our babies are perfect. And we're not going to worry about them. We might be dumb, but we got married, *then* made those babies . . ." A shadow crossed his face. "Because we love each other. No matter what. We haven't given up on each other, have we?"

"No, Jazz. We haven't." I straightened my back. Squared my shoulders. "But don't call me Bell." I winked at him. "I'm Jane."

I'd never tire of seeing him smile at me. "So, Jane," he said, "in the Bible story, the baby was born, then died a little bit later. Right?"

"Exactly. David's baby got sick and died in seven days."

"How did Thunder's baby die?"

"That's just it. He didn't say. At the time I thought he may have been speaking metaphorically. I figured the baby could have been stillborn or she could have aborted it—any number of things. SIDS didn't readily come to mind."

I went on. "David's baby got sick. But what if Thunder's first baby with Nikki didn't? How could someone murder a baby and make it seem like the child had been sick?"

"I think we're on the same page, Bell. I was thinking about how Nikki's rousing speech at Zeekie's funeral garnered her instant celebrity status of sorts. And how anytime a woman is pregnant or has lost a baby, she gets all of this attention."

"Exactly!"

"That's like that weird mental illness. What's it called? They showed it in *The Sixth Sense*."

"Munchausen syndrome by proxy."

"What is up with *that*?" His eyes sparkled. He loved it when I did my psychologist thing, that is, except for when I used my skills to torture him.

"Many professionals view MSP as a form of child abuse. The parent's MO is pretty much to make the kid sick so they can get the attention of doctors, neighbors, and concerned coworkers. It's like, 'Wow. Look at what a great mom Psychotica is. She's so dedicated to that sickly child. Poor Psychotica.'"

Jazz rubbed his chin. "That's freaky weird. And what do you say about all this, Jane?"

He's so good-looking, I hardly noticed I'd slanted my body so Jazzward that I had to rest my forearms on the table. A curtain of braids swept down my shoulder, and I took great pleasure in whisking them back like I'd turned into one of Charlie's Angels. I could tell by how he narrowed his eyes and parted his lips a bit that he took great pleasure in the gesture.

"Did I tell you how good you look today, Jane?"

I tapped my index finger to my temple. "Hmmmm. I can't recall. Perhaps you should do it again."

"You look gorgeous today, Jane. Now hurry up and ask me your question before I take you home and get us both in trouble."

I hesitated. On purpose.

He cracked up. Licked his lips and made me want to never ask that question. But I had to play hard to get.

"The question . . ." I said, with a big-time pause . . .

He slouched in his seat and scowled at me. "Tease."

"The question is, *Who* do women kill?"

Jazz didn't hesitate. "They tend to pick victims who are close to them. Husbands. Children. Strays they pick up whose social security checks they cash while the missing person rots underneath their rose bushes."

"Exactly! Now, let's isolate the victims. *How* do women—mothers—kill their own children?"

He effortlessly rattled off the answers. "They abandon newborn babies in garbage bags, they drop, shake, beat, poison, suffocate—"

"And drown."

A thoughtful look softened his features. So, you're thinking Nikki has this Munchausen syndrome by proxy?"

"Maybe I've been around you long enough for you to rub off on me, but . . ."

Jazz took a sip of his honey steamer. We'd both ordered them—he to stand in solidarity with me and to help me act like I wasn't drinking a cup of hot milk. "Uh-oh," he said. "Don't tell me I've corrupted your good manners."

I considered that. Shoot. In some ways, he had. "In *this* instance, through all the stories you told me, not to mention the warnings you frequently give me, you've actually given me a different perspective of murderers."

"Yeah. The world is no joke. There are a lot of nutjobs out there."

"That's precisely what I mean, detective. Maybe a few months ago I would have seen a woman with Munchausen's and thought she was some poor soul who'd been horribly abused or neglected in childhood and lacked the appropriate skills to empathize with others."

"Yeah, blah, blah, blah, yakety smackety."

I laughed. "I found out Friday that Rocky's parents completely emotionally neglected him, but he's one of the most empathetic people I've ever met."

Jazz grudgingly agreed.

"And Nikki Thunder is, according to every report I've gotten—with the exception of her husband's—completely attention seeking and narcissistic, with no concern for anyone *but* Nikki Thunder . . ."

"You used the 'N' word. So, besides being a narcissist, with a capital 'N,' you think she's got this Munchausen's thing?"

"I don't think she's got Munchausen's at all."

He raised an eyebrow. "Do tell, Jane?"

"I think she's the 'P' word and the 'S' word."

He leaned across the table and gave me a delicious grin. "You're a lot of fun, Jane."

"You think so, detective?"

"Tell me what the 'P' and the 'S' words are."

"Lieutenant Brown, it's my professional opinion that Nikki Thunder is a psychopath and a serial killer."

———————

That whole serial killer thing killed our flirtatious, playful mood. Jazz retreated inward, saying little while he sipped his steamer. I didn't try to fill the quiet with idle chatter. We'd long grown comfortable with silence. If only we could become comfortable with more than just silence.

When we got back to Jazz's car, he kept up his good manners. He opened the door for me, seated me, and didn't try to flirt with me. He took me back to the Rock House well before the dinner hour. Walked me to the door.

I almost wished I'd saved my assessment for later. I enjoyed being Jane for him. I enjoyed having overpriced milk and honey with him. Shoot. I enjoyed *him*, and I didn't know how to extend our evening and not disappoint Rocky or renege on the promise I'd made him.

As if Jazz read my mind, he drew closer to me. Hemmed me against the front door of the house. His scent filled me, with no hint of alcohol, only a faint trace of cigar smoke and Irish Spring soap. He bent to kiss me, and I put my index finger on his lips.

"No mixing business with pleasure, detective."

He gently took my hand away and held it. He pressed his body close to mine. "May I speak to Jane?"

"This is Jane."

"I want full-time wife and mother Jane."

"Jack Daniel's ran her off."

"Touché. I haven't had a drink all day."

Goodness gracious, he stood too close. He made me feel all tingly. I wanted to touch him.

"Come back home," he whispered.

I turned my gaze away from him. Stared at the ground. He didn't lift my head this time. He grazed my cheek with his own. Stubble had just begun to emerge, and the friction felt so good that I had to stuff my hands in my coat pockets to keep from laying them on him.

He whispered, "I'm sorry I got drunk."

"I need to work through something, Jazz. I can't come home."

Maddening man! He kept murmuring—his soft, sexy voice and warm breath tickling my ear. His hands found my waist.

"Come home with me. Don't even get your stuff. Let's go."

"I want to . . ."

"Then let's do it."

"The way you're pushing up on me, I think you want to do more than go home."

"I'm not drunk, and that's exactly what I want to do."

"Jazz you need to listen to me."

"I did listen, Bell. I'm not drunk on anything but the vanilla and sweet amber I smell in your hair."

I couldn't help myself. I swept my hands up and down his cheeks and let them make their way to his curls. He turned into a beast, furiously kissing me.

"We should stop."

"We're married."

"We're having—"

"A really good time, as soon as I get you home. Let's go."

"Jazz, that isn't going to solve our problems."

"It'll solve one of mine. Come on."

I didn't answer. Let his kisses carry me someplace I'd been before, but didn't stay nearly as long as I should have. I ached to return. "Okay," I said.

He stopped. Stared at me, his expression almost comical. "Did you say 'okay'?"

"Yes."

He grabbed my hand and got me off that porch like *it*, not

him, was about to explode. I trailed a little bit behind him. He didn't seem to mind until we got to the car. He went to open the passenger-side door, hesitated, and looked at me. He took his hand off the door handle. "I know you want to go."

"You're right, Jazz. How could I not?"

"Give me another chance, Bell. I won't disappoint you."

"I said okay."

"Okay is different than yes."

"Semantics, Jazz."

"Touché."

"Why do you want me to go?"

He sighed. "You're my wife, and you belong with me. My babies belong with me."

"Will you start pounding your chest like King Kong, shouting what belongs to you? I am alpha male. Hear me roar?"

His features darkened in anger. "Do you have to ridicule me?"

"Jazz, I'm not trying to ridicule you. It's just that sometimes you say things that . . ."

His mouth tightened in a flat line. "Things that what?"

I paused, debating whether I should say it. I decided to be honest.

"Things that remind me of Adam."

I couldn't have surprised him more if I'd slapped him. "Adam? The nutjob who beat you? Do I need to remind you that I've never laid a hand on you?"

"Sometimes you make me sound like inventory. 'You're mine. Do this. Do that.' Even the way you said, 'Come home with me.' A demand. You didn't really ask."

He leaned against the car. The cold and his anger reddened his cheeks and nose. Even angry he looked beautiful. For a long time he didn't say anything. Then finally, "You told me that there is a serial killer in that house. I'm going to say this one more time, Bell, because sometimes in life you have to act and you can't coddle and placate. You have to say, 'Move!' or 'Watch out!' And you may lose your decorum in that instance. You may have to physically remove the person against protest. But you do it so you won't have to scrape them off the bus tires." He gave me a look as hard as the one he'd given me on our wedding night before he stormed out of my life.

All that, and I hadn't even told him about the threat she'd made. He went on. "If you don't get in that car and come home with me, I promise you, I will call my lawyer as soon as I get home, and when the time comes, I will sue you for custody of my children."

I could feel the rage coiled tight as a spring slowly unfurl. My legs trembled and my hands burned to scratch or slap or punch him. I tried not to think about the fact that he'd just threatened to take away my children. A number of unpleasant names crouched at the tip of my tongue. I dared not speak because I knew if I did, something would come out and do the kind of damage one can't easily undo.

If felt like my throat was slowly closing. My lungs hurt to breathe. I lifted my head and looked at him, and his expression had turned from anger to alarm. I began to count to calm myself enough to be able to speak and put an end to this conversation, put an end to the fiasco we'd called a marriage. Ten, nine, eight, seven, six, five . . .

Lord, have mercy; Christ, have mercy; Lord, have mercy.

Four, three, two, one . . . Deep breath, in and out, again.

Finally I could speak. "Then I suggest you get a scraper, because you'll scrape me off those bus tires before I go anywhere with you. I'll see you in court."

I turned and walked away from him only to feel his hand clamp over my wrist. My rage became incarnate.

Dear God, I'm going to hurt him. Protect my babies because I'm going to . . .

He grabbed my wrist. "Get in the car with me."

The porch light came on, and Rocky opened the door. All I had to do was lash out, and Rocky would help me.

"Is everything all right out there?"

"I'm taking her home."

Rocky stepped toward us. "Jazz, let Bell go."

"This is my wife. She's coming with me."

Rock took another tentative step. "Jazz, dude."

Jazz exploded, "You stay back, or I will hurt you, Rocky. I played along, earlier. Now I'm taking my wife home."

"Let her go, Jazz."

He held me fast, with me resisting him. We were frozen in that nightmare, neither one of us willing to surrender. Or so I thought.

Jazz let me go.

I stood there a moment, unsure if I should flee or fight. None of us moved. Elisa waddled outside and took Rocky's arm.

He looked at her, clearly annoyed. "Babykins . . ."

"This is a husband and wife, Rocky," she said.

"She doesn't want to go."

"I know she's your friend, but she's his wife. Has he beaten her?"

Rocky's puppy eyes searched mine.

"No," I said.

Elisa continued. "Did he cheat on her?"

I shook my head.

"Bell, why don't you want to go with him? What does he want that you don't want to give him?"

I didn't answer her. She addressed Jazz directly.

"Jazz, what is it that you want?"

"I want to protect her. She knows that's all I want."

"He wants to own me."

"I do own you. You are mine."

Rocky stepped closer to me. He looked at Jazz as if he were asking for permission. Jazz obviously gave it.

"Jazz. You need to rethink the scriptures. Marriage is about serving one another. It's not a slave thing."

I could sense Rocky's fear of Jazz's aggression. None of us knew what Jazz would do. Rocky spoke tentatively.

"Babe, I know I asked you to play hard to get. But this is taking things a bit far. You're welcome here anytime. But I think you need to have a talk with your husband tonight."

Jazz spoke. "No, that's okay, Rocky. Don't help me. If it takes all that to get her to come home, then she doesn't want to be home." Jazz threw his arms up. "I'm done." He lowered his arms. "Forgive me for all the drama. I may not be like you Rocky, but I love her. More than you do. See, I'm *one* with her. I'm in her and she's in me. And that's not just a sex thing. I used to think it was. I was married before, or I thought I was, and I had a lot of women, but I wasn't *one* with anybody. I'm only *one* with her."

He walked to the driver's-side door and opened it. Jazz took one last look at me, then got into the car and drove away, leaving me standing in the driveway with Rocky and Elisa.

Three o'clock in the morning, and I tried to discreetly unlock my three locks and quietly enter my apartment. I met with no resistance. I swung open the door and looked around. All things Jazzy had been stripped from my apartment. My husband and all his stuff had vanished from my life.

After I settled in, I picked up the telephone. Dialed a number I almost never did. Heard my father's voice, thick with sleep.

"Daddy?"

"Princess, is that you?"

"It's me. Daddy?"

"What's the matter?"

"I keep making a mess out of my life. That's all."

"Everything okay with you and Jazz?"

"Why didn't you prepare me, Daddy? Why didn't you tell me I was strong and beautiful and worthy? Why did you leave me when I needed you the most? Carly got that part of you. I missed it."

"Do you want me to come over there?"

"I don't need you to come over here. I need my husband to come over here. And bring his stuff back. But you know what, Daddy? I don't even think I really want that because he's drinking so much, he can't begin to be a good husband and father. And you know what I really want to know? How did I end up marrying you?"

Daddy didn't speak. The phone stayed quiet until I hung it up, angry. I thought he'd fallen asleep on me.

I was wrong. An hour later he was at my door. A tall, brown brick of a man. Woolly white hair. Skin the color of pecan shells. Dancing eyes full of compassion. Paint stained his clothes from his making art all day. He brought me Starbucks.

He sat beside me on my sofa. "Go ahead and rage, princess. I'm up for it."

We stayed up all night, him nodding his head and listening while I raged. He stayed until I was spent.

"Princess," he said, as the light of dawn began to emerge through my blinds, "everything you said to me is true, but I need to say something to you that's true."

I waited.

"You're not a teenager. You're an adult. You're acting like a child emotionally, but you are not a child. You have to tell that teenage girl who's running your life, 'Thank you, but I don't need you anymore. I'm adult Bell, and I have to take over now.'"

The truth of his words caused me to sag against my sofa cushions. He went on. "All that you told me about Ezekiel Thunder, your fractured faith, your disappointment in the God who doesn't always do a miracle, your confusion about Ezekiel Thunder's gifts, your anger at me—they're all your teenager stuff, Bell. Your never-healed teenager stuff."

"I'm thirty-five years old, Daddy."

"But not in these matters. In these things, you're fifteen."

"How can God use Ezekiel Thunder? He's awful. But, Daddy, he knew about my tumor. He knew Jazz's name without ever being told. He prayed for my ankle, and the next day the pain was gone."

"Gifts and callings are without repentance, sweetie. Look at Saul. Look at David."

And then the big ones.

"Look at you, princess. And me."

My daddy had changed, just like I had. He hadn't had a drink in years, and yet I still punished him as often as I could like he was still a sloppy drunk.

"I'm sorry I keep bringing up your past. I know you're a different man now."

"It's my chickens coming home to roost, princess. I deserve all your wrath and more. I did all that drinking. The least I can do is be here now when you call for me, which isn't often, though I wish it were."

Daddy let me fall asleep with my head on his shoulder. He kept my hand in his, and I drifted off into a dreamless slumber, hearing his voice telling me that, in the end, God will redeem it all, and everything we suffered will be clear to us. Love really will win in the end, he said.

I believed him. After all, he was my daddy, and despite himself I loved him.

chapter
twenty-one

I TRUDGED INTO WORK at the jail an hour and a half late, barely functional. Finding clothes to fit my ever-expanding voluptuous frame took some time. Before I went to my desk, I saw one of my pals, Detective Jeff Winslow. I caught Jeff hanging around the front desk and pulled him aside. I'd hoped I could buy him off with a bag of Famous Amos Cookies. I headed over to the vending machine, Jeff following.

I pulled three quarters and a dime out of my handbag. Plopped them into the vending machine. Jeff caught on immediately when I pushed the numbers and his favorite chocolate chip cookies fell out.

"Uh-oh. A bribe."

"Jeff, you worked on the case with Ezekiel Thunder, right?"

He eyed me warily. He was a big, blustery man, blond, blue-eyed, just shy of handsome. Bushy hair. Overweight. He talked like he had chronic breathing trouble. "Why d'ya ask, Amanda?" He had that smirk on his face like he wanted to say, "What is she about to do to get beat up now?"

"Two words: Nikki Thunder."

"For her I got one word, but you're a Christian, so I won't say it."

I took the cookies out of the vending machine and handed them to him. He took them, reluctantly.

"What if I told you I've heard that she had three other babies who died? Two cases of SIDS and one mystery death I haven't gotten the details about yet?"

"I'd ask you how you could prove they were homicides."

"Wouldn't that be your job?"

"I've done my job. I investigated. Got the medical examiner's report, and it says her kid had no indicators of child abuse to suggest that his death was anything other than an accident."

"What about that story, Jeff? A kid goes to the bathroom and walks out leaving his almost three-year-old, very busy brother who dies?"

"It raised flags, sure, but we couldn't find anything amiss other than that incredulous story the kids didn't budge from. And truth be told, it wasn't so incredulous. Kids drown in bathtubs."

"He was a firecracker, Jeff. He'd have taught himself to swim in that tub before he drowned in it."

"We got nothing for the DA. What can you do?" He shrugged his wide shoulders.

"What if I had a name you can run a check on? Her *real* name. See if the police in Philly want her on something. Come on, *two* SIDS babies? Another baby dead of unknown causes? And a toddler who drowned in the bathtub after that?"

He leaned against the wall. A few people shuffled into the area—an officer and a nervous-looking older couple probably hoping to bail out some wayward soul. "Amanda, maybe the woman has tough luck. If nobody else prosecuted, they didn't have enough on her. You know how hard it is to prove a SIDS death is a homicide. Babies don't fight back."

"How many babies have to die before she's stopped? She's a serial killer, Jeff."

He wheezed. Surreptitiously glanced around. Slanted toward me. "Lower your voice, Amanda. *Sheesh.* You can't just go around accusing people of being serial killers."

"I'm sorry, Jeff. I'm just frustrated."

"And what is it with you and murderers? You a homicide cop now, like your hubby?"

"My hubby got suspended for drinking on the job."

He placed his hand on his double chin. "No stuff?" Only he didn't say "stuff." "When did this happen?"

"A lot has happened. It's crazy." I tried to give him the puppy eyes. "Jeff, I know she's a psychopath. She's gotta go down."

He put a beefy hand on my shoulder. "It's not your job to take her down. You can't just charge in there like you're Christie Love." He thrust an imaginary gun at me, with both hands, his arms extended. He used a falsetto voice, "You're under arrest, *sugar*!"

I cracked up. "I *cannot* believe you remember *Get Christie Love!*"

"Remember it? I was in love with Teresa Graves."

I shook my head. "I'd better get to my desk. As it is, I'm late and have been absent again. Plus, I'm afraid you're sweet on black women now. I'm not sure I can trust you anymore, you rascal."

He roared with wheezy laughter. When he'd calmed he said, "Your boss isn't the only person around here worried about you, you know."

"I know, Jeff. I have two very good reasons to behave myself now."

"Congrats on the babies, Amanda."

News travels fast at the Washtenaw County Jail. "Thanks, Jeff." I turned to go to my desk.

"Amanda," he said. I turned back to him. "Sometimes you have to let it go. We don't win 'em all. I wish we did."

I nodded and waved good-bye to him. But I couldn't let it go. Not when all those kids in my dream were crying out for help. I couldn't help them all, but I could help my little Thunder boy. At least I hoped I could.

———————

Two hours after my chat with Jeff, I sat at my desk amid piles of manila folders. The work had piled up while I spent a week with my husband, the craziness of Zeekie's funeral, exorcisms, and finding out I was pregnant. My fabulous life as Jane sure did make my job at the jail look boring.

Before I had time to muse about it, a female uniform—a redhead named Rebecca Burns—summoned me to a meeting with Eric. She almost winced when she told me he wanted to see me in the conference room. When she left, I rolled my eyes and took a deep breath. The conference room. He'd give me "the talk"— employer's version.

It felt like I walked five miles down the hallway to get to him. He could have just as easily told me, again, that he didn't appreciate my frequent absences without the fanfare of having to go into the conference room.

I knocked on the door, and like a doctor, didn't wait for him to say "come in" before I barged into the room. One look at his face and I could tell that he wanted to talk about more than my attendance.

He didn't stand when I came into the room, not quite the perfect gentleman. He nodded to a chair in front of his desk. "Dr. Brown, please, have a seat."

Dr. Eric Fox had the cool persona of a Vulcan. Honestly, the man even looked like Dr. Spock sans pointy ears. Tall, always immaculately dressed, thin, dark-haired—with a shock of black hair constantly falling across his forehead—and anal retentive. He always seemed to be preoccupied.

"Good afternoon, Eric."

"And speaking of afternoon, you got to work late today, Amanda."

"I'm sorry, Eric. My dad was over, and I didn't sleep. I'm dragging around this morning, and a lot is going on. You know I'm rarely late for work."

"Yes, and perhaps that's because you rarely come to work."

"That's not fair, Eric. I've worked here for years, and you've never had any problems with me. I know that the past five months have been—"

"Amanda, I like you. You know that. I've been very patient with you, but in truth, the past five months have been unacceptable. You continue to involve yourself in police matters to your own peril."

I couldn't deny it. "Eric, I was absent this week because I found out I'm pregnant with twins, and I have a medical condi-

tion that will make that precarious. My mother said she spoke
to you."

"She did, and congratulations on the babies. I know you've
wanted this for a long time, and you deserve it."

"Thank you, Eric."

"Dr. Brown, we both know a pregnancy with twins is going
to be high risk."

"I'd hope to address that later on down the road. I'm only
about seven weeks along, though I *look* four or five months—"

"You've already missed three days of work, and you only just
found out about the babies."

I looked at my hands wringing in my lap. Generally speaking, Eric didn't intimidate me, but I had that sinking feeling. And
I could see what was coming. "Well, one of those days I had to
go to a loved one's funeral. The fact that I had to be hospitalized
doesn't necessarily mean that I'll continue to miss work. I don't
know how things will progress. I've never been pregnant with
twins before."

"Didn't you have a miscarriage once, Dr. Brown?"

"You know I did, Eric. A long time ago."

"Surely you're concerned."

"Of course I'm concerned."

"And frankly, I'm disappointed that you talked to Detective
Winslow this morning about Nikki Thunder."

I couldn't hide my own disappointment that Jeff had ratted
me out. Eric must have seen it in my face.

"Now, now, don't look like that, Dr. Brown. He only spoke
to me out of concern. Several people have confided in me about

how alarmed they were at your unorthodox decisions to involve yourself in homicide cases."

"Them and *everyone* I know. Like I said, I know the past few months have been—"

He cleared his throat. "I don't want to fire you, Amanda. You're a fine psychologist and a wonderful colleague."

My heart felt like it had dropped down to the kitten heels of the purple boots I had on. "I don't *want* to be fired, Eric."

"I think it would be best for everyone if you resigned. I'll be happy to give you a good recommendation."

I'd always played nice. I'd never been fired before in my life. I didn't love the work. I should have been courageous enough years ago to let the job go and do some work that I did love. But it offered the security of excellent benefits. How in the world would I pay for my prenatal care and the birth? What if I needed a C-section? What if something was wrong with the babies?

I felt sick to my stomach. I couldn't blame Chantilly because Eric didn't wear it. A headache bit at my temples. If I sat there much longer, I'd end up weeping into my palms.

Be brave, girl. You can do this. If thou canst believe, all things are possible.

I stood, kept my posture erect, and extended my hand to shake his. He stood in turn and met mine across the table. His concerned expression let me see he'd had a hard time with this.

"I'll put together a letter of resignation today. With two weeks' notice?"

"There's no need for you to continue on for two weeks. You can leave now if you'd like." He released my hand. "I'm truly sorry, Amanda. I really do think this will benefit you and your new family in the long run."

I shrugged and bobbed my head about in a not quite affirming nod and a not quite disagreeing shake. "Thank you."

I swallowed the huge bitter pill I'd been given without any water. I walked away, trying to keep my knees from trembling and my hands from shaking.

I walked to my desk and begin to clear out my personal mementos. I didn't have many.

Everyone avoided me, except for Jeff. He approached me reticently. "I didn't know he'd fire you, kid." Jeff was only ten years older, but he always called me kid.

"It's not your fault."

"Need some help?"

A tear strayed beyond my control. I swiped at it. Shook my head.

Jeff gathered me in a hug. He emboldened a few others to do the same. I even got a woman or two in the office to cry with me.

"Hey! You'll have plenty of time to take care of those babies. And you gotta let us see the twins when they get here," Rebecca the redhead said.

Despite their generous good-byes, I couldn't get out of there fast enough.

My legs felt like they were made of lead. I trudged to the car and then home, feeling completely defeated.

Jazz doesn't want me to work anyway.

Score one for Jazz.

Just then, my cell phone rang. I rarely charged it, so whoever tried to contact me caught me in good form. "This is Amanda," I said.

"Bell, it's Elisa. Rocky is sick. He's in the hospital."

That hale and hearty man is rarely sick. My heart dropped to my shoes. "What happened, Elisa?"

"We don't know," she sobbed. "He just got really sick. Vomiting. Diarrhea. Spitting up blood. They say he has severe gastroenteritis. I think he's dying, Bell."

I couldn't think. One mantra repeated in my brain.

Help him, God. Help him, God. Help him, God. Please, help him!

When my thoughts could move past my litany of terror, Nikki Thunder's face flashed before me. Her words: *an accident could happen to someone you love.*

I had very unflattering names for her in my mind.

Nikki had made good on her threat. I knew it with everything in me. But could I prove it? Who else did she harm? Had she been in contact with Jazz? Dear God!

"Where are you?" I asked.

"I'm here at the U with him. He's in intensive care!"

"How long has he been sick?"

"Since this morning."

Oh, God. Oh, God. What to do?

"Listen to me, Elisa. I think he's been poisoned."

"Poisoned? Bell, that can't be."

"Make them check him for poison."

"What kind of poison?"

"I don't know. Anything."

I could hear the frustration and hesitation in her voice. "Why would somebody poison him?"

"You have to trust me. I can't tell you everything now, but I guarantee you a threat was made and that Rocky was poisoned. Make them listen, Elisa. Let me save Rocky's life like I saved yours."

I heard her sniffle. She must have been gathering her courage. "Okay. I'll try."

"Do it, or he's gonna die, Elisa."

"I love him."

"Then make them listen to you. I'll prove it. I'll prove it all. Just give me a minute."

She started sobbing uncontrollably.

I hung up the phone, praying I was right. I needed to make another call; I called on Jesus.

I knew Carly had taken me off her favorite persons list, but I didn't care. I called her cell phone and prayed she wouldn't be so upset at my neglecting her in her Timothy crisis that she would refuse to talk to me.

"Hi, bunny!" she said cheerfully. She was so not mad after all.

"Don't tell me. You and Timothy got back together."

"Of course we did. I'm Carly Brown. Men don't break up with me. He was temporarily insane."

"Speaking of insane, Carly, I think something happened to Rocky."

"So?"

"Carly, this is urgent." A pause, where she no doubt decided I meant business.

"What's going on, Bell?"

"He's at the U. They say he has severe gastroenteritis. I think he's been poisoned."

"Bell, I'm not liking the sound of this."

"What kind of poison would give those symptoms?"

A big pause.

"Carly!"

"Don't do this. You have babies. You can't. Don't, Bell."

"She tried to kill him."

"I don't know what you're talking about, and I don't want to know. Don't get involved."

"He's the best friend I've ever had. I'll be lost without that catatonic-going goofball. I can't let him die."

"Bell. I don't know what's going on, but I don't want any part of it."

"Nikki Thunder poisoned him. She threatened me. She said somebody I love could have an accident, and now Rocky is in intensive care."

"I don't want to hear this."

"Carly, please, he may be dying. Please help me."

She sighed into the receiver. "Arsenic mimics gastroenteritis, and it's easy to get a hold of. Common rat poison is full of arsenic. I'll make some calls to the U. I've got a few friends, but what I am supposed to tell them?"

"Tell them you've got a hunch. Pull a favor. Do what you gotta do, sis, but don't mention Nikki Thunder."

"You'd better be careful. You can't afford to get hurt again."

"I will. I promise. Thank you, Carly."

"I'll come by after work. How are the babies?"

"Fine," I said. *By faith,* I added to myself.

My nerves felt as taut as rubber bands stretched to capacity. "She hurt my friend," I said in a faltering whisper. "That evil woman hurt my sweet friend."

Carly's steely voice snatched me from the brink of despair. "You listen to me, Bell. I know you don't believe this, but I trust you. I trust your instincts, even though I'm scared to death you just stumbled into something else that can hurt you. So you can't fall apart. You have to be strong. If we can find out what poison he ate, we might be able to save him."

"I'm not strong."

"You *are* strong, Amanda Bell Brown. You think of your namesake. She wouldn't have you fall apart. What would she say?"

I tried to pull myself back from that precipice I teetered on. "Let the weak say, 'I'm strong.'"

"You go with God, girl. And don't let Rocky down."

"I won't."

I flipped my phone shut and took a deep breath.

Man up, girl. Or lose your friend.

I got into my Love Bug praying, *I am strong, I am strong, I am strong, I am strong, I can do all things through Christ, who strengthens me.*

All the way to the hospital.

chapter
twenty-two

I WALKED INTO THAT HOSPITAL, my entire being aware of every step I took. This wasn't Niagara Falls. This evil that had visited my friend was far more insidious. Step by step. Inch by inch I moved closer to an edge I didn't think I could keep from falling off. And Rocky! My poor sweet Rock couldn't die. How would I ever laugh again without seeing that goofy grin of his? Those eyes.

Yea, though I walk through the valley of the shadow of death, I will fear no evil. Please, God. Whatever it is, let us find a way to help him in time. Please, please, please, God.

God's sweet Spirit spoke to me. Softly. *If thou canst believe, all things are possible to him that believeth.*

God, I prayed, *It's been a long time since I believed anything with my whole heart, but I am giving you every little bit of faith I have right now. I believe you can help my friend. I believe. Please, God, help him. Don't let him die. He's twenty-eight years old. Don't let her get away with this.*

Peace washed over me like rainwater on the desert. I didn't know what the outcome would be, but God heard me. His peace comforted me. Whatever would happen, God would fix it. He already had.

Rocky wasn't in the Dream.

That's right! Hope fluttered about my belly. It was Jazz who was in mortal danger in my Dream, and my babies.

The realization hit me with sickening force. I started praying again.

Hard.

chapter
twenty-three

All things are possible to him that believeth.

Go inside, Bell. You may not be able to let Grandma Bell be in charge of your life, but you sure can borrow her great faith.

I stepped inside the hospital room and found Elisa standing over Rocky, still crying. I felt like I had stepped into a dream, oddly detached. Like at any moment I'd float right out of my body and hover around the ceiling. I didn't want to take in what I saw. Rocky, paler than I'd ever seen him. Ghostly next to white sheets. Tubes snaking in and out of his body. Struggling to breathe. Raspy, labored breaths forced out of his lungs.

I felt my own breath coming out with similar difficulty. Elisa grabbed me in a fierce hug. But I didn't have time for her.

"I need to be alone with him," I said.

She must have known I meant business because she fled the room like I'd threatened her.

I walked up to my frail friend. I'd had never seen him this sick. Rocky had to be one of the healthiest people I knew. His happiness and faith kept his body strong. And this sociopath wanted to snuff him out.

Oh no. Not on my watch.

I leaned over the bed. Touched Rocky's face. "Rock," I whispered.

He could barely open his eyes, but he tried at my voice. Tears streamed down my cheeks. He couldn't say anything. His puppy eyes shut again.

"You do one thing for me, babe," I said. He loved it when I called him babe, God help me. "You stay alive," I whispered. "I know you want to see Jesus face-to-face, but you can do that when you're an old, old man. And I know you want to be loved, just like me. I never knew you hurt so badly, Rocky. I thought your love tank was full to overflowing. If I wasn't so self-absorbed, maybe I would have seen how love-starved you were, but now I know. So, you can't die, because there is too much love left for you to get, including from me, my friend. Maybe especially from me."

I began to sob. "Forgive me my debts, Rocky, and I owe you a lot. But I'm going to make it up to you if you stay here. Trust me. Okay, babe?"

And, God bless him, he nodded, just a tiny little nod, before he went back to sleep.

I kissed my pal on his ashen forehead and got the heck out of there. I needed to find out a little more about Toni Thunder's sickness.

All things are possible to him that believeth.

I needed the reminder. As I walked out of the hospital, a sharp pain seized me.

Not again!

I hoped it wouldn't get as bad as the horrible/precious day

when Jazz had to carry me to Dr. McLogan's and I found out
about my babies.

My babies!
My Dream!
Oh God.

chapter
twenty-four

BEFORE I LEFT THE HOSPITAL, I wrenched out of Elisa the whereabouts of the Thunders. She'd frozen in fear and didn't know what to do or whom to trust. I finally broke her down and found out they were keeping a prayer vigil for Rocky at the Rock House. I needed to see them. I needed to end this reign of terror.

I drove back to Ann Arbor as increasingly painful spasms threatened to take me out. The Jesus Prayer, simple and manageable, rode shotgun with me. I had no idea what I was doing. I was relying on mercy, and mercy held me up.

Still, the monkey chatter in my brain continued unabated. All the way to the house my thoughts buffeted me.

What kind of circumstances created a woman who could kill again and again, especially victims as powerless as babies, toddlers, uncommonly kind middle-aged women, and blond boy toys—holy and stuff. *If* those were her only victims. I knew all the clinicianspeak to explain someone like Nikki Thunder. I even knew the copspeak. But my soul grieved within me. How must a loving, good God feel in the face of such evil?

After spending time with Ezekiel and Joy, I had no reason

to suspect they had anything to do with Zeekie's death. I hadn't gotten to spend time with Zekia and Zeke, as I'd wished, but I felt certain they either knew what happened to their little brother or they knew Nikki and Sister Lou knew.

What happened, God? Give me wisdom.

Nikki *had to* have coerced them into doggedly clinging to her fabrication. How did she do it? They seemed too sweet to take a bribe from her. What did she threaten them with?

I thought about those children. They must have been wee ones at ten and seven or so when their mother died, with little Miss Psychopathica right in the thick of things. Would she be crazy enough to have told them that she'd been the one who caused their mother's death? If she had, she might have told them that if they didn't keep quiet about what really happened in the bath, she'd hurt their father, too—and get away with it. A psychopath would do just about anything for self-preservation. But that seemed like too bold a move, even for her. *Wisdom, God. Give me insight into this.*

Maybe she told little Zeke she'd seen him drown his brother. That he'd go into a juvenile detention facility. She could have done the same to Zekia. They were just kids. They wouldn't know how to defend themselves against her.

God, I could speculate all day.

I had to get those kids to trust me enough to divulge information that could steer me in the right direction. And Nikki had probably joined herself to their little hips at this point. How could I get them to talk if she was in the house, hovering over like a green sky preceding destruction?

That still, small voice said something to me.

Go to Lou.

I didn't have any time to argue with God. The hospital was five minutes from the Rock House. I made a detour and high-tailed it back to the U.

Lord, I need an ally right about now. I need Lou or the kids or someone to give me some evidence strong enough to take down Nikki or at least tie her up long enough for us to gather more evidence to nail her. Make me a girl Columbo for real. I know he is only a TV character. I'm just asking that you make me as wily and wise as he is.

Jazz's blood pressure would spike and he'd keel over from a stroke if he knew I'd prayed to be like Columbo.

I parked the car. Noted my space number on my parking ticket and took the elevator to the Taubman Center. In the elevator I nearly doubled over in pain.

God, help me.

From there I weaved my way to the floor where psychiatric patients are cared for. *Take it easy, girl. Try to hold on to these babies as best you can.*

I got to the locked doors on the psych floor, said who I was and who I'd come to see. You can't just go to the front desk at a hospital and ask for Louella Dickson. A psychiatric patient's name wouldn't be released to visitors—a privacy perk. If you knew she was there, however, and came to this door, you'd get access. Besides, most of the staff knew Eric Fox and me. I'd have little trouble getting to her.

Someone buzzed me in, and the bored-looking nurse at the nurse's station told me recreation time would begin shortly. She told me what Lou's room number was, although she acted as if the effort to find the number caused her pain. I found the room with no problem. Louella sat on the bed, wearing regular clothing and no Chantilly oh-the-toilet. I thanked God I was able to see her. It always amazed me that some people have to get psychiatric health care without any support whatsoever.

I stood leaning against the doorjamb. "Hello, Sister Lou."

She startled, and scurried against the headboard like I'd come to harm her.

"May I come in?"

She didn't say anything.

I eased into the room and sat in an awful pea green chair. "How are you today?"

After a long pause she answered. "Blessed."

"That's good."

"Are you looking forward to going home soon?"

Her eyes darted around the room like I'd brought a lairful of demons with me that she'd have to cast out. She nodded her head.

"I'm not going to take up too much of your time, Lou. I was concerned about you. This is the first time I've been able to come see you since I brought you here, remember?"

Her eyes softened. Her gaze rested on me a few more seconds before she looked away again.

God knows, I didn't want to upset her. I silently prayed for wisdom and waited. Lou surprised me with a question. "He ain't raise Zeekie from the dead. Why ain't he raise him?"

"Maybe it wasn't God's will, Louella."

"I had done fasted and prayed. We anointed that child and baptized him."

We? Baptized him? When did this happen? Pentecostals don't baptize toddlers.

Lou rattled on. "Some don't go out but by prayer and fasting. You gots to get them demons or they take you over. Like you— you got a nicotine demon, gal."

"I think you have me mistaken for my sister. I don't smoke."

Lou pointed her gnarled finger at me. "You gots a spirit of nicotine that wanna keep yo' temple of the Holy Spirit corrupted." She started speaking Klingon again, but she didn't come near me. Just kept speaking in tongues until she finally said, "Demons everywhere. All in the house. All in the children. Zeke shoulda raised the baby up. He was 'spose to raise him from the dead. She told me he would."

"Who told you that, Sister Lou?"

She rocked, banging her back against the wall. "Demons all in the house. All the people round here got demons. The woman of God got to cast them out. The prophetess gots to discern them foul demons, then they gots to be cast out. Ezekiel knows he should have raised that child from the dead."

Are the woman of God and the prophetess two different people?

"Did Nikki tell you that Ezekiel would raise Zeekie from the dead? Did you try to cast the demons out of Zeekie, Lou?"

"All them children got demons. You got a nicotine demon, gal." She went on and on with her circular reasoning, never answering my question, and finally retreating back to speaking in tongues. I let her go on about ten minutes until the twins compelled me to take a trip to the bathroom.

I figured Lou had answered the questions she wanted to, so it

was time to go. Even though she was ill, she'd had enough lucidity to communicate *something*. Before I left, I asked nurse Chronic
Fatigue to have Lou's doctor look in on her.

She'd likely be released on medication, with instructions for
her family to follow up with their own doctor at home.

The Thunders were probably anxious to leave Rocky's house,
especially with Nikki's star now rising. Dear Lord, I could hear a
different kind of ticking clock now. I knew if I couldn't confirm
my suspicions soon, they'd be completely out of reach, and she
might get away with this.

Over my dead body.

But, God, what if I'm wrong about all of this?

But I'm right!

*Am I right, Lord? Did Nikki Thunder want to be a Gospel-
preaching superstar?*

She seemed to thrive on attention. I needed to pick her brain,
but could hardly stand to be in a room with her. She didn't like
me anyway, and she had the hots for my husband.

*Am I just crazy? Emotional? Did I make all this up because I feel
threatened by her?*

I made my way through the hospital again and back to my
car. *Oh, Lord, this pain. Protect the babies.*

I believe.

I didn't know what I was doing, but God have mercy, I was
going to do *something*. For Zeekie. In honor of all the infants in
my dream who died at the hands of their own mothers, including
my own child since I'd allowed a madman to kill her.

But don't let this hurt my babies. I believe!

Remembering my dream about Zeekie brought to mind

my God Dream. I prayed, prayed, and prayed for Jazz's safety. I prayed marginally for Nikki Thunder's, but I did pray! Maybe she's the one I should have been praying for most. But perhaps I'd seen enough psychopaths to know they don't change. How God would redeem someone like Nikki was a mystery to me. Again the scripture came to me.

All things are possible to him that believeth.

Could God reform Nikki Thunder? God could do anything. *Would He?*

My daddy said God wanted to redeem all things back to Himself. Even Nikki Thunder could go under that umbrella of grace. I said a prayer for her.

Your will, God. Have mercy on her. God knows that was one weak, halfhearted effort. But I didn't have any more to offer.

Perhaps working with criminals had affected me in the same way working homicide had affected Jazz. I couldn't imagine Nikki Thunder going to heaven. I didn't happen to be a spiritual romantic—not when I'd dreamed of her taking my husband. God forgive me, but that murderess could wear the black wedding dress I dreamed of and go straight to hell. I'd do whatever I had to do to keep her from hurting anybody else.

She was on my watch, and I had my eyes wide open.

chapter
twenty-five

IT SEEMED TO TAKE FOREVER to get to the Rock House. I dragged myself out of the Love Bug and shuffled into the church, my pelvic area screaming with pain.

I tried not to think about how Rocky wasn't there. The thought matched the agony of my physical pain as I walked into the sanctuary. Ezekiel sat in the front row with the children, Zekia with her head on her daddy's shoulder. Zeke knelt on the floor by his leg. The poor child prayed in earnest. Joy sat next to Ezekiel, rocking in silence, her Bible on her lap. All greeted me warmly, but with the ragged edge of concern in their voices.

Ezekiel spoke first. I don't know whether he could read my face or God had spoken to him again. "You heard about Rocky?"

I nodded. I went to each of them, passing out hugs despite my pain. "Where's Nikki?" I asked, thinking she needed to be accounted for at all times.

Ezekiel answered. "She said she needed some time alone. Too much has happened, Bell."

Indeed it had.

Thunder had on a gray wool turtleneck sweater and black

twill pants. He looked great. If he'd had on a silk smoking jacket, the only thing that would have surprised me is that he smoked. He had an old Hollywood-glamour quality, like a darker version of Duke Ellington.

"She didn't take her bodyguards with her?" I asked.

Sister Joy rolled her eyes. "They're at the house eating poor Rocky out of house and home."

And Rocky could care less about their excesses, bless him. One morning he'd confided, "Those are big dudes. They need a little more than the rest of us." They probably ate an entire Black Angus cow for breakfast after they'd drained the thing of all her milk. But Rocky would have prayed for more food to feed them instead of complaining.

I sat on a chair near Ezekiel, and Zekia put her head on my shoulder, as if it were perfectly natural for her to do so. The sweet girl. Ezekiel smiled when he saw it, as did Joy. They loved those kids.

Zekia patted my tummy, lightly, but it had begun to really ache and I jumped.

She bolted up, apologizing profusely. "I'm so sorry, Mrs. Bell."

"Oh, no, honey, put your head on my shoulder again. I'm just a little achy today."

Joy frowned at me. "Are you hurting, sweetness?" Thank God I'd won her over, too.

"I am, but I'm on my way home. I stopped in because I went to see Sister Lou after I saw Rocky."

Ezekiel looked surprised. "That was awfully nice of you, sissy."

It grated me when he called me that, but this was not the time for me to play the name game. "I was happy to do it, Ezekiel."

Ezekiel said, "You're a psychologist. Do you believe my big sister is what they say she is?"

"Do I believe she's a paranoid schizophrenic?"

"Yes, or do you believe it could be—"

I couldn't take his deliverance spiel. "Your sister isn't possessed, Ezekiel. She's sick." He didn't say anything to counter what I'd said. I went on. "I agree with her diagnosis, but she has some moments of lucidity that I found revealing."

"What do you mean?" Joy asked.

I looked at Ezekiel. "Maybe you should have the children leave the room."

He looked at them. Zekia sat up and reached for my hand. He shook his head. "No, I'd like them to hear. They're old enough to be included in everything now."

Relief relaxed the tightness I didn't realize I'd held in my shoulders. I thought he'd made a good decision, one that would make what I needed to do easier.

"At the hospital I tried to talk to her, but she's not communicating much. She's retreating inward."

"She did that with us, too. She seems stuck on the idea that I should have . . ."

"What you should have done, you did. You released your son to Jesus and buried your child."

"I believe God could have done it. He could have raised Him."

"Yes, but He just doesn't seem to be passing out resurrections nowadays, does He?"

I looked at this man who'd hawked his miracle prosperity oil to the gullible masses. The anger that I'd barely kept in check since I'd walked away—been fired!—from my job seeped out at Thunder.

"Why do you continue that fiasco, Ezekiel? Can't you save that for the camera?"

The kids looked away. Little Zeke looked up at me with an expression of shock on his face. He turned back to his dad, but at least I knew he heard me.

Ezekiel didn't hide his own frustration. "You don't know anything about my faith, young lady."

"I know you were on the comeback trail, and come on, resurrections have got to be great television, whether or not they work."

"I wanted my son back. Haven't you lost a child? Didn't you want her to live? Didn't you want a miracle?"

I blinked at him. I hadn't expected him to volley the question back to me. I thought of my little girl, impossibly tiny, but alive in the palm of Miriam's hand. Adam had beaten me too badly for me even to reach up to hold her, not that they'd have let me. My baby girl took a single breath. Just one—a tiny little squeak that I think I heard only because that child consumed me. And then she went quiet and still, and Miriam whisked her away. Only later, when I could walk again, did I go to Adam's backyard, to the spot where the grass had been disturbed. I knelt down where she lay under the dirt. I told her I was sorry. I tell her to this day.

I'm sorry, Imani.

"Yes. I wanted a miracle, but not a media event."

"I didn't, either," he said. "I didn't want any media events at all. Ever! Unless I could win more souls to Christ through them. I started preaching when I was still a boy. I never wanted to be famous. I wanted to bring people to Jesus, but everybody around me pushed me because I was good-looking and had the gift of gab."

Joy interrupted our argument. "You had a God-given gift, Ezekiel, and people loved to hear you talk about the Lord."

He hung his head for a moment, then looked back at me. "The next thing I know, I had a board of directors and a Christian marketing company making up mail-order miracles in exchange for donations."

"How could you allow that?"

"I wasn't the one making all those decisions! You think I believe in miracle prosperity oil? I only wanted people to have some point of contact to activate their faith. I didn't even think of it myself. I had a team of people deciding everything. Making up the miracles. But, Bell, sometimes God would answer prayers. Sometimes he would show up and heal. Or deliver. Or change. It was never me."

I thought about my ankle. God showed up and healed it. Ezekiel didn't take a bit of credit for it.

"I was a country boy who suddenly had the attention of millions of people, including women. Good Christian women, who weren't quite as good as they should be."

"But you were the star. You could have stopped it all."

"I wasn't a star! I was a dumb hick who'd gotten too much power too quickly. Do you think anybody prepared me to be famous? To have money I didn't think possible, all the while having a team of people telling me it's all from God. It's a *blessing*. I came from sharecroppers, sissy. I had no idea how to be the famous Ezekiel Thunder."

He shook his head. Grazed his hand over his mouth before he spoke again. "Women wanting a piece of the man of God. Christian women putting their phone numbers in my *front* pocket like my wife didn't matter. Well, everybody knows what happened. I had affairs. And then Toni became too good to be a real wife to me. My 'people' covered my sin, and not in a godly way. Nobody challenged me, because I was the anointed one. We had a huge ministry that did a lot of wonderful things for the kingdom of God. We fed hungry children. We got Bibles to people who never owned one. I felt obligated to go with the charade because I thought if it all fell apart, more people would be hurt than if we kept it together. I hoped God would help me change."

I'd never envisioned him as what he described. I always saw him as a hustler and a ladies' man. I saw him as a narcissist like Nikki, only concerned about himself and his own interests. When I didn't speak, he went on.

"Even though I was a grown man, I still felt like that kid I used to be, preaching 'cause the older folks thought it was so wonderful to see a young man love God. They pushed me forward way before I was ready. And it all ruined me. In spite of all the pressure, I knew I was responsible for my own self, and I tried to change—God knows I did. I stopped the affairs. I tried to get my life right.

"Twenty-some-odd years ago, I confided in a young girl who worked as my assistant. We spent many hours on the road and in my office alone, but I had no intentions toward her. She wasn't even a pretty, fast gal. But she had a good heart, and I needed a good person in my life. I came to love her, and she loved me. She was going to be eighteen in a few months. I wanted to marry her.

"One lonely night, just one, we made a mistake. She loved Jesus enough to leave me before she could do any more damage to her soul. Neither of us meant for what had happened between us to leak. A friend told the press. It was like David said, 'I was wounded in the house of a friend.' And nobody was more like David than I was."

He looked down at his hands again. Joy spoke for him.

"He stepped down from the ministry. He dealt with all the shame, but he lost the woman he'd fallen in love with. All the people he made so much money for treated him like a leper. There was no more ministry. Ezekiel spent the next several years getting right with God."

"You every hear of St. Mary of Egypt, Bell?" Thunder asked.

I had, but I couldn't resist hearing her story again.

Thunder continued. "Mary was a prostitute who didn't work out of need—as many women who were alone in that time did. She did it because she loved men. One day she paid for a journey to Jerusalem using her body and considerable skill. A group of pilgrims were going to venerate the true cross, and she thought she'd go along for kicks."

His honey voice and delightful drawl captivated me.

"On the trip she serviced every man who'd have her and a few who didn't want her at first. When they got to the holy city and to the church, which housed the cross where Jesus paid the penalty for our sins, she couldn't enter the door to get into the church."

The rat. He could really tell a good story. I wanted more.

"She tried three times, and an invisible force barred her. She stepped away from the church and saw an icon of the Virgin Mary and baby Jesus. She was overcome by her own sinfulness. She said to the Lord's mama, 'If you help me get in, I'll serve your Son for the rest of my days.'"

I nodded, as if I were hypnotized. "Then what happened?"

"The blessed mother answered her and allowed her entry."

"Wow," I said.

"That's not the amazing part. Mary became a believer that very day and took Communion. She went with three small loaves of Communion bread to the desert to pray. She spent the next forty-seven years living wild for God in the desert, repenting. Forty-seven years. I'm gonna need a little longer than that," Ezekiel said wistfully.

"But if you've repented, why have you been seeking all this media attention?"

"I wasn't."

Joy spoke up. "That young gal came into his life. She wanted him to be famous again. One look at him, a few stories about the things he'd once accomplished, and she decided to resurrect the dead herself. She talked him into that whole television thing, including the new version of miracle prosperity oil."

I considered the children. He and Joy spoke freely around them. They must have talked all these matters through before. I admired him for that. "Did she talk you into that before or after Toni died?"

"After."

"Ezekiel, what happened to Toni?"

"I told you. She got sick and died."

"How did she get sick?"

"She kept having stomach problems. We were sure it was from stress. She was kind of delicate, you see."

"Tell me about the stomach problems."

"She couldn't keep much down. In the end she kept vomiting blood. Couldn't hold her bowels. It was terrible, but the doctor said it was natural causes. Gastroen—"

"I know what it is, Ezekiel." I didn't mean to be rude, but I could barely hold on, the pain had gotten so intense. "Was Nikki around her? Did she feed her? Help her in any way?"

"Nikki was a godsend, despite what had happened between us. She cared for Toni while Joy cared for Zekia and Zeke. She had a little medical training. Had studied to be an MA."

Shazam! A very unfortunate profile had emerged. Knocking off babies. Killing the people she should have been caretaking. A stone-hearted murderer.

"How could she have stayed on after Toni found out about the affair?"

"She begged Toni to forgive her and not to kick her out. She had no place to go. Toni looked at her as a misguided child. It was me she punished."

Misguided child, my eye. I'll bet her performance eclipsed all Hollywood had to offer, surpassed only by her act at her son's funeral.

"I wanted her to leave, but Toni felt sorry for her."

"Ezekiel, how did the baby—the little girl you and Nikki had—die?"

Under stress his accent stretched out. His drawl had a far

more exaggerated quality. This wasn't his TV voice. "Just liiiiiiike Daaaaaavid's baby; she never thriiiiiived. Seven days after she was born she diiiiied."

I imagined Ezekiel had fed Nikki his "I'm like David" garbage. Actually, it was true, but I didn't like it. She'd know exactly what buttons to push to maximize his guilt. *Lord, have mercy.*

My abdomen area not only burned but shooting pain doubled me over. I tried to hide it, but my breathing became ragged.

"Bell, you're not okay." Ezekiel said. "Let me pray for you again."

"Not yet. I want to ask you one more thing."

"What is it, sissy?"

I smiled at him. He'd managed to become *human* in my eyes. I liked him a little more. "Don't call me sissy." I winked at him.

He tried to suppress a smile. "Yes, ma'am."

"I mentioned I talked to Sister Lou. She didn't say much before she went back to speaking in Kl— in tongues. But she did say, 'He was supposed to raise him from the dead. She told me he would.' Who was the *she* Lou was talking about? Nikki discouraged you from praying for God to raise him, correct?"

He nodded.

"Who else could Lou have meant?"

He looked thoughtful. "I honestly don't know."

"Did you talk to her about raising your kids from the dead before anybody died?"

"Of course not."

"Have you actually raised *anybody* from the dead?"

He shook his head.

"Ezekiel, I think Nikki talked Lou into doing something to

the baby and told her that you would raise him from the dead if anything went wrong. Have you known Nikki to be a liar. At all?"

His mouth opened. Nothing came out.

Joy answered. "She lied constantly. She'd say anything to get what she wanted or to cover her tail."

Like most psychopaths.

I looked Zekia right in the eyes. "Baby, why did you give Zeekie the bath?"

A look of terror crossed her face. She answered too quickly. "I wanted to. I want to be a mama one day."

Joy broke in, shaking her head vigorously. "They loved their brother, but he was a handful. He got on their nerves. She wouldn't want to give him a bath, never showed any interest in such a thing."

I looked at the younger Ezekiel. "Zeke, what did you do in the bathroom?"

"Huh?" He looked afraid. "I—I, uh, just used it, ma'am, and then I left."

Zeke began to cry. "Mrs. Bell, Zeekie must have fallen down or something after I left the bathroom."

I spoke softly. "You would have told your sister you were out of the bathroom, and she probably would have known when you came out of the bathroom, anyway, if she was giving him a bath in the first place. None of it happened. Zekia didn't give Zeekie the bath, and you didn't let him drown after you got out of the bathroom, did you?"

Both kids started wailing. Zeke jumped into his father's arms, and Joy nearly toppled me over to get to Zekia.

"I'm sorry, Ezekiel. I don't want her to get away with it because they're protecting her. They don't know any better."

Ezekiel's eyes had filled with his children's pain. "Of course they wouldn't want to get their auntie in trouble. She's a sick woman. You see she's in the hospital."

I raised my voice. "Ezekiel! Sister Lou isn't the sick woman little Zeke is protecting. In fact, the woman he's protecting isn't sick at all. She's a psychopath, and I believe she's one of the most dangerous people I've ever met."

I tried to calm myself. By now I hurt badly. I needed to get out of there. I lowered my voice. "Look, I don't know what you were thinking when you got with Nikki, but I can imagine. We all make mistakes. God knows I have. I have no right to judge you for your sins when I need to go to the desert for forty-seven years myself. Maybe fifty.

"Ezekiel, I think she wanted the glory you lost. Do you remember that woman at the funeral who Nikki said she didn't know? Nikki knew her. They used to be partners in crime. She said Nikki had two babies before you met her, starting when she was fourteen years old. Both babies died of SIDS, but I think she suffocated them when they were no longer useful to her."

Ezekiel violently swiped at his tears. The anger on his face chilled me. I thought he'd have come after me if his boy wasn't in his arms. "That can't be true."

"I think she killed four children; four that I know of, two of them your own. She's a serial killer. I think she may have killed your wife, and I think she's done something to Rocky. She threatened me at lunch—a very subtle threat, but she made good on it. I need to know what she could have given Rocky, because he's fighting for his life. And what's next? Now that she's a media darling, she won't need any of you anymore. Who else is going to have an *accident?*"

It felt like the pain would slice me in half.

I made one more appeal to Thunder. "If you are as smart as I think you are . . . if you really want to make it up to God, even though you can't, I'd take Joy and these children promptly to the Ann Arbor police. I can't get Zekia and Zeke to talk, but you can. See, I think she threatened to do something to you, and these kids would rather take the blame for Zeekie's death than lose their only remaining parent."

Joy's shoulders convulsed and she dissolved in tears. "Lord, I shoulda known what was going on."

Zekia burst out with, "They gave him a bath in water and miracle prosperity oil. They said he was possessed because he always got into stuff. They said they were going to baptize him in the tub."

That was all I needed to hear. "I'm confident Nikki intended for him to die and then threatened the kids."

"She told us that Daddy would go to jail if anybody found out. She said it was an accident, but we would all get in trouble because we believed in deliverance and sometimes bad stuff happens when you try to set somebody free, like what happened with Auntie Lou a long time ago."

I squeezed that sweet girl. "It's okay, baby. You tell the police what you know. Tell them everything."

I said to Thunder, "Go to the police and ask for Jeff Winslow. I know this will be hard, but you should have Toni's body exhumed. Killers often use the same method if they were successful. You need to have your late wife's body checked for poison. Arsenic in particular. Then you and Joy—the woman you know you're in love with—need to have that little skank put away before she kills anybody else. Get out of here like a ghost. Leave right now."

I stood. "Pray for me. I need to get home."

I shot out the door, not bothering to hug them good-bye. I fumbled with my keys and got into the Love Bug. I tore out of the parking lot, praying like my life—and my babies lives— depended on it. I could feel my faith diminishing as my womb twisted inside me.

Jesus, I'm so stupid, always trying to help somebody else. I put my own babies at risk trying to save somebody else's family.

The small, still voice within: *Rocky is your family.*

Yes, Lord, he is.

I needed more than mustard-seed-sized faith—if I even had that now.

I believe you can help me. Can't you?

I could scarcely think anymore, my own thoughts battered by the thought of losing not just one baby, but *two*—along with my best friend. And that Dream. In my God Dream, Jazz was at risk. Where is he?

I clung to the scripture.

Lord, I believe. I believe you can save them all. All things are possible to those who believe, and I believe.

Keep telling yourself that, Bell.

I believe in miracles. I know you can do it! Please, Jesus. I'm sorry for all my sins. I'll obey my husband. I'll be a good wife. Please help them all.

I wiped my eyes. I couldn't very well get me and the babies killed because I couldn't see to drive. I thought of what Dr. McLogan had told me once before. He'd said that if I was having a miscarriage, nothing I did could stop it. I thought of the directions he gave me. Go home and lie down if I was in pain. Stay off my feet. Take the painkillers. If it gets worse, call him, and we'd go from there.

But my God Dream!

Dr. McLogan said the babies were perfect. Please, God, I believe.

Mostly, I believe.

My faith wavered to and fro, and I didn't want it to. I felt scared that if I doubted even a little bit, everything would fall apart. *Help my unbelief.* I fumbled in my purse to find my cell phone. I punched in Jazz's cell phone number. He answered, his voice filled with anxiety.

"Baby? I'm glad you called. I need to talk to you. I'm—"

"Jazz, listen to me. I'm in a lot of pain."

"Is it the tumor?"

"Probably. Maybe. I don't know."

"Go home and get in bed. I was on my way to your apartment. I've been thinking about some things, but we'll talk about that later."

"I lost my job today."

"Aw, baby." A pause. "I'll take care of you. Bell, I'll take care of you."

"Okay, Jazz."

"I love you."

"I love you, too, baby," I sobbed into the phone. "Jazz, there's one more thing."

"What's that, Columbo?"

"Rocky is in the hospital. He may be dying. She poisoned him, Jazz. She threatened to hurt someone I care about, and she did it."

A torrent of curses exploded out of him. "I told you she was dangerous. I told you. Where is Nikki now?"

"I don't know."

"She may be lying in wait. Go somewhere safe, Bell. Don't go home."

"I have to get in bed. Ezekiel said she just went out for a bit. She doesn't know where I live."

"Anybody can find out where you live."

"I need to take my medicine. I promise I'll be careful."

"You don't know *careful*, Bell. You can't even say 'careful.' Can't spell it. Can't sound it out phonetically. You don't grasp the concept of *careful*."

"Jazz, please. I just want to go home."

"Fine. I'll be there in fifteen minutes. Stay safe. Do you hear me, woman?"

"I hear you. God is with me."

"That's all good, baby, but I'm Catholic. I grew up hearing martyr stories of people dying terrible deaths when God was with them. Excuse me, but I'm not feeling the comfort here."

"He'll keep me safe. I need a break. I've gotta get a break this time around. I can't get hurt every time I help somebody, can I? I'm having babies. I'm trying to keep Nikki Thunder from victimizing someone else. God will keep me safe. *Won't He?*"

I hoped so. Jazz didn't answer me.

chapter
twenty-six

I GOT TO MY APARTMENT, hoisted myself up those endless steps, weeping profusely I hurt so badly. I wiped my eyes when I finally saw apartment 3B. I don't think I could have been happier if I'd made it to the promised land.

As soon as I got inside, I called Dr. McLogan. Told him what was going on and got his medical advice. It was as he said before: Get to bed. Take the pain reliever, and if I wasn't feeling better within an hour, have Jazz take me to the emergency room.

I quickly obeyed. I took comfort in knowing Jazz was on his way. He'd make me a bath maybe. Climb in bed with me. Hold me. Maybe he wouldn't be intoxicated. Maybe I'd tell him how I missed him. How I wasn't going to let the youthful, Adam-damaged me be in control. Inner child therapy had become popular, but inner grown-ups—when they weren't tormenting you, like, say, Sasha—were so much better at the helm of your heart.

I climbed into bed. Waited for my husband until a few minutes later I heard him knocking.

Knocking? Why didn't he use his key?

I thought about that. The last time he'd left me, he threw his keys at me. Maybe he'd left them somewhere in the apartment when he moved out. But that wasn't like Jazz. He had an uncanny ability to have my keys on his person.

Still. I got up and went to the door. Jazz said he'd be along promptly. I opened those stupid three locks to let him in.

Only it wasn't Jazz.

Nikki Thunder pushed me away from my door and let herself in. She locked the three locks behind her, and she was smart enough to put on the chain.

All I could think was how many times Jazz had told me not to open the door without finding out who was there. And about all the times he had told me to put the chain lock on the door when I was home.

"What do you want, Nikki?"

"I want to know why my family isn't at the Rock House."

"What makes you think I know?"

"Because you seem to know a little too much, *Amanda*."

I backed away from her. Slowly.

Easy, girl. Just keep her talking. Jazz is on his way. "I don't know much at all. For example, I don't know why you killed your two babies in Philly."

"I didn't need them anymore."

"What about the boyfriend? And the woman you took care of? The one Neicy told me about."

"Again. No longer needed them." She took a menacing step toward me. I took another step back.

"I guess you didn't need Toni anymore, either."

"Nope."

"Where'd you get the arsenic?"

Her cold, dead gaze locked with mine. She shrugged. "Hardware store. You have to admit, it's clever. Nobody looks for arsenic anymore, especially when you've got a hypochondriac like Toni."

"Why did you do it, Nikki?"

"Because. She was stupid. They all are. Look at Joyce Meyer's ministry. She reaches millions. He could have kept doing that, too, the old fool. But me, I could take it further than he did. I could be bigger than Joyce Meyer."

"Impossible," I said.

"What makes you think so?"

"People *like* Joyce Meyer. But you, your sickness doesn't take long to see. You've deluded yourself, Nikki."

"I'm going to be on the Good News Network. They *ate up* that tragic story I gave them."

"No, you're not going to be on the Good News Network. You're going to be on truTV. Maybe the GNN was impressed with you, but anybody who spends more than a few hours with you can see the ugly between the cracks. You're crazy, Nikki. Worse than crazy. You're a psychopath, and your family knows it."

"They don't know anything. They don't have the good sense God gave them."

"Maybe not, but I gave them a whole lot to work with. It's over, Nikki."

"It's over, all right," she said, as she pulled a gun from her purse. She'd gotten a Saturday Night Special. I'd seen them before. The .38 caliber weapon would give her six to ten shots, depending. I may be resilient, but I didn't happen to be bullet-proof. Those martyr stories Jazz spoke about suddenly made me wish I'd gone through a Catholic catechism. I'd missed all those saint and martyr stories as a Protestant.

She bared her teeth at me in a frigid grin. "Say hi to Jesus for me, okay?"

"I will, especially since you'll probably never see Him."

"You should have left it alone. I would have been famous."

"You still will be," I said.

I could hear Jazz turning his key in the locks. She turned. I could have lunged at her, but honestly, I didn't know what to do.

Jazz tried to open the door and the chain caught it.

"Bell," he said, "open up."

"Jazz, Nikki is here."

For a second—just a moment!—she looked at me, gun poised at my head, and then just as suddenly, she spun toward the door and fired.

The sound echoed in my head. *Pop! Pop! Pop! Pop! Pop!* Five shots like firecrackers. Silence. A scream lodged in my mouth. Stuck. Horror washed over me. She killed my husband.

Nikki Thunder killed my Jazz.

I couldn't move. Couldn't think. Just felt like there was nothing left to me. I had to be dying. *God, please let me die.* Moisture trickled between my legs. Slow and steady like blood. I smelled gun powder rising from her weapon toward the ceiling, like some profane incense.

My voice returned with a single-word prayer. "*Nooooooo.*"

She laughed. Her hollow voice spoke to me in mocking tones. "I've got one more. I saved it for you."

And I didn't mind it. I closed my eyes and waited for her to fire. The Browns were going to meet Jesus on the family plan. And I didn't mind.

*B*ANG!
One big sound, but I felt nothing. And then more sounds. My door blasted open. Jazz's voice shouting, "Drop your weapon." Nikki Thunder gasping.

Holy guacamole! He was alive! My husband was alive. I could hardly process it, but Nikki snapped me back to reality. She waved the gun wildly between Jazz and me. And finally settled on me.

"You drop yours, Jazz."

He repeated, his voice as cold as hers, "Drop it, Nikki. I won't hesitate to kill you."

"I'll blow her away first. If you want your wife and babies, drop your gun, Jazz."

"You may have killed your babies. But you won't kill mine. Last chance, Nikki. Drop your weapon."

This was their stand-off. Every second seemed to last a year. I held my breath. *If she's going to kill somebody, let it be me not him. He can meet us in heaven.*

Finally, with a snicker, Nikki said, "I'm going to make sure you remember Nikki Thunder for the rest of your life."

She moved the gun so that it pointed to her own head.

"Drop it, Nikki," Jazz said. But she didn't look like she was about to squeeze the trigger. She was up to something. In a flash it dawned on me that she was trying to fake him out.

Fear incapacitated me. All I could think was, *Lord, no.*

"*Jazz!*" I cried out.

His attention went to me and in an instant Nikki fired her gun, striking my sweet husband in the chest.

Jazz clutched his heart. Fell on his back outside my apartment door.

I screamed.

Jazz tried to speak, blood spurted out of his mouth.

Nikki laughed. Like a Southern belle she said, "Don't y'all forget me now."

Everything seemed to go in slow motion. I flew to my husband. Laid my body on top of his.

He managed to choke out the words, "I told you I'd die for you." Then he closed his eyes.

I wished I could have climbed inside his body and stayed there. My head completely shut down. I had been plunged into some surreal nightmare. My husband was dead, my babies were dying, and there was nothing I could do. I heard someone screaming, "*Kill me, too! Kill me, too!*"

I didn't realize it was me.

Nikki must have changed her mind about me. As blood trickled down my legs and pain wrenched my belly, I felt a bullet burn its way through my back.

At least we'd go together. The last thing I heard was Nikki Thunder laughing.

chapter
twenty-eight

I REMEMBER WAKING UP FROM SURGERY, my mother and Carly by my bedside. I didn't care about a thing in life. All my desire to live died with my husband and babies.

My eyes fluttered open, and I saw my mother and sister. They tried to speak to me, but I tuned them out. I started singing to myself.

"Hush-a-bye don't you cry
Go to sleepy little baby
When you wake you shall have.
all the pretty little horses."

I shouted the words to drown out Sasha and Carly. Screamed them. When they tried to stop me, I did my best—even in my weakened state—to fight them, and I'd never in my life raised a hand to my mother. I didn't need her to tell me my husband and babies were gone.

And I had to go with them.

I was determined to be with Jazz. In a frenzy I pulled whatever tubes the doctors had put in me right out of my body, ignoring my pain.

And nobody but Jesus would stop me.

————

Blessed sleep overtook me. I didn't dream of anything, just floated on a sweet wave of euphoria. Also known as morphine.

I slept a long time. And even when I awoke, I didn't open my eyes. Just lay there thinking of my man. Some grace from heaven put a montage of him in my mind. I remembered all the good things, and we did have good things sometimes. I should have cherished them instead of giving him so much grief.

And, Jesus, we were so happy.

He died for me.

God bless you and keep you, Jazz.

God smile on you and gift you.

God look you full in the face.

And make you prosper . . . in heaven.

Until we meet again, my love, and hey, kiss all three of my children for me. I'll be there very soon.

————

He died for me, but he wouldn't want me to die for him. In fact, if he were here he'd yell at me like he always did and tell me if I died he'd *kill me.* And I'd tell him, "That's a bit redundant, Jazz." And he'd laugh and tell me I always had to win the argument.

I finally opened my eyes and looked at my mother, who cried when I reached for her.

I was still in a weird, drugged haze, but I wanted to get up. I wanted to live because he'd want me to, but how I'd do it without him, I had no idea.

"Mama," I said.

"Yes, baby," she said.

"Take me to him. I want to see Jazz."

She paused. "He's not in good shape, baby."

"I don't care. I want to see him."

"I don't know if you can."

"Ma, just get my clothes and take me to him."

Carly spoke. She had gone to get coffee; she had a cup of Starbucks in her hand. "Bunny!" she said. Her eyes filled with tears.

"I want to see my husband."

She wasted no time. She handed the cup to my mother. "Come on," she said.

"Carly," Ma said, "I don't think she should do that. She's been shot. And the babies."

I felt as if she'd kicked my empty womb.

"Mother, the babies will be fine. We're just going downstairs. I'll take her in a wheelchair. Give me a break. I'm a doctor."

"But all your patients are dead," I said.

"Not all of them," she said with a hint of a smile. "Not today."

I stopped. "Wha—What do you mean, Car? What do you mean 'the babies will be fine'?"

"Honey, your husband called it right when he said you were a soldier. You got shot in your shoulder. You've been through surgery, your fibroid tumor twisted on its stem and began to bleed, and you still hung on to those babies."

I knew the drugs were in my system and God knows I felt woozy, but it sounded like Carly said I was still pregnant.

"Carly?" She must have seen the confused expression on my face. "What?"

"The babies are fine. The fibroid is actin' a fool, but your babies are safe for now."

My hand flew to my belly. I hadn't thought I could cry anymore. "I'm still pregnant?"

"As pregnant as you can be, baby."

I hugged her and we cried, two sisters. We'd never been closer than this moment.

She looked at me. "Come on, girl. Let's go see your man. He's just a few floors down."

"Oh, Carly, how am I going to do this without him?"

"You won't do this alone. Trust me."

"I wanted to die, but I knew Jesus wanted me to go on. And Jazz would want me to go on."

"You better believe he would."

I sat on my bed and waited until she got me a wheelchair. I didn't worry about clothes or even shoes. I thought it odd that they'd brought him to the hospital when he was dead on the scene, but what did I know about how the ME operated in Ann Arbor?

She took me to the elevator, and we went down several floors to the Burn and Trauma unit.

"What is this, Carly?"

"I'm taking you to your husband."

"I thought we were going to the morgue."

"If we were going to the morgue, I'd have made you get

dressed. I've got a few friends over there. We Brown women gotta represent."

I was still confused. "Why do you think they brought him here?"

"Because the burn and trauma unit here is one of the best in the nation."

You can't just waltz back into the burn and trauma unit; it's locked. But they must have recognized Carly.

She got us buzzed in, and I finally jerked my hand out of hers. "Carly . . ."

Anger rose in my voice. I didn't appreciate her if this was a ploy to get me up and about. I'd made peace with God. I told him I'd live. This was cruel.

I got up from the wheelchair, still loopy from the sedatives, and stood in a wide hall. The rooms had large panes of glass, as if the patients needed to be watched at all times, even from outside the room.

"Pumpkin?" *Pumpkin* was a new one for Carly. "Jazz was hurt badly, but he's going to make it. That's what we were trying to tell you when you started that awful screaming lullaby. The worst is over. He pulled through his surgery. He was wearing one of those Saint Christopher medals, good Catholic boy that he is. Chris got the worst of it. Not to say that Jazz fared well . . ."

I stood there, my mouth agape. My heart did the Snoopy dance, God help me.

"Carly?" I didn't know what else to say. Words failed me.

"You helped save his life, too, Bell—not just Saint Christopher. When you lay your body on his, you put pressure on his wound. The bullet went into his chest cavity. It punctured his lung but missed his heart. He's going to have a rough go of it with his lungs for a while, but he's going to be all right. Especially when he sees you. Now stand up. Your man is anxious to see his family. Give him something to live for."

I wanted to believe her, but it seemed too good to be true. When I lay on top of him why didn't I feel his heart?

You were in shock. God gently whispered to me. *All things are possible to the one who believes.*

I started sobbing. "He's alive?"

Carly pulled me forward. "Look through the glass. Who's that fine man in that bed?"

I have no memory of walking into the room. I may have floated about three feet off the ground—and not just from the morphine. I only know that I found myself staring at my husband. Every kind of tube imaginable snaked in and out of his body, and I'd never seen him so pale. Jack and Addie flanked me on either side. I don't even know where they came from. I didn't care.

My beloved. Alive.

He breathed in and out, though the breaths were ragged and wheezy.

His mother spoke to him. "Jazz, baby, say hello to your family."

His eyes fluttered open, and he fixed them on me.

I thought my heart would burst. Tears streamed down my face, and I covered my mouth. Why, I have no idea. I couldn't have spoken if I'd tried.

He gave me a tiny smile. "Jane," he said.

I leaned over the bed rail, even though it hurt like crazy, and kissed my man. "You lived for me."

"For a long time, baby." Then he closed his eyes and fell back to sleep.

Jack laughed. "He got to calling for Jane when he woke up, and we didn't know *what* to think. We thought he had another woman. We were horrified."

"He has four Janes, but I know exactly which one he wants now."

Full-time wife and mother Jane, and by the grace of God, he had her.

"For a long time, baby," I repeated back to him. Somehow, I knew he heard me.

chapter
twenty-nine

W E HAD A LONG RECOVERY ahead of us. I got home
ten days before Jazz and seven days after Rocky, who
responded beautifully to the poison antidote, had di-
alysis briefly, and was not much worse for wear. I didn't sustain
any major damage. I think Nikki shot me someplace she didn't
think would kill me because she wanted me to suffer living without Jazz.

On Valentine's Day I was still in the hospital. Rocky wanted
to cancel the Rock House traditional Valentine's Day feast and
postpone his and Elisa's wedding so their "best person" would
be available. I insisted they go forward. The feast went on—for
the sake of love—but without Rocky and Elisa. She went into
labor at seven in the morning. Since we were all at the University of Michigan, Mason May married Mr. and Mrs. Rocky
Harrison, with a nurse, his parents, and several Rock House staff
and friends present. They even had their best person, in a lovely
hospital gown, dragging my IV with me. Twelve hours later,
the happy couple became the proud parents of a seven-and-a-
half-pound, gorgeous, white-chocolate-kiss-colored, green-eyed
baby boy, Rocky St. James Harrison. Since papa Rocky didn't

have a middle name, he insisted on using Elisa's maiden name, that way her name, which Gabriel had once stolen from her, would live on.

They came to see me after the baby was born, and Elisa looked radiant. And honestly, little Rocky had to be the cutest baby ever.

Two days later, Ezekiel Thunder came to see me at home. I invited him in, and we sat at my dinette table, he having a Pepsi, and me a cup of warm milk.

"I don't know how to thank you, Bell."

"You did what I asked you, and you protected your family from any more harm. I'm sorry you've lost so much, Ezekiel."

He looked sad. "There were more losses," he said.

I thought he may be speaking of Louella. The DA's office was trying to decide if she was competent to stand trial. She'd likely be charged with manslaughter, but I doubted if in her mental state she'd do any time. "I don't think she'll go to jail, Ezekiel, and even more, she'll get the help she needs."

"I should have seen to it that she got help years ago. I mean real help, but I didn't imagine she'd do anyone harm. I couldn't imagine. I've been such a fool."

"Don't beat yourself up. We've both made incredibly foolish choices. I could have lost Jazz and my own life, along with our babies. I kept thinking of that scripture you gave Rocky as a child."

"All things are possible," he said, his eyes lighting up.

"That's the one," I said. "But even with believing, you know it could have gone very differently. People believe all the time and still have losses. I know what my husband means, now, about

God being a mystery. I have a lot more respect for God. And reverence."

"You know why I called you sissy that first time?"

"Why?"

"Because I saw the same sorrow in you that I have. I recognized in you a kindred spirit. Bell, I never wanted that insanity that I let my life become, just like you never wanted your life to get so crazy with that man who was so cruel to you. And neither of us have fully recovered from the losses we suffered through those things."

"You're right. You've made me see that we are all a lot more alike than we may think we are. I guess that's yet another reason Jesus told us to judge not."

His expression sobered. "Sissy?"

I didn't tell him not to call me sissy.

"Nikki is dead," he said.

My hand went to my mouth. Despite my Dream, her death still shocked me. I reached for his hand. "What happened?"

"She met her match in jail. Nikki got into a fight with another inmate and was beaten to death."

I told Ezekiel about my Dream, how it all was freakishly accurate, though things hadn't turned out as I'd feared they would —because of the power of prayer, no doubt!

"Oh, Ezekiel. I couldn't stand her. I should have prayed as heartily for her as I did for Jazz and my babies. Forgive me."

"I'm just as much at fault. I should have been praying more for her, too. I should have done a lot differently, but we both know that."

"May God have mercy on her soul," I said sincerely.

"May he indeed, and mine, too."

"What will you do now?"

"Sis, I want to get my sister settled and take my kids somewhere so we can all heal."

"Is Joy going with you?"

"She always has. And I'm blessed that she *still* wants to go with me. I should have married her long ago. I was a weak, sinful man. I'm still sinful. Still weak, but so help me God, I don't want to do anything but spend the rest of my ragamuffin life making her happy."

"Are you a Brennan Manning *Ragamuffin Gospel* fan?" I asked, grinning.

"I think he wrote that book for me."

"No, he wrote it for me."

He gave me a soft hug, so as not to hurt my shoulder. "You are my sister."

I hugged him back. "You are my brother, and friend."

I never knew ten days could stretch out so long. I hated the nights Jazz sent me home from the hospital. I missed him so. In a short time, he and I had changed so much. My own apartment wasn't home without him.

I welcomed my king home on a bright Tuesday morning. I'd have carried him up those stairs myself if I could have. He braved them like a soldier.

He was still very weak and slept a lot, but I cuddled with him, careful not to hurt him. With all that had gone on, we hadn't exchanged Valentine's Day gifts. I hadn't gotten him anything and felt bad, but he said the twins and I were all he wanted.

I didn't expect a gift from him, but one night, several weeks later, he was watching the news in our bed and I was reading my Bible—*The Woman's Study Bible,* New King James Version, not *The Message.* I still hadn't quite forgiven Eugene, especially about that *whoring* thing. Jazz flicked off the television with the remote control, reached under the bed, and pulled out a box.

It was bigger than a ring box, and besides, he'd already chosen the perfect wedding ring for me—a one-of-a-kind band of lilies and vines crafted by my favorite artist, his mother, Addie Lee.

"Happy Valentine's Day," he said.

"You silly guy," I said. I kissed him and opened it. I startled when I saw it and slid it out of the box, sentimental tears springing to my eyes.

He'd given me another Addie Lee creation, my Marriage Wish necklace. His mother made one for each of her children when they got married. She even made one when she found out that Jazz had married Kate—just before he divorced her. By that time he and Kate were already separated, and she'd gone to live with his partner, Detective Christine Webber.

Jazz wouldn't let his mother give it to her. Now he delivered mine himself.

I fingered the delicate necklace, created with multiple strands of cream-colored, white, and luminous gold peyote beads, mixed with funky hand-blown glass beads—all kinds, all gorgeous. My Marriage Wish necklace was completely different from Kate's, with a more fun, more whimsical quality. I laughed as much as I cried at the charms she'd chosen. Unlike Kate's, the charms on this necklace were made of fourteen-carat gold.

There was a crab, which Jazz said was for his mother's crab cakes that I loved. I told him it represented his attitude. There were two baby shoes, a Love Bug, and a dollar sign, to represent Addie and Jack's hope for our success in life. I don't know where Addie found the little Kool-Aid pitcher charm, smiling face and all. That was for Jazz giving up alcohol. He didn't go to AA, and he didn't promise he'd never have another beer in his life, but he definitely got real about his abuse and did what any good man would do—he acted in the best interest of his family. To top off everything, he'd commissioned his mom to paint a portrait of me pregnant. He said she didn't give him a discount, but I was worth it.

When we'd finished marveling at the necklace, I told him I felt bad that I didn't have anything for him.

"There is something you could give me." He gave me that mischievous look and trailed his finger up my arm. "It would be the perfect gift."

"I don't know," I said. "I haven't seen sexy Jane for weeks. I'm not even sure she stuck around."

"She stuck around," he said, unbuttoning my pajama top.

"How do you know?" I asked, every part of me becoming alive.

"Because I know what she likes."

I knew what she liked, too, and I also knew that not only had Jane stuck around, but she was feeling mighty good tonight. But it was fun to play a little hard to get.

"Whatever could that be, detective?"

"Call me Tarzan. It's been way too long, baby," he said. He

unbuttoned until there were no more buttons left. "And I'll do you one better, I'll *show* you what she likes."

And that's just what he did. But he was wrong about one thing. She didn't merely like it . . .

She loved *him*.

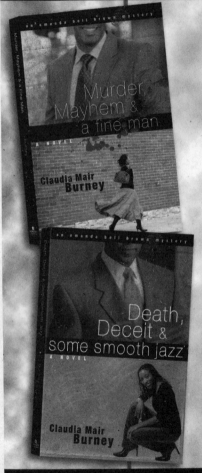